I0772582

THE CRYPT

BOOK TWO:
VOIDSTRIKE

SCOTT SIGLER

aethonbooks.com

VOIDSTRIKE
©2026 SCOTT SIGLER

**BOOKS IN THE
SIGLERVERSE CONTINUUM:**

The Crypt Series

Shakedown

Voidstrike

Fratricide

Kissyman Era

Kissyman & The Gentleman

Modern Day Era

Infected (Infected Trilogy Book I)

Contagious (Infected Trilogy Book II)

Ancestor

Nocturnal

Pandemic (Infected Trilogy Book III)

Earthcore

Mount Fitz Roy

The Galactic Football League Series

Book I: The Rookie

Title Fight (novella)

Book II: The Starter

Book III: The All-Pro

The Rider (novella)

The Detective (novella)

The Reporter (novella)

Book IV: The MVP

The Reef (novella)

Book V: The Champion

The Stone Wolves (novella)

Book VI: The Gangster

The Generations Trilogy

Alive

Alight

Alone

NON-SIGLERVERSE BOOKS:

The Man in Gray Series

Slay

Media Tie-Ins

Aliens: Phalanx

The Color Series short story collections

Blood is Red

Bones are White

Fire is Orange

*This novel is dedicated to Lt. Col. Maryann Radulski
and Lt. Col. Jake Radulski. Thank you for your service—and for
raising a daughter whose strength,
humor, and integrity helped shape this story.*

No Spoilers!
If you review this novel in any format or discuss it online—be it on
social media, in blogs, or anywhere else—please don't spoil the big
moments for others who have not yet read it.

I only get one chance to delight a reader.
If you—in wondrous enthusiasm or rage-read annoyance—reveal the
key moments and concepts in *Voidstrike*, or in Book I, *Shakedown,*
I lose that rare opportunity.

We live in a shared world. Please be considerate of others.

***The Crypt* Galactic Map: scottsigler.com/map**

Voidstrike involves a complex, covert mission that crosses several borders. If you'd like to see the political boundaries involved, I've posted the galactic map at my website. This map focuses on the *Galactic Football League* era of my continuum—set 200 years after *The Crypt* series—but the borders are essentially the same.

And if you're intrigued by the idea of a sprawling sci-fi quest set against a backdrop of multiple sentient species locked in lethal combat on the gridiron, check out *The Rookie*, Book I of my Galactic Football League series. Learn more at scottsigler.com/the-rookie.

This book is part of the extended Siglerverse continuum. If you'd like to see the events that led to the various political alignments and entanglements, check the Galactic Timeline at the Siglepedia wiki: scottsigler.com/timeline

Keeling's surface looked like a forest of pointy tree stumps the color of freshly hammered copper.

Bethany Darkwater walked through those stumps, her vacsuited hand lingering on the curved, rough surfaces. Each spire was about a meter in diameter at the base, tapering up two meters to a wicked-looking barb. The hangar's many lights made the burnished surfaces seem to glow from within.

Her fakegrav boots kept her attached to *Keeling*'s hull, although whether the irregular, green-patinaed surface between the spires was the actual hull or some kind of coating atop it, she did not know. That particular detail remained a mystery. The spires were so thick they almost blocked her view of *Keeling*'s superstructure, its angular architecture softened by the same spiky, asymmetrical coating.

Despite the cylindrical hangar being fully pressurized, Bethany wore a standard-issue, light blue vacsuit as a precaution. A wise one, she knew, considering the damage inflicted when the chrysalis first formed. Better safe than sorry. Battered support beams and cracked panels stood as witness to *Keeling*'s violent "cocooning" incident. The hangar's shell hid blocked views of both the vastness of space and the dead rock known as Pearson's Planet, around which Gateway Station orbited.

While she'd choose *safe* over *sorry* every time, she hated wearing the vacsuit. No matter what internal temperature she specified, she always felt cold. For that matter, everywhere on Gateway seemed a bit chilly to her. She hadn't felt warm since she'd evaced from *Keeling* three weeks ago, moments before this lumpy, spiky coating covered the ship.

Bethany wanted to be warm again. She wanted to be in the beautiful atrium. She wanted to be near the heartstone and bask in its golden glow. She wanted to be in *the Mud* again, where, sometimes, God communed with her.

Oh, the wondrous things she'd seen...

"Ensign Darkwater, sir, does this spot look good?"

Bethany turned to face Spec-1 Michael Camp, machinist mate. He, too, wore a vacsuit, his wide visor letting Bethany see his entire face, his expression of annoyance.

She'd lost track of time. Again. She'd meant to give this section of hull a slow walk, to see if she might be inspired by a deep divot here, a fracture there, but she'd found no breaks in the chrysalis's rough, undulating surface.

Behind Camp stood Spec-1 Leona Romanik, a xenobiologist. She gripped the drive-bar of a thick sled, upon which sat the intermolecular grinder, a compact device about the size of a dorm fridge. Romanik didn't look annoyed. She looked scared. Bethany couldn't blame her. Romanik did not yet know the glory that was *Keeling*.

It still struck Bethany as a bit odd to have people reporting to her. As an Ensign, or *O-1*, she held the lowest officer rank in Fleet, yet she outranked every enlisted sailor, no matter how experienced they might be. That included, obviously, the rank of Specialist-1, or *E-1*, which sat at the very bottom of Fleet's hierarchy.

Bethany and Camp each had one *Keeling* deployment under their belts. Romanik, on the other hand, had yet to see the ship's interior. She'd been at Gateway for all of a week. What had the woman done to be assigned to *Keeling*? Bethany did not know.

Bethany didn't know Camp's violations, either, but from the way he leered at her and always tried to find a reason to press his body against hers in *Keeling*'s close confines, she suspected his crimes were of the sexual nature.

"This spot is as good as any, I suppose," Bethany said. She pointed to a space between two spires. "Let's start there."

Thousands of spires—4,473 of them, to be exact, she'd done the count three times—dotted the chrysalis covering *Keeling*'s 110-meter-long hull. One hundred and *twelve* meters, actually; the chrysalis added to *Keeling*'s overall length. While no two spires looked exactly alike, any differences were lost amongst their sheer volume.

Bethany thought she saw something recognizable embedded in the chrysalis. She knelt for a closer look; the remnants of one of the many sensors that made up *Keeling*'s complex optical system, which allowed them to see the Mud—a good thing, as it was rumored that seeing the Mud with the naked eye made people go mad.

This particular sensor had once been a small disc, about three centimeters in diameter. Perhaps for radio or IR, she wasn't sure. Either way, now it was junk, bent, broken, and half-buried by the chrysalis. It looked like a coin caught in metallic magma that had first warped it, then cooled around it.

Before the chrysalis formed, hundreds of these tiny sensors had been spaced across the hull—like an insect's compound eye, with each ommatidium set meters apart from the next. Bethany didn't know the system's finer points, as her department wasn't responsible for it.

Bethany stood as Romanik activated the sled's fakegrav base and secured it to the hull. Camp began unfolding the grinder's compact drilling arms.

With Colonel Hasik gone—to where, Bethany did not know—and Lead Xeno Jenn Hathorn dead, the mystery of the chrysalis fell to Bethany. *We need her back on the line*, Epperson had told her in his quiet voice that still, somehow, felt like he screamed every syllable. He needed his prized, classified warship for a new mission. What was that mission? Bethany didn't know that, either.

Hathorn. Another group therapy session coming up in a few days, when she would have to talk about Hathorn again...

So what *was* going on with *Keeling*? Bethany hadn't a clue. The ship possessed the most advanced technology she'd ever encountered, and she'd spent her entire professional life in the study of automatonics. That was when she'd been *Susannah Rossi*, though, before Admiral Bock strong-armed her into becoming *Bethany Darkwater* and made her spy on this ship and its crew.

Bethany didn't like to think about *Susannah* anymore. That era of her life had been one of pain and betrayal. Lost years. She had a new life now, in the service of God and in the field of xenomechanics, a.k.a, *unknown alien technology*.

"We're ready, sir," Camp said.

"Proceed," Bethany said.

The intramolecular grinder—*IMG*, for short—marked a last hope of sorts. She needed to take a sample of the chrysalis material back to Gateway's labs for detailed analysis, but they couldn't break off even the smallest bit of it. Diamond-tipped drills ground to dust. Laser cutters proved worthless. Plasma torches that burned hotter than the corona of a typical G-type star didn't leave a mark. While she knew using high explosives and/or penetrator munitions would work, she—and Epperson—were hesitant to do anything that might damage the ship beneath the chrysalis.

The IMG utilized gravitational waves to move material in opposite directions, in a back-and-forth motion so powerful it literally split molecules. If the IMG couldn't get the sample, they'd have to use ordinance.

"Initiating first cut," Camp said. "Romanik, go ahead."

Romanik gripped the cutter's boom. She knelt and placed the fist-sized drill head against the smooth surface. A small light atop the drill head shifted from red to green. The IMG produced a vibrating, thrumming sound.

"Instruments register a split," Camp said. "It's working."

He sounded excited. Bethany certainly was. With a sample to analyze, she could—

She sensed movement behind her. She turned, looked at one spire, then the next, then the next. Had they shifted?

A wave of fear ripped through her.

What were Romanik and Camp doing?

Why were they *hurting* her?

Panic building, *anger* building...

Bethany realized those emotions were not *hers*.

"*Shut it off*," she said. "Specialist Camp, shut it down right—"

A sound like the tinkling of metal wind chimes. Two coppery spires *moved*, rigid as steel one moment, flexible as dough the next. One spire curled down like a striking snake, its wicked barb piercing the IMG in a crunch of metal and plastic.

Romanik stood, leaving the drill head in place. She, too, saw the second spire's movement, but too late—the narrow barb drove straight through her chest. The spire bent upward, lifting her into the air, then, like a cracking whip, smashed her down hard against chrysalis's surface.

Bethany couldn't move. Couldn't think.

Camp ran, panicking so badly both feet lost contact with the surface. He drifted away from the ship, arms and legs flailing. A spire stretched out toward him, thinning as it lengthened. Bethany thought it would run him through, but instead the material wrapped around one ankle, then quickly and gently drew him back to the hull until his fakegrav boots clonked down.

Bethany was distantly aware of a voice inside her helmet, yelling at her, demanding her attention, but she could not listen—not when she faced God's wrath.

For a long moment, she and Camp stood still, frozen with fear, watching the spires return to their original, upright orientation.

They moved no more.

A new sound, like dozens of guitar strings being tightened all at once—thin threads of copper extended from the hull and stretched across Romanik, who was on her back, making the feeble, ineffective movements of one hurt and dying. A blob of dark, rubbery material marked the spot where her suit had sealed the bloody, fist-sized puncture. That was what vacsuits did, sealed holes to maintain internal pressure and air integrity, but that automatic response would do nothing to stop her internal bleeding.

If they could get Romanik to medical, they might save her still...

That thought vanished as the wires thickened, tightened, began to pull *down*.

Bones snapped.

Romanik let out a sound, a horrid sound, a desperate, wheezing moan of pain as the strands widened, *spread*, overpowering her, dragging her *into* coppery metal that flowed like water.

In seconds, she vanished from sight. The chrysalis reformed above her, with nary a dent or divot to mark the spot.

A heartbeat. Another.

"Ensign Darkwater, can you hear me!"

The voice inside her helmet.

"Yes... I can hear you."

Her own words sounded distant, somehow separated from reality.

"Fast response is en route," the voice said. "Can you tell me what's going on? What just happened?"

Wasn't it obvious?

"We cut into the hull," she said. "The ship defended itself."

1

TRAVIS

Lieutenant Travis Ellis checked his service uniform in the mirror. Everything was crisp and sharp. He'd always taken pride in his appearance, but as he looked himself up and down, he realized that—for the first time in his career—he didn't feel comfortable all buttoned up and proper. During his two weeks aboard *Keeling*, he'd grown an appreciation for coveralls with arms tied around the waist to give some relief against the constant heat and humidity, and for sweat spotted T-shirts that should have been changed but why bother when the next one would become comparably rank in mere minutes? No one on *Keeling*, including Captain Kiara Lincoln, gave a damn about razor-sharp seams or polished boots.

Still, he was about to see Admiral Epperson, the bastard who'd put him on that ship of nightmares. Epperson was a stickler for appearance. Epperson was a stickler for *everything*.

Satisfied with what he saw, Trav sat at his desk. His Pier Two quarters were four times the size of his tiny *Keeling* compartment. Most of his current space went unused; he didn't want to become accustomed to extra room. Anything not hanging in his closet he stored in his footlocker.

He checked his in-box. Nothing yet. He was expecting a message from Molly.

Many lightyears separated Gateway Station from his home at Crindalon Base, which orbited Neptune. Messages to or from his family traveled via punch-relay, one vessel carrying the message from one punch-point to another, then transmitting the message to a waiting ship before that ship then traveled to the next stop. Every message from his wife was at least a standard week old before it reached him.

And that was *before* Bureau of Information and Intelligence studied each one. BII agents searched for phrases, gestures, or even facial expressions that might constitute a possible breach of secrecy.

Six months, one week, and six days since he'd touched Molly, since he'd held their daughter, Aven. His second daughter, Kinley, still in Molly's womb, was due in two months. Would he be there for her birth?

Travis stood. He paced—something he could actually do in this room as opposed to his tiny compartment aboard *Keeling*. Once upon a time, Gateway Station housed ten thousand permanent staff and accommodated crew from dozens of ships docked there. These days, the huge facility went largely unused. Piers One, Three, and Four sat empty, their long framework arms stretching out into space. Three of Sixth Group's warships—frigate *Talita*, destroyer *Richthofen*, and light cruiser *Winghead*—were docked at Pier Five, two kilometers away from *Keeling*'s hangar. The rest of Sixth Group—destroyer *Fu Hao*, carrier *Shu*, and supercarrier *Akathaso* orbited farther out, some three thousand klicks from the station.

The *Ishlangu* crew—those few who'd survived, anyway—were supposedly somewhere on the century-old station, receiving medical care and recovering from their ordeal. They couldn't simply go home or be sent to another duty station, not when they'd been aboard the Union's biggest secret. BII evaluated each person, ensuring they would not tell tales out of school. Travis assumed *Keeling* crew endured a similar process when their mandatory two-year stint ended.

Two years, of which Travis had ninety-eight weeks remaining.

Ten minutes until he had to leave for the debriefing. Since *Keeling*'s return after extracting Paul Cooley from Purist Nation territory, Epperson had spoken to Travis only once, when the admiral castigated him for engaging the Purist warships that ambushed *Ishlangu*. Epperson even hinted that Trav's death sentence for cowardice in combat—a sentence that would be wiped clean if Trav completed his two-year hitch—remained a very real possibility. The dressing down ended abruptly when *Keeling* extruded a strange coating that sealed the ship off completely. No one had been inside since.

Every effort to penetrate the coating came up wanting. Yesterday, Darkwater tried a new method, which resulted in the death of Spec-1 Leona Romanik, one of the few replacements who had reported for duty.

Today, Epperson wanted answers.

Answers Travis did not have—*Keeling* remained a terrifying mystery even to those who crewed her.

Ten minutes... now nine... might as well study.

He sat at his desk, called up the interface.

Fleet Command had pushed through an upgrade of the CMS—*contact management system*—that every warship used to track friends, foes, and others. New protocols for nav-orbs, new naming nomenclature for any and all contacts. Such "improvements" happened from time to time. Travis and every other crewmember who operated in *Keeling*'s CIC needed to know the new terms like the back of their hands.

He'd mastered it, but it didn't hurt to make sure.

The desk chimed: *new message*. Travis reduced the CMS information and called up his messages.

New video message from Ellis, M.

His chest felt pinched, twisted.

Travis opened the message. A first-frame still of pregnant Molly, sitting on their living room couch. No Aven on her lap. The look on his wife's face... the deep sadness ringing her eyes...

The waiting "play" button seemed like the trigger of a suicide device.

Holding his breath, Travis clicked it. When he did, the love his life, the mother of his children, spoke to him.

"Hi, Travis. I... there's no easy way to say this, so I'll just say it. I can't do this anymore." She choked on the next word. Her lips pressed into a tight line. Travis saw her muster the will to continue. "It's not good for the kids. It's not good for me. I'm filing for divorce and full custody. I hope you'll do the smart thing, because if you fight me on this the court is going to take my side. I know this hurts you, and I'm sorry. It hurts me, too. A video is an awful way to tell you, but I have no idea how long it would be until I could do it face-to-face. This is the right thing, for all of us. Let me know when you'll get parole, or leave, or—" she shrugged, sniffed back tears "—or whatever it is, and I'll arrange for you to see Aven. And, probably by then, your new daughter. Goodbye, Travis."

The screen went black.

Divorce.

Divorce.

From an early age, Travis had dreamed of three things: escaping the prison of living with his abusive grandmother; captaining a warship; and being a family man, a good husband and father. He'd achieved the first goal. He'd given up on the second—after his court-martial, he knew he'd never get a chance. And now, the third and final goal looked to be at the end of a slow, consuming death.

If Molly left him, what would he do? What meaning would his life still have?

His watch buzzed; time to leave for the meeting with Epperson.

His heart a dead thing not yet ready to accept—or even understand—what had just happened, Travis stood. He gave his uniform one last examination, then left his quarters.

2

SASCHA

When Pier Two served four, five, or even six Fleet vessels at a time, the Pier Two Barracks Lounge might have been a hot spot. Room for a hundred in here, easy. With only the *Crypt* moored, though, the lounge was a ghost town. Empty chairs, empty tables, empty couches, empty terminals with blank displays.

Huddled at a corner terminal, Ochthera engineer/gunner Rudolf Friseal, who went by the call-sign "Good Dog," off duty and dressed in civvies, typed away. An evaluation exam, most likely, one of many required for entry into pilot training.

At one table by the far wall sat Sergeant Paulo Fuentes, lead propulsion tech, and Spec-1 Li Ying, propulsion mate. They each read from a tablet. Maybe they were studying. Fuentes wore standard-issue sweats and a T-shirt. Perhaps he'd just come from the gym. Ying was in light gray service coveralls. She always wore coveralls—even in the heat and humidity of *Keeling*'s lower decks, she wanted to hide the pale-white vitiligo patches that dotted her almond-colored skin.

She couldn't hide her face, though. Makeup didn't fully conceal the irregular splotches marking her cheeks and forehead. Genetic therapy to remove them was more expensive than a sailor could afford. If she'd been born in the League of Planets instead of the Union, they'd have fixed her condition before she was old enough to crawl. The League had better bioengineering tech. And had money to burn, it seemed.

Other than those three, only two people occupied the lounge: Lieutenant Sascha Kerkhoffs, engineering department head, and Warrant Officer Junior Grade Doug Erickson, navigation chief. They sat at a long table in the room's center, speaking in hushed tones and peering at a tablet laid flat.

"Impossible," Sascha said. "Check it again."

Erickson shook his head. "No. It's correct."

He was a selfish jackass, but the man knew his mass spec. He'd started his career in engineering before transferring to operations and pursuing a navigator track.

After the battle against the Purist destroyer and corvettes, in which *Keeling*'s superstructure armor failed, Sascha followed standard post-conflict procedure and collected samples of the damaged material. Upon arrival at Gateway—and before the strange, metallic skin encased *Keeling* from stem to stern—she'd turned most of those samples over to Admiral Epperson's people. They, in turn, passed them on to the Bureau of Science & Technology, the Union's military science division. BST studied armor strikes, always searching for ways to make the multi-layered material better, more resilient.

Sascha had turned over *most* samples, but not all. A few she'd kept for herself. She didn't trust Epperson, and she didn't trust BST.

Corporal Cass Mollen died because a single Purist missile penetrated *Keeling*'s armor, armor that should have handled the strike with ease. Sascha wanted to know what went wrong. Captain Lincoln said she would make the enquiries and ordered Sascha to leave it be.

But Sascha didn't trust Lincoln, either.

In a way, Sascha hadn't disobeyed the order. She hadn't researched the armor—she'd made the silver-tongued, natural-born conman Erickson do it for her.

He'd filed a statement saying he suspected density variation between the port- and starboard-side armor might cause navigation complications while in the Mud. Therefore, he needed to know more about the armor's material composition and manufacture. Lieutenant Alex Plait, the ship's operations department head, gave Erickson leeway to pursue anything critical to *Keeling*'s function and survival. Anything potentially affecting navigation fell under that umbrella.

Erickson's tactic pursued the same info Sascha wanted, but from a different angle. He wasn't looking for *failures*, he was looking for *solutions*, a subtle difference let him look where Sascha could not.

"You're *sure*," Sascha said. "*Keeling*'s armor was originally installed on the *Boudicca*?"

Erickson nodded. "One hundred percent sure."

During the Battle of Asteroid X7, Purists captured the light cruiser *Blackmouth*. Travis Ellis, who'd been in command of the frigate *Schild* at the time, ordered his damaged vessel to retreat, leaving *Boudicca* unprotected—*Blackmouth*'s guns tore her to pieces.

Some of those pieces wound up installed on *Keeling*'s super-structure.

"We got repurposed armor," Sascha said, "but from a *destroyed* ship? How could they think the armor was combat worthy? Did they test it?"

Doug shrugged. "If they did, I can't find the test results. At least not in Gateway's database. We'd have to file a records request with Epperson's office. If you want to do that, go crazy, but leave me out of it."

Things didn't add up. *Keeling* was the Union's secret weapon, a ship that did something no other ship in existence could. *Keeling* had a black budget—so why was everything on it so *cheap*? The Raider platoon's old TASH rigs. Reused armor plating. Obsolete Ochtheras.

"Check requisition orders," Sascha said. "See if there's a line-item cost for the *Boudicca*'s armor."

"Line-items costs also necessitate direct requests to Epperson. He controls the purse strings. Look, I did what you asked. Like I said—from here on out, leave me out of this."

Sascha understood her own actions, her own *choices*, landed her on the *Crypt*. Do the crime, do the time, but she was doing that time because Doug Erickson ratted her out.

They and their little crime crew made a tidy sum defrauding Fleet. When any ship Sascha served on needed maintenance, resupply, or modification, she and Doug used their influence to make sure Hunata Industries got the contract despite Hunata always coming with the highest bid, and by a good margin. A healthy chunk of that fee got kicked back to Sascha, Erickson, and the others in their cadre. It wasn't even a *crime*, really—Hunata did good work. And hey, it was taxpayer's money, who was going to miss it?

The bean-counters at BII. That's who.

They'd busted Erickson. In an attempt to save his own hide, he'd given up the rest of the ring, including Sascha and Daniel Monstranto, *Keeling*'s supply chief. Erickson's betrayal didn't save him—his sentence put him aboard *Keeling* alongside those he'd ratted out.

"Find a way around the regs," Sascha said. "Like you did for years before you got caught. Put those skills to work. Get me those costs."

He flashed her a comforting smile, the same easy grin that once made her believe he knew what he was doing, that they could run their victimless supply scam indefinitely and never be caught. The smile crinkled his eyes, eyes so brown she should have always known he was full of shit.

"Look, Sascha, I just want to serve my time on the *Crypt*. I don't want any more trouble. I helped you. You take it from here. All right?"

Erickson was a weasel in human form. She despised the man.

"Warrant Officer JG Erickson," she said, quietly but with force, "you will address me as *Lieutenant Kerkhoffs. Lieutenant*, as in *five ranks* above you."

He tried to hold eye contact but withered under her unabashed hatred.

"I'm entombed on *Keeling* because of *you*," she said. "You will do what I say, when I say, or I'll make your time harder than it already is."

He huffed. "Harder than it already is? What are you going to do, *Lieutenant Kerkhoffs*—sentence me to the *Keeling*?"

She leaned closer. He didn't lean away, but that clearly took all the will he possessed.

"You *owe me*," Sascha said. "A debt unpaid until I say so. If my rank isn't enough to make you comply, I'll play dirty. I know where to find you, Doug. Once we're underway again, there's no place you can hide."

The words flowed out like molten magma coursing into the sea, boiling and hissing with steam. She'd never spoken to anyone like that before—it felt *good*.

"You're threatening me," he said. "I could report you. What if that's enough for Lincoln to replace you with Ledford?"

During the last deployment, Corporal Barnes Marchenko—then Staff Sergeant Marchenko—secretly machined crude blades from the ship's copper alloy. Those blades resulted in the death of Jenn Hathorn, Phillip Eskander, and nearly the death of Colonel Hasik. Chenk didn't remember making the blades. Lafferty found a note with five of his thumbprints made with his own blood; Chenk had apparently used the shivs to cut himself as a bizarre, final quality control measure.

For making weapons that resulted in two deaths and two additional assaults, Lincoln busted Marchenko down from staff sergeant to corporal. Sergeant Zhen Smith replaced him as Auxiliary Division Chief. That Marchenko wasn't wasting away in a brig was testament to the secrecy surrounding *Keeling*—a sailor experienced with the ship was not to be tossed away for something so trivial as causing the death of two sailors.

Marchenko was under Sascha's command. Any action of a subordinate rolled up to the department head. Lincoln had ripped Sascha a new asshole, threatened to replace her as engineering department head as soon as they returned to port. Lincoln hadn't pulled the trigger on that yet, but she'd made it clear who would replace Sascha if she did—Warrant Officer JG Adam Ledford, *Keeling*'s propulsion division chief.

If Lincoln did make that move? Sascha honestly didn't give a shit.

"Go ahead and rat me out, Erickson," she said. "That's what you're good at, right? Just know that if you do rat me out again, for *any reason*, I will hurt you. If you like your shriveled-up bitch balls connected to your body, you'll do what I say."

He couldn't hold her gaze. He had ten centimeters and forty pounds on her, but Doug Erickson was *soft*. He was a coward.

"I'll keep looking," he said.

She stared at him a bit longer, just to make sure he knew the score.

"Good," she said. "Now go get at it."

3

JOHN

Smoke drifted through the passageway, partially masking the insane combinations of colors and patterns swirling along the deck, overhead, and bulkheads.

Corporal John Bennett's TASH armor kept the smoke out of his eyes and lungs, prevented sounds of close-quarters combat from damaging his ears. RR-36 stock tight to his shoulder, he knelt at a corner junction. Leaning out, he sighted through the haze and fired—more smoke billowed from his backblast tube as the 20-millimeter round covered the short distance in an instant. He hit his target but did not put it down.

"Cross on my mark," John said. "Beaver first, then Abs. Abs, flasher!"

Spec-1 Neal Abshire lobbed a grenade down the passageway. It bounced off a crazily strobing bulkhead and skidded across the deck before erupting in pulsing, plasma-bright light.

"*Go*," John said.

Spec-1 Jim "Beaver" Perry ran for the far corner. He was the fastest in the squad—in the entire platoon, really—but compared to the enemy, he moved like a puppy stepping through tar. Rounds whizzed by him, barely missing their mark.

He reached the corner, knelt, and sent covering fire toward the enemy.

"*Go*," John said.

Abshire crossed the intersection—a shot clipped his left leg, flashing on impact. He stumbled but stayed on his feet, passing Beaver to reach cover.

Beaver waved John in, then laid down more suppressing fire, his RR-36 kicking out plumes of smoke.

John stood and sprinted across the passageway. Madly swirling, alien designs on every surface toyed with his depth perception. An enemy round glanced off his helmet—his HUD registered the hit but showed no damage.

He passed the corner as Beaver yanked a grenade from his hip mag-mounts. John found Abshire standing, rifle mag-clamped to his chest. His gauntleted fingers worked at his lower left leg, pressing at recessed controls.

"Compensator's jammed," he said. "Can't get it to adjust. Leg's out of commission."

The rest of the platoon was already dead—John, Abs, and Beaver were the last ones standing. With Abs impaired, it was time to evac.

"*Frag out*," Beaver screamed, so loud his voice distorted the audio. "Eat tinsel, motherfuckers!"

John heard the grenade's detonation, heard the tinkle of "shrapnel" skitter off metal walls. That would hold off the enemy for a few precious seconds.

"I'm point," John said. "Abs, stay close. Beaver, cover the rear. Move!"

John fast-walked down the passageway. He eyed his HUD's rear-cam panel, saw Abshire hopping along, his suit's internal gyros adjusting for the off-balance movement. Behind Abs, Beaver shuffled backward, his RR-36 ready to fire at any pursuers.

All the mad colors on the walls... all the insane patterns...

John tried to block out memories of his friends dying in a passageway similar to this one, memories of screeching, see-through

Sklorno coming at them like suicide savages desperate to tear flesh from bone.

Tear it free... and *eat* it.

Up ahead, on the right... that opening should lead to the hull-adjacent passageways. Any escape hatch could get him and his men into the void's embrace where they could jet away to safety.

But from that same opening came six black-as-space soldiers in TASH rigs sleeker and less bulky than John's, moving faster than anything John had seen before.

"Contact, front!" John dropped to a knee and shouldered his rifle. Enemy fire poured in heavy and dense. A round hit his chest, his raised knee, his left shoulder. Those areas of his armor froze. He fell to his side, his RR clattering to the crazy-colored deck.

Abshire went down next, a headshot dropping him like a sandbag. Red lights on his back pulsed rapid-fire—he was dead.

Beaver stepped past John and Abs both, knelt close to the bulkhead, opened up on full auto, 20-millimeter rounds punching momentary negative-space trails through the smoke.

John tried to rise, tried to find the balance to do so when half his armor wouldn't react. He reached for his rifle, looking down the passageway as he did.

So *fast*.

Three Raiders closed in. Perfect fan formation, all clear of each other's backblast, all firing simultaneously. A round hit John square in the chest. His armor froze up completely—he was out of the fight.

Beaver took a hit, fell to the deck in front of John.

"Fucknuggets," Beaver said. "They got me."

John couldn't move. A TASHed enemy knelt in front of him, rifle clamped to his chest, big Raider knife in his hand. The name DIET-RICH on his left breast. On his right, the Raider symbol and the four down-pointed chevrons of a Master Sergeant. Below that, in smaller letters, the word AKATHASO.

"Hey there, Old Man Bennett," Dietrich said. "Look at you with one little chevron. A corporal now, huh? Whose wang did you gobble to finally get a promotion?"

Fucking great. Had to be *this* asshole.

"Hey, Master Sergeant Dickdrip," John said.

Dietrich tapped the knife blade against John's helmet.

"I haven't heard that nickname in a while, Bennett. Probably because anyone who says it gets their jolly jumblies sliced off. I'm sure yours are shriveled like raisins and dangle to your knee, which will make 'em easier to cut. We should spar sometime soon."

A thing John did *not* want to do. Dietrich was a puma in man-form.

"*I'll* spar with you, Master Sergeant Dietrich," Beaver said, sounding quite chipper for a man who'd just burned to death. "Anytime, anywhere. It would be fun!"

"Shut up, Spec," Dietrich said. "Bennett, I've never seen your ship, but I hear it's even uglier than your wrinkled old nutsack of a face."

Anger twisted John's heart. Disrespecting a Raider was one thing. Disrespecting a Raider's *ship* was another.

"Nice rig," John said. "That a V15 you're wearing? I see you needed the latest and greatest to beat us."

Dietrich laughed. "*Sure,* old timer. Blame it on your gear. Pathetic."

Old timer. True enough. Dietrich was pushing forty—John was old enough to be the man's father. Hell, he was old enough to be Beaver and Abshire's *grand*father.

"Speaking of rigs," Dietrich said, "let me leave a little something on yours. You know, to remember me by."

John sat there, motionless and seething, as Dietrich use the tip of his knife to carve a "D" on the side of John's helmet.

4

BETHANY

"I keep telling you, I don't remember," Bethany said. "I mean no disrespect, Lieutenant Issac, but until my recollection improves, which may or may not happen, your continuous repetition of this question seems like a waste of time for everyone."

Lieutenant Nikki Issac tapped her stylus against the flexipaper resting on her lap. She was always doing that. She tapped it with her right hand, of course, because she had no left arm. The left sleeve of her BST service tans was neatly rolled up and pinned just below the stub that remained beneath her shoulder.

She made a note; she was always doing that, too.

Barnes Marchenko sighed. "What the fuck are you writing down, Doc?" He crossed his thick arms, leaned back in his plastic chair. "Ensign Darkwater says the same shit every goddamn session."

Marchenko was short and solid, thick like a blast door. He was a nice enough guy, Bethany figured, but anywhere other than aboard *Keeling* he seemed perpetually impatient and endlessly irritated.

"Kindly let me do my job, Corporal Marchenko," Issac said. She finished her note, lightly tapped the stylus tip on the flexi. "Warrant Akagi, how does what Ensign Darkwater said make you feel?"

Bethany bit her inner lip to keep from saying something. Always the same question with this hack of a psychologist—*how does that make you feel?*

Raider Warrant Officer Brendan Akagi, crawler co-pilot, call-sign *Brainiac*, sat slumped in his chair, staring blankly at the floor. He hadn't shaved in the three weeks since *Keeling's* chrysalis formed, resulting in an unkempt, worn-out paintbrush of a black beard. That was against regulations, but Fleet regs weren't a thing Captain Lincoln worried about all that much.

"It makes me feel sad," Akagi said. "All right? It makes me feel sad."

Issac tapped the stylus and made a note.

Marchenko rolled his eyes. "For fuck's fucking sake, you worthless *slug*. Let the man be."

Slugs. Because people in the Bureau of Science & Technology didn't go "over the top" from their trenches to attack, like Raiders did. Nor did they guide warships into combat, like sailors did. When a fight came, BST personnel just sat there—like slugs. Bethany didn't appreciate the pejorative, but she understood the nomenclature's logic.

Katharina Winter, Raider platoon executive officer—*PXO*—leaned forward in her chair, elbows on her knees.

"Chenk, knock it off," she said. "We'd all rather be somewhere else. Let Lieutenant Issac do her thing."

Marchenko leaned back in his chair, crossed his arms, and said nothing.

Winter outranked Marchenko, but that wasn't why he complied, Bethany figured. Warrant Officer Winter could probably snap the man in half without breaking a sweat.

Bethany found herself wanting to like Winter, but the Raider was beyond her understanding of the universe. Bethany had lived in a lab: solitude, quiet, peace. When that lab went away, she'd lived in a convent: solitude, quiet, peace. Winter, in contrast, lived in a tumult of violence. She *fought*, in *battles*, like something out of a story.

Bethany was short and thin. Winter was taller, only by a little, true, but thick with muscle, with shoulders so broad she probably had to angle herself a bit to get through some doors. And her keloid scars, so terrifying—a constellation of dusky streaks upon her beige skin—left when molten metal burned through a TASH visor.

The group session included people who had done violent things while in the Mud. *Really* violent things, that was. If they included everyone who threw a punch, half the crew would be here. At *least* half. As it was, the group included those who'd committed assault with a deadly weapon against their crewmates, those who provided weapons used in such assaults, and those—like Bethany—who had *killed* their crewmates.

Raiders Winter, Dave Starr, and Chris Brogan were in the first category. Marchenko and BII operative Jester Gillick were in the second, Chenk because he'd crafted the copper blades, Gillick because he'd used one to stab Colonel Hasik in the thigh, almost killing the man. The third category included Akagi, who'd bludgeoned Bhola Nessa to death with a pipe wrench, and Bethany, who'd apparently used one of Marchenko's blades to cut Jenn Hathorn's throat.

In the Mud, bad things happened.

The goal of this group was to help the perpetrators cope with any residual guilt, and to—hopefully—ensure they didn't repeat the performance on the next deployment.

Issac tapped her flexi. "Spec-one Brogan. How about you? Any new memories float to the surface since the last time we met?"

Brogan's pale blue eyes had a piercing quality to them, reminding Bethany of the Siberian Husky her neighbors owned when she was little, if Ol' Chomper had a buzz cut. He always sat as straight and as thin as a two-by-four, eyes forward. Unlike most of the sailors and many of his platoon mates, he had not relaxed into Lincoln's less-than-rigid ways. Brogan took being a Raider seriously. Maybe too seriously, but it wasn't Bethany's place to judge.

"Yes, Lieutenant Issac," he said. "I'm still not one hundred percent sure what happened, but I think I remember a... ah... a small creature telling me that Tatianna was going to murder my mother."

Issac made a note.

"Except... my mother's been dead for years." Brogan shifted in his seat. His hard stare softened. Bethany's heart broke from the shame written on his face. "But I guess that didn't matter. The voice told me to kill Tatianna. I... I still don't recall what happened after that."

Bethany knew the sense of helplessness that came from not knowing what had happened, from not known *why* you did something violent. Brogan was all of twenty years old. *Keeling* was only his second deployment. He remained in the crew. Raider Spec-1 Tatianna Dobrevski, on the other hand, had been declared medically unfit to serve after Brogan stabbed her with his combat knife.

"I see," Issac said. "Can you describe this small creature for us?"

Bethany had an idea of what Brogan would say. While the in-dim hallucinations varied wildly among the crew, there was one image that several people had mentioned—at least those few who actually shared what they saw.

"My recollection is a bit fuzzy, sir," Brogan said. "It sort of looked like a prawn. A furry prawn." He held his hand out, chest-level, palm-down. "Maybe this tall. I think it had three eyes... kind of a satin-gray color. Really wide head. And some green stuff coming out of its chin."

Issac made a note, but Akagi sat up straighter.

"*Green stuff,*" he said to Brogan. "Like a stiff beard, kind of?" Akagi put the back of his hand to his chin, waggled his fingers. "Or like... *ferns* or some shit?"

Brogan's brow furrowed. "The fuck is a *fern*, Brainiac?"

Of course Brogan didn't know. He was from the Vosor 3. He wouldn't know a fern from a fungus.

"Ferns are a vascular plant," Bethany said. "Polypodiopsida. Instead of leaves, they have fronds that unfurl in a spiral called a *circinate vernation*. Ferns reproduce with spores, not seeds."

Everyone looked at her, *squinted* at her.

She shrank into herself. Had she said something wrong?

"*Circular nation*," Brogan said. "What does that mean?"

Bethany shrank further. She wanted to hide. She would never, ever, learn how to talk to Raiders.

"It's a fucking *fern*, Jizzy," Marchenko said. "You know, like a bendable fishbone made of thin little green leaves."

Jizzy. Where *slug* was the common pejorative for BST personal, sailors called Raiders *jizzies*, because in combat, Raiders were shot out into space. So crude.

Akagi and Brogan both brightened.

"Like a *fishbone*," Akagi said, again wiggling his chin-fingers.

"Yeah, kinda." Brogan looked at Bethany. "Why didn't you just say that?"

Never, ever, *ever* learn how to talk to Raiders. Except for Nitzan. Talking to him had been easy. He'd...

Bethany pushed the thought away. She didn't want to think about Nitzan Shamdi or what Anne Lafferty had done to him.

"It's clear Warrant Akagi and Spec Brogan feel they have similar recollections," Issac said, writing on her flexi. "Warrant Akagi—tell the group about your experience seeing this vision. Was it the reason for your aggressive actions toward Ochthera pilot Nessa?"

Akagi again slumped in his chair, a balloon with half its air let out. He said nothing further.

Now all eyes switched to Issac. Bethany's included. Issac was bad at her job. Akagi clearly remembered more than he let on—perhaps memories of caving in someone's skull with a pipe wrench were not easily discussed.

Issac forced a smile. "How about you, Warrant Officer Gillick? Did one of these small creatures speak to you before your actions against—" she glanced at her flexi "—Colonel Hasik?"

Anywhere other than the group, Gillick talked a mile a minute, striking up conversations with anyone about anything. Typical for a BII spy, especially one tasked with spying on his own crewmates. In group, though, he watched and listened far more than he spoke.

"I have no recollection of the event," he said.

Marchenko huffed. "You mean other than your schnoz?"

When Bethany first boarded *Keeling*, Gillick had been handsome, with jet-black hair that matched his black BII uniforms, a smooth, steep-angled nose, and handsome, friendly, almond-shaped eyes. Now, yellow and purple patches hung under those eyes, some of the bruising coming from the headbutt he'd received from Nitzan Shamdi, and some of it from two surgeries—so far—to repair his badly broken nose.

"Eventually, my nose will look better," Gillick said. "Too bad we can't say the same for your leg."

Marchenko had lost his lower left leg in some battle somewhere. He wore a prosthetic made of solid metal. Aside from a slight limp, the fake leg didn't slow him down in the least.

"Fuck you, Gillick," Marchenko said.

Issac made a note.

"Lieutenant Issac," PXO Winter said, "perhaps it's time to end this session."

Issac looked up, realized that six people—each of whom were here because they had killed or *tried* to kill someone—were staring at her, none too happy with her approach.

"Ah... yes." She clipped the stylus to the flexi. "I will see you all back here in four days." She stood, quickly enough to make her chair squeak as it slid backward a few centimeters. "Good day to you all."

She tucked the flexi under her severed left arm and was out the door before anyone spoke a word.

"Fucking slugs," Winter said. She glanced at Bethany. "Not you, though, Darkwater. You're all right."

Bethany knew the Raiders thought she was *all right* because she'd figured out how to send *Keeling* into the Mud and escape the Purist task force, therefore saving the ship and all aboard. In the midst of brutal combat, it hadn't been a Raider or a sailor who saved the day— it had been a lowly *slug*.

If that was the reason the Raiders seemed to accept Bethany, that was fine with her. Raiders were a mean and scary bunch. Better to be on their good side.

"Thanks, PXO," Bethany said. "I appreciate it."

And in a bizarre, very un-rational, un-scientific, *primitive* way, she really did.

5

ANNE

Major Anne Lafferty did not like the look in Admiral Epperson's eyes.

"I want an explanation," he said. "If you four can't give me one, I will be disappointed."

You four, lined up shoulder to shoulder at parade rest in front of Epperson's desk, including the triumvirate command of *Keeling*—Captain, XO, and Intel Chief. Beth, a lowly ensign, was the only member of *Keeling*'s xeno department on-station, which made her the department's de facto commanding officer. In addition, a crewman's death occurred under her leadership; this meeting would not go well for her, Anne knew.

"We do not yet have an explanation, sir," Captain Lincoln said. "We're working on it. It would be most helpful if Colonel Hasik took charge. May I ask when he will return?"

Anne cringed inside. Lincoln had responded to an admiral's question with a question of her own. Disrespectful and dangerous, but Kiara Lincoln, above all others, embodied an ethos that permeated the crew—*What are they going to do, sentence me to the* Crypt?

Anne, the XO, and Beth were dressed appropriately for a meeting with an admiral: Ellis in his service grays, looking sharp as a tack;

Beth in her BST service tans; and Anne in regulation-perfect BII service blacks.

Lincoln, on the other hand, wore the same light gray coveralls she wore aboard *Keeling*. Her stupid red bandana finished off her rumpled, wrinkled, and all-around *embarrassing* appearance.

"Hasik is not here," Epperson said. "You are."

The office, which Epperson commandeered from the base commander, was over a century old and it showed—patched walls, scratched bookshelves, bumpy gray paint. The admiral, though, looked every bit the part of the crisp, sharp leader he was. Service grays spotless and pressed. The four stars on each collar gleamed, as did the metal of his wireframe glasses. His freckled pate reflected the overhead lights. The wrinkles around his eyes had deepened a bit, maybe due to a lack of sleep. Or maybe it was from constantly kissing the ass of Malcom McKinney, president of the Planetary Union. Their close friendship was no secret.

McKinney, who was fighting impeachment for his handling of the war. And for his womanizing. And for alleged corruption. Anne bet BII higher-ups, her father included, knew plenty about that, but such things were above her pay grade.

"Admiral," Lincoln said, "my people can only do so much when they're not privy to the full body of research regarding *Keeling*. In addition, the shell the ship grew is new to everyone. Ensign Darkwater has had only weeks to study it. She's doing the work on her own. As I've told you before, she needs assistance."

Lincoln wasn't backing down. Beth needed help. Anne had asked her father, General Bart Lafferty, head of BII, if someone could be sent to assist. Daddy had been disappointed Anne let her emotions dictate her actions to the point where she asked him to use his influence. Nothing unusual there—Daddy was disappointed in her more often than not. That would change, Anne believed with all her heart.

It would change because she was better now.

She would never again feel that insistent *tapping* at the base of her skull.

Never feel the need, the *heat*.

She was better now.

She was better.

She had mastered her little problem and made it a thing of the past.

Still, though, Daddy had tried. He'd reached out to Epperson directly, resulting in the only replacement crewmember so far—Spec-1 xenobiologist Leona Romanik, fresh out of the Academy. Following Romanik's grisly demise, Beth was once again on her own, at least as far as trained scientific help was concerned.

"Excuses are like buttholes," Epperson said. "Everybody has one." He stared at Beth. "I want your take, Ensign, and I want it now. Tell me what happened."

Anne wanted to step in, but she could not help. At least Beth knew she was on the spot, hence her meticulous uniform and freshly trimmed, short black hair. Anne's red hair was even shorter, thanks to shaving it for her undercover mission on Varaha two months earlier.

Varaha... where Anne's best friend Olivia lived. Anne missed her. That was okay, though. Life moves on. Anne had a new best friend now.

"Admiral," Beth said, "are you talking about the *mechanical* aspects of what happened, or are you asking about the *principle?*"

Epperson leaned back slightly. "Excellent question. Mechanical first."

"Both the chrysalis material and the ship proper are automatonic in nature," Beth spoke with confidence, but Anne heard a tremor of fear lurking in her words. "Their inherent structure is akin to that of a multicellular organism, able to generate new material just as we might grow new skin or bones. The chrysalis material, though, is far more malleable. I've never seen anything like it. It is capable of going from a solid to a gel-like—or even *fluid*-like—consistency in an instant. The closest analogy is Prawatt minid tech, but Prawatt tech operates at nanoscale level, whereas the chrysalis's ductility is likely executed at the *molecular* level. As we are unable to gather a sample, my study is at a standstill."

"I'm familiar with your inability to gather samples, Ensign," the Admiral said. "In short, you're telling me you have no idea as to the mechanical nature of the tech that killed Spec-One Romanik. Now, as for the principle—*why* did it happen?"

"It's obvious," Bethany said. "The ship was defending itself."

Epperson's eyes narrowed.

"There were three people on the cutting team," he said. "So if the ship defended itself, why aren't you and Spec-One Camp in body bags?"

Beth half-nodded, as if answering some internal question.

"It's possible Camp and I weren't killed because *Keeling* knew us," she said. "We spent two weeks aboard. Romanik had never been inside. *Keeling* didn't recognize her as *crew*—it believed she was an unknown threat."

"It *believed*." Epperson leaned forward. "Ensign, are you telling me the ship is *sentient?* That it thinks for itself?"

His tone and body language told Anne this wasn't the first time he'd discussed the concept. No surprise really; aboard *Keeling*, Anne and her BII team had heard sailors and Raiders whispering similar thoughts.

"No, sir, I am not saying the ship is sentient," Beth said. "*Keeling* is an automatonic construct, clearly designed to take in data, categorize the data, and react according to preprogrammed behavioral models. While the method of defending itself makes it *appear* to be sentient, what the ship did is conceptually no different than an automated weapon defending an objective against attack."

Anne noticed something about her friend's carefully chosen words. Bethany had said *I am not saying the ship is sentient*. She had *not* said it *wasn't*.

The admiral leaned back in his chair. "Do you think Romanik's body is inside the chrysalis? Or possibly inside the ship?"

Epperson wasn't asking if there was any chance Romanik still lived. He'd seen the footage, as had Anne, Lincoln, and Ellis.

"I assume her remains are under the chrysalis," Darkwater said. "She was taken in by a form of phagocytosis. It's possible her body is between the chrysalis and the hull, an inverse relationship to a grain of sand between an oyster's shell and its mantle."

An *oyster?* Could the ship make Romanik into some kind of human pearl? Anne didn't even know what to think about that.

"Very well, Ensign," Epperson said. "Do you have any other ideas on how we might penetrate the... *chrysalis*... and gain access to the ship? We need *Keeling* back in service as soon as possible."

Epperson didn't care about Romanik's death. He probably didn't care about any of the people who'd died on *Keeling*'s last run. Or prior runs, for that matter. Anne didn't judge him—to reach Epperson's level, to command as many people as he did, his heart had to be iron. He likely saw sailors, Raiders, and strikers as little more than soldier ants.

"Admiral, my recommendation is to leave *Keeling* be for now," Beth said. "We've seen one defense mechanism. There might be more."

Epperson glanced from Beth to the XO, to Anne, then to Lincoln.

"It seems we don't have any other choice," he said. "Ensign, you are dismissed."

Beth left the office.

The admiral leaned forward again, rested his elbows on the desk, steepled his fingers.

"I need your ship back in action," he said. "We have a critical mission only *Keeling* can accomplish."

Anne's heart beat a little faster. For a moment, she thought Epperson might spill the beans, but he said no more. What a tease.

"I assume the mission involves Sklorno," XO Ellis said. "Our Raiders spent the last week combat-drilling in Sklorno ship mockups. I'm sure the admiral is aware our platoon is nine Raiders short of a full complement? We need time to integrate newbies. And they need better gear. Sir."

Say one thing for Ellis—he cleaned up real nice. When Anne first met him, he he'd been all spit and shine and looking fine. During the last deployment, though, his discipline slipped away. At times he was as bad as the belowdecks grunts: stubble on his face, hair a mess, coveralls rumpled, T-shirt sweaty and stanky.

Now, though, his perfectly combed jet-black hair looked soft and pullable. And those odd, amber eyes of his. So interesting. Some thought the XO had a cold, soulless gaze, like he stared straight through you. Anne agreed; she kind of liked it. Too bad he was married. Or, at least, too bad he honored those vows. In a ship filled with more rutting than a rabbit farm, the XO partook of nothing.

"I'm well aware of your complaints about gear, Lieutenant," Epperson said. "And *tired* of it as well. There's a war on. We make do with what we have."

Before the chrysalis formed, *Keeling*'s Raiders had taken their rigs and weapons off the ship to perform maintenance. Standard procedure. If they hadn't, the rigs would still be trapped inside.

"Replacement sailors and Raiders should arrive tomorrow," Epperson said, then turned his glare toward Anne. "Major Lafferty, your people will manage the intake. Kindly do a better job at watching these new crewmembers. We certainly don't want a repeat of the Shamdi situation."

Another rush of emotions, this time embarrassment and shame. Anne was *Keeling*'s Intel Chief. The responsibility to find any spies among the crew fell on her shoulders. And yet, blaming her for Nitzan Shamdi's rampage was like blaming a dinner guest for a chef's shitty cooking.

"Shamdi was a deep-cover operative well before he was assigned to *Keeling*," Anne said. "To do my job correctly, I need to be part of the crew selection process, not saddled with people others choose to send my way."

Hell, if Lincoln was pushing the admiral's boundaries a little bit, why couldn't Anne give it a try?

"The selection process is above your pay grade," Epperson said. "Speaking of doing your job correctly, if you'd done so, we'd have a lot more survivors from *Ishlangu*, now wouldn't we?"

That pissed Anne off. She'd risked her life to save those people. Shamdi had flown his TASH suit clear across an active battle space to reach the hauler flown by Beth—by brave, selfless Beth. No one saw Shamdi's betrayal coming. Not Anne, and not *super-spy* Paul Cooley, who'd been aboard *Keeling*.

Sometimes, in the grand chess match of clandestine operations, the foe changed the rules and simply outmaneuvered you.

"Yes, Admiral," Anne said. "Based on the Shamdi incident, though, I repeat my request for access to the crew's full jackets. Knowing what they did to wind up on our ship would help me focus my energy on more likely suspects."

She expected Epperson to bite her head off, but he seemed to consider the idea.

"Request denied, Major," he said. "For now. But I'll give it further consideration. All of you, find a way to bring *Keeling* back online. Dismissed."

Lincoln and Anne turned to leave, but the XO remained at parade rest.

"Admiral, if I may have a moment alone to discuss a personal issue?"

Anne and Lincoln paused. A personal issue? An issue with his family, perhaps?

"Of course, Lieutenant," Epperson said. "Kiara, Major Lafferty, shut the door behind you."

Anne wished she was the BII analyst reviewing incoming and outgoing messages for *Keeling*'s crew, but Epperson had his own handpicked people doing that task. Anne didn't know who they were. She'd have to find another way to learn what was going on with the XO.

She followed Captain Lincoln out of the office, and, as instructed, shut the door.

6

TRAVIS

"Make it quick," Epperson said.

The expression on his face, like this was an annoying check-box on his to-do list. The bastard *knew*. He knew what Travis wanted to ask. He knew about Molly's message.

Of course he did. His people screened every ingoing and outgoing message from *Keeling*'s crew.

"My wife filed for divorce," Travis said. "Since *Keeling* is effectively mothballed for now, I request leave to return home and address the situation."

In other words, *let me try to save my marriage.*

"Request denied," Epperson said. "Current crew leaving port, for any reason, is prohibited. Your personal life is no exception, Lieutenant. Dismissed."

Just like that. No pretense of sympathy or understanding. Not even a perfunctory *I'm sorry to hear that.*

Epperson had known known what Trav would ask, had known his answer, yet had let Travis ask anyway.

Anger and frustration clawed at Travis. Rage so raw it made his teeth ache. His wife, his children, he needed to fight for them, right now before it was too late...

...but the authority before him, the four stars on Epperson's collar. The Academy, drilling into him blind respect for command. Ten years in Fleet, conditioned to obey every order, *every order*...

He had to make his case, he had to make it now, he—

"I dismissed you, yet here you stand," Epperson said. "You are disobeying my orders, just like you did when *Ishlangu* was ambushed. Is that it, Lieutenant?"

That was a battle, people's lives were at stake, Travis had done what had to be done...

"Well, Lieutenant? Answer me."

Epperson hadn't spoken to Travis since the chrysalis formed. He'd thought Epperson had gotten over his anger. Travis had fought for the lives of the *Ishlangu* crew. Wasn't that what a Fleet officer was supposed to do?

"I... no, sir, I am not disobeying orders, it's just that—"

"May I remind you your sentence for cowardice in combat is *suspended* while you serve aboard *Keeling*. I can end that suspension any time I like."

The sentence... execution by venting...

"Yes, Admiral," Travis said. "I appreciate the opportunity, but since we are stuck here, I—"

"*Dismissed*, Lieutenant!"

Travis found himself at the office door, through it, out it, closing it behind him, the creeping specter of being blown out an airlock into the vacuum of space on his heels.

Epperson. An admiral. Commander of Sixth Group. King, emperor, even *god* of Gateway Station. There was no one above him, no higher power who might grant Trav's request.

No chance to see Molly, to stand in front of her and beg for more time.

Head roiling with anger and frustration, with a sense of utter helplessness, Travis was halfway back to his room before he realized what he'd done. Just like at Asteroid X7, he'd *run* from the fight.

That was why Epperson railroaded him aboard *Keeling*, wasn't it? Because the admiral believed if Travis wound up in command, when the shit hit the fan, Travis would run, thereby preserving Epperson's secret weapon.

In the Battle of *Ishlangu*, Travis hadn't run. He'd stayed. He'd found a way to win. But now, in port, with his family on the line, he'd backed down with barely any fight at all.

That son of a bitch... Epperson had used Trav's *marriage* as a fucking *test* to see if Travis was the same *yellowbelly* he'd been before.

Apparently, Travis was.

He'd missed his chance to stand up for himself. If he went back to Epperson now, he might receive that sentence after all. And if he did, his daughters would grow up without any father at all rather than one who lived thousands of lightyears away.

He felt ashamed. He felt weak. No wonder Molly wanted a divorce.

Travis headed for his room. As he walked, he thought of the message he would send home, another desperate Hail Mary that his wife wouldn't even watch.

7

BIGGIE

Warrant Officer Danielle "Biggie" Bang had three combat flights to her name. Three Raider Claws, the decoration given to APC crews each time they delivered Raiders onto the hull of an enemy ship. One Expeditionary Medal, for those who engage in combat outside Union territory. And one Fleet Arrow, the decoration given to the crew of a Fleet warship that destroyed an enemy vessel—all *Keeling* crew, even the dead, received one after the Battle of *Ishlangu.*

She was always ready and willing to fly an Ochthera into enemy fire and deliver a payload of armor-clad doom.

She was a warrior.

She was a bad motherfucker.

She was blue twisted steel and sex appeal, yet they had her doing a *literal* milk run, using one of *Keeling*'s two old-ass Ochthera-Bs to haul cargo from Gateway Station out to the Fleet's largest carrier.

"Lemme tell you something," said her co-pilot, Torchia Dudgeon. "That there is one goddamn big ship."

Biggie heard the laughter of engineer/gunner Dalia "Knuckles" Nikula, hidden away up in the Occie's top turret.

"I see you finally got a promotion, Torch," Knuckles said. "From *Corporal Dudgeon* to *Captain Obvious.*"

Akathaso's size defied logic. It was like an optical illusion you couldn't quite grok until you got close. At over a kilometer long, it took fifteen minutes to walk from the prow to the rear chemjet cones. Two hundred meters wide, close to forty meters tall for the main hull, then add another ten meters for the superstructure. Biggie figured fifteen *Keelings* might fit inside *Akathaso*. Maybe more. And the carrier's crew complement? Over *ten thousand* sailors, strikers, and Raiders.

Voidcraft flew in and out of *Akathaso*'s four flight bays. Rumor was, passageways the size of train tunnels connected the bays. If one bay took damage preventing launch and landing, its assigned voidcraft could be internally taxied to an undamaged one.

The carrier had officer's clubs and enlisted clubs. Salons. Movie theaters. Liquor stores. Two full-on supermarkets. A frigging *shopping center*.

Serving on that city in space had to be something special. Not that Biggie would ever find out; Fleet command didn't take kindly to pilots who went AWOL, especially those who stole a voidcraft worth millions to do so.

She'd been given a choice—*Keeling*, or twenty years in prison. In prison, you didn't get to fly anything. Not even old-ass APCs. Not much of a choice at all, really.

"A ship that big, you'd think they have a whole wing of transport craft," Torch said. "Those *chingados cabrones*, press-ganging us into schlepping stuff around."

"That's the price for clearing out an entire station so no one sees the *Crypt*," Knuckles said. "No in-house haulers, no hauler crews."

Gateway had once housed thousands of on-base pilots and crews, hundreds of transport craft. Without them, anything that *could* be used for hauling *was* used for hauling.

"Ah, crap." Torch tapped a gauge, the fingers of her formfitting armor—a *LASH* rig, lighter than the heavy TASH rigs used by Old Man Bennett and the others—clacking against plastic. "Looks like coolant pump three is losing pressure again."

Biggie sighed, long-since resigned to her bird's constant problems. It was an Ochthera-B, a good twenty years old (older, even, than the two Ochthera-Cs she'd flown while on *Keeling*). Both of those, sadly, had been sent to the scrap pile.

She switched to the flight-control channel.

"*Akathaso* control, this is Ochthera Kilo Echo One. We are inbound, requesting landing instructions to deliver cargo lot—" she glanced at her console screen "—*hotel romeo two-niner echo*. I say again, *hotel romeo two-niner echo*."

Every Fleet ship, base, or station had a short-code, usually the first two letters of the ship's name. Hence, *Kilo Echo* for *Keeling*. Those two letters, plus the class name (in this case, *Ochthera*, although some flights used the common term *Crawler*) and the craft's number created the comms identifier.

"Copy, Kilo Echo One." Flight control sounded like flight control always did—scratchy and tinny, like words spoken through a child's toy microphone. "Uh... we don't show a scheduled shipment for lot hotel romeo two-niner echo. Do you know what's in it?"

Torch keyed the Ochthera's internal channel. "This BS again? They're moving so much cargo they're as confused as a fart in a fan factory."

It would be one thing if this was the first time it had happened, but it wasn't—it was the third out of the last eleven runs.

"*Akathaso* control, we didn't exactly stop off at the nearest asteroid and take a little peeky-poo inside the cargo crates," Biggie said. "How can you not know what the hell we're delivering?"

A pause.

"One-five-nine, I, ah... this cargo has the *hotel-romeo* prefix, which means only the sender and those cleared to take possession of it know the contents. The flight deck is a little busy today. Maintain your position in starboard delta for the next ninety minutes. We should have space clear by then."

Ninety minutes? What a waste of time. Biggie had important things to do. Like take a nap.

"Control, the three crates we're towing can wait that long, but we have several smaller containers in our troop area," Biggie said. "Between you and me, when we loaded up, I overheard the crew there say something about ice cream for a fancy party your admiral is throwing. Ice cream shipped all the way from *Earth*. And here we are, in an APC that's probably older than you, that has *all kinds* of overheating problems."

Another pause.

"Uh, one-five-nine, please proceed to bay four and set down on pad seventeen," control said. "Sending coordinates now. Over."

That was more like it.

"We appreciate it," Biggie said. "Coordinates received. We're en route. One-five-nine, out."

8

JOHN

Say one thing for Gateway Station—it had yet to run out of beer. John appreciated that.

Pier Two's enlisted club could easily seat two hundred patrons. With only a dozen or so off duty *Keeling* crew spaced out at the tables, the place somehow seemed lonelier than if it had been empty. John's table held six—the platoon's two squad leaders and four fireteam leaders. Each had a brown glass bottle of beer in front of them.

Sergeant Renee Jordan commanded Alpha Squad. Corporal Sharma Sarvacharya led fireteam Alpha-One. John, Alpha Squad's second-in-command, led Alpha-Two. Corporal Kimberly Torres led Bravo Squad. Corporal Pippa Remic was her second-in-command and leader of Bravo-Two. Corporal Dave Starr, that oh-so-delightful man, led Bravo-One.

"Fuckers had *V15s*," Jordan said. "I didn't even know those rigs were *out* yet, let alone given to *Akathaso* douchebags."

Jordan wore fatigue pants with a bright white tank top that contrasted with her black skin. She loved to show off her muscled arms any chance she got. John, Starr, Torres, and Remic hadn't both-

43

ered to change out of their fatigues. Sharma had, opting for jeans and a gray flannel. She preferred civvies whenever off duty.

"*Douchebags*," Starr said. "Ain't that the truth? They kicked our asses, though."

He scratched at the bite-sized scar on his face. That scar came courtesy of Delaker Oneida's teeth during a Mud-driven tussle, during which Starr put his thumb through Oneida's right eye. Oneida had been cycled out due to the injury, but Starr remained entombed —hard to say who got the better of that deal.

The post-exercise debriefing hadn't gone well, to say the least. Platoon Commander Gary Lindros, platoon XO Katharina Winter, and platoon Sergeant Francis "the Book" Sands had torn into them, citing everything from bad marksmanship to poor unit cohesion.

Sharma stood and carried her empty beer bottle to the recycling bin. "We can't blame it on our rigs." She pulled two fresh bottles from a cooler next to the bin, then returned to the table, setting one in front of Torres. "If we go up against crickets for real, they're not going to give us a break because we have old gear."

Sklorno were an ugly species, so much so that many Human parents used them as a modern bogeyman—*behave, Little Sammy, or a Sklorno will eat you while you sleep.* See-through bodies. Tentacles instead of arms. Dangling, drool-dripping raspers. And those hideous heads. While they didn't look much like Earth insects, they looked more like Earth insects than anything else. Hence, their powerful, back-folded legs generated one of their many speciesist slurs: *crickets.* The name applied to the females, anyway—the far smaller males looked so different from females that many thought they were another species altogether.

Not that the difference mattered. Males didn't fight. Females did, and to the death.

Crickets did make for a good bogeyman, John had to admit. They didn't communicate with Humans like the Ki, Harrah, or Whitokians did. Hell, thousands of the latter two species were Union citizens, working away and paying taxes just like everyone else. Sklorno, while sentient, were as close to the old fictional about murderous aliens as it got. Even though that perception, for the most part, came from the media and Fleet propaganda, John knew first-hand that the truth was far worse. He'd boarded their ships. He'd fought them. He'd killed them. He'd seen them kill his comrades.

Torres let out a belch. She was already on her third beer.

"Beer's better outta glass bottles," she said. "Not that I'm complaining 'bout the plastic bottles on the *Crypt*. I mean... at least it's still *beer*, you know?"

John and the others kept a wary eye on Torres—she got belligerent when drunk. Torres wore her auburn hair in a short Mohawk. When she spent time on it, it looked damn cool, all spiky and straight, with the words *¿Quién quiere vivir para siempre?* tatted in script from her right temple to behind her right ear. At the moment, though, she hadn't spent time on it—her helmet hair hung limp and greasy over the tat.

"It wasn't their tech advantage that un-alived us," she said, opening her bottle. "Yeah, their V15s are superior to our V11s and V12s, but that's not the main problem. Our rigs are *shot*. We can't even get good replacement parts."

She'd taken over Bravo Squad from Malik Blanding, who died while boarding the Purist corvette. During the shakedown cruise, Bravo had lost four of their eleven Raiders; two KIAs, and two wounded deemed *medically unfit to serve.*

"Torres is right," Starr said. "The rig room looks like a fucking junk shop."

The rig room, located close to the pier, was meant to house an entire company's weapons, armor, and gear. Over 150 stalls sat empty. In seven stalls, recently delivered TASHes—four V12s and three V11s—awaited the platoon's replacement members.

Bad gear. John *hated* bad gear.

"Abshire's leg compensator crapped out in the middle of the fight," he said. "That happens in a real mix, he's toast. Anyone else have rig trouble in their squads?"

"We did," Sharma said. "Basara's HUD blanked out. He was as useless as tits on a bull."

Sharma shook her head. "When is that meathead *not* as useless as tits on a bull?"

Meathead was a common descriptor for Raiders, most of whom took their physique seriously. Basara, though, looked like an amateur bodybuilder. He was the biggest Raider in the platoon. Would have been the biggest person on the ship if not for Bradley Henry—how Combat Cook maneuvered around that tiny galley, John had no idea.

"We had trouble, too," Torres said. "Pippa here didn't get in the mix at all."

Pippa Remic was solid. Reliable. Her ebony skin had a subtle tinge of dark blue to it, hinting at Satirli 6 heritage. Remic had the worst nose in the platoon, by far. John wondered how many times her schnoz had been broken.

"My right shoulder seal failed before hull breach," Remic said. "Compromised my rig's atmospheric integrity. I had to tap out before we encountered the enemy. Goddamn printed parts. The fabbers here are garbage. I put in a requisition for a replacement, real OEM stuff, but you know how that goes."

John knew they weren't the only ones in Fleet with gear trouble. With the war dragging on, equipment took damage and components wore out. Obtaining OEM—*original equipment manufacturer*—replacement parts was hard enough without factoring in the logistical barriers brought on by *Keeling*'s isolation.

Fireteam leaders filed parts requests with squad leaders, who passed them on to platoon sergeant Sands, who in turn routed them to Gateway's quartermaster. If the gear was in Gateway's warehouses, the Warthogs got it, but there weren't a lot of replacement parts for their antiquated rigs.

The quartermaster printed some replacement parts easy enough. Fasteners, clamps, armor plates, CO_2 scrubbers, basic boards... Gateway's fabbers kicked them out quick. Quality varied, to say the least. Anything complicated, though, like micromuscle, magic goop, or most circuit boards, had to get requisitioned from the depots. Didn't mean you got what you needed. Supply requests disappeared into the void like everything else.

"We're on a ship so secret no one is allowed to *look* at it," Jordan said. "You'd think we Warthogs would get top priority for gear, but they give us scraps while *Akathaso*'s Raiders get V15s. Fucking bull-shit, man."

"I'll drink to that," Torres said, and she did.

Warthogs. The unofficial name for the *Crypt*'s crew. When aboard *Keeling*, sometimes you had to wallow in the mud just like those ungodly ugly Earth animals loved to do.

"It's ridiculous," Starr said. "Damn rigs already got one of us killed." He raised his bottle. "To Laior."

John and the others raised theirs.

Laior's death still burned hot in John's chest. In a training exercise to simulate repelling boarders, she'd lost contact with the curving trench wall right when *Keeling* made a sharp evasive maneuver. Her helmeted head smashed into the trench. Her armor should have handled the impact with relative ease, but two of the four inertial dampening cylinders on her collar failed—her neck snapped, killing her instantly.

Admiral Epperson was the big boss. At the end of the day, responsibility for shitty gear rolled up to him. John hated the man.

"We have to do something," Remic said.

Sharma shook her head. "What the hell *can* we do? We put in requisitions. Lincoln is trying to back our play. Even that useless piece of shit Lindros is trying—"

John raised a finger, a small, subtle motion, yet it stopped Sharma mid-sentence and drew everyone's attention. Maybe they didn't respect Lindros, but John did.

"We don't talk about the LT like that," he said. "Especially among platoon leaders. Yeah?"

Sharma met his eyes, ready to challenge, ready to fight, then she looked down.

"Yeah," she said. "My bad, Old Man."

John noticed the crimson dot on her forehead, just between her eyebrows. A bindi. Was she Hindu? She hadn't worn it on the last patrol. Maybe a few weeks entombed had her re-thinking her religious stance. She wasn't the only one, John knew, nor did it surprise him—the madness of the Mud drove people to seek comfort and hope in various ways. Hell, if he'd ever been religious, maybe he'd be doing the same thing.

Torres drained her beer. "Sharm, didn't you serve on the *Richthofen*? It's here at Gateway. Can you try reaching out to someone there?"

Sharma laughed quietly, shook her head.

"You pounded too many brewskies, Torres," she said. "Like we can contact *anyone* that's not in our crew." She eyed John. "How about you, Old Man? You been around the block. What can we do to fix this?"

Everyone again looked at John, this time as if his nearly forty years as a Raider gave him insights they didn't have. No such luck.

"We keep our eyes and ears open," he said. "Sometimes the gods of war smile down upon you. Sometimes they don't."

More like *most times* they didn't. Those gods were nothing if not capricious. John would keep his eyes open, but he wouldn't hold out much hope. On Gateway, in Sixth Group, there was only one god of war.

His name was Admiral Mathias Epperson.

9

BETHANY

Bethany Darkwater sprinted down the *Keeling*'s gently twisting passageways, her shoes slapping against the fakegrav deck plates.

It was after her—whatever *it* was.

She *heard* it, a crackling sound like snapping tree branches, if tree branches were made of brittle metal. She heard screams, too—the screams of her crewmates, dying, pleading for help that would not come.

The sound grew louder, closer. The atrium... if she didn't reach the atrium and seal herself inside, she was lost.

A cry of pain, one she *felt* rather than heard, felt in her heart and her head. Desolation, desperation, crushing *loss*... like her soul was being ripped in half.

Bethany ran, her lungs a stinging pinch of inadequate air, her legs on the edge of surrender. She reached the passageway that led to the atrium, raced around the corner expecting to see the atrium's sphincter oval up ahead—it wasn't there. The passageway extended for many meters, bending slightly right and down, then up and left.

Had she taken a wrong turn?

Behind her, the shattering clockwork sound drew closer... *louder*...

Bethany turned. She saw it—a thicket of metallic segments, each thin as a pencil, advancing down the passageway. When a segment reached about a meter in length, its end split with a ringing ricochet sound that birthed two more segments. An ever-expanding hydra. Some segments locked onto deck plates or pressed against bulkheads, while others stretched toward her before bursting forth their own extensions. The rods *filled* the passageway, top to bottom, side to side, a bursting latticework reaching for her.

She turned to run, felt the agony of low-gauge needles punching into her lower back and legs. Her spent legs gave out, but she didn't hit the deck—the cold twigs held her aloft even as more of them lanced into her shoulders, her spine.

Somehow, she knew what came next, and yet that instantaneous eventuality seemed to take a lifetime, the last moments of her existence before the end began...

Something hot and hurtful flooded into her.

It burned...

...it filled her, *scorched* her, signaling her death...

...boiled alive from the inside out...

From somewhere came a new sound, a *bang-bang-bang* thudding.

Bethany dangled like a puppet. She couldn't move. Her right hand was out in front of her—as she watched, her skin blistered and puffed, it *split*, releasing jets of steam. Her flesh sagged like melting wax, dripped down to splash against the deck...

———

She screamed herself awake. Chest heaving, she looked at her right hand.

No wounds.

No damage.

She grabbed at it with her left, squeezed and probed, searching for injuries, for blisters.

Nothing.

Bang-bang-bang.

"Beth, are you all right? Let me in!"

Anne Lafferty.

Bethany shivered, both from Gateway Station's ever-present chill and from a fear of something even worse than the nightmare—the real-life monster that tormented her, refused to let her be.

Was Lafferty here to kill her?

There was nowhere to run. One door. Bethany couldn't get away.

"Beth, honey... open the door. *Right now.*"

Bethany sucked in a deep breath, tried to calm herself. Time to act, to be someone she wasn't. She had to be sharp, had to be on point —the image of Nitzan Shamdi's mutilated body and pleading eyes were never far from her thoughts.

"I'm all right," she said. "Hold on."

Bethany thew off the covers and got out of her bunk. She slept in a Fleet T-shirt and sweats. After a decade in a Purist convent, she didn't feel comfortable being naked, as an unclothed Human body generated nothing but sin and shame.

She opened the door. "Hi, Annie."

Anne Lafferty pushed past Bethany into the room, eyes whipping across the small space. She shut the door. She knelt, looked under Bethany's bunk, then opened her locker.

"I had a nightmare," Bethany said. "I'm alone."

Lafferty turned sharply. "A nightmare about *what?* Romanik?"

Bethany's heart hammered. Romanik. Since the meeting with Epperson, Bethany hadn't thought of the woman all that much.

Should she be thinking of Romanik? *Should* she be wondering who might be next to die?

"No, not Romanik, Annie. I was aboard *Keeling*. We were in the Mud. There were these... *growths.* They burrowed into the ship. They chased me and... they *melted* me."

Lafferty's hard stare vanished, replaced by her oh-so-friendly expression.

"Melted people. That sounds awful. I have just the thing to soothe your mind—I'm taking you to lunch to celebrate!"

Had she smiled like that when she'd hacked through Nitzan's leg? When she'd cut his tongue from his mouth? When his blood spattered all across Paul Cooley's porn-filled hauler?

Bethany couldn't remember. Like so many other things, she couldn't remember.

"Uh... celebrate, Annie? Celebrate what?"

"You're being promoted," Lafferty said. "They are bumping you up to Lieutenant JG. I wanted to be the first to tell you. *And*, you are now *Keeling*'s lead Xeno. A new Xeno Mate is en route to Gateway."

Bethany's head swam. She was taking over Hathorn's position as lead Xeno, number two under Colonel Hasik. Hopefully, that meant more access to study *Keeling*'s alien technology. The pay bump wouldn't hurt, either—not that there was anywhere to spend what little money she had.

Still smiling, Lafferty opened her arms.

"Well don't just stand there—come give us a hug!"

Bethany hesitated, but only for a panicked moment before she *realized* she was hesitating. She rushed into Lafferty's arms.

Lafferty held her tight.

Inside, Bethany's soul twisted and churned, every ounce of her screaming *get away*. But she dared not flinch, dared not show any sign of the revulsion overwhelming her.

She had to pretend she liked Lafferty. Had to pretend to be Lafferty's friend. If Bethany didn't, she might wind up like Nitzan.

"Thank you, Annie. I feel better now."

Lafferty stepped back, her face beaming. "And I have a little secret to share. We were both nominated for the Fleet Cross. We didn't get it, but I'm sure that's only because our last mission was *beyond* classified."

The Fleet Cross—the Planetary Union's second-highest combat decoration.

"Don't tell anyone," Lafferty said. "We're not supposed to know, but Daddy let it slip. Keep it our secret, okay?"

Bethany pantomimed locking her mouth and throwing away the key.

"The secret is safe with me, Annie. Was the nomination for our... I mean... for what happened in Cooley's hauler? With the *Ishlangu* survivors..."

Lafferty shook her head. "Mine was for that. Your recommendation was because you got *Keeling* back into the Mud during the battle. You saved the crew. And Cooley's intel, whatever it is. You saved *me*, Beth. You saved all of us."

Fragmented memories swirled, ghostly fragments of that fight in the atrium against Hathorn. She didn't remember much. The official story was that Hathorn attacked her with a homemade copper blade, similar to the one Lafferty used to torture and kill Nitzan. Hathorn had been bigger, stronger, but somehow Bethany took the blade from her and used it to kill the woman.

Self-defense. That's what Lafferty said. That's what Lincoln and Ellis said. That's what would have gone on the official report, were such things recorded anywhere.

Afterward, Bethany apparently found a way to power up the previously drained transdim drive, which let *Keeling* escape certain destruction at the hands of Purist Nation warships. She still had no idea what she'd done to get it working again.

Bethany remembered holding the blade, but not what she did with it...

She remembered the blood, but not where it came from...

The thing she did remember, though, was a feeling of *oneness* with the ship, with High One himself...

"Hello, Beth?" Lafferty snapped her fingers. "Annie to Beth. Come in, Beth."

Bethany blinked, came back to the moment.

"Sorry. I blanked out a little."

"You've been doing that a lot lately," Lafferty said. "Could be PTSD. How's your therapy coming along?"

She wanted to know how Beth was doing with therapy? *Lafferty* was the one who needed therapy. Or a firing squad.

"Really well," Bethany said. "We're making good progress. We're all healing."

Healing? Lafferty would see right through that bullshit.

"Wonderful," Lafferty said. "I'm so happy to hear that. You deserve to be at peace with what happened."

Bethany didn't know what to say. Did Lafferty really think group therapy for *slitting a woman's throat* would make things better? How skewed was her marked deficit in affective empathy?

"Seriously, though, keep quiet about the Fleet Cross thing," Lafferty said. "Friends keep each other's secrets. Right?"

That wasn't mere lip-service. Lafferty knew Ensign Bethany Darkwater was, in fact, Susannah Rossi, placed aboard *Keeling* as a spy for Admiral Adrienne Bock. As far as Bethany knew, Lafferty hadn't told anyone. Bethany, in turn, hadn't breathed a word about what Lafferty did to Nitzan.

"Bock's people haven't made contact with me," Bethany said. "You know I'll tell you if that happens, right?"

Lafferty pursed her lips, nodded. What did that mean? Was it a genuine emotion, or yet another of her prefabricated expressions?

"I know you will. And it's a *when*, not an *if*. Bock didn't put you here for shits and giggles. Now, let's not discuss that anymore." She clapped her hands three times. "Time to celebrate! Food! Drinks! Shower up and meet me in the officer's club. Wear your service uniform, and don't forget your new rank insignia." She ruffled Bethany's hair. "I'm so *proud* of you, Bestie."

Her touch felt like the loving caress of a spider.

"Thank you, Annie."

Lafferty left, shutting the door behind her.

Bestie. So messed up. They'd been *besties* for all of two weeks. Lafferty seemed to believe the friendship was real.

Bethany had no choice but to play along. Lafferty was a decorated BII Major and *Keeling*'s Intel Chief—it was her *job* to catch Purist spies. If Lafferty thought for a moment that Bethany might talk about Nitzan, Bethany might wind up in the brig.

Or facedown somewhere with a bullet in the back of her head.

Or... or Lafferty could get Bethany alone, somewhere isolated, and use the same copper blade she'd used to carve up Nitzan. *That* particular blade hadn't been reported to Lincoln. Did Anne still have it?

Bethany wanted all this to go away. She wanted High One to help her, to *deliver* her. She wanted back inside *Keeling*, the only place where everything made sense.

But first—lunch with a sadistic murderer.

Bethany headed for the showers.

10

BIGGIE

"I'm bored," Torch said.

Her quiet grumbling and grousing was getting on Biggie's nerves.

"At least you have some company down there," Knuckles said. "I'm stuck up here in the turret and you don't hear me bitching. Read a damn book or something."

To be fair, Knuckles didn't bitch about anything, really. Except, maybe, about other people bitching.

"I don't like reading," Torch said. "I'm not just bored. I'm bored and *annoyed*. How much longer do we have to sit here?"

The woman's ADHD... never a quiet moment when she was involved.

"We sit here until we don't have to sit here," Biggie said. "Torch, you're killing me. Shut your pie-hole for a while."

Torch huffed then stared out the cockpit window.

They'd landed two hours earlier. A crew came for the ice cream, but the remaining cargo had yet to be offloaded. Biggie, Torch, and Knuckles wanted to step out, stretch their legs a little and see what *Akathaso*'s pilot lounge offered. Flight control, however, ordered them to stay in the Ochthera.

Bay Four was a shitshow. Half the sprawling space was dedicated to one of *Akathaso*'s fighter wings, and a quarter to Ochtheras used by the carrier's Raider platoons. The rest of the bay was a log-jam of transports waiting for cargo to be unloaded and towering stacks of already unloaded cargo that needed to be delivered. A wide, two-lane road led deeper into the ship. A queue of empty, flatbed wheeltrucks stretched through the bay's big internal pressure doors. Dozens of LASH-suited sailors checked registries or did whatever it was they did with the tablets they held, then directed overhead cranes to load crates onto the trucks.

"Look at this crap," Torch said, unable to stay quiet any longer. "Those eight Occies over there are all Model-*E*s. State of the art. See them, Knuckles?"

"Yeah, I see them," Knuckles said with a sigh. "But fancy new crawlers don't have the charm of our old *B*. Now shut up, I'm almost to the dirty part of my book."

Biggie understood Torch's frustration. Over the last thirty years, the GU-44 Ochthera line had gone through major upgrades, from the original *A* model up to the *E* models here on *Akathaso*. The bird she sat in now (a repeatedly updated *B*) had been state of the art once—when Biggie was all of seven years old.

"We should have a new bird," Torch said. "As soon as *Keeling*'s copper condom pops, you know we'll be back in the mix. This big, beautiful carrier stays lightyears away from any real action."

"Yeah," Knuckles said. "*Akathaso* only teams up for the clean-up."

Epperson kept his flagship out of the big battles. When he did commit *Akathaso*, it was usually to finish off targets softened up by other warships. Some thought that branded Epperson a coward. Biggie didn't agree. As ancient philosopher-general Sun Tzu wrote, *victorious warriors win first and then go to war, while defeated warriors go to war first and then seek to win.*

Under Epperson's command, Sixth Group had won four major engagements. He had yet to be defeated in battle.

"I'm just glad McKinney's last term is almost up," Torch said.

"When we get some new blood in the President's Palace, maybe we get out of this stupid war."

Good lord, now the chatterbox wanted to talk politics?

"If *ifs* and *buts* were candy and nuts what a wonderful Christmas it would be," Biggie said. "McKinney's going to get impeached before his term is up, but while we're on this military mission, how about we not talk poorly of our *commander-in-chief*."

Torch sat quietly for almost ten seconds.

"Our shift was over an hour ago," she said. "I hope these numb-nuts hurry up and unload us already. I'm bored."

Once back at Pier Two, the Warthog platoon's techs would give the crawler a once-over before the next crew started their shift of cargo runs. *Keeling's* three flight crews—pilot, co-pilot, and engineer/gunner—rotated through the ship's two Ochtheras. Even in high-use times like this, each crew got eight hours of rack time. Sleepy pilots and snoozy gunners made for bad business, something to be avoided whenever possible.

The flight control channel squawked.

"Ochthera Kilo Echo One, this is *Akathaso* control. A team is coming to unload you now. You are third in line for departure."

Torch started pre-flight checks.

"Control, this is Kilo Echo One," Biggie said. "Copy on unloading and departure. We *so* enjoyed our grand tour of your fine vessel. Thank you so much for your hospitality."

"Kilo Echo One, a little advice," control said. "Jokes, or paltry attempts at them, are not part of how we do things here. *Akathaso* control, out."

Torch shook her head. "Sounds like that kid needs to get laid."

That kid wasn't the only one. Biggie had an itch that needed scratching. She had no intention of hooking up with fellow Raiders, but there were a few *Keeling* sailors who'd made passes. Ted Mi-Suk, an electrical mate, shined her up on the regular. He wasn't Biggie's cup of tea, though. That young lead torpedoist, Caleb Haddad, on the other hand? Now *he* was worth consideration.

"Unloading crew's approaching," Knuckles said.

Finally, Biggie and her crew could head home. Time to get some sleep.

Or, maybe, see if Caleb was off duty.

11

TRAVIS

As he walked through the ghost town that was Pier Two's admin building, Travis tried to focus on the task at hand—getting information on *Keeling*'s replacement crew.

Tried and failed, for the most part.

He wasn't the first sailor to be distance-dumped by a spouse or significant other. Thousands of men and women—people who dedicated their lives to the military—endured the same kind of pain he carried with him now. That particular sense of community didn't lessen his burden in the least.

Travis had sent a video, asking—pleading? *begging?*—for Molly to reconsider, but knowing her she might delete the message without watching it. Molly rarely second-guessed herself. When she made up her mind about something, there was no turning back.

He wanted to see his wife.

He wanted to see his daughter.

He wanted to keep his family together.

Thanks to Epperson, going home wasn't an option.

Travis stopped, checked the signage mounted on the wall. Epperson's personnel officer had set up shop in Room 1402, one of the admin building's many empty offices. The sign's number range pointed down the hallway. Travis continued on.

Normally, crew changes were implemented via computer. The instant a sailor, Raider, or striker was selected for transfer to a new ship, officers on that ship received complete personnel records. Not so where *Keeling* was concerned. Travis did not yet know names or even ranks of the replacements. Such information remained secret as long as possible, lest enemy agents acquire those names, those records, and use them to track down distant family members, friends, lovers—anyone who could be used to pressure a crewmember into becoming a spy.

After Nitzan Shamdi, Travis knew spies were all too real.

He found the office. He knocked.

"Enter," came a woman's voice.

Travis did so. Major Maia Whittaker sat behind the desk. He'd never met her in person, but he knew her name. She'd interviewed many of the crew prior to assigning them—sentencing them?—to *Keeling*. Most of them blamed Whittaker, specifically, for their current lot in life. *Epperson's Executioner*, they called her.

She'd come to Gateway Station to oversee *Keeling's* crew replacements.

A stack of manila folders sat on the desktop. Real paper. So rare.

Travis saluted. "Lieutenant Travis Ellis, executive officer of PUV *James Keeling*, reporting."

The major returned the salute.

"Just you, Lieutenant? Is your captain coming?"

"No sir," Travis said. "Captain Lincoln instructed me to handle this."

"Well, she's been through this process before, so fine with me." Whittaker opened the first folder and read from the pages inside. "First, all brevet promotions and demotions have been finalized. Zhen Smith promoted one grade to sergeant. Barnes Marchenko demoted two grades to corporal. Raider John Bennett promoted one grade to corporal." She looked up from the folder. "John Bennett, a *corporal.* The old buzzard didn't try to tank his promotion?"

The warmth in her expression told Travis she'd met Bennett, and that she liked him. Damn hard to *not* like the guy.

"I didn't give him a choice," Travis said. "He should have been promoted long ago."

Whittaker huffed. "XO, you don't know the half of it. On to new promotions." She again read from the folder. "Specialist-Two Colel Citalmina is promoted two grades to corporal. She'll be your lead ECM now."

ECM—*electronics countermeasures.* The lead ECM needed authority conveyed by rank to manage the three-person team responsible for wreaking havoc with enemy tech such as comms, computers, and the tracking systems in torpedoes and missiles. Citalmina, a smart if slightly overzealous sailor, was taking over for Corporal Cass Mollen, who died during the last battle. Travis recommended Citalmina's promotion; Lincoln had agreed.

"Specialist-Two ECM operator Brinson Sorro is promoted one grade to spec-three," Whittaker said. "And gunner's mate Peredur Geraint is promoted one grade, from specialist-three to corporal."

Geraint was taking over for Anna Ling, who'd died in the Type24 turret alongside her gunners Jessica Painter and Scott Canuk. Geraint would be the turret master for the port-side turret when—and if—*Keeling*'s coating receded.

Travis remembered each name of the dead and wounded, just as he remembered each name of the casualties suffered on *Schild* during the Battle of Asteroid X7—the conflict that led to him being assigned to *Keeling.*

"In your xeno department," Whittaker said, "Ensign Bethany Darkwater is promoted to Lieutenant JG. She'll be number two in Xeno, beneath Colonel Hasik."

That particular promotion didn't make sense.

"Darkwater endured a traumatic experience," Travis said. "She was attacked by a superior officer and forced to defend herself with lethal force. She shouldn't be in a position of higher responsibility right now."

Whittaker shrugged. "Not my circus, not my monkeys. In other words, Colonel Hasik requested the promotion. Admiral Epperson approved it. Any questions?"

Her tone of voice made it clear Darkwater's advancement was not up for debate.

"No, Major."

"Good," Whittaker said. "Epperson will perform a promotion ceremony in Pier Two's reception center for all the promoted individuals. Brevet promotions included. Full dress. I'll coordinate with Chief Sung."

A ceremony would be nice. The promoted crew deserved to be recognized.

"I'll let Chief Sung know," Travis said. "He'll be happy to oblige."

Which couldn't be further from the truth. If the word *surly* could be formed into a piece of walking gristle, that mix would produce something exactly like Warrant Officer Eloi Sung.

"Excellent," Whittaker said. "On to crew replacements. The new member of the xeno department will arrive in two days. The remainder of your replacements are already on base and undergoing BII evaluations."

Already on base? Had they come in on another pier, or been brought in by Sixth Group's ships?

"When did they arrive, Major?"

"They've been at Gateway two weeks now," Whittaker said. "All seven are former crewmembers from *Ishlangu*."

What were the odds seven survivors from *Ishlangu* had done something bad enough to deserve being entombed on the *Crypt*?

Then it hit him—they'd likely done *nothing* wrong. Nothing other than being inside of the Union's biggest secret. Epperson wasn't going to send them home any more than he would send Travis home.

Instead, for their heroism and service, seven *Ishlangu* survivors got assigned to *Keeling*. What better way to keep them from *talking* about the secret ship than condemn them *to* the secret ship?

How unfair. How utterly and unforgivingly unfair. And how on-brand for Epperson.

"I understand," Travis said. "When can we talk to them?"

He needed to prepare the newcomers for their upcoming ordeal.

"Not until BII vetting is complete," Whittaker said. "The vetting process does not include Major Lafferty, by the way. She'll get her turn when they report for duty."

Anne Lafferty remained on the spot for not knowing a Purist spy had been aboard *Keeling*. Many others missed Nitzan Shamdi's true allegiance as well, so it wasn't entirely Anne's fault. She'd been the last in line, though—she bore the lion's share of the blame.

Anne's brave attempt to rescue *Ishlangu* crew was likely the only reason she retained her position as *Keeling*'s intel chief. It probably didn't hurt that her father was General Bart Lafferty—BII's director—but as far as Travis was concerned, Anne had proven her mettle beyond any shadow of a doubt.

Seven members of *Ishi*'s crew assigned to *Keeling*. One member in particular concerned Travis the most.

"Major, may I know the names of my new crewmates?"

"Not yet." Whittaker opened a second folder, looked at something inside, then closed it. "I can tell you this, though. Consider it a favor. My records show you had a prior relationship with Vesna Jakobsson, former captain of *Ishlangu*. She is not among the replacements."

As far as Travis knew, Vesna remained on Gateway Station. He hadn't seen her since she'd disembarked *Keeling*.

"What about the losses in our Raider platoon?"

"Those will be filled in the, ah... more *traditional* way," Whittaker said. "Traditional for *Keeling*, at least."

"Convicts and newbs fresh out of boot?"

Whittaker smiled. "You said it, not me. We're done here, Lieutenant. Dismissed."

"Thank you, Major."

Travis saluted again. Whittaker again returned it.

He turned on one heel and left the office.

He was no sooner in the hallway, heading out of the building, when thoughts of his impending divorce punched him in the heart.

12

ANNE

With *Keeling* locked up tight, some departments had little or nothing to do. Not Intel, though—a BII agent's job was never done. Anne's department occupied space in Building C. Three adjacent offices and one meeting room served as *Keeling*'s temporary "Spookhouse."

"We *will not* have another Shamdi on board," Anne said. "I want to learn as much as we can about our new crewmates before the ship opens up again."

If the ship opened up again. Who could say? Because if Beth didn't know, Anne didn't think anyone else would. Beth had an affinity for the ship, some kind of *connection* to it.

"It's bullshit they blame us for Shamdi," Akil Daniels said. He tugged absently at one of his cornrows. "I mean, you're not the one who assigned him to *Keeling*, Chief. You'd think they would have caught the guy in boot, or on his two prior deployments."

Yes, one would think so. And yet, Shamdi slipped through. No, not just *slipped through*—Shamdi excelled as a Raider. So fully did the Purist spy fool everyone, he'd been assigned to the Fleet's biggest secret.

"That's facts," Jester Gillick said. "Shamdi had *documented kills* against Purists. How were we supposed to know?"

Warrant Officer Daniels and Corporal Gillick were both suck-ups, trying to tell Anne what they thought she wanted to hear. That was the thing with BII agents—you never really knew when one was telling the truth.

It didn't matter, though. They were in the same boat as she was.

"If there's a spy among them and we miss it, it's all of our asses," Anne said. "Sixteen newbies. Seven sailors, nine Raiders. We don't know a damn thing about any of them."

She still had trouble reconciling the secrecy surrounding every crewmember, from command staff down to the lowliest grunt. She was the ship's intel chief—she should know *everyone's* background. Maybe Epperson would change his mind about that soon, give her the tools she needed to do her job. Maybe not.

"The sailors are all *Ishlangu* survivors," Gillick said. "Pretty unlikely they could be spies, considering they barely escaped with their lives."

Now why would he say such a thing? Was Gillick that oblivious —or was he trying to cover up for someone?

Daniels glared at Gillick, his hazel eyes narrowing in anger. A genuine emotion, or was the warrant officer putting on an act? Hard to tell with him—Daniels had skill.

"Use your head, Corporal," he said. "The key is they *did* survive. Hundreds of others did not. We still don't know how the Purists jumped *Ishi* at the rendezvous point. Any of the survivors could have leaked those coordinates."

Gillick's eyebrows rose slightly. He even flushed a bit.

"Good point," he said.

A very good point. Daniels was sharp enough to see it without being told. Gillick, apparently, not so much,

"Assume nothing," Anne said. "If Shamdi got through, so can someone else. It's our job to find them. Daniels, schedule every new crewmember for a face-to-face with you and me both. Gillick, you make yourself available in the barracks, the mess, the mixed club, and anywhere else they'll be. Make friends. Get people talking."

Gillick nodded. "I'm the most helpful pal a newbie could ask for."

Seasoned sailors knew BII's job was to listen, to dig and pry, to look for disloyal crew, and—most of all—to find spies. Ergo, most sailors didn't trust BII agents. Or at least they didn't *want* to trust BII agents. Maybe Gillick wasn't the sharpest mycoware on the table, but his easy charm and fast wit made people relax around him. Made people *like* him. Within days, Anne knew, he'd have some newbs spilling more secrets than if they were being interrogated under the knife.

"The Raiders, too, Gillick," Anne said. "Cozy up to them. Make sure you're spending extra time in the mess hall when they're off duty. Oh, and ask Lindros for hand-to-hand training time. Nothing gets those jarheads comfortable like punching each other in the face."

Gillick's shoulders sagged. "Major, can I skip sparring this time? I'll wind up going against Beaver again. I'd rather slide down a rusty razor into a vat of gasoline."

When it came to sparring, Spec-1 Jim "Beaver" Perry dominated. He'd even bested Sergeant Major Sands. If Beaver remained in the platoon a few more months—and if he was allowed to integrate with non-*Keeling* units—Anne wouldn't be surprised to see Lincoln enter him in the Fleet Combat Games. Nothing brought honor to a ship like having the Raider heavyweight champ on your roster.

"Then get yourself some chainmail underwear," Anne said. "I need you in there."

Gillick's head drooped comically. "Yes, Major. If my teeth get knocked out, I'll make them into a necklace for you for Valentine's Day."

Was that a joke, or was he hitting on her?

Gillick was Anne's subordinate. If she was going to have some fun while onboard, it certainly wouldn't be with the people in her department.

And besides—Anne wondered if the man was up to something. His round face bothered her. So did his broken nose and the yellowish bruises under his eyes, as well as the fact that Nitzan Shamdi had put him down with a single head butt. Embarrassing that one of her direct reports hadn't put up a better fight. If he had, Colonel Hasik might be dead, and Beth as well, but still—it made BII look bad.

It *had* been a long time since Anne shared her bed with anyone, though. Too long. The fact that Lincoln allowed fraternization among the crew boggled Anne's mind. Such things were forbidden on most ships. But, when in Rome, Anne had the option of doing as Romans did.

Maybe things with Beth would go to another level. Other than Beth, Anne was attracted to only a few crewmembers. Spec-3 Brinson Sorro's ass was so tight it could deflect bullets. Sascha Kerkhoffs's whole *oops, I'm always sweaty* thing caught Anne's eyes more often than not. The new pilot, Lekan, had bedroom eyes that could make panties spontaneously combust. Anne had never slept with a blue-skin before. Might be worth a whirl.

And then, of course, there was XO Ellis.

His shipboard quarters were next door to hers, after all. Hard to find a bang buddy more convenient than that. Such a shame he was so prudish about his marriage.

"A necklace of teeth," Anne said. "How heartwarming. Make sure you floss before you spar with Beaver. Let's get to work, men. We've got spies to catch."

13

BETHANY

"May I take your order, Lieutenant?"

The man's voice startled Bethany. A *waiter*? He wore a sailor service uniform: light gray blouse with black slacks. Bethany didn't recognize him—he wasn't *Keeling* crew.

"The lieutenant isn't ready yet," Lafferty said. "We'll order from the table."

The waiter nodded once and walked away.

Bethany had spent most of the last three weeks either on *Keeling*'s hull, in improvised lab space in a Pier Two warehouse, or asleep. Other than visits from Lafferty—which terrified Bethany, as did all interactions with the woman—she'd seen no one other than her shipmates.

This was her first trip to the officer's club. She'd dressed for the occasion, wearing the BST service uniform of tan blouse and black slacks. Lafferty wore her service uniform as well—all black, like everything BII wore.

"You almost jumped out of your seat," Lafferty said. "You're a bit on edge today."

Bethany was *always* on edge when around this killer, analytically conscious of every word, every gesture, every facial expression. Around her "bestie," Bethany needed to appear relaxed at all times.

"I'm fine, Annie. I wasn't aware outsiders were allowed on Pier Two, that's all. He gave me quite a start."

Lafferty's face took on that blank, indiscernible expression so common when she was on duty. Not a good sign.

"You didn't see the waiters and bartender when we walked in here?"

Bethany glanced around the room, saw their waiter standing at the bar with a second waiter, and a bartender as well. Other than Alex Plait, eating alone, the rest of the tables sat empty. Three patrons in a space made for a hundred or more. When she'd entered, she hadn't looked around in the least—all her focus centered on being "relaxed" and "easy" around Lafferty.

Bethany forced out her best fake laugh. "I didn't notice them at all! So silly of me. I guess I'm lost in my thoughts. With the ship, I mean. You know me, Annie... my head's always in the clouds."

Lafferty's face became human again. She smiled.

"Sad, but true. Your big, beautiful brain can do quantum physics yet not see the nose in front of your face."

Bethany forced another laugh, one she thought sounded sheepish and embarrassed.

"Guilty as charged," she said. "How long has this place had waiters?"

Lafferty tapped the center of the table. A menu appeared above the white tablecloth, showing images of beverages, sandwiches, entrees, and side dishes.

"Wait staff started two days ago," she said. "You'd realize that if you weren't working all the time. Lincoln complained about her crew having to grab sandwiches and drinks out of bins. For once, someone listened. But watch your tongue around these *waiters*, Beth—they're all BII."

She said it loud enough to be heard by the three staffers, but they didn't react.

"I understand," Bethany said. "Does the mixed club have staff, too?"

"Of course." Lafferty tapped an image of a cheeseburger and fries, selected *rare*, then added an old fashioned. "Epperson wants to know if enlisted and NCOs are running their mouths just as much as he wants to know if officers are. Hurry up and order, I'm hungry."

Bethany reached to tap a salad but quickly changed her mind. She ordered the same thing Lafferty had. That made Lafferty smile, which was the point.

Keeping Major Anne Lafferty happy was *always* the point.

These little get-togethers exhausted Bethany. She endured fight-or-flight mode every single second. The moment Lafferty thought Bethany, or rather, *Beth*, wasn't her "bestie" was the moment things would get even more desperate.

"Some people *need* to be monitored," Lafferty said. "Speaking of which, what are your thoughts about Jester Gillick?"

The major masked her emotions, but Bethany detected a trace of a recognizable tone in her voice—a tone heard two weeks earlier, when Lafferty first asked Bethany about Nitzan Shamdi.

"Corporal Gillick," Bethany said, pretending to think deeply on the name, using that bit of delay to figure out what Lafferty wanted to hear. "Well, he stormed into the atrium when we were in transdim. He had one of those... ah... those copper blades. He stabbed Colonel Hasik."

And would have stabbed Bethany, maybe, if Nitzan—the same man Lafferty later butchered with a similar blade—hadn't stepped in, along with John Bennett, the old Raider...

...Hathorn...

...the heartstone, so *bright*...

...Nitzan...

...Bennett, the *Empty Man*, a man to be *feared*...

"Bestie?"

Bethany blinked. Where was she? White tablecloth. She was sitting across from Lafferty.

Lafferty, who'd carved up Nitzan like a hog on a spit.

"Beth, are you all right?"

"Um... yes. I just... well... Gillick attacked us. It's... I'm sorry. Remembering the incident upsets me."

Lafferty liked to hear such things, liked to think of Bethany as a delicate flower who needed protection. Which, maybe, wasn't all that far from the truth.

"Of course it upsets you," Lafferty said. "Difficult memories, I'm sure. Aside from that unfortunate interaction with Gillick, and him later bringing you to see me in the Spookhouse, what are your thoughts on the man?"

Why was she asking about one of her own subordinates?

"I don't really have any thoughts on him," Bethany said. "He lost it in the Mud. Happens to a lot of people."

The waiter approached and delivered their drinks. Bethany saw his rank and last name: KAVALCHUK, *Spec-3*.

"Your food will be right out," he said, then returned to the bar.

Bethany picked up her drink, looked at the amber liquor and the single, swirling big rock. An actual orange peel. It smelled lovely. A world of difference between being here and being aboard *Keeling*, where all plates, cups, and utensils were made of fungus fiber.

"Real glass," she said. "Funny how basic glass seems like advanced alien technology after weeks of mycoware."

"And nice to have a drink that doesn't taste like mushrooms." Lafferty took a sip. "Ah, that's good." She set the glass down. "Beth, I'm asking about Gillick because I wonder if you have sensed the same thing from him you sensed from Shamdi. Do you think Gillick might be a Purist?"

The air pressed in on Bethany, *squeezed* her.

Lafferty's soulless green eyes.

...copper blade...

...Nitzan, tongueless, lipless, bloody, *mangled*, begging...

...*Err-raa-ree... hep eee...*

"I don't think Gillick is a Purist," Bethany said, the words flowing from somewhere inside her, driven by her lizard-brain's survival instinct. "I mean, with what little I've interacted with him, he doesn't strike me as a Purist at all. I could be wrong, though. I have been before."

Across the table, Major Murder studied Bethany. Examined her. *Hunted* her.

Bethany let some of her fear show. Not all of it, just enough to reveal she knew Lafferty held—and would *always* hold—the upper hand in this relationship.

"Well, that's good news." Lafferty smiled. "Isn't it? Time to eat."

The waiter returned. He set a plate with a cheeseburger and fries in front of each woman.

Bethany stared at her burger, at the patty's edge, glistening and still sizzling slightly. She rarely ate meat. The burger smelled abhorrent to her. Traces of red blood, gleaming with globules of melted fat ...

When the voice came over the PA, Bethany jumped and let out a yelp.

"*Attention, attention. Lieutenant JG Bethany Darkwater, report immediately to Building C, Room 1402. Lieutenant JG Bethany Darkwater, report immediately to Building C, Room 1402. That is all.*"

Bethany's heart kicked. Her head hurt. Fight or flight, every damn *second*.

"Oh, poo," Lafferty said. "I'll get yours boxed up. Come pick it up at my room when you're done talking to Epperson's Executioner."

The major picked up her cheeseburger and took a bite. Her eyes narrowed in pleasure. A trickle of red drilled down her chin.

Blood... on the skin of a killer...

"Thanks," Bethany said. "I'll talk to you later. Bestie."

She hurried out of the Officer's Club.

Five of them wore chains, each with a Raider in full TASH armor standing close behind, towering over them.

Three had it even worse, in John's opinion—no chains, but they bore the wide-eyed look of a newbie fresh out of boot.

Only one wore no restraints yet also exuded the easy air of confidence found in veteran Raiders. That one, however, was obviously high as a kite.

"Quite a haul," John said.

"That it is, Bennett," Sands said. "Only the cream of the crop for us."

Platoon Sergeant Francis "Book" Sands held a flexipaper in one hand. He wore his eight-pointed cover, bent bill set low to hide his dark brown eyes. It also somewhat hid the scar on his right cheek from when PXO Winter sliced him open with a homemade copper shiv.

They stood in Pier Two's reception center, an industrial building used for ceremonies, formation training, and to process the station's new arrivals. On the concrete floor, painted lines crossed over each other in various colors, marking multiple basketball, volleyball, and tennis courts, all within the boundaries of a regulation soccer pitch surrounded by a six-lane running track. The cavernous space was large enough for a thousand sailors, Raiders, and strikers to line up in queues. With only sixteen people present—a number that included John, Sands, and the five armored guards—it felt empty. Every small sound echoed off the gray walls.

Sands glanced at his flexi. "Corporal Bennett, let's get this party started before one of these hooligans attempts another crime."

John drew in a deep breath, put on his best scowl, and let loose his *Noncoms Are Very Loud* voice.

"New arrivals, *fall in*! When your name is called, step onto the white line!"

The ten Raiders formed up shoulder to shoulder behind the line.

Sands stepped forward, spoke in his rusty steel wool voice.

"I am Master Sergeant Francis Sands. You will refer to me as *Master Sergeant Sands*. You *will not* refer to me as *Top*."

The speech sounded similar to the one Sands gave when John reported to Gofannon Station for deployment to *Keeling*. Sands even tucked the flexi under one arm, just as he'd done at Gofannon.

"For those of you who arrived in restraints, I have the right to keep you in them as long as I deem necessary," Sands said. "I trust that if I—in my immeasurable foresight and unrivaled comprehension of the human condition—decide to release you from said chains, you will behave like proper Raiders and not embarrass me in front of the honored ghosts of soldiers past. Am I correct in this assumption?"

"*Yes, Master Sergeant*," the five chained Raiders said in unison.

"Maaaagnificent," Sands said. He looked to the TASHed guards. "Escort detail, release these warriors on my recognizance."

One of the armored Raiders stepped around the new arrivals, heavy boots clicking on concrete—John's stomach pinched in anger when he saw the Raider's nameplate.

"Hello, Sands," Master Sergeant Cletis Dietrich said. "You *sure* you want me to release them? From what I've heard you Warthogs do to newbies, I figure you'll have an easier time of it if they can't resist."

Sands unrolled his flexi, looked at it as he spoke, not giving Dietrich the respect of eye contact.

"Cletis, why don't you head back to your fluffy pillows and pleasure lounges on *Akathaso*? The people who do the real fighting have a busy schedule."

Behind the helmet's visor, Dietrich smiled down. The thick, smooth armor made him a head taller than Sands.

"We whopped your asses in training and sent y'all whimpering back to your copper turd of a ship," Dietrich said. "I carved my mark on the helmet of that old fossil standing next to you. That *real* enough, Francis?"

Copper turd? Had Dickdrip seen *Keeling*? Maybe, or maybe he'd just heard whispers. The ship was a secret, yes, but word had gotten out. Word always did.

"Cletis, defaced gear can be repaired or replaced," Sands said. "A deficiency of moral fiber, on the other hand? That is what separates a proper soldier from one who's turned sycophancy toward command into an Olympic event—you're a gold medalist in posterior diplomacy."

Dietrich's face wrinkled. He didn't know what Sands was saying. John didn't either. Sands had a way with words.

"Say, Corporal Bennett—" Sands crooked his head and looked at John's right shoulder as if what he saw there confused him "—what in the name of all that is sartorially sacred are those embroidered artifacts affixed to your uniform sleeve?"

John reached up, brushed his shoulder, felt the five hammer patches stitched on his jacket. You could always count on Sands for the perfect setup.

"Master Sergeant Sands, these are *Raider Hammers*," John said. "They represent the five times I've boarded an enemy vessel, thereby fulfilling a Raider's ultimate purpose."

Dietrich's face burned with envy.

"*Maaaagnificent*," Sands said. He looked at Dietrich's armored shoulder, squinted theatrically. "Cletis, how come *you* don't have any hammers?"

Dietrich had none because—like most Raiders—he'd never boarded an enemy vessel. Most never got the chance. Of those who did, few returned to tell the tale.

"Fuck you, Sands," Dietrich said.

He walked back behind the line. He and the escort detail removed the chains. Without another word, the five Raiders from *Akathaso* left the building.

"Penis Dickdrip is quite the charmer," Sands said. "We need to get back at him for marking your rig."

John nodded. Paybacks were a bitch. He didn't know what that payback would be, but when he figured it out, he would wallow in it —as a warthog does.

Sands addressed the platoon's new members.

"My apologies for such an unfortunate distraction," he said. "Step on the line when I call your name. Those fresh out of Hotel Brittmore first."

Brittmore Base, a.k.a. *Hotel Brittmore*, the crucible in which young men and women transformed from dumb-ass civilians into void-chewing Raiders.

It seemed like only yesterday that Sands had been a bug-eyed boot, eager to prove himself but equally terrified at the thought of battle. John had taken the man under his wing, just as he'd done with so many others over the years. Now John took orders from him, something that made John immensely proud.

"Spec-One Vera Pola," Sands said. "Spec-One Jason Carpenter. Spec-One Jasmine Miroslav."

The three boots stepped onto the line. The two women— Miroslav and Pola—and the man—Carpenter—all looked afraid. What lies had Dietrich told them about *Keeling*? Not that lies were necessary; the *Crypt* had plenty of genuine, Grade-A terror readily available.

"Pola, I see you completed corpsman training," Sands said. "You patched anyone up yet?"

"Yes, Master Sergeant. I field-dressed two minor wounds in combat drills."

"That's good news, Spec." Sands glanced at John. "We'll just have to make sure all our wounds from here on are *minor*, then."

"Yes, Master Sergeant," John said. "No major wounds from here on out."

Pola seemed oblivious to the light teasing.

"Moving on," Sands said. "Onyeka Ayo..." he peered at the flexi, tried to parse out the name, "Ayo... *deal?*"

One of the men who had worn chains stepped to the line. "*Ayodele*, Master Sergeant. It rhymes with *belly*. Most everybody just calls me *Yo-Yo*."

Fresh-faced Ayodele was obviously fresh out of boot, but he'd arrived in restraints? The man must have gotten into some serious trouble at Brittmore. A big, solid kid, Ayodele had pronounced features, almost comically so, as if someone had started to whittle a Raider from plascrete and stopped halfway through before getting to the detail work. Dark lips, but lighter than his skin, an odd genetic combo found only on a particular group of small stations in the Venus Net Colony, as far as John knew.

"Now for the vets," Sands said. "Corporal Linda Reiner."

A tall woman with a red buzz cut stepped to the line.

"Spec-One Fatima Mukami," Sands said.

A bulky woman stepped up. She wasn't a boot, John could see, but the look on her face made it clear she hadn't been out of Hotel Brittmore for long.

"Spec-Two Dubaku Handan," Sands said.

The one who'd arrived stoned to the gills languidly stepped up, a dreamy, half-smile on his tan face. John wondered how he'd managed to score while in chains and under supervision. That was the thing with the hardcore druggies—they always found a way. In any other outfit, that doped-up grin alone might get him tossed out, but *Keeling* was shorthanded.

"Spec-Three Ricky Chidimma," Sands said.

A dark-skinned man with a shaved head stepped forward. Anger in his eyes. He had what John liked to call a *resting murder face*. Most times in the world of the Raiders, a RMF was a good thing. On *Keeling*, though? Perhaps not. Time would tell.

"Warrant Officer Kuzman Lekan," Sands said.

A man with the blue skin of a Satirli-6 native stepped to the line, a winged crawler beetle pilot pin above his name tag. He was the replacement for Bhola Nessa, killed by her co-pilot, Brendan Akagi. Did Akagi wear chains for that murder? Nope. No punishment for him, because the incident happened while *Keeling* was in transdim.

In the Mud, bad things happened.

"Corporal Bennett," Sands said. "Let's escort these extraordinarily well-behaved warriors to the rig room and find them fashion suitable for a night on the town."

15

BETHANY

What are you in for?

While underway, Bethany hadn't spent all her time in the atrium. She'd cross-trained in engineering, fabrication, firefighting, and even knew the basics of operating the AP6 rotary cannons and the big Type24 artillery batteries, which sometimes crew referred to as a *deuce-quad*.

During that cross-training, while rubbing elbows with sailors in propulsion, electrical, gunnery, and fire control, she heard one whispered question more than any other—*what are you in for?*

Damned crewmembers wanted to know why fellow crewmembers were equally damned.

Most didn't answer the question. If they did, they claimed they hadn't done anything wrong, said they didn't deserve to be entombed on *Keeling*. Suspicion abounded. Was the man working next to you there for sexual assault? Was the woman watching your back in for murder? Was your favorite shipmate a coward who would not stand strong in the face of enemy fire?

Many asked their superior officer about a particular mate's prior offenses. Those officers invariably said they didn't know. Bethany believed them. Even that psycho Lafferty—*Keeling*'s Intel Chief—

didn't have access to personal histories. Some suspected Lincoln knew all there was to know, but if so, the boat's commander kept that info to herself.

Bethany wondered, occasionally, what it was like for Lincoln and XO Ellis to lead people while not knowing if those people were thugs, thieves, rapists, murderers, con artists, or had committed any number of other crimes.

And now, for the first time, Bethany understood how challenging that lack of knowledge must be.

"Where did you do your xenomechanics undergrad, Ensign?"

The woman seated next to Bethany—in her forties, her short blonde hair streaked with gray and buzzed at the temples—forced a smile, but it was the woman behind the desk who spoke.

"You know you're not supposed to ask that, Lieutenant," Major Whittaker said. "Ensign Martigral wouldn't be here if she wasn't qualified for the job."

Not even the basics, not even small-talk courtesies. Whittaker had an open folder in her lap, tilted down from the desk so Bethany and Martigral couldn't see the contents. The paper inside alone likely held more information about Martigral than Bethany would ever learn.

"My apologies, Major," Bethany said.

Martigral was the new xeno mate, taking over the role from Bethany just as Bethany advanced into Jenn Hathorn's position as number two in the department behind Colonel Hasik.

Hathorn, who had attacked Bethany... whom Bethany killed in self-defense...

At least that's what she'd been told. She didn't remember. The only clear recollection she had of that incident was God telling her to *fight back.*

Bethany had killed Jenn Hathorn.

Bethany had killed Major Bratchford.

Would she have to kill Ensign Mindy Martigral as well?

Love wins, my child.

Would she have to—

"Lieutenant Darkwater?"

Bethany blinked, returning to the moment. She'd blanked out, let her thoughts consume her. Had that been the voice of God in her head again, or an echo of a memory?

"Lieutenant," Whittaker said, her voice stern, "are you all right?"

"Yes, of course." Bethany forced a smile. She was getting good at that. "I'm fine. It's just... my apologies, the recent incident on *Keeling*'s hull still weighs heavily on my mind."

Whittaker nodded quickly, as one does in sympathy to a stranger.

"I read the report on Leona Romanik," she said. "Quite tragic."

Whittaker read a report? In a beyond-secret, *need-to-know* environment, Romanik's death wasn't something Bethany thought a personnel officer would need to know.

Bethany turned slightly in her chair, faced Martigral.

"Ensign, I'd welcome you aboard *Keeling*, but since that's not possible at the moment, welcome to the crew."

Martigral was a small woman. She and Bethany probably wore the same size uniform.

"Thank you, Lieutenant Darkwater," Martigral said. "I'm looking forward to it."

Crewmembers often commented that Bethany seemed too old to be an ensign. Martigral was even older, clearly, but her age wasn't an issue in Bethany's book. The Planetary Union had activated almost all reservists. When that wasn't enough, especially in the sciences, they offered large signing bonuses and promises of rapid career track advancement. Ensigns in their thirties and forties weren't unheard of.

Martigral held a degree in xenomechanics—the study of alien technology. Bethany had hoped for someone well versed in automatonics, like she was, but no such luck. Fleet seemed to think of *Keeling* as a piece of alien equipment rather than see it as Bethany did, as a self-assembling construct closer in theme to the biomechanical Prawatt race.

Whittaker closed her folder and put it in a drawer, leaving her desktop empty.

"That should do it for now," she said. "Lieutenant, Admiral Epperson arranged a secure room for you to bring Ensign Martigral up to speed on your department's functions and knowledge. Verbal communication only, I'm afraid. The room has no computer, per the admiral's instructions. Until the ship is accessible again, you'll have to make do. Any questions?"

Bethany had only one. "Do you know when Colonel Hasik will return?"

"That information is classified," Whittaker said.

Of course it was.

For now, Bethany was in charge of a two-person department. A department that could literally do *nothing*.

"You're dismissed, Lieutenant," Whittaker said. "I have a few more things to cover with Ensign Martigral."

Bethany left without another word.

Martigral and Whittaker knew something that Bethany did not. Once again, Bethany was on the outside looking in.

16

BIGGIE

LASH suit on, helmet dangling from her pinkie, Biggie walked toward Pier Two. Time to meet the new pilot and see what he was made of.

She liked Gateway Station. Maybe because she rarely saw anyone in the building corridors, connecting tubes, or the exterior walkways. She preferred the walkways—being "outside" was a privilege she didn't get aboard *Keeling*, which didn't have a bubble deck. During the day, Gateway's crysteel bubble let in the dim light of Pearson's Star. During the night, an endless expanse of glittering glory stretched out forever. The station faced away from Pearson's Planet; it was a dead rock, nothing much to see there.

Gateway's design harkened back to an earlier time. The central hub was 1.75 kilometers across. Full atmospheric pressurization let personnel walk around the campus without exosuits, although exosuit lockers were plentiful and never far away. Constructed with war in mind, every building was designed for strength (not aesthetics, that was for sure) and had its own pressure integrity in case the station's bubble failed.

It was often said the Union wouldn't—and couldn't—build another facility like Gateway. *Wouldn't*, because big stations that couldn't punch from one place to another had fallen out of favor decades ago, during the First Galactic War. *Couldn't*, because Fleet didn't have the money to build another Gateway. The Planetary Union was not the economic giant it had once been. Federal debt had hit insane levels and was climbing steadily. Just the interest alone (paid on loans from the League of Planets and the Ki Empire, mostly) added hundreds of trillions to the Union's national debt every year.

Even though Gateway was a century old and had plenty of issues from age and overuse, Fleet wasn't about to scrap it. Its proximity to the Tower Republic and the Leekee Collective would let the Union launch full scale campaigns against those allied governments, should hostilities ever break out. And Gateway's proximity to the Zone of Interference proved invaluable to science nerds studying that odd patch of the galaxy.

All in all, the mostly empty Pier Two Sector felt like Biggie's personal estate, made for an empress just like her. She would have called it a "ghost town," but she served on the *Crypt*—she knew what a real house of horrors was all about.

She reached the pier itself, a wide, crysteel-bubble-covered jetty stretching a half kilometer out from the crysteel-bubble-covered station. The pier gate's cargo airlock—the big one that allowed wheel-trucks to roll through—was closed. Had been since *Keeling*'s crazy metamorphosis. A Raider in full TASH guarded the smaller, pedestrian-only lock, which sat open, the logic being it could slam shut in an instant if something breached the pier's crysteel bubble.

"Hey there, Biggie. I think you're late."

Raider Spec-1 Clifton Bishop, who served under squad leader Dave Starr. Bishop's TASH hid his scrawny frame. Crazy how the heavy armor made everyone look like a thick bodybuilder, while the lighter version (like the one Biggie wore when she flew) tended to make everyone look damn near feminine in comparison.

"Come on, Cliffie," Biggie said. "You should know by now I'm *never* late. I'm always right on time."

Clifton waved her through. Farther into the base, at the access points to Pier Two Sector, security was tight. Epperson didn't want unknowns gallivanting around his secret ship. Once inside, though, security was mostly a formality handled by Raiders in her platoon. With a small crew like *Keeling*'s, you knew everyone by sight.

Keeling's big, white hangar sat midway down the pier on the starboard side. While *Keeling* wasn't a big ship, the hangar was the largest Biggie had ever seen. Ships that size didn't *get* hangars. There was no need for them. If the unthinkable happened and an enemy attacked a station, you wanted all guns available to fire. You did *not* want to wait until a ship exited a hangar to get line of sight on the attackers. *Keeling*'s enclosure served one purpose and one only—to hide it from view.

Between the hangar and the airlocks (also on the starboard side) were gangway tubes leading to armored launchpads. Most pads lay empty. Two held *Keeling*'s Ochtheras. At the hatch entrances of those tubes stood Lieutenant Lindros and PXO Winter, in full TASH save for their helmets, which were mag-clamped to their hips. Lindros's pencil neck looked funny even without the armor. With the rig on and helmet off, it was downright comical.

While Raiders wore heavy TASH—*tactical assault suit, hermetic* —pilots and crews wore the thinner, more formfitting *light assault suit, hermetic* rigs. Torch, Knuckles, co-pilot Victor "Swamp Rat" Alyona, engineer/gunner Silva "Bankshot" Lehtonen, and the new guy wore their LASH rigs, their helmets in-hand.

"Flight leader Bang." Winter pantomimed a glance at an imaginary watch, as if there was a watch anywhere that would fit her armored wrist. "So glad you could join us."

Torch and Knuckles gave Biggie mock dirty looks, scolding her tardiness.

"Aww, PXO, that's so nice of you," Biggie said. "You know you're my *favorite* platoon executive officer in all the galaxy, right, man?"

Winter rolled her eyes.

Biggie was five minutes late. She'd meant to be on time, but she was still a bit high from a breakfast benzo. PXO Winter didn't mind, not really—you survive a *Crypt* deployment together and things lighten up a bit.

"Unacceptable," Lindros said. "Don't be late again, Warrant Bang. Got it?"

Well, things lightened up a bit for *some.* "Dork" Lindros was laying down the law? A tiger with no teeth. Hard to be a badass when you're too busy running around naked every time the ship dipped into the Mud. The dude had yet to fight. Until he did, the Raiders tolerated him more than obeyed him. He knew it. Maybe he had to put on airs for the newbies.

"Got it, LT," Biggie said. "Hey there, new guy. Introduce yourself."

The flight team's sole replacement was a blue-skin. Biggie hadn't expected that. You didn't get a lot of blueys in the pilot ranks.

"Warrant Officer JG Kuzman Lekan," he said. "Happy to be here."

LEKAN on his name plate, and below that, in Raider aviator fashion, a second, slightly smaller plate: "HANDSY."

"Nice call-sign," Biggie said. "Got anything to do with why you were sent to the *Crypt?*"

The bluey grinned, his purple lips twisting—more sneer than smile. The look in his eyes... this one had *creep* written all over him.

"I got the handle because I'm good at cards," Lekan said. "I'm good at lots of things. As for why I'm here, I had a sit-down with a Major Maia Whittaker. She said y'all needed the best of the best." He gestured to himself, languid fingertips sweeping from his chin to his waist. "And here I am."

Many of *Keeling'*s crew had met Whittaker. In a way, Epperson's Executioner was like that mythological figure Charon—Maia Whittaker sent people to the land of the dead, a.k.a., the *Crypt.*

"I heard of you," Lekan said. "*Biggie.* Aren't you the one who stole Commodore Garrant's shuttle and barrel-rolled past his tower?"

"*Allegedly,*" Biggie said. "Allegedly *borrowed,* by the way, not *stole.* You've met your crew, Handsy?"

Lekan glanced at Swamp Rat, a here-then-gone thing, then his eyes lingered on Bankshot, subtly looking her up and down. Bankshot clearly felt his gaze—she looked away, out past the launch pads.

"I have," Lekan said. "I'm sure we'll get along famously."

Definitely a creep. Biggie would keep an eye on this guy.

"Saddle up," she said. "My crew in Occie Two. Handy's crew take Occie One. Basic formation flying first, then a mock combat landing at pier's end, then a mock dogfight. LT, PXO, I assume you're riding in Handsy's troop compartment?"

Lindros pulled on his helmet. "Something you'd already know if you'd been here on time, flight leader Bang."

Lindros and Winter would test Lekan's comms techniques, make sure he knew how the Warthogs did things.

"Solid," Biggie said. "Take copious notes for me, man. We'll see if *Handsy* really is good at *lots of things*. Let's get to it."

17

SASCHA

The last time Sascha wore her dress whites had been her court-martial.

They should have held the promotion ceremony somewhere smaller. Every footstep, every light cough, every cleared throat, and squeak of the folding chairs echoed in the big, empty reception area. That made Sascha—and everyone else—talk a bit quieter. Anything over a casual level of volume reverberated like a fart in church.

"All these fancy clothes and not even a couple of balloons," said Alex Plait, seated at Sascha's left. "Got to be some ribbons in this old base somewhere, huh?"

His cover hid his bald head. Sascha could just make out the black elastic band that wrapped around the back of his head and attached to the temples of his glasses, keeping the black frames firmly on his nose.

Keeling's command staff sat in the front row: Captain Lincoln directly in front of the glossy black podium, XO Ellis on her right, Major Lafferty on his right. Chief of the Boat Eloi Sung sat to Lincoln's left, then Sascha, Plait, Cat Brown, and Bethany Darkwater, who occupied the xeno department head's seat because Colonel Hasik wasn't present.

Everyone wore full dress white. Rows of pressed uniforms and spotless white covers, save for Lafferty and her BII guys in their ominous dress blacks, and Darkwater—the sole BST crewmember present—in dress tans. The *Keeling* crew all polished up, spit and shine.

To the right, separated by a meter-wide aisle, stood the Raiders. *Stood*, not *sat*, like the sailors did. Sascha had to admit the jizzies looked sharp—every one of them ramrod straight, their charcoal gray dress jackets, white pants, gloves, and barracks covers immaculate. Every brass button, black shoe, and cover visor gleamed. In the front row, Lieutenant Lindros, Master Sergeant Sands, and PXO Winter wore pearl-handled daggers in black scabbards.

Sascha remembered seeing those same Raiders—most of them the same, anyway—as a motley group on the bubble deck of *Ishlangu*. They'd come a long way as a platoon. She wondered if that was the influence of Sands and Winter rather than Lindros, even though the young lieutenant was the unit commander.

Plait nudged Sascha.

"Look at that podium," he said. "Does Epperson travel with that thing?"

The podium was some ten meters in front of double entrance doors. Epperson wanted to be close to an exit at all times, maybe.

"He does," she said. "I saw him speak a few years ago at a commissioning ceremony."

Not a single ding, divot, or scratch marred the black-lacquered podium. On its front, in polished brass, hung the circular sigil of Sixth Group, and below that, in polished brass letters: ADM. MATHIAS EPPERSON.

A few meters behind the podium, three flags hung limp from poles on portable stands: the silver-starburst-on-black banner of the Union, the Fleet's indigo flag, and the blood-red flag of the Raider Corps.

"This'll be short," Sung said. "Won't even take ten fucking minutes, I bet. Bunch of crap."

He barely looked like the same man. Warrant Officer Sung stalked the corridors of the *Crypt* with his coveralls unfastened to his navel, a sweaty white T-shirt clinging to his chest and beer belly, always on the hunt for out-of-line sailors who needed to be put *back* in line with a swift kick in the ass. His peaked cap bore decades of sweat stains and had been crumpled in his angry hands so many times the creased-and-cracked bill looked like it had been run over by wheeltrucks. In dress whites, though, and with an unblemished cover, he looked like a respectable sailor. Somehow, the clothes even made the pockmarks on his face less pronounced, less noticeable.

Sascha understood the COB's anger. In Fleet, promotions were a rare thing for individual sailors. A ceremony like this was usually a time for COs to shower the promotee with praise for all the hard work and sacrifice. A time for the promotee to say a few words. A time for family members who could make the trip to see their sons and daughters shine.

Not this time, though.

Epperson's people had informed Captain Lincoln there would be no speeches from anyone save for the admiral himself, and that his speech would be brief. He wasn't even going to pin on the new rank insignia, as the unit commander usually did. Lincoln would do so after he left.

It wasn't just a break from tradition, it was an insult—Epperson clearly didn't have the time or the desire to celebrate his people.

The double doors opened.

Two Raiders in full TASH marched through, their steps perfectly synchronized.

"Detail, ten-*hut!*" Sands's bellow echoed off the walls

Sascha and the sailors stood.

Major Maia Whittaker, in dress whites, entered next, following the Raiders. She carried a manila folder in one hand, a black case in the other.

Sascha felt a burst of anger—she was on the *Crypt* because Whittaker had put her there. Sascha figured she wasn't the only one who despised the woman.

The two Raiders took positions wide left and wide right of the podium. Whittaker stood a few steps back from the podium's right.

Epperson entered, followed by two more Raiders in full TASH.

"*Admiral on deck,*" Sung called out.

Epperson stepped to the podium.

"Crew of the PUV *James Keeling,* good morning," he said. "Be seated."

A rustle of uniforms and creaking plastic as all on the left side of the aisle sat. The Raiders remained standing, as they always did for formal ceremonies.

"We gather today to recognize the achievements of men and women who have proven themselves in the crucible of service," Epperson said. "Their commitment, performance, and courage have earned them the trust of their superiors and the right to wear a new rank."

Epperson put his hands on the podium.

"This is not just an administrative step. It is a covenant between the individual and the Union. With every increase in authority comes a heavier burden of responsibility. These promotions are approved by Sixth Group Command under the authority of the Office of the President, Malcolm McKinney, and in accordance with the Fleet Code of Conduct."

The admiral and McKinney were buddies, supposedly. They'd been in the same class at the Academy. McKinney served eight years in Fleet, then cycled out and got into politics. Epperson, most thought, would *never* cycle out.

The admiral reached a hand toward Whittaker; she handed him the folder. He set it atop the podium and opened it.

"When your name is called, step forward and remain at attention. Brevet promotions are now made permanent by order of Sixth Group Command. Zhen Smith, promoted one grade to Sergeant. Raider John Bennett, promoted one grade to Corporal."

Smith and Bennett approached the podium, Smith with some degree of formality, Bennett moving with the rigidity of a robot.

From the case she carried, Whittaker handed each man a small black box containing their new rank insignia.

"Permanent promotions, effective immediately," Epperson said. "Specialist-Two Colel Citlalmina, promoted two grades to corporal and assigned as lead ECM. Specialist-Two Brinson Sorro, promoted one grade to specialist-three. Specialist-Three Peredur Geraint, promoted one grade to corporal and assigned as Type-24 port turret master. And Ensign Bethany Darkwater, promoted to lieutenant junior grade and assigned as lead Xeno."

The called sailors joined Smith and Bennett. Darkwater looked so *small* standing with them all, the lone tan uniform in a line of mostly white. Whittaker handed each their box.

"You are hereby promoted to your new rank," Epperson said. "These ranks carry not only the weight of command, but the burden of expectation. You represent the Union. You represent Sixth Fleet. You represent *Keeling*. Raise your right hands."

The line did as they were told, holding their boxes in their left hand, raising their right.

"I, state your name, do solemnly swear," Epperson said.

The promotees repeated his words, and all that followed.

"To support and defend the Constitution of the Planetary Union... against all enemies, foreign and domestic... to bear true faith and allegiance to the same... and to obey the orders of the officers appointed over me... according to regulations and the Uniform Code of Military Justice... so help me God."

Epperson closed the folder, handed it to Whittaker.

"Congratulations," he said. "Dismissed."

With that, he and Whittaker walked out the doors, the Raiders who'd been behind leading the way, those who'd been in front bringing up the rear.

A dry ceremony. Formal, yes, but without passion, without the unabashed pride Sascha usually saw from commanders in such ceremonies. If Epperson had emotions other than annoyance and anger, he'd chosen to not share them.

Some of the sailors went forward to shake hands, to congratulate their shipmates. The Raiders stayed where they were. Still stiff as a board, Bennett returned to his position. Sands called out an *about face*. The platoon marched out, maintaining their formality.

"Congrats to those promoted," Lincoln said. "Let's pin those new rank insignia, then those not scheduled for duty can join me in the mixed club. First round is on me."

The sailors cheered, a burst of happiness that seemed to have been kept bottled up by Epperson's perfunctory manner.

A drink. That would be just the thing.

18

ANNE

Onyeka "Yo-Yo" Ayodele sat ramrod straight in his chair.

"No, Warrant Daniels," he said. "I'm not religious. Definitely not a Purist, if that's what you're thinking."

Arms crossed, leaning against the office's back wall behind Ayodele, Anne stayed quiet, let Akil Daniels do the work. Akil sat on a chair in front of the young Raider, elbows on knees, totally relaxed —just two guys having a friendly chat.

"Come on, Yo-Yo," Akil said, flashing his oh-so-charming grin. "You're not religious at all? Not even a *little*, from your parents? Did you know eighty-four percent of Humanity is affiliated with a religious group?"

Ayodele's gaze flashed down, only for a second, to meet Akil's eyes before returning to his straight-ahead-stare-into-nothing.

"My parents died when I was little," the young Raider said. "Don't know if you know what the Venus Net Colony foster system is like, but it ain't all milk and cookies. Churches run it. Gave me a bad taste for religion. *Eighty-four* percent? Really?"

Akil nodded, glanced off as if contemplating something. The gesture was pure affectation, part of a physical repertoire meant to relax a subject, to make them think they were in a conversation and not an interrogation. If Anne hadn't been taught the same repertoire, she might have fallen for it—that's how smooth Akil was.

"Yeah, true facts," Akil said. "I mean, at least that's what the eggheads in BST say. But you can only put so much trust in the word of people who don't carry a weapon and man a post, am I right?"

Anne smiled. Akil was going for *validation* and *common ground* in the same stroke. By and large, Raiders were well aware they didn't possess the kind of intelligence prevalent in Fleet's scientists. The knuckle-draggers compensated with the belief they performed the only part of military service that actually mattered—shooting the enemy. Akil catered to that sentiment. And wore a pistol in a hip holster, right out there in plain sight. It didn't matter the thing wasn't loaded, what mattered was the symbolism—he carried a weapon for his job, just like Yo-Yo did.

"I hear you there, Warrant Daniels," Yo-Yo said. "I'll take street smarts over book smarts any day. But still... eighty-four percent is like... well, that's like most people."

A real brain surgeon, this one. Not that Anne judged such things. She had nothing but respect for Raiders. Next to going undercover in enemy territory, they had the most dangerous job in Fleet.

"Yep, *most* people," Akil said. "But not you. Right? No sympathy for the Purists? I mean, I don't like to admit it, but the Purists have dealt with a fuckload of persecution over the years. Pretty unfair, if you ask me."

Normalization and *empathy* in one stroke. A little more forced than Akil's earlier ploy, but not bad.

"With all due respect, sir," Yo-Yo said, "I don't have sympathy for churchie terrorists. They kill civilians. Women and children. The only good eight-head is a dead eight-head."

Eight-head. Purists confirmed in their church tattooed an infinity symbol on their forehead. Looked like a sideways number eight. *Churchie* was the more common pejorative, but *eight-head* was far more offensive to those of the Purist faith.

Akil smiled. That smile could charm the pants off a statue. Anne would bet money that Akil's smile—and his bright, hazel eyes that screamed *I am very interested in you*—was the thing that sealed the deal with recruiters and put him in Blackhall, the BII's training academy.

"Spec, I commend your intensity," Akil said. "But let's keep this respectful. We have Purists in Fleet's ranks."

Ayodele sat up straighter.

"Yes sir. Sorry, sir."

Poor guy. Wouldn't want to offend anyone's religious sensitivities, now would we? In Fleet, you couldn't belittle even the religion of the goddamn *enemy*.

Ayodele was the last interview. While Anne had watched, and occasionally participated, Akil politely grilled the replacement Raiders. As with the sailor replacements from *Ishlangu*, Anne hadn't picked up any tells pointing to a spy from the Purist Nation or any other government. Not any clear tells, anyway.

Anne planned to keep a closer eye on a few of them, though. Spec-1 gunner's mate Serena Comtois was new to the ship, on her first-ever Fleet deployment; no better time to turn someone then when they were under twenty and still in training or fresh out of it. Spec-3 fire controller Fern Hardy, from *Ishlangu*, had shifty eyes and couldn't answer a straight question to save her ass. Spec-3 Raider Ricki Chidimma looked like he wanted to kill everyone he met.

With Akil's skill, Anne now knew what several people had done to wind up on *Keeling*. Chidimma admitted he'd been convicted of second-degree murder. Raider Vera Pola confessed to being arrested for narcotics possession, and for use of the same while on duty. Raider Dubaku Handan hadn't admitted to anything, but he was *on* something, no question. Druggies—always a problem.

Anne hadn't figured out everyone's secrets. She would, though. Eventually. For now, she wanted to know what Yo-Yo had done.

Akil could use the man's cute little nickname, because Akil was the "friendly" one. Anne had the higher rank and was far better at projecting the cold, dismissive air of a superior officer. She'd improved her performance in that role lately—she'd learned by watching Epperson.

"You arrived in chains," Anne said. "Must be upsetting. What crime did you commit, Spec?"

Ayodele started to turn in the chair, to look at the person who'd spoken to him.

"Eyes forward," Anne snapped.

Ayodele obeyed instantly. "Sir, yes sir."

"Answer the question, Spec," Anne said. "What are you in for?"

The young Raider hesitated.

"Sir, I was told that information is confidential," he said. "That means I don't have to tell anyone."

Anne suppressed a smile. *Confidential* was four syllables, after all. Maybe that was a lot for Ayodele, maybe he felt the need to define it.

"You are part of a secret mission here, Spec," Anne said. "I'm the head of intelligence. That makes me the boss. So tell me what you did."

Like everyone else on the crew, Ayodele wasn't obligated to say a damn thing. The ploy didn't work on everyone. Pola and Chidimma had been dumb enough to fall for it, so maybe Ayodele would as well.

"I... I thought that's why I volunteered to serve here," he said. "So it will be like what I did never happened."

And there it was.

Some crewmembers aboard *Keeling* had done nothing wrong. They were assigned to the ship because they had no connections that could keep them off the roster, and because they didn't have family that would make a stink if they weren't heard from for years. Beaver Perry, Neal Abshire, Clifton Bishop, and others fell into that category.

But not Ayodele. He'd *volunteered*, which meant Major Maia Whittaker had offered him a choice—two years on the *Crypt*, or he could serve whatever sentence Fleet had given him, a sentence hidden in the parts of his records Anne could not access. Two years entombed would wipe his slate clean.

Anne felt sorry for the kid. Barely nineteen years old. If he lived to twenty-one, he'd get a fresh start. But such sentiments were for the weak. She needed to know what she could.

She nodded at Akil.

"Yo-Yo, tell the major what you did," he said. "It will go easier that way."

Akil put exactly the right amount of fear in his voice. He was an excellent actor. Or was he not acting? Was he really afraid of Anne? If so, even better.

"My drill sergeant," Ayodele said. "He wanted... *stuff* from me."

Fear in his voice, too, but no acting for him. Fear and shame. For the *stuff* this drill sergeant wanted, or for what Ayodele did to wind up here?

"We know about your instructor," Anne said, an easy lie. "We can't mention the name, but we know. You weren't the first person the instructor tried it with."

Anne had no idea which of the hundreds of instructors at Brittmore might be the culprit. Leave out the gender, cover up the lack of knowledge with "secrecy," and stupid people sometimes bought it.

Ayodele said nothing.

"Tell us what happened, Yo-Yo," Anne said. "If you don't, that deal you took might get pulled."

Akil looked up sharply at Anne. She had no right to make such a threat, and zero authority to back it up. She stared back, daring Akil to say so. He did not—instead, he lowered his gaze.

"Tell her, Yo-Yo," he said. "You don't want to get on the major's bad side."

Smart boy, that Akil. He understood how things worked on the *Crypt.*

"All right," Ayodele said, his voice tight from a dark memory.

"Drill Sergeant Capistrano got me alone. He told me if I didn't do what he wanted, he'd make up some shit about me and kick me out of the Raiders. I got real mad. I hit him. A couple of times." He cleared his throat. "More than a couple of times. I didn't mean to kill him."

This kid killed a drill sergeant with his bare hands? Impressive. Ayodele was telling the truth. Anne knew such things.

"That's a rough deal," Akil said. His eyes flicked up to Anne's. "It's difficult when people threaten you with things that aren't true."

An ominous bit of irony, considering what Anne had just done. She'd make a point to steer clear of Ayodele, in case he figured Anne wasn't supposed to ask what he'd done, and *definitely* not supposed to pressure him into revealing it. Yo-Yo was a killer. Maybe he wouldn't do anything to Anne considering her rank and position, but in the Mud, bad things happened.

"Thank you, Spec Ayodele," Anne said. "Your secret is safe with us. Mention this conversation to no one. Go join your platoon."

Ayodele was up and out the door in a heartbeat.

Akil's accusatory stare fell on Anne again.

"He was the last one," Anne said. "I want your full report on all newbies by oh-eight-hundred tomorrow. Dismissed."

Akil left. Slower than Ayodele had, but promptly all the same.

Did Anne need to keep an eye on Akil as well? She still didn't know what he'd done to be entombed.

But then again, he didn't know what she'd done, either.

Considering they worked so closely together, perhaps that was a fair trade.

And, if her instincts about Gillick turned out to be accurate, Anne might need Akil to help bring Gillick down.

19

TRAVIS

Mouth wide open, drool running from the corner of her mouth, little Aven Ellis *screamed*.

"Hush, baby girl," Travis said. "It's all right. Daddy's here."

He bounced the two-and-a-half-year-old on his knee, held her little body close with one hand, petted her hair with the other. His heart and soul twisted and frayed, the unstoppable anguish of a parent with a child in pain—he didn't know what was wrong, and she didn't have the words to tell him.

Aven stopped wailing only long enough to draw in a wet, choking breath, then her tiny lungs pushed that air out in an even louder scream that hurt Trav's ears.

"Dammit, Aven," Travis said. "*Stop it.*"

No, not *said*—he had *yelled*.

He'd let his frustration boil over into anger. What kind of a father was he? She was just a child. A child in pain.

"Daddy, *it hurts!*"

"I'm sorry, honey," Travis said in a soft, sing-song voice. "Daddy's sorry. It's okay, baby girl. It's okay."

But it was not okay. Something was wrong. Where was Molly? Molly would know what to do.

Aven started twitching and thrashing. Travis held her tighter, not knowing how to help. He whispered *shhhhhh*, as if that would do anything.

Aven started to *kick*.

Travis looked down at her chubby little legs…

…at the wrinkled, wet, pink *thing* chewing on her feet.

A newborn baby, skin smeared with pasty vernix caseosa—a term perpetually lodged in Trav's head from Aven's birth, when he'd watched her emerge from his wife's womb. The whitish stuff covered the newborn like the fading greasepaint of a clown. A newborn, but with *teeth*, a mouth full of blood-streaked, needle-sharp teeth that chomped down on Aven's tiny foot again and again and again.

Travis yanked Aven upward, above his head, trying to separate her from the threat. Jaws clamped—the newborn clung to Aven's foot, its weight pulling her leg straight, then Aven's skin ripped free like a sock sliding off. The newborn dropped, thudded against the floor. Travis reared back to *kick* it, to *kill* it, but stopped cold.

Somehow, he knew this monster baby.

Somehow, he knew it was *Kinley*, his second child, whom he'd never seen, because she was still in her mother's belly…

Aven screamed.

And *screamed…*

Kinley flopped on the ground in that awkward, uncoordinated way of an infant, then she rolled to her hands and knees. She looked up at Travis with the same piercing, amber eyes that stared back at him every time he looked in the mirror.

She has her father's eyes…

Blood-streaked greasepaint lips curled back in a horrifying carnivore's smile.

Kinley crawled toward Travis, little hands leaving splotches of red and smears of clumpy white on the floor…

Aven screamed.

And *screamed…*

Travis sat up sharply, his breath a deep wheeze of panic and disorientation, his heart kicking his chest.

He was in his quarters, alone...

A dream.

A nightmare.

But... if he was awake, why did he still hear his daughter's screams?

Because it wasn't a scream—it was a klaxon.

A pounding on his door.

"XO, wake up!"

Travis threw off his blanket, rushed to the door and yanked it open, not caring he wore only boxers.

Eloi Sung, the Chief of the Boat—his mangled hat off for once, revealing thin strands of salt-and-pepper hair sticking up in all directions—stood there, anxious and intense, as if he'd witnessed something he couldn't quite process. Something that terrified him.

"XO, it's *Keeling*. The chrysalis is moving."

BETHANY

Terrified shrieks sliced through Bethany's awareness.

She felt *terror*.

But not hers.

Suffering... pain...

High One. God. *Keeling*. Lost. Crying out in incoherent confusion...

Bethany felt it in her soul—something was coming.

Something *wonderful*.

She raised her head. She'd fallen asleep at her improvised lab desk again. A klaxon alarm blared.

Bethany ran her fingers through her hair. She rubbed at her face, trying to bring herself fully awake.

Something wonderful.

Love wins, my child.

She hurried to the door and headed for *Keeling*'s hangar.

BIGGIE

LASH armor rattling slightly, Biggie raced down Pier Two toward her Occie's pad, Torch and Nikula close behind. Farther down, *Keeling*'s huge, white hangar shuddered and trembled from some unknown force slamming against it...

...from the *inside*.

Biggie turned right down the gangway that connected to her bird's launchpad, pulling her helmet on as she did, sealing it tight. Her suit pressurized. At the gangway's end, a Raider in LASH stood waiting at the airlock door—Sergeant Robin Taylor the crawler crew chief.

"Haul balls, people!" Her voice rang loud in Biggie's helmet. "Cap wants you out there on the double!"

Which Biggie already knew, hence her sprinting, even though she and her battle sisters had no "balls" to actually haul.

Chief Taylor double-checked the seal indicators on Biggie's suit, then did the same for Torch and Knuckles—all green. Taylor spun the wheel to open the outer airlock door. The four women rushed into the small compartment. Taylor shut that door; the ceiling light glowed green. She pulled the lever to vent the airlock. The light switched to red. A moment later, the compartment's air vented into the vacuum of the void.

Taylor spun the wheel for the space-side door.

Knuckles rushed through before it fully opened, scrambled up the ladder to the top turret. Biggie went up her ladder and into the Ochthera's open cockpit. She buckled her restraints as Torch swung into the co-pilot's seat on her right, buckled in, and began pre-flight checks.

"Sealing cockpit." Biggie flipped the switch to lower the canopy. "Pier Two control, clear us for emergency takeoff."

The crysteel canopy closed, its full seal marked by a small light on the console shifting from red to green.

"Top turret sealed," Knuckles said.

Biggie glanced up through the clear canopy, saw the armored hangar's roof retracting, exposing the endless, star-speckled black.

She felt a slight shudder ripple through her Ochthera. Whatever was happening in the *Keeling*'s hangar, it was getting worse, so powerful it vibrated the entire pier.

She had to get her bird clear, pronto.

"Pre-flight complete," Torch said. "Good to go."

Biggie gripped the cyclic. "Control, Ochthera Kilo Echo One. If you don't clear me, I'm leaving anyway."

"Kilo Echo One, Pier Two Control. You are clear for emergency takeoff. There is no traffic in your immediate area."

"Copy," Biggie said. "Kilo Echo One departing."

She triggered a short burst of the Ochthera's VTOL chemjets; the bird rose up and out of the hanger. Biggie angled the crawler away from the pier and applied three seconds of full forward thrust, inertia slamming her back into her seat. She rotated 180 degrees and triggered counter—thrust, again forcing her back. A quick partial rotation: her Ochthera faced the starboard center of *Keeling*'s 130-meter-long white hangar.

What in God's name...

"Control, Kilo Echo One," she said. "Are you seeing this? Do you have visual?"

"Kilo Echo One, Control." Whoever was on the mic, they sounded as dumbfounded as Biggie felt. "We have visual."

The hangar wall thundered and bucked outward, spots in the thick metal bending like tinfoil, white composite shattering and scattering. A rent raced along the side, exposing a ragged gap some ten meters high, thirty meters long, the cyclone of escaping air roiling broken composite out into space like snowflakes in a blizzard.

Through that gap, Biggie saw the spike-covered chrysalis. It *moved*, a football-field-long worm violently contorting, spikes whipping like massive, spasmodic flagella. How could something so big move like that, *heave* like that... like a thing alive?

Like a thing fighting for survival...

"A la verga," Torch said.

The spike-covered copper mass contorted, seemed to compress lengthwise, then expanded explosively. The battered hangar bay doors—each three stories high, ten meters wide—broke free, silently spinning away amid a storm of large-scale shrapnel.

"Ochthera Kilo Echo One, Control. Ochthera Kilo Echo Two is preparing to launch to support you. We need eyes inside the hangar, right now."

"Copy," Biggie said.

She put more distance between her bird and the buckling white tube as she flew to the hangar's end. She and Torch watched for large pieces of wreckage that might pose a collision threat, but there was no need—the detritus moved *away*, inertia carrying it on an infinite journey.

The Ochthera flew wide of the hangar's end. Biggie again expertly stopped on a dime and rotated to look inside.

Her blood chilled.

"Fuck this nonsense," Knuckles said in a disbelieving monotone. "Fuck this completely."

Through the 20-meter-wide, 30-meter-tall oval opening and

down the hangar's 130-meter length, the few lights that remained unbroken shone upon the wriggling, rippling chrysalis, reflected off hundreds of long spikes that trembled with incessant, sickening undulations. The copper sheath covering the ship's aft end—the end that had slammed into the huge bay doors and sent them hurtling into the void—began to *tear*.

Keeling's bizarre tail horns burst through the chrysalis, the three long, wicked-looking barbs extending a good fifteen meters beyond where the bay doors had been moments before. Shreds of copper sheath clung loosely to the barbs, hanging like sloughed, spiked skin.

As Biggie watched, that sloughed skin began to move again, but in a different way.

"Lord save us," Torch said. "I didn't sign up for this."

Neither had Biggie. Neither had Knuckles. *No one* had.

"Control, Kilo Echo One," Biggie said. "Confirm visual—are you seeing what I'm seeing?"

22

ANNE

Anne ran for the pier gate, the legs of her exosuit *zip-zipping* against each other like snowsuits she'd worn when she'd been a little girl and Daddy took her on skiing trips.

Anger and fear fought for dominance—how could her best friend be so *stupid?*

"Beth, get your ass out of there! *Right now!* Lincoln ordered everyone off the pier."

Biggie's live footage played in the HUD projected onto the interior of the exosuit's visor. At a full sprint, watching the jostling image, it was hard to make out what was happening. What Anne could identify, she didn't like.

"Annie, I'm fine." Beth's voice in the helmet speakers, calm and relaxed. "It's so beautiful."

She didn't sound injured. She sounded *crazy*, sure, but unhurt. Had she already been in the hangar when *Keeling* started doing whatever it was doing? Or had she been the first to realize something was wrong, her preternatural affinity for the ship sending her racing to the hangar?

Ahead, at the pier gate, Anne saw five TASHed Raiders stretched out in a defensive cordon, rifles mag-clamped to torsos. The guns and their imposing black armor sent a clear message—they wouldn't let anyone in.

Major Anne Lafferty wasn't just *anyone*.

As she sprinted to the gate, one of the Raiders stepped toward her, armored hand outstretched, palm-up.

"Hold on, Major," Corporal Bennett said. "No one allowed on the pier. Captain's orders."

Anne stepped closer. It was like standing toe-to-toe with an obsidian gorilla.

"Let me pass, Corporal. Darkwater is in that hangar."

"Yes sir, XO Ellis is aware," Bennett said. "He ordered Lieutenant Darkwater to leave. As soon as she exits the hangar, Alpha-One and Bravo-Two are ready to take her to safety."

Anne glanced past the access gate. Little clusters of flickering lights moved around it—Raiders using their rigs' chem-thrusters, hovering close to the long, battered, white hangar.

"Lieutenant Darkwater *refuses* to exit," Anne said. "I'm going in to drag her out of there."

She moved to step around Bennett—he stepped sideways to block, his rig's artificial muscle letting him maneuver far faster than she could. Two of his squad came closer, flanking him. She took in their name-plates: Spec-1 PERRY and corporal REINER.

They were starting to piss Anne off.

"Corporal Bennett, your crewmate is in danger," she said. "I know where she is."

She couldn't *order* him to help; the captain's orders always superseded Anne's. He could call it in and wait for permission or he could take the initiative and decide for himself.

"You know where she is?" Bennett asked.

Anne nodded.

"Reiner, take command of this post," Bennett said. "Report in that Yo-Yo and I are going to assist a shipmate in danger. Abs, Beaver, stay here. Major Lafferty, we'll get you there quick. But if there's trouble, I will maneuver you to safety with or without your permission. Is that clear?"

He was coming with her. And, in a way, *he* had given *her* an order. Such steel in his voice. How was this old man only a corporal?

"Crysteel clear," Anne said.

Bennett opened the pedestrian airlock. The pier's atmo integrity hadn't been breached, so it didn't have to cycle. As Anne stepped through, she glanced at Ayodele. Did he know she'd lied to him about having to reveal he'd killed his drill sergeant? Armored-up Ayodele carried an RR-36, which, considering the situation, Anne assumed held live ammo. If he wanted to, he could shoot her dead and claim it was an accident.

There wasn't time to order Bennett to take someone else, nor was there time to rationalize that demand—Beth was in danger.

Anne felt Bennett's armored gauntlets grip her sides.

"Yo-Yo, stay behind-right," Bennett said. "Do not touch your weapon unless I tell you to."

And then Anne was flying, Bennett's TASH thrusters accelerating her down the pier's length faster than her exosuit's basic thrust could have managed. They closed in on *Keeling*'s hangar.

"Take me to the amidships airlock," she said.

Once there, Bennett set her down without the slightest jostle. Anne rushed into the gangway tube. She didn't need to look back to know Bennett and Ayodele's thick armor slowed them in the tube's narrow confines.

Anne reached the closed airlock, the very same one she'd gone through with Bennett, Colonel Hasik, and XO Ellis when the chrysalis first formed. The red light above the door meant the hangar had lost pressure, something already made obvious by gaping cracks in the bulkhead around it. The lock's keypad remained lit—it still had power. Anne punched in a security override. The airlock opened, but not all the way, shuddering to a halt as broken internal mechanics ground against each other.

There was just enough room...

"Major, *wait*," Bennett said. "Wait for us!"

Ignoring him, Anne slipped through. She made it three steps before the stunning scene stole her thoughts.

Up and down the ship, the pointy metallic spikes sagged, deflated, retracted into themselves. Their collapses rippled across the coppery surface like rocks dropped into a 120-meter-long tubular pond, multiple impact rings expanding over one another in mad, circular crisscrosses.

Off to the right, a person in an exosuit, a *short* person, hands locked on a rail that had buckled and warped from *Keeling's* mad convulsions.

Beth.

Anne ran to her, grabbed her arm and started dragging her toward the airlock door.

Beth stood firm, a snap of her shoulders freeing her from Anne's grip.

"I'm staying," Beth said. "I must *witness*."

Her icy, unforgiving tone stunned Anne. Meek Beth—*compliant* Beth—would not be moved.

"We *have* to get out of here," Anne said. "*Look* at that thing! You're going to get hurt!"

Beth stared up at the rippling behemoth, taking it in as if it were some artistic masterpiece to be endlessly admired.

"*Keeling* won't hurt us," she said, her voice again peaceful, almost hypnotic. "*Keeling* knows us. *Keeling* loves us."

She wasn't afraid—but Anne was.

The *Crypt* vibrated like a globule of molten metal floating in zero-G, a globule with an obfuscated yet still distinctive peak of the super-structure. By Fleet standards it wasn't a big ship, not even close, and yet here, standing only a few meters away, Anne felt like an ant on an alien shore, waiting for a tidal wave of liquid copper to crash upon her.

"Everything will be fine," Beth said. "Everything will be okay. Oh, *look*, Annie... it's receding!"

The liquid metal tightened around the vessel. No, not *tighten*—it *flowed* inward, a three-dimensional lake drying up before her eyes. The ship's familiar, gnarled texture appeared, at first obscured by a shimmery glaze, then, when that glaze dribbled away like globs of draining mercury, was just as rough and mottled as Anne remembered it.

The chrysalis, the shell—whatever it may have been—vanished, leaving no trace it had ever existed.

Beth clapped her hands, bounced up and down.

"Astonishing! It's *a miracle*."

Striations lined *Keeling*'s curved hull, rippled streaks and bands that were a lighter, brighter copper color than the gnarled, weathered hull Anne remembered. Hundreds of those striations, almost like...

...like stretch marks.

"Astonishing," Beth said again, her voice lilting and reverent. She looked left, down the hangar, leaning out over the bent rail. "Look at the tail!"

Far to Anne's left, *Keeling*'s tail and its long barbs stretched a good ten meters past where the bay doors had once been.

Impossible...

Anne looked to her right, to the bow. The lower prow pressed against the hangar wall, was *embedded* in it a little, as if *Keeling* had drifted in with too much inertia to stop before crashing home.

But... before... *fifteen* meters had separated the upper prow and the hangar's end.

Impossible. *Impossible.* And yet, what other explanation could there be?

"Beth... did *Keeling*... did it..."

Anne couldn't quite speak the word, because that word simply could not be reality.

"It did, Annie," Beth said. "Our ship *grew*."

23

SASCHA

Sascha Kerkhoffs had never been face-to-face with an admiral before.

Epperson sat across the table from her. Master Warrant Officer Brooke Ralston sat next to him, a tablet in her hands. Epperson had an air about him—simultaneously commanding, dismissive, and heartless, and he had yet to say a single word. Ralston's glossy, brunette hair was pulled back so tight, Sascha wondered how the woman managed to blink.

Captain Lincoln, XO Ellis, and mousy little Bethany Darkwater were on Sascha's side of the table. Like her, Ellis and Darkwater were buttoned up and sharp, as one should be when meeting an admiral. Lincoln wore coveralls and a red bandana. How did she get away with that?

The meeting room bore the dings and dents brought on by over a century of use, gray walls patched in two dozen places to cover up damage, to repair crumbling plasquick, or to fill in holes left by equipment that had once been state-of-the art but eventually faded into obsolescence. Wild to think the first meeting in this room had occurred decades before Sascha's grandparents had been born.

She had performed a quick and dirty evaluation of the ship's exterior, recording changes and documenting what equipment had been damaged or destroyed. Presumably, that was why she'd been included in this briefing—or did Epperson know she'd been quietly researching purchase orders and supply requisitions? Had she really been called here so Epperson could eviscerate her in front of her commanding officers?

"Let's get down to it," the admiral said. "First off, I can see with my own eyes *Keeling* is bigger. What are your measurements, Lieutenant..."

His voice trailed off. He glanced at Ralston. She angled her tablet toward him, tapped a spot on the screen.

"Lieutenant *Kerkhoffs*," Epperson said. He looked at Sascha. "The new measurements?"

He didn't know her name? Sascha would have been offended if that hadn't been a good sign—if he didn't know who she was, he was likely oblivious to her snooping.

"*Keeling* was one hundred nine point seven meters long," Sascha said. "That's measured from the tip of the dorsal barb to the forward point of the lower prow. The same span is now one hundred thirty-six point five meters. *Keeling*'s beam was ten point two meters—it is now twelve point three. While we haven't been inside yet to measure internal volume, for all intents and purposes, *Keeling* is twenty percent larger."

It sounded crazy to say those words out loud, yet they were true.

"Lieutenant Darkwater," Epperson said, "with Colonel Hasik away, you are the acting xeno department head. Tell me what happened."

Darkwater laughed. Sascha felt anxious—she'd never met an admiral, but she assumed admirals did not like to be laughed at.

"Is something *funny*, Lieutenant?" asked Epperson.

Darkwater's smile vanished. She stared down, not meeting his callous stare.

"I'm sorry, Admiral," she said. "It's not *funny*, exactly, it's just that... well... the question surprised me. It seems obvious what happened. The ship grew."

Epperson leaned forward, elbows on the table.

"In my thirty years of service, I've never known a ship to *grow*," he said. "I understand Prawatt ships increase in size as time goes on, but *Keeling* isn't a Prawatt ship. I'm asking *how* it grew. *Why* it grew. What is the mechanism by which this warship's length increased by some twenty-six meters? Will it grow again?"

Darkwater's eyes flicked up to Epperson, but only for an instant before she again looked down. Sascha found Darkwater's behavior odd in a way she couldn't specify. So... *deferential*, but not in a military sense.

"I don't know the answers to those questions, Admiral," Darkwater said. "The event is barely two hours old. I haven't had time to evaluate. I haven't even been inside yet."

Epperson nodded. "I suppose that's true."

"I need Colonel Hasik." Darkwater finally looked up, this time holding Epperson's gaze. "May I ask when he will return?"

Sascha expected Epperson to bite Darkwater's head off again, to establish his dominance, but the question didn't anger him.

"I'll have Colonel Hasik here as soon as possible," he said.

Epperson could have ordered Hasik whenever he liked, yet he had not. What could be important enough to keep *Keeling*'s xeno department chief away all this time? The ship had grown a damn *shell* and killed a crewmember, for fuck's sake.

The admiral sat up straight. "Captain Lincoln, I need your crew back at their posts immediately. We have a critical mission that only *Keeling* can perform. You ship out in twelve hours."

Twelve hours? That was insane. The ship needed to be studied and analyzed—for *months*, at a minimum—not sent out willy nilly on an unknown mission.

Now it was Lincoln who leaned forward, like she might in a boozy bar if someone insulted her and she wanted them to know a second insult would be met with fists.

"Admiral," she said, "the ship has just undergone a... a..."

She couldn't find the word.

"A *metamorphosis*," Darkwater offered.

Lincoln's jaw muscles twitched. "Whatever we call it, there are structural changes to the hull. We don't yet know the extent of any internal damage. We need time to ensure *Keeling* is safe for the crew. We have to identify what repairs need to be made, what equipment to replace, what—"

"Time is a luxury we don't have," Epperson snapped. "This mission has a fixed operational window. Success could change the course of the war."

What objective could be so important? The Raiders had been drilling in Sklorno ship mockups. Sascha hoped *Keeling* didn't have to go up against those insane savages.

"Admiral," Lincoln said, "our point-defense guns were sheared away. All three need to be replaced. We have yet to install the port Type24 turret destroyed during the Battle of *Ishlangu*. No one has been *inside* yet—we don't know what new problems await us there."

Darkwater's inappropriate laugh had stressed Sascha, but Lincoln's borderline aggression hit another level altogether. Epperson's high-handed capriciousness had ruined many a promising career, or so the rumors went. Everyone in Fleet feared him. Everyone, it seemed, except Kiara Lincoln. She stared at the admiral, not bothering to hide her anger.

Anger that didn't bother Epperson in the least.

"Then get your people inside and determine what needs to be fixed," he said. "Ralston, what do we have available for repairs and restock?"

Ralston tapped at her tablet, a hungry bird pecking for food.

"Three AP6 VODS are in central storage," she said. "I'll have them on Pier Two within the hour."

The AP6 void defense system, or *VOD*, was *Keeling's* point-defense weapon. The 20-millimeter, 6-barreled rotary canons were used against any incoming threat, from torps to voidcraft to exo-troops.

"The replacement Type24 turret will be installed within six

hours," Ralston said. "Composite armor plate to replace the damaged segments, replacement equipment for the fabrication room, the replacement Raider terminal... everything you need is in Warehouse Two-Three."

Replacement armor—would it also be second-hand shit from *Boudicca,* or some other scrapped Fleet vessel?

"Your Mark 16 and Mark 15 torpedo resupply is ready," Ralston said. "Plus, you've been allocated six Mark 14s."

That was good news. The STC manipulation fields generated by Mark 14 scrambler torps were stronger than those created by artillery-launched STC blazer rounds, though still not nearly as powerful as a ship's internal space-time corruptor. Fourteens couldn't "think for themselves" like the bat-brain-guided Mark 16s, but they could be preprogrammed with a specific route or logic tree—an *if-X-then-Y* structure.

Fourteens weren't as readily available as fifteens and sixteens. That supply gave *Keeling* six of them meant Epperson considered this mission vital to winning the war.

"What about the ODAIA?" asked Lincoln. "The chrysalis destroyed every single sensor."

Ralston looked down at her tablet.

"The *ODAIA,*" she said, pronouncing it as a single word—*ohdaiah*—just as Lincoln had. "I'm not familiar with that system."

"*Optical dimension analysis and interpretation array,*" Sascha said. "We mostly just call it *optical.* It's how we see our surroundings when we're in the... ah..."

She glanced at Epperson for approval.

"Warrant Ralston is read-in, Lieutenant," he said, irritated. "Continue."

Obviously she was read-in, or she wouldn't be here.

"Right, of course," Sascha said. "When we're in transdim, looking at our surroundings with the naked eye can cause... *problems.*" That seemed like a good word for *driving people insane,* which was how Colonel Hasik phrased it. "Regular cameras don't work. Everything in the other dimension comes back as white light. ODAIA—*optical*—incorporates hundreds of tiny sensors detecting multiple input types. The data feeds into an internal analog processor to give us a 360-degree view."

That view fed into the nav-orb. The minimum focus length meant *Keeling*'s crew couldn't see anything within a hundred meters or so of the hull, but past that, optical let them see a long, *long* way.

Ralston entered data. "Is the ODAIA's internal processor working?"

"We don't know," Lincoln said. "Because we *haven't been inside yet.*"

Ralston nodded, ignoring the biting tone.

"Ah, here it is," she said. "Warehouse Two-Two has a full set of replacement sensors. We have a dedicated engineering crew on-station, with full clearance, to install the Type24, the AP6 point-defense guns, and everything else external, but your people will have to install and connect the ODAIA. How long will that take?"

Lincoln looked to Sascha.

"If the internal wiring is intact, eight hours," Sascha said. "If not, three days. Maybe four."

"Then pray the internal wiring is intact," Epperson said. "Captain Lincoln, I suggest you get your people into your ship and let Ralston know what needs to be fixed. The twelve-hour deadline is firm."

"Admiral, I must object," Lincoln said. "The safety of my crew is—"

Epperson slammed his fist on the table, cutting Lincoln off.

"Your *crew* serves on a Union *warship*," he said, his words ringing off the walls. "We are at war. *Keeling* is the only ship that can execute this critical mission. If you persist in your objections, I will relieve you of your command. With or without you at the helm, Kiara, *Keeling* punches for New Earth in twelve hours. Do I make myself clear?"

Lincoln kept her anger under control, but in no way did she hide it.

"Yes, Admiral," she said. "We'll begin prepping for departure immediately."

Epperson nodded. "That's what I thought. Your mission orders are classified and will be delivered once you are underway. There's one more thing. Ralston here will arrange for the delivery of several crates. These crates are sealed. They are not to be scanned or tampered with in any way. Your orders will explain their purpose. You are all dismissed. Get to work."

Chief of the Boat Eloi Sung barked at the crew, ordering them to stack neat piles of duffels and other gear near the access gate but clear of the main road. Two wheeltrucks, loaded with provisions, idled on that road, both driven by *Keeling* crewmembers. Alex Plait, the ship's ops department head, and Daniel Monstranto, the supply chief, examined the contents of a third truck stacked high with crates.

The crew prepared to board, but Lincoln wouldn't allow it yet. Travis stood with her just inside the pedestrian airlock. Both wore exosuits. Lindros was with them as well, in full TASH.

A squawk in Trav's headset.

"XO, Lafferty. Do you read me?"

Lincoln had put Travis in charge of preliminary ship evaluation. He'd sent Lafferty and her BII team in first, escorting Sascha Kerkhoffs to the CIC, all wearing LASH rigs for safety.

"Copy, Major," Travis said. "Go ahead."

"Internal power is out on Decks One and Two," Lafferty said. "Kerkhoffs wants to go down to engineering and see what's what. Topside sphincters are functioning."

Travis fought the urge to glance at Lincoln, to get her permission to make the next choice. He was learning that when she wanted to take over, she'd say so. If she didn't, her last instructions stood.

"Negative, Major," Travis said. "Stay in the CIC for now. I'll have Raiders do a compartment-by-compartment check of the lower decks." He turned to Lindros. "I want one Raider squad to enter through the pouch. Have them do a visual of the torpedo bays first. Put the second squad on standby, ready to go in and support."

Behind his visor, Lindros nodded.

"One squad through the pouch, a second on standby," he said. "Aye-aye, XO. But should we only send in people who were on the last deployment? If *Keeling* killed Romanik because the ship wasn't familiar with her, should we keep new personnel back?"

A good question, one Travis had already discussed with Darkwater. In any other situation, sending armed-and-armored Raiders into their own ship would seem like overkill. But *Keeling* had killed one crewmember—Captain Lincoln and Travis needed to know what would happen.

"As long as none of your people try to cut into the ship or damage it in any way, we should be fine," Travis said. "Newbies have to board at some point anyway, so we might as well make sure the first newbies in are wearing TASH."

Would that armor protect them from any danger? Darkwater didn't know for sure.

Danger... bloody greasepaint face... needle teeth...

Travis pushed the memory away. He didn't have time to dwell on bad dreams.

Only *Keeling* crew on the pier, save for two Raiders in full TASH who guarded a stack of four crates set off to the side. The Raiders' ship insignia showed they were from *Akathaso*—DIETRICH, a master sergeant, and CHINOOK, a sergeant. Epperson did allow some outsiders to see his secret ship, it seemed.

"Lieutenant," Trav said to Lindros. "Go tell Dietrich that we'll load those crates as soon as the ship is cleared."

Lindros walked toward the Raiders.

"Eng, XO," Travis said.

Kerkhoffs came back instantly. "Eng here, go ahead, XO."

"When the lower decks are cleared, check the curvine room first," Travis said. "Report back to me on the status, then deal with the power situation. Darkwater will check the atrium."

Aven screaming... Kinley (was it Kinley? Couldn't be Kinley) chomping down on Aven's precious little foot...

"Curvine room first," Kerkhoffs said. "Aye-aye, XO."

Travis stared down the long pier, pretended to look at the battered white hangar. He couldn't shake the horrific vision of his monstrous daughter.

He'd had a *nightmare*. Not a *hallucination*, because he wasn't in the Mud.

Did that make it better... or worse?

25

JOHN

He felt so at home in his armor.

John and the Raiders of Alpha Squad flew through the space between the battered hangar and *Keeling*'s underside, their rigs' extended chem-thrusters propelling them along.

"Hey, Sarge," Beaver said, "I think the ship got the clap."

John winced. Beaver never knew when to stop talking.

"Shut your trap, Spec Perry," Sergeant Jordan said. "Alpha Lead to Platoon Lead. Are you seeing this? There are some kind of growths on the hull. They look like... pimples. They're all over."

Lieutenant Plait and Warrant Gillick procured dozens of powerful portable lights to compensate for those destroyed during *Keeling*'s "hatching," if that was the right word. Those lights gleamed off the bright copper lines and zigzag metallic striations laced across the ship's gnarled belly, and other things that hadn't been there before the chrysalis formed—lumps the size of half a beach ball, each crusted in pointy spikes. It made John think of the skin of a horned toad.

"Copy, Alpha Lead, we have visual," Lindros said on the platoon channel. "I'll have Bravo Squad survey the hull and get a count of those... ah... additions. Continue on to the pouch."

John and his squadmates moved along *Keeling's* underside, examining the changes. The ship had grown. Unreal.

"Aft torpedo bay looks intact," Corporal Sarvacharya said. "Striations around it, but I don't see any cracks in the armor."

Like the topside superstructure, the squat, rectangular, bottomside torpedo bays—one forward, under the base of the lower prow, and one aft, where the midsection and tail joined—were add-ons to *Keeling's* hull. Torpedoists basically lived in those tight confines, maintaining the weapons, gear, and constantly tending to the living brains of bats used for torpedo navigation.

Alpha squad continued on. There was nothing like flying alongside a warship. Even a relatively small vessel like *Keeling* made you feel tiny and insignificant. In the grand scale of the Milky Way galaxy, an individual person was nothing more than an infinitesimal blob of matter.

"We're approaching the pouch," Jordan said. "Bennett, Alpha-Two goes in first. Slow and steady wins the race. We don't know what might be waiting for us. Remember—this ship killed a clam a few days ago. Be on the lookout for her body."

The ship, or the coating or whatever, had pulled Spec-1 Romanik in. No sign of her body on the hull. Lieutenant Darkwater speculated Romanik's corpse had been pulled inside the ship, somehow, or had dissolved in the chrysalis—like an amoeba dissolving dinner.

"Copy, Alpha Lead," John said. "Slow and steady."

He often dreamed of dying in battle, of bringing honor to the Raiders. Wouldn't it be a kick in the pants to get killed by his own ship instead?

All four fire teams had members new to the Crypt. Lincoln and Lindros opted to keep the fire teams as-is instead of culling off *Keeling* vets for this task. John didn't agree with that decision, but it wasn't his job to agree. He was a corporal—superior officers made choices, he implemented those choices.

"Alpha-Two," John said, "form up on me, but stay as spread out as you can. Once inside, Beaver takes point. Abs, Reiner, cover his flanks. Yo-Yo, you stay with me."

In the three days since the replacements' arrival, Corporal Reiner had proven her worth as a skilled operator. In drills, her combat experience showed. Bennett already trusted her. Yo-Yo, on the other hand, was so fresh out of boot the kid could barely operate his TASH rig. The lack of parts didn't help—Yo-Yo's hip-flexor micromuscle had gone bad, and his helmet's neck-seal clasp was so stripped from long use it wouldn't properly seal. The quartermaster printed a replacement clasp. John cannibalized some muscle from one of the platoon's two dead rigs.

John continued flying along the ship's underside. At amidships, he clicked his heels twice, activating his armor's counterthrust. He slowed, came to almost a full stop in front of *Keeling*'s closed "pouch," the internal area that housed the flight bay.

The pouch's entrance, closed up tight, looked like the pursed lips of some massive fish, or perhaps the mouth of Jonah's biblical whale. The mouth sat almost directly below the CIC, which was in the superstructure three decks above. The pouch's interior ran forward from the mouth, meaning anything flying out of it was initially oriented toward *Keeling*'s aft.

Now came the interesting part—the pouch mouth was usually opened from within the flight bay. Until now, no one had tried opening it from the outside.

On and in *Keeling*, "sphincters" took the place of hatches and airlocks found on most ships. Exterior sphincters—meter-wide circles of copper-colored metal—had lines and wrinkles so organic-looking they bore an unfortunate resemblance to a Human butthole. The crew referred to them as "spanuses," a portmanteau of "space" and "anus."

Spanuses opened or closed at the slide of a hand along their unfortunately named "rims." No end of jokes from the Raiders for that nomenclature. When John was eighteen or twenty—the typical age of most jizzies—he would have found such jokes absolutely hysterical.

"Attempting to open the pouch now," John said.

He placed his armored hand against the lower copper lip, swept gently from left to right.

There was a pause, then the metallic lips opened, one curling up, the other curling down, exposing a cavernous, dark space inside.

"Internal power appears to be out. Alpha-Two, lights." John tapped a button on his helmet. Small but powerful lights blazed from the helmet's sides and from each hip, piercing the darkness. His teammates did the same. "Alpha-Two entering now. Beaver, go."

Beaver flew in slowly. The fist-sized thrusters at each end of the thin X-arms extending from his lower back pulsed in staccato bursts of yellow fire. Like everything else Raider-related, Beaver made the complex task of zero-G maneuvering seem effortless and natural. Reiner and Abs entered next, Reiner on Beaver's left, Abs on his right. Abshire didn't have Beaver's skill—he made constant micro-corrections to counter too much thrust this way, over-rotation that way. Reiner made it look almost as easy as Beaver did.

Almost.

"Yo-Yo, with me," John said. "Remember, don't over-thrust. Less is more. And don't even think about touching your weapon unless I order it."

John half expected to hear Yo-Yo refuse the order. This was the kid's first time seeing *Keeling*'s interior—flying into a dark monster's gaping maw made one hell of an impression.

"Copy, Corporal Bennett," Yo-Yo said.

A bit of a tremor in the kid's voice, but he didn't complain. A good sign.

John applied thrust. He flew through the gaping mouth and into the pouch. He'd been in here dozens of times, but with the power out it was like floating into a cave lit up by the headlamps of five eager spelunkers.

He moved past the empty spaces on the port side where the

platoon's two Ochtheras would rest, then past the maintenance frames, tool storage, and empty armament storage racks. Soft reflections from the silver cross-hatching in the microfilament zip-ties Chief Taylor and her techs used to lock down anything and everything, to secure racks and equipment in the unconventional, oddly shaped landing bay. TASH lights sweeping across the curved, coral-patterned overhead, the gear racks, and the dark openings of cubbyholes gave the place haunted house vibes.

Lindros on the squad channel: "Alpha-Two lead, see anything unusual?"

As if anything on *Keeling* could be considered usual to begin with.

"Looks how I remember it, LT," John said. "Except... I think it's bigger in here."

Maybe that was to be expected, considering, but it still felt weird.

"Alpha-Two lead, take your squad through the tunnel to Raider Land," Lindros said. "Jordan, move Alpha-One into the pouch. PXO Winter and I will be there shortly with the crawler tech crew."

John acknowledged the order.

"The Dork is coming in," Beaver said on the fire team channel. "I feel safer already."

Abshire laughed.

"Spec Beaver," Reiner said on the same frequency, "you're aware platoon command can listen to all channels, simultaneously, yeah?"

Only a few days in, and she was already helping manage the fire team. John appreciated it.

"Uh... no, Corporal Reiner," Beaver said. "I wasn't aware of that."

If Lindros had heard Beaver's joke, discipline would ensue. Most likely in the form of many pushups. Beaver could rip off 150 of them before even breaking a sweat. He'd probably enjoy it.

John flew to the rear of the landing bay and dropped down. His armored boots clanked home on the fakegrav deck.

"Alpha-Two, entering the tunnel," John said. "Abs, take point. Then Beaver, then Reiner. Yo-Yo, on me."

While the exterior sphincters were round, those within the ship were more oblong, just wide enough for TASH armor to fit through. Abshire slid a hand along the textured rim. The living metal pulled back, revealing the dark tunnel that led to Raider Land.

"Gross," Reiner said. "The way this stuff moves. You told me about it, Bennett, but now that I see it up-close? It's nasty."

While she wasn't wrong, he looked forward to her first unarmored slide-through the exterior sphincters. Now *that* was gross.

"This tunnel is twenty meters long," John said. "Or at least it was before the ship grew. The tunnel runs forward through the lower amidships area to platoon quarters. We've been through it a hundred times."

A hundred times before the chrysalis formed, at any rate. A hundred times when the lights strung down the ceiling's length lit up the copper walls and fakegrav deck plating below.

"I don't like it," Yo-Yo said. "It's dark, like... like a throat ready to swallow us or something."

"You know all about swallowing," Beaver said. "That's what Abs told me, Yo-Yo. Right, Abs?"

Abshire had the good sense to keep his mouth shut.

"Beaver," John said, "you're one more dumb joke away from a blanket party with me, Mafi, and Basara. Copy?"

Mafi and Basara were the biggest men in the platoon. One-on-one, Beaver could whip either of them. Pinned down by a blanket in his bunk, though, Beaver wouldn't be able to do a damn thing while people took turns wailing on him with a bar of soap whipped around inside a sock like some medieval mace.

"Copy, Corporal," Beaver said. "I'll behave."

Abshire entered the tunnel. His rig's lights played off the coral-patterned, dull copper walls. Beaver followed.

"Tunnel's wider," Abs said.

John entered next, found that Abs was right. Before, the tunnel's narrow width forced TASH-rigged Raiders to walk with shoulders at a slight angle in order to fit through. Now he had a good thirty centimeters on either side.

"Wider like your asshole, Abs," Beaver said. "After Mafi gets done pounding it."

Yo-Yo laughed, a bit too loud. Kid was trying to fit in.

"Beaver," John said, "what did I tell you about jokes?"

"You said dumb jokes would get me in trouble, Corporal," Beaver said. "Gaping asshole jokes are always smart jokes."

A squelch on John's private channel with Lindros.

"Alpha-Two Lead, get your people under control," the lieutenant said.

John gritted his teeth. He should have warned his team about excess chatter at a time like this.

"Copy, Lieutenant." John switched to the team channel. "Beaver, I won't warn you again. Everyone get your game faces on. Stay focused on the task at hand."

And what an odd task it was: move through your own ship with the same caution you'd use boarding a derelict vessel that might have enemy troops hiding behind every corner.

"Approaching tunnel exit," Abs said.

"Abs, move into the training area," John said. "Hold there. Beaver, cover his right, Reiner his left."

His people moved forward and spread out.

"Training area is clear," Abs said. "Rig room hatch looks damaged. Visible damage to workout gear."

John exited the tunnel into the small open area Raiders used for briefings and hand-to-hand training. Workout area to port: the four treadmills that had been neatly arranged side by side now sat at shallow angles to each other, as much as a meter of space between them; of the six strength resistance arrays bolted to the coppery bulkhead, two had bent frames and another two had completely popped free from their mounts. To starboard, the rig room's heavy, reinforced steel hatch painted a picture of the shifting forces at play: upper hinge broken, bottom one visibly bent, door itself bent inward at the middle as if the overhead and deck had pushed toward each other.

"LT, Alpha-Two Lead," John said. "Rig room door is damaged, might not be secure. Repeat, might not be secure."

"Copy, Alpha-Two Lead," Lindros said. "Alpha-One Lead, take your squad into the rig room. I need a damage assessment ASAP. Alpha-Two, move forward."

Abshire continued on, leading the team between the head and showers, on the port side, and the LT's small compartment, to starboard.

Past those, the platoon's "nuts to butts" racks, which stretched forward into the narrowing compartment that was *Keeling*'s lower prow. Three bunks to a rack, laid out in three rows of four racks each. One row ran along the port side bulkhead, one along the starboard, and one up the middle between them with only a meter of space on either side. Or, at least, there had been only a meter of space—now it was a meter and a half in some spots, two meters in others, as if the floor had been haphazardly stretched beneath them. The racks in the rows themselves had butted right up against each other, end to end; now some showed three or even four meters of distance between them, broken bolts and fasteners showing where they'd been pulled apart.

"Fucking hell," Beaver said. "Looks like someone threw a wild party in here and didn't invite us."

On the deck, fakegrav plates once tight as tiles on a kitchen floor now had varying space between them, showing the oddly textured copper beneath. Some plates were cracked, others broken in two from the ship's shearing forces.

John's ship had not only widened, it had *stretched*, the prow far more so than the midsection.

"LT, Alpha-Two Lead," John said. "Raider Land is bigger. By quite a bit. No movement. We'll check between each rack to be sure, but the compartment looks clear."

As far as John knew, his little imaginary rat-shrimp buddies could be hiding in the dark spaces. Probably not, though, as those guys were hallucinations that only visited him when *Keeling* was in the Mud.

"Copy, Alpha-Two Lead," Lindros said. "Hold your position, I'm coming in."

Beaver turned, his face bright behind his visor, ready to drop another stupid one-liner. John grabbed Beaver's wrist, opening up a private touch-channel.

"Don't fucking say it." John let go. "Alpha-Two, spread out. Check all spaces. Make sure the LT doesn't come in here and find a nasty surprise."

26

BETHANY

Bethany leaned against the bulkhead, trying to make as much room as she could in the small compartment. She ran a towel over her hair and face, wiping off the ship's lubricant. Far more of it than normal. Three weeks since anyone entered through the sphincters—the gel must have built up.

"Ensign Martigral is next," Bethany said. "It's her first entry, so be nice."

A stack of white towels draped over her forearm like an over-worked sommelier, Fire Control Chief Constance Alabama grinned.

"Absolutely, Lieutenant," she said. "We take great care with delicate virgins."

Yet another sex reference. Why were sailors so *crass*?

Bethany felt a stab of jealousy at Alabama's hair—not a trace of gray in those close-cropped, strawberry blonde curls. The warrant officer had to be half her age. Perhaps a year or two *less* than half.

A pair of goo-slimed boots poked out from the sphincter above, kicking spasmodically.

"Ajeet, help her," Alabama said. "She's fighting it."

A man working with Alabama—MAHINDER on his light gray

coveralls, a Spec-3 sensor operator Bethany knew by face only, mostly by his sleepy left eye—grabbed the boots and pulled.

Mindy Martigral slid out of the sphincter along with globs of purple gel that splattered Mahinder and fakegrav plates alike. He managed to keep Martigral from falling as she thrashed and gasped for breath, trails of the thick lubricant dangling from her lips and jaw.

"What the *fuck* was that?" Martigral scooped goop from her eyes. "Why didn't anyone tell me it was like *that*?"

Bethany had told her. So, too, had Chief Sung.

"Clean yourself up, sir." Alabama pressed a towel against Martigral's chest. "And please make room for the next crewmember."

Martigral grabbed the towel, then shoved the larger Alabama against the bulkhead.

"Touch me again, Warrant, and I'll have you up on report!"

Martigral was so *angry*.

"Ensign, that's enough," Bethany said in her best *command* voice, which wasn't very commanding at all. "Stop being a baby. Come with me."

Martigral's hateful gaze swung to Bethany. Purple gel coated the woman's face, clumped in her short, graying blonde hair.

"Yes *sir*," she said, sneering. "Lead the way, *Lieutenant*."

Martigral did not act like a fresh ensign, of any age. Maybe she'd been a powerful person in the private sector before enlisting. Well, she wasn't powerful now.

"Follow me, Ensign."

Bethany was halfway down the ladder to Deck Four when it hit her—she was leading Martigral to the atrium just as Hathorn had led Bethany.

In life, things changed. Death was the only constant.

They reached Deck Four. Martigral scrubbed at her face and hair with the purple-streaked towel.

"That's the environmental control station," Bethany said, pointing out a block of devices mounted against the bulkhead.

Martigral pulled at her coveralls collar. "Does environmental even work? Why is it so hot down here?"

Bethany smiled. Heat and humidity were part of the deal. The atrium was hotter. And wetter.

"You'll get used to it," she said. "Machining compartment to port, curvine room in the middle, fabrication compartment starboard. This way."

Martigral's hands-on examination of those areas would likely come soon, as XO Ellis and Captain Lincoln insisted on extensive cross-training.

"It looks so strange in here," Martigral said, still toweling off. "Why aren't these passageways straight?"

The answer was so obvious any first-year automatonics student would see it instantly. The ship hadn't been *built* in the traditional sense, it had *formed*, self-assembling materials following a prepro-grammed plan just as living creatures grew from single cells into animals with arms, legs, a spine, a brain, etc.

Martigral's lack of knowledge didn't exactly fill Bethany with confidence in her new xeno mate. Then again, Martigral's back-ground centered on xenomechanics, not automatonics. There wasn't time to worry about it—for now, Bethany would convey the same message she'd been told over, and over, and over again.

"Ensign, if no one told you not to ask questions on this ship, let me be the first," Bethany said. "*Don't ask questions.*"

She led Martigral through the narrow, curving passageway, pointing out the wrinkled, organic-looking sphincter leading into the ACIC, then the engineering controls room with its traditional gray bulkhead and hinged pressure door, and, finally, the xeno depart-ment's storage space, also with a standard pressure door.

That storage space... the same room where Bethany had eaten cake with Nitzan Shamdi... where Anne Lafferty threatened her with that crude copper blade...

Bethany pushed those thoughts away.

She stopped at Deck Four's forward-most door, another closed sphincter. She could barely contain her excitement. *Three weeks* since she'd been here, in the only place that felt like home, in the place where she truly *belonged*.

And, the last place on the ship that hadn't been seen since the chrysalis retracted. No one had found Romanik's remains—could they be in the atrium?

Bethany hoped not.

She slid her hand along the furrowed rim, reveling at the feeling of her skin against the semi-living material. A pucker at the sphincter's center expanded outward; the glossy, wrinkled metal receded into the rim. Thin curls of warm mist seeped out.

"Ensign Martigral, welcome to the xeno department."

Bethany and Martigral stepped through. Bethany ran her hand down the inside of the rim. Without a sound, the dark copper material extruded back into place, sealing the sphincter.

Wide-eyed, Martigral looked around. "What in God's name is this place?"

In God's name. Had anyone ever asked a more appropriate question?

"This is the atrium," Bethany said.

She'd missed gazing up through the thin mist at the thick vegetation clinging to the conical ceiling, which rose to a point some seven meters above. She'd missed the bright flowers dotting the dark green leaves, missed the thick, dangling tendrils pulled taut from the weight of huge fruits and vegetables they bore, all dotted with droplets of condensation as if it were perpetually the break of dawn.

"I've never seen anything like this," Martigral said, loosening the chest of her coveralls. Sweat beaded on her forehead. "Why is the produce so *enormous?*"

The question made Bethany look up again, examine things anew. Tomatoes as big as basketballs. Head-sized strawberries. Bean pods longer than her arm. Portobello caps spanning nearly a meter. Eggplants so long and girthy they looked downright obscene.

Spots of blackening rot dotted some of the crops. It had been too long since a harvest—food was dying on the vine.

"We're not entirely sure," she said. "Aside from confirming nutritional value and ensuring there are no poisons or contaminants, the plants haven't been studied that much." She pointed to the bumpy, glowing object that pulsed from within, a rough crystal cylinder resembling—if you squinted enough—a gnarled glass tree trunk filled with the fires of creation. "The gigantism is likely due to light provided by the heartstone."

Bethany's soul ached at the beauty of it. At the *majesty* of it.

Keeling had grown—and so had its heartstone. The incandescent mass had swollen, *thickened,* warping the metal-grate catwalks lining each side and the one arching over its midpoint.

The atrium itself had expanded as well—a good sixteen meters wide where before it had been ten, and roughly twenty meters long, up from fourteen.

The three individual bunks, the three lockers, and the three workstations remained roughly where they'd been before, although all were now covered in flat rivulets of copper foil that expanded from the ship's hull like slow-growing mold. Bethany's station, Hathorn's old station, and Colonel Hasik's station were so covered with the stuff they almost looked gilded.

Bethany felt so much love in her heart. So much *joy.* Nightmares were to come, for certain, because God worked in mysterious ways. For now, though, she had to train Martigral.

"The *heartstone,*" Martigral said. "That's the coupler? That's what takes the ship into another dimension?"

Bethany nodded. They weren't entirely sure how *that* worked, either, although she suspected Colonel Hasik understood the transdim mechanics far better than she did. He chose not to share his higher levels of knowledge.

"First, we look in here for Romanik's remains," Bethany said. "*Don't touch* anything. Then I will teach you how to operate the protuberance. When I do, pay close attention, as your life, and the lives of everyone aboard, may soon depend upon your ability to do things *exactly* as I show you."

Sascha stared into the fabricator's open rear panel. Peggy Keahloha, electrical chief, stared along with her.

"There's no wires," Sascha said. "Where did the wires go?"

Keahloha shrugged. "I don't know, Lieutenant. No trace of them. Everything works, though. As far as we can tell, these veins replaced the wires."

What the fuck was going on?

"*Veins*, Chief?"

If Sascha had to pick one word to describe Keahloha, that word would be *gristly*. The woman's voice sounded like that of an angry toad. She'd worked her way up from rank Eo, Recruit, to W1, Warrant Officer JG, and had undoubtedly seen some shit. Her twenty years of service had come and gone, yet here she was, still working hard.

"That's what Dimo called them," Keahloha said. "She found them first. The word seemed appropriate to me."

Spec-1 Hyeon Dimo, propulsion mate. She and sergeant Kishor Bakshi, electrical mate, were replacements from *Ishlangu*.

Veins was a good word, Sascha had to admit. That's what they looked like—thin, branching, frozen rivers of shiny new copper, extending from the coral-patterned walls, stretching under and across the deck, reaching up onto equipment housings, lumping on various ports like globs of fresh solder.

"Veins carry power and signals both," Keahloha said. "Exposed surface areas are insulated, somehow, so they're safe to touch. Initial tests show signal flow reliability improved by eleven percent over the previous wiring. And the signal paths themselves are more diverse, Lieutenant. Veins are spread out all over the compartment, on the bulkheads, even under the deck plating. They interconnect like a big spider web. That creates multiple connective redundancies. I bet you could blast a hole the size of a cow in this bulkhead and any piece of equipment that isn't destroyed will operate fine. The signal they carry is analog—where they connect to equipment that has optical or digital input-output, the veins convert those signals, re-convert them on the other end."

All-analog transmission. That meant they would likely function well in the space-time manipulation that came with close-in combat. And the redundant connections made them more reliable—seemed like ideal tech for a warship.

"Do a systems check," Sascha said. "Everything in this compartment."

"Did that before I called you. Nano-molecular assembler, quantum microfoundry, particle ablating and resurfacing array, the general-purpose fabricator... everything works great. Some of it better than before."

Keahloha should have called Sascha first, prior to testing anything. Sascha wasn't going to worry about that right now.

"Test it all again, Chief. Right now. I want to see this myself."

Keahloha got right to it. She ran systems checks on the fabrication compartment's equipment. Saws and drills spun up. Grinders whirred. She fired up the CAD system: the nano-molecular assembler printed a test cube, the quantum microfoundry kicked out a transistor; the particle ablating and resurfacing rid produced a sample strip; and the general-purpose fabricator spit out a plastic and composite pivot bearing.

Everything worked.

"Test comms," Sascha said.

Keahloha called up to the CIC; the deck watch officer heard her clearly, and vice versa. She used the sound-powered phone to call the curvine room—like everything else, the SPP worked fine.

When the chief finished, she didn't say *I told you so.* Sascha was grateful for that.

"Lieutenant, there was no one in the ship," Keahloha said. "The whole time the *Crypt* was wrapped up, there was no one in it, no one in this compartment."

She didn't need to say the rest. No one had been in here, which left the obvious conclusion—*Keeling* replaced the ship's wiring with a system of its own.

"How, though?" Sascha shook her head, wondering how she could explain this to Captain Lincoln and XO Ellis. "*How?*"

"I'll tell you what I think it was," Keahloha said. "That damn foil we had to scrape away all the time? With no one here to scrape it, maybe it crept up into the equipment, replaced our wiring with these copper veins."

The foil. What a pain in the ass it was, spreading across decks, equipment, railing... anything and everything. The crew spent far too much time scraping the stuff away.

Had the ship been extending that foil because it was trying to find ways to... to...

...No, that was impossible.

"It's almost like the *Crypt* wanted to improve on our systems," Keahloha said. "Like, it *knew*, somehow, what kind of wiring we had, and it gave us something better."

Exactly the *impossible* thing Sascha had been thinking.

"Chief, let's say the foil did make these veins," Sascha said. "What happened to the old wires?"

Keahloha scratched at her ear.

"Ship must have absorbed them, I guess. Wires, coating, solder, connectors... not a trace of any of it."

That scared Sascha more than the veins did. The ship giveth, the ship taketh away.

In the briefing with Epperson and Ralston, Sascha wondered if *Keeling*'s internal wiring remained intact. It did not—it had been replaced.

"Chief, you told me Dimo found them first. How are she and Bakshi fitting in?"

"So-so," Keahloha said. "Bakshi hates it here. He doesn't bother to hide that fact. Like it's our fault he got entombed, right?"

Sascha couldn't blame Bakshi for feeling that way. Unlike many in the crew, he'd done nothing wrong to draw this assignment.

"How about Dimo?"

"She's the opposite," Keahloha said. "Little Thing loves it here."

Little Thing. A fitting nickname for Dimo. At a hair under five feet tall, she was the shortest person in the crew.

"Dimo is a bit... *odd*," Keahloha said. "Always running her hand along the copper bulkheads, the door rims, looking at them like they're priceless art or something. Reminds me of how Darkwater adores the ship, you know?"

Darkwater's admiration for all things *Keeling* bordered on obsession.

Sascha realized she'd briefly focused on Dimo and Bakshi because doing so let her *not* focus on the situation at hand, a situation she wasn't sure she wanted to deal with. How did this ship keep getting stranger? Keep getting *spookier?*

What she wanted didn't really matter, though—she was the engineering department head. Before she reported this to Lincoln, she wanted to know all she could know.

"Check *everything*, Chief. Machining, environmental, all connections in the flight bay. I'll get propulsion and aux on the same task. Atrium and Raider Land as well. I'll check the optical array's connections myself."

Sascha stepped to the comm handset and dialed in 42MC.

"CIC, Engineering. We have a situation."

28

TRAVIS

They'd only been aboard a few hours and already the CIC smelled of sweat. After three weeks of proper environmentals and clean air, Travis had forgotten that stink. He knew he'd quickly get used to it again, or as used to it as one could get. In a confined space like this, olfactory fatigue was a sailor's best friend.

The *Crypt* was a madhouse. Loading a 110-meters-long ship—correction, now a 136.5-meters-long ship—took time, especially when everything had to be carried in through the sphincters or flown in through the pouch.

From the pier, *Keeling* looked like an insect hive, swarming with workers carrying food, tools, parts, weapons, and ammo inside, stashing those treasures away not only in assigned racks and storage bins but also in the many small cubbyholes that dotted the ship's thick copper bulkheads. There was no way of knowing if *Keeling* would return to Gateway after this still-unknown mission.

Or if they'd be assigned another objective.

Or if they'd have to flee the target zone and run for their lives.

Or if they'd get stuck in the Mud for God knew how long.

"Ops," Travis said, "resupply update."

Alex Plait worked his console. "One moment, XO."

Travis stood at the command slate, reading lists of information scrolling across the flat surface. He pulled at the sweat soaked collar of his undershirt. While much of the ship had changed, the claustrophobically small CIC remained the same—save for higher temperatures and increased humidity the enviro controls had yet to compensate for. Copper foil covered many areas of decks three through five, but not so in the superstructure's two decks. Stations here suffered only flecks of it, if any, while the overhead tangle of pipes and wires remained untouched.

"XO, starboard Type24 battery is fully loaded," Plait said. "All three AP6 point-defense turrets fully loaded. Galley stores will be topped off in another thirty minutes to an hour. Torpedo bays fully loaded. Port deuce-quad battery installation should be completed in two hours."

Trav looked to the forward clock-timer, the one mounted above the pilots' stations: two hours, forty-six minutes remaining until Epperson's specified departure time. They'd be cutting it close.

He glanced back at Captain Lincoln, who leaned against the xeno loft's base, her arms crossed. She preferred to observe, only speaking when Travis missed something she wanted done. Sweat sheened her skin and dotted her red bandana. She nodded at him once—her way of saying *good job so far, keep at it.*

That nod was as close to an *attaboy* as Lincoln got.

"Weps," Travis said, turning back to the slate, "is the wiring inspection complete on all weapons? I want to test-fire all guns the instant we get clearance."

Cat Brown, head of the weapons department, didn't seem to know how to answer. She rubbed the stubble atop her shaved head. Her scalp showed no gleam of perspiration. She'd grown up on the planet Jones, which had the highest average temperatures in the Planetary Union. Jones also boasted the Union's strongest gravity in the Union—its 1.3g contributed to Brown's short, thick stature.

"I guess that's a multiple-choice question, XO," she said. "Weapons wiring inspection is complete, except there's no wires. I mean, other than the ones now being run for the port deuce-quad. As for the starboard deuce-quad, the point-defense turrets, and both torpedo rooms, veins replaced all wiring. All signal tests check out fine, though. Better than it was before, even. Doesn't appear to be any problems at all. We'll find out when we test-fire."

Wiring gone on decks three through five, inexplicably replaced by something *Crypt* decided to grow on its own, yet that didn't matter to Epperson. His response to the unprecedented situation was the Twenty-Sixth Century equivalent of *damn the torpedoes, full steam ahead.*

Darkwater said the veins posed no safety threat to the crew. Travis would have rather had Colonel Hasik's take, but Hasik had yet to report. Travis had a feeling, though, that even if Hasik did object to this rushed mission, Epperson wouldn't give a shit.

As for the new "pimples" on the hull, Darkwater still didn't know what they were. She and Kerkhoffs were taking a closer look.

For any other ship, shocking developments like the veins and the pimples alone would put it on ice indefinitely for intense study, reliability testing, and more. Fleet's scientists and engineers would analyze every last detail. Not so for *Keeling.*

"Excellent work, Weps," Travis said. "Torpedo crew status?"

"Bat-brains already locked in and ready for departure," Brown said. "Aside from the port deuce-quad, all weapons are good to go."

This would be Brown's third *Keeling* deployment. She knew her business.

Travis looked left, to where Lieutenant Lindros sat at the new Raider Liaison terminal, a replacement for the one destroyed in the battle.

"Raider Liaison, status?"

"TASH rig stowage continues apace, XO," Lindros said. "Weapons loaded and secured, full ammo complement as well. I will notify you when all rigs are locked down."

Travis didn't know what the mission entailed. Would they really tangle with Sklorno warships? If so, he'd have his hands full maintaining crew morale—facing an enemy that *ate* prisoners generated new levels of tension.

Forward of the Raider Liaison station sat the ECM station, manned by newly promoted lead signaler Colel Citlalmina. The CIC's dim lighting brought out the reddish hue of her brown skin. She had her thick black hair pinned back by plastic barrettes the shape of a corporal's single downward chevron. The showoff. She was proud of her new rank. Good for her.

Forward of ECM sat the signals station, manned by Lead Signaler Sara Ellison. Forward of signals sat the darsat station, manned by Lead Darsat Operator Kanya Saetang.

Up front were the pilot and co-pilot stations, manned by Lars Nygard and Colin Draper, respectively. Navigation chief Doug Erickson sat at the nav station, just behind and between Nygard and Draper, so close to them he could read over their shoulders without leaning forward.

To Trav's right, Plait at the ops station. Forward of Plait, Brown at the weapons station. Forward of her, artillery chief Dardanos Leeds at the guns station.

At the CIC's center, directly in front of the command slate, sat the navigation orb that tracked everything and anything *Keeling* command needed to see. On the last voyage, that orb had turned into a giant, malevolent black widow spider that spoke to Trav with the hate-filled voice of his long-dead grandmother.

Would he see and hear that again once the ship dove into the Mud?

Behind Trav and to his right was the Intel Loft, currently manned by Jester Gillick, one of Anne Lafferty's two subordinates. The xeno loft—behind Trav and to his left—sat empty, which again begged the question: where was Colonel Hasik? Would he arrive before *Keeling* departed?

Unlike the last time Trav shipped out, everyone in the CIC had at least one *Keeling* run under their belt. There was no substitute for experience.

Would any of them succumb to the Mud's murderous influence? No way to tell.

In the Mud, no one was sane. Not fully.

A light flashed on the comms panel: 5MC, flight bay.

Travis lifted the handset. "XO here."

"XO, we finished the sweep," Chief Sung said. "Top to bottom, stem to stern. All compartments and cubbyholes, every nook and cranny. No sign of Romanik's body."

Yet another mystery to deal with. Even if they'd found her remains mangled beyond visual recognition, that would have been better than no remains at all. What had the ship done with her?

"Thank you, Chief," Travis said. "Get on the hull and see what help you can provide with optical installation."

"Optical installation, aye-aye. We got a problem with head-count, though. Akagi and Camp haven't reported. They're not answering calls. You want me to grab some Raiders and round them up instead of helping with optical?"

Travis glanced at the clock-timer: two hours, thirty minutes until departure.

Akagi, a crawler pilot. If he didn't show, Epperson's Executioner would have to quickly grab a pilot from another ship. And Camp, a machinist/gunner... his experience on *Keeling* could not be easily replaced.

Travis hesitated. There was a specific protocol for this situation, and a specific department assigned to handle it—it would not go well for Akagi and Camp. Travis wanted to send someone to quietly remind the men what might be in store for them if they didn't report ASAP, but he didn't have anyone to spare.

"XO," Lincoln said, "what's the issue?"

He covered the handset speaker and told her.

She took the handset. "Chief Sung, this is the captain. Get on the hull as the XO ordered."

Lindros turned in his seat. "Captain Lincoln, I can send some Raiders to find Akagi." He'd clearly overheard Trav's explanation, heard the mention of his newest pilot not reporting. "PXO Winter is about to go over transdim instructions with the platoon. That can wait until all my people are present."

He, like Travis, knew the proper protocol and was hoping for a quiet resolution instead. Lincoln, though, didn't have that same desire.

"Focus on your duties, Lieutenant," she said. "Let your people know to continue on as scheduled. You will see to it that Akagi gets brought up to speed when he arrives."

She was pissed. Travis could hear it in her voice.

"Aye-aye, Captain." Lindros turned back to face his station.

Lincoln switch the comms to MC33—the Spookhouse.

"Chief Lafferty, we have an issue," Lincoln said. "Draw sidearms from the small arms locker. Warrant Brendan Akagi and Spec-1 Michael Camp haven't reported. I want them on board, right now."

29

JOHN

Thirty-four Raiders had packed into the small training area, standing in heat and humidity damn close to sauna levels. PXO Winter held the comm handset, listening to Lieutenant Lindros.

The old, broken fakegrav plates had been repaired. New plates filled in the spaces created by the ship lengthening and widening, resulting in differing shades of gray on the Raider training area deck. Someone had put the four treadmills back in place. The resistance arrays had yellow tape wrapped around them—they were not to be used until they were re-bolted to the bulkheads. The rig room door showed fresh welding lines around newly fabricated hinges.

Everyone seemed nervous. John included. Nervous about departing for a mission on a ship that killed its own crewmembers, yes, and nervous about pending transdim dives that might drive Raiders temporarily insane and pit them against each other, certainly, but what really had them off-kilter was the fact that there should have been thirty-*five* Raiders present.

"Copy, Lieutenant," PXO Winter said. "I'll proceed as scheduled." She hung up the training area handset and turned to face the assembled Raiders, murder in her eyes. "Warrant Officer Akagi must have slept in. The poor, tired lad. Lafferty and her people have been sent to fetch him."

Well, shit. A black mark on the Warthogs. Nothing quite so embarrassing as one of your people deciding they didn't want to do their duty.

Winter looked at Biggie Bang, packed in with her flight crews and crawler techs.

"*Lead* Crawler Pilot Bang." Winter's voice growled low and thick with threat. "Care to explain to me why one of *your* co-pilots decided he couldn't be bothered with showing up?"

John saw Biggie silently mouth a plethora of frustrated curses in a matter of seconds, not meant for Winter, but rather for her errant pilot.

"Akagi has been in therapy," Bang said. "He's... ah... having some problems, PXO."

Problems. That was one way to put it. The guy had trouble coping with the fact he'd crushed a fellow Raider's skull while caught up in the throes of transdim madness.

"I don't give a shit about his *problems*," Winter said. "Akagi is *your* responsibility. I don't get a wet tit-fuck about *therapy*. You make sure he doesn't do it again or I will address the issue with *both* of you. Copy?"

Bang mouthed another three or four silent curses.

"Copy, PXO," she said. "I'll talk to him."

John had to admit—when Winter talked like that, all angry and such, it turned him on. When they were alone, that was *exactly* how she talked to him.

"Moving on." Winter held up a set of heavy canvas straps, each with a thick cam-lock colored in Raider black. "The first legs of this mission are via standard punch-space. You're all familiar with punch-space, even you wet-behind-the-ears newbies. I don't know our final destination, but I do know that in a few days we'll go transdim, also known as *diving into the Mud*." She held up the straps. "When we dive, all Raider newbies will be restrained to their bunks with these. No exceptions. Don't even *think* about complaining."

A burst of embarrassment brought heat to John's face, made his ears tingle—he recognized the little cartoon bunny rabbit drawn in permanent marker on the cam-lock. Last night, in one of Pier Two admin building's many empty offices, Winter had bound him with that same set of restraints. His wrists still hurt. So did his dick. Winter fucked like she fought—hard and without mercy.

As casually as he could, he checked his sleeves, making sure they covered his wrists. Winter had broken one of their little rules—the restraints left bruises.

"Hey, Sarge," Beaver said. "Newbies didn't get strapped down before. What changed?"

Beaver had his shirt off. He did that whenever possible. The kid loved to show off both his physique, which was impressive, and the SCREAM AIM & FIRE tattoo across his chest.

"The last mission was the *Crypt*'s first Raiders onboard," Winter said. "It seems Captain Lincoln didn't like the amount of violence begotten in Raider Land. So, newbs get strapped to their bunks, as does everyone who has a history of violent outbursts. That includes me and Lieutenant Lindros. When we dive, Master Sergeant Sands is in command until he determines that I, and-or the LT, am of sound mind. Now, finish policing your team's section. Look for things that could be turned into a weapon. Sharp objects. Scraps of metal. An inexplicable paper clip. *Anything*. Use your imagination. Get to it."

The group split up. John walked to his bunk in the barracks area, gesturing for his fire team to follow. Beaver, Abs, Yo-Yo, and Reiner joined him.

"Corporal Bennett," a wide-eyed Yo-Yo said in a hushed whisper, "we don't *really* get strapped down to our bunks, right? This gotta be some kind of first-cruise prank on us newbs. Right?"

John felt sorry for the kid. Straight out of boot, and Yo-Yo was about to undergo something no one had trained him for, no one *could* train him for.

"It's no prank," John said. "You'll see soon enough."

Reiner laughed, crossed her arms, looked down at John. Good lord the woman was tall.

"Something funny, Corporal?" asked John.

"Not a thing." The smirk on her face said otherwise. "Just make sure you pervs don't accidentally cop a feel while I'm all tied up. Because I keep score, and at some point, I'll be *un*-tied. You get me?"

Beaver smiled wide. "You mean like we'd *fight*, Corporal Reiner? Because if you want to spar, I'll spar with you."

John wanted to ask him not to talk so damn loud, but what was the point? Beaver didn't get it, would probably never get it.

Reiner stepped closer to Beaver, stood nose-to-nose with him. She was the only woman in the platoon who could look him eye-to-eye.

"Beaver," Reiner said, "why are you *always* shouting?"

Beaver's face wrinkled with confusion.

"I'm not shouting," he shouted. "This is my inside voice."

Sadly, he wasn't joking.

Beaver had fifty pounds on Reiner. Still, she had more combat experience, so John wouldn't bet against her.

"Reiner, relax," John said. "No one is going to touch your jumblies."

"Unless you *ask* someone to touch your jumblies," Abs said. "Then I'm sure you'll get volunteers."

Reiner's hard glare made it obvious Abs now had a mark on her scorecard. He would likely learn the hard way you don't mess with an E-4.

"Watch your mouth, Spec Abshire," Reiner said. "A lot can happen to a guy in his sleep."

Abshire held up both hands, palms out. He couldn't fully hide his smile.

"No offense intended, Corporal," he said. "You should know the rules of fraternization aren't exactly enforced here on *Keeling*. Ask Bennett, he'll tell you."

Beaver giggled and covered his mouth like a schoolboy who'd just heard a dirty joke.

John's face flushed hot again.

"Enough jibber-jab," he said. "You heard the PXO. Police your racks. *In* them, *around* them, *under* them. Broken bolts, loose screws, hex nuts rolling free, that kind of thing. Look *close*. Yo-Yo, Reiner, trust me when I tell you that anything you miss could wind up getting someone hurt. Or killed. Yourselves very much included."

Reiner squinted down at John like she didn't quite believe him, but she would still do as asked. Yo-Yo, on the other hand, looked like he might throw up.

"I don't like it here," he said, his voice almost too soft to hear. "This sucks."

Oh, he had no idea how *much* it sucked. When it came time to dive, he'd learn the hard way.

"Get to work," John said. "Don't miss a thing."

The battered hanger surrounded them, taking up the view on all sides save for forward, where the missing hatch-gate revealed a billion stars blazing bright, an endless expanse of infinity.

Sascha stepped carefully along *Keeling*'s hull. To her right, Bethany Darkwater kept pace, far enough away—hopefully—that a whipping copper tentacle couldn't take them both out at once.

"Relax, Lieutenant," Darkwater said. "I swear I can hear your heartbeat through your mic."

Relax? The ship had *slaughtered* a sailor right next to Darkwater. How could *she* relax?

That said, it was Sascha—not Darkwater—who'd ordered the engineering crew onto the hull to install hundreds of new optical sensors, a job they needed to finish before Epperson's launch clock ran out.

Sascha felt like a flea clinging to a hairless dog, a dog that might scratch at any moment. She'd seen the footage of Romanik's death— what a horrible way to go.

"Makes me nervous, is all," Sascha said. "What the hell happened to Romanik's body, anyway?"

Darkwater didn't seem bothered by the missing corpse. Sascha thought that strange, considering Darkwater had been *right there* when it happened, had faced the same bizarre, brutal death herself. Michael Camp had been there, too, and now he was afraid to set foot on the hull. Camp wasn't crazy about being inside of it, either. No one was.

No one except Darkwater.

"I don't know what happened to her body," she said. "Not yet. But don't worry, Lieutenant—we're not hurting *Keeling*, so *Keeling* won't hurt us. You'll be fine. Come join me, please. This is the biggest one so far."

Wondering if each step might be her last, Sascha walked closer. She knelt next to Darkwater, felt the fakegrav of her exosuit's knee guard clamp down on the hull just like the soles of her boots did.

The bump, or *pimple*, looked small from a distance, but it was as big as Sascha's chest. The spiked exterior seemed like a visual warning that screamed *DANGER! DO NOT TOUCH!*

"What do you think it is?" asked Sascha.

"I couldn't say," Darkwater said. "They're evenly distributed across the hull, each about ten meters from its nearest neighbors. That's a mathematical distribution, very common in automatonic growth. My guess is the ship formed these in reaction to some kind of stimulus."

The person on the ship with the most knowledge about what *Keeling* was and what it could do had no idea what the pimples might be? Great.

"Think Colonel Hasik would know?"

"We'll see," Darkwater said. "I hope he gets here in the next ninety minutes, before we depart. Maybe he'll think of something I didn't. Testing anything on the hull, or even getting samples, could be... problematic."

Darkwater and Romanik had been trying to collect samples. Saying it was *problematic* was like saying the void was *kinda large*.

Darkwater looked up from the pimple. "Your people haven't found anything inside?"

"Not yet," Sascha said. "The pimples don't extend to the interior bulkheads. They're on the surface only. Could they be a result of the spikes that were on the chrysalis?"

Darkwater glanced around, shook her head.

"The spots don't line up," she said. "And there were far more spikes than there are pimples. This is something that formed under the chrysalis."

Darkwater stood. So did Sascha. They both stared down.

"We have no idea what these things are," Sascha said. "For all we know, they could explode while we're in punch-space. Or in the Mud."

Sascha didn't say what she really thought: *I can't believe that dickhead Epperson is sending us out.* As far as she knew, the admiral was listening in.

"Everything will be okay," Darkwater said. "Trust *Keeling*, Lieutenant. Everything will be okay."

Wasted words. Sascha didn't trust Epperson. She didn't trust Darkwater.

And she sure as hell didn't trust the *Crypt*.

31

ANNE

Pathetic.

Anne had never seen such a pathetic little worm of a man.

"Send me to the brig," Akagi said. "I don't care."

Warrant Officer JG Brendan Akagi, call-sign *Brainiac*, sat on his bunk, in his room, staring at the floor. Anne stood a few feet in front of him, Daniels at her side, Gillick at the door.

Akagi hadn't even tried to run. Not much point in that, as there was nowhere *to* run. Pier Two Sector was locked down. Only four points of egress, all of which were heavily guarded. Even if he could have slipped through those gates, where could he go and not be found? Gateway Station's cameras and bio-detectors would rat him out no matter where he tried to hide.

"Get your ass up," Anne said. "You will report to *Keeling* immediately."

Akagi slowly shook his head.

"I can't go back," he said. "I won't. The things I saw. I'd rather serve my original sentence, all right? Ten years in the brig is better than going back to the Mud. It's funny, you know? If I'd just served my time for going AWOL in the first place, I wouldn't be AWOL now."

Ah, so that was why he'd arrived in chains. Anne filed that knowledge away.

What a *worm*. This was what passed for a Raider aviator these days? They should have never lowered the educational requirements. Volunteers were drying up, though, Anne knew. President McKinney was considering implementing conscription for the first time in a century. Maybe soldiers like Akagi were the best the Union could hope for.

"A lot of people saw a lot of things," Anne said. "Those people are all already on board, ready to do their part. Sack up, Akagi."

He looked at her from under hooded brows. Haunted eyes. Perhaps *cursed* eyes was a better term. The defeated gaze of a man on death row.

"*Sack up*," he said. "What did *you* see in the Mud, Major?" He looked at Daniels. "And you?" He looked to Gillick. "And you? What did you see before you stabbed Hasik and Shamdi fucked up your nose?"

Gillick took a half-step out of the room, his face went white as a sheet.

Jesus Christ... was Anne surrounded by cowards?

She drew her sidearm and pressed the muzzle against Akagi's forehead, a gentle kiss of metal on flesh. Her fast draw caught him unawares—without moving his head, those cursed eyes flicked up, looked at the steel.

His fear... what a rush.

"Akagi, I have another worthless coward to collect, and I have to do it quick," Anne said. "You volunteered to serve on *Keeling*. Your former sentence is no longer available as an option. You are *AWOL*. As Intel Chief, I am well within my legal rights to use lethal force. In other words, the exit wound of this ten-millimeter round is so large that, a week from now, custodians will *still* be finding little bits of bone and brain. So, I will count to three. Either you agree to get back on that ship and take your chances at living, or I hit *zero* and save you the trouble. One..."

"I'll go," Akagi said. "I'll go. Right now. I'll go."

Maybe he was a coward, but he wasn't stupid. He believed Anne would put him down. Perhaps *Brainiac* wasn't such a bad call-sign for him after all.

Anne holstered her weapon. She grabbed Akagi's collar, yanked him to his feet, pushed him toward Daniels.

"Cuff him," she said. "Take him to *Keeling*. If he gives you any trouble, *shoot* him. Shoot to *kill*. Understand?"

Daniels was almost as wide-eyed as Akagi. Gillick just stood there, jaw hanging down like a fool.

"Aye-aye, Major," Daniels said.

He pulled flexicuffs from his belt and bound Akagi's wrists. Akagi gave no resistance. Daniels walked him out of the room.

Anne tapped her earpiece. "Central Security, Lafferty. Current location of Spec-One Michael Camp?"

She glanced at her watch: less than thirty minutes before scheduled departure.

"Camp appears to still be in his quarters," the voice came back. "Biometrics detecting one individual in room three-four-niner."

Appears to be. No cameras allowed in barracks rooms, thanks to the legacy, bleeding-heart policies of the previous presidential administration.

Anne strode out of the room. Gillick fell in behind her.

She shouldn't be doing this idiotic babysitting duty. She should be aboard, watching everyone go about their pre-departure business, looking for various tells that might indicate the stress of a spy knowing they had to go out with no support, had to be isolated for who knew how long.

And *Gillick* was her backup? Awful. But then again, Anne could watch *him* for those same tells. He was still high up on her list of suspects.

They went up one flight of stairs and reached Room 349. Door closed.

Anne stepped back.

"Open it," she said.

Gillick looked like he might throw up, but he did as he was told. Hand on the grip of his holstered pistol, he opened the door and stepped inside, only to be knocked off his feet in a head-rattling flying tackle that took both him and Camp to the ground. Camp, in his light gray coveralls, landed atop Gillick, in his BII blacks. Camp straddled Gillick, rose up, raised both hands high—in them he held a butter knife.

"*I'm not going back*," Camp screamed. "We're doomed! We're *doomed*! I'm not going back!" He drove the knife downward. Gillick raised an arm in defense; the blade punched through his palm, jutted out the back of his hand. Blood spattered on Gillick's face.

Camp had found a way to sharpen the butter knife. What a goddamn pain in the ass.

Anne drew her pistol and shot Camp's left shoulder.

The sailor grunted in surprise, roll-flopped off of Gillick and fell to the floor.

Gillick, on his back, bleeding and moaning, a butter knife through his hand.

Camp, on his side, bleeding and moaning, clutching his left shoulder.

Anne checked her watch: twenty-five minutes until departure.

She tapped her earpiece. "Central Security, Lafferty. Shots fired, two wounded. I need two stretchers here on the double. Get *Keeling*'s medical team out here ASAP. We'll be taking both wounded back to the ship."

32

BETHANY

"I'd prefer not to scrape any more foil," Martigral said. "It's too hot in here to do that. I hate this ridiculous mist. Why don't you just leave me alone?"

Bethany stood there, staring. *I'd rather not?* What was this woman's problem?

"Ensign Martigral. I outrank you, and you are under me in this department. You better..." Bethany groped for the right words "...you better *shape up!*"

High One, did that sound stupid.

"*Shape up,* huh?" Martigral crossed her arms. "How about you stop pretending to be an officer and get the hell out of my face?"

Bethany hadn't had an order refused in... what... over a decade? She didn't know what to do, what to say. She was a lieutenant. Martigral was an ensign—she was supposed to do what she was told. Bethany had even asked nicely.

Well, maybe the time for being nice was at an end.

"You will scrape that foil, Ensign, or..."

Bethany trailed off again. Or what? What was Bethany going to do to the woman—sentence her to the *Crypt?*

"Honeeeey, I'm hoo-ome!"

Bethany turned to see Colonel Zvanut Hasik limp into the atrium, laboring under the burden of an overstuffed duffel slung over his shoulder and the heavy data drives he carried in each hand. The mist curled in his wake.

He wore a service uniform, clean save for a few damp patches from the spanus. Perhaps the lubricant levels had returned to normal. At any rate, seeing Hasik in anything other than a soiled tank top was a rare thing indeed.

As he limped by her on his way to his workstation, Bethany saw a line of fresh stitches across his forehead. A purple-and-yellow bruise marred his right eye, the colors running down almost to his cheekbone.

The limp was a result of Jester Gillick stabbing him in the thigh three weeks back. The rest of the damage came after *Keeling* docked and Hasik left.

"Colonel," Bethany said, "what happened? Did you get into a fight?"

Hasik didn't seem to notice Martigral, who stood there silently, arms still crossed, that annoyed look still etched on her face.

"Nothing so grand as a fight." Hasik set the heavy drives on his desk. He let his duffel drop to the mist-spotted deck. "Fell down a ladder. Quite clumsy of me."

There was a hollowness to his words that reminded Bethany of her days in the Purist convent. Many of her sisters had taken the cloth, not out of deep devotion to the church, but rather as the only method available to escape abusive husbands. Some who arrived at the convent bore marks of recent beatings. Without fail, every one of those women claimed they'd fallen downstairs, or walked into a door frame, or had been in a car crash—anything but admit where their bruises and cuts really came from.

Hasik had a man's voice, yet he sounded like those sisters all the same.

Where had he gotten those bruises and that cut? Had someone mugged him?

The *how* didn't matter. He didn't want to talk about it, and it wasn't Bethany's role to pry. If and when Hasik wanted to share, she'd be ready to listen.

At his station, he slid one drive into its slot, pushed until it clicked home, then did the same with the second drive. From under his collar, he pulled free the key he wore on a plastic lanyard. He locked each drive in place and dropped the key back down his shirt.

He looked around, blinking.

"Ensign Darkwater... is the atrium... *bigger?*"

Had he not been informed?

"It's *Lieutenant JG* now, Colonel," Bethany said. "And, yes, the atrium is both wider and longer, relative in proportion to the ship's overall dimensional increases."

Hasik removed his steamy glasses, squinted at her as he wiped the lenses against his sleeve.

"*Lieutenant JG?* Ah, yes, I see your rank tab. Your promotion went through. Congratulations."

Bethany heard the pride in his voice. It surprised her to realize how good that made her feel.

Hasik slid the glasses back on. "What do you mean by *the ship's overall dimensional increases?* Are you claiming the ship itself is larger?"

He'd left within hours of the chrysalis's formation. He'd been gone for three weeks. Had no one kept him in the loop?

"Colonel," Bethany said, "do you know *anything* about what transpired here during your absence?"

The expression on his face provided all the answer she needed. Hasik looked like a man lost.

"Epperson told me you would bring me up to speed," he said. "I'm gathering the changes are extensive. It seems insane he's sending us out so soon, but if I've learned anything during my involvement with *Keeling*, it's what the admiral wants, the admiral gets." He finally looked at Martigral. "Who the hell are you?"

Her hands dropped to her side. "Ensign Mindy Martigral, Colonel. Xeno Mate."

"Hathorn's replacement," Hasik said, nodding. "Very well." He dragged his duffel to his bunk, unzipped it, and pulled out a plastic two-liter bottle filled with amber fluid. "Xeno Mate Martigral, come over here and have a seat. You, too, *Lieutenant JG Darkwater*. Let's drink to celebrate my return."

It didn't sound like he was in the mood to celebrate. It sounded more like he had sorrows that needed drowning. The poor man. Maybe soon he'd feel the joy Bethany felt, feel the love she knew every minute she spent in this room.

Doubt on her face, Martigral glanced at Bethany. Martigral probably thought this was some trick, her department head seeing if he could trick her into drinking on duty.

Bethany walked to her bunk and sat. Hers was the middle of the three, with Hasik's on her left and Martigral's on her right. Bethany took the bottle from Hasik and unscrewed the cap—the contents smelled like a swamp. She took a drink. *Tasted* like a swamp, too. A swamp made of burning garbage. She *hated* alcohol. She offered the bottle to Martigral.

"You're *drinking*," Martigral said, her tone alarmingly harsh. "Drinking *alcohol* on duty. What is wrong with you people? I will have you written up on report."

Hasik stared. Bethany did, too. Junior personnel didn't speak to superior officers like that. They simply *did not*.

It seemed Martigral finally understood that. She squared her shoulders. She knew she'd gone too far.

"Ensign, you have much to learn," Hasik said, a cold burr in his words. "Lesson one—*don't fuck with me lest I fuck with you back*. I have neither the patience nor the disposition to deal with whatever the hell you think you are. While you have my sympathies for being entombed with us, you'll find the atrium a good place to work. Once you get used to the heat, of course. And the humidity. But I digress. If you make things difficult for me, I'll have you mucking out each and every head aboard, *starting* with the ones in Raider Land."

Yet again, Bethany didn't know what to say. Hathorn had given Hasik shit all the time. He'd never spoken to her like that. Of course, when he offered Hathorn a drink, she'd drank.

Hasik pointed to Martigral's bunk, which had been Hathorn's bunk.

"Sit down, Ensign," he said. "Let's get to know each other a bit."

Martigral's scowl deepened the wrinkles at the corners of her eyes. She walked to her bunk and sat.

"You'll find we have certain privileges in the atrium," Hasik said. "Lieutenant JG Darkwater offered you a drink. So *drink*. That's an order."

Now things were getting weird. Weirder than they already were, of course, which on the *Crypt* was saying something.

Martigral took the bottle. She gave it a sniff, winced.

"Oy vey," she said. "Smells like its drained straight from a bog. Islay?"

Hasik brightened. "Spot-on. Old Earth is still good for something, at least. It's Bruichladdich. You'll have to trust me on that—glass bottles are not allowed on *Keeling*."

"So I've been told," Martigral said. "For our *safety*, right? That's dumb." She took a cautious sip—her face screwed up like she'd drank kerosene. "Oy *vey*." She leaned across Bethany's bunk, handed the bottle back to Hasik. "What did you mean when you said I was *entombed*?"

Hasik laughed. "You know, *entombed*. Because you're buried in the *Crypt*."

Martigral's face twisted into a dismissive sneer. Some people were just mean inside. However long she remained aboard, it would be too long.

"*The Crypt*," Martigral said. "What does that even mean?"

She'd never heard of it. A bit surprising, perhaps, although

Bethany hadn't heard of it before Admiral Bock "recruited" her to join the crew.

"The *Crypt* is what some people call this ship," Hasik said. "Did Lieutenant Darkwater not share this tidbit with you?"

Bethany realized she had not. And why should she? It was an ugly word. Dark and depressing. The ship should have a glorious nickname, like *Light of the Heavens*, or something along those lines.

Martigral glanced at the conical, fruit-heavy greenery dangling above the heartstone.

"*Keeling* is called the *Crypt*," she said. "Why? I don't get it."

Hasik took a drink of Scotch. A big drink.

"We'll address that later," he said. "For now, catch me up on what's happened while I was away. I have to report to Captain Lincoln shortly. Darkwater, you'll attend with me. Ensign Martigral, while we're gone, you will scrape the deck and remove the copper foil polluting *my* department. Unless you're eager to begin wiping up misplaced Raider piss?"

Bethany blinked. Had he been standing outside when Martigral refused to do the chore?

Martigral's scowl deepened. "I'll scrape the foil, *sir*."

"Excellent," Hasik said. "Darkwater, when I boarded, Chief Sung mentioned a crewmember died, someone assigned here in my absence." He took a deep swig. "Start with that."

He didn't know anything. Where had he been for the last three weeks? What had he been doing?

"Her name was Spec-One Leona Romanik," Bethany said. "She was a xenobiologist."

33

BIGGIE

As *Keeling* slipped free of its battered hanger and accelerated away from Gateway Station, Biggie Bang headed for the infirmary. Scuttlebutt belowdecks said Spec-3 Watson, a medic, was the person to see.

Six weeks entombed. Twenty-two and a half months to go.

There were bad people aboard. Rapists. Murderers. Scammers who sold out their own comrades for a few dollars more. Probably pedophiles, too, although if she learned of any she'd find a way to smoke those assholes.

What are you in for?

People had their hunches about everyone, but no one knew for sure. *Keeling* crew kept their crimes close to the vest.

So what had Biggie done?

She'd *run*.

Sure, she'd taken the oath of service. Sure, she'd given her word. But there was a difference between giving one's pledge with all the earnestness a nineteen-year-old can muster and living up to that word when you saw war up close, when you learned you were expendable, a token pushed about on a map by people who saw you as nothing more than a game piece—if they saw you at all.

The battle known as "Solomon's Surprise" was supposed to bring a quick end to the Third Galactic War. It started with the Churchies getting cocky. They sent twenty warships to attack planet Tower, seat of the Union-allied Tower Republic. Things don't always work out as planned—Republic forces kicked the Purists square in the ding-ding. Eleven Churchie ships busted up like Quinceañera piñatas, nine more limping home with tails tucked between their legs.

Union brass, in their infinite wisdom, decided that was the ideal time to strike. Second Group, run by Commodore Emil Garrant, got the call: take planet Solomon. Three destroyers, a heavy cruiser, a pair of assault ships (including *Karengetang*, Biggie's ride at the time) and a shiny-ass flagship carrier. On paper? Second should have steamrolled the Churchies. Each assault ship carried four Raider battalions. Their job? Seize control of Solomon's orbital defense network and hold it until Second Group's four Sumpters dumped 100,000 Union ground-pounding grunts onto the surface.

Bing-bang-boom.

Planet captured.

Purist Nation takes the *L*.

Everyone goes home fat and happy (other than the Churchies, of course, who should have been praying to their imaginary "High One" for mercy and forgiveness).

Except for one wee little problem—Garrant underestimated the Purist Nation's Watchtower system. The network of signal-detection stations logged Second Group's staging at Rodina. Purist eggheads calculated Second's likely punch-out point. Instead of punching into nice, open space with plenty of time to form up and deploy, Second Group popped ass-first into a welcome wagon of twenty-five Purist warships. Hence, *Solomon's Surprise*.

Biggie didn't know a lot about the battle other than that she was in it. Most of the fighting remained a blur, but there were some things she would never forget. Things like the stench of her co-pilot, Abigail "Spicy" Spagnolla, burning to death in the seat next to her. Things like her engineer/gunner, Clay "Hard-Six" Peterson, crying in the turret, begging for his mother to save him while Biggie tried to bring her shot-to-fuck Occie in for a landing on the shot-to-fuck carrier *Theia*.

After that debacle, Second Group (or what was left of it, anyway) gathered at Vishvakarman Station orbiting Thomas 3. *Karengetang* and *Theia* needed major repairs. For a couple of months, Biggie had nothing to do but drink, drug, fuck, and try to forget.

She still didn't know how much rum she'd guzzled when she found herself in *Karengetang*'s flight bay, there to examine her replacement Ochthera. Lo and behold, there were several other craft present as well—including Commodore Garrant's personal shuttle.

His shuttle, with its *identify-friend-or-foe* beacon that let it go wherever the commodore wanted it to go.

While a breadcrumb-trail of bad decisions marked Biggie's path through life, that day brought her greatest fuck-up of them all. She'd walked onto the shuttle like she owned it. In a moment of infinite optimism driven by copious amounts of alcohol (as well as some pills, some weed, and some shrooms, because she wasn't one to pass up a good time) Biggie stole Commodore Garrant's personal shuttle.

Oddly, she still remembered her grand scheme: steal the shuttle, full-burn down to Thomas 3, dump that bad boy in the ocean, swim to shore (she was a kick-ass swimmer, always had been) and start a new life under a new name.

Trouble was, radio signals traveled a helluva lot faster than a shuttle did.

She never even made it to shore; MPs snatched her right out of the ocean.

When they brought her up on charges, she figured she'd do time in one of Fleet's long-term prisons. Addelson Consolidated Brig. Leavenworth Disciplinary Barracks. Or even Karuntun Gulag, the hellhole prison on Thomas 3's moon. She'd spend a decade incarcerated, maybe. She'd done the crime, she'd do the time.

Turned out, the charges were more than she'd bargained for. *AWOL*: sure, couldn't deny it. *Wrongful appropriation of military assets*: yeah, you steal a commodore's shuttle (even when it was a harmless drunken accident) and they'll hit you with that. *Destruction of military assets*: no argument there, as she had put a multi-million-credit asset on the ocean floor.

The charges she hadn't thought about, though, were on another level altogether: *Espionage, Conspiracy,* and *Aiding the Enemy.* The cocksuckers claimed she'd stolen the shuttle in order to sell it to the Purists. Bullshit, obviously, because the only way a pilot of her considerable skills put a bird in the deep drink was because said pilot *wanted* to put said bird in the deep drink.

A decade in prison for theft was one thing—execution for treason was another.

They made her an offer she couldn't refuse.

They told her they'd fudge the incident report to say she'd "borrowed" the shuttle, as a prank, and buzzed Vishvakarman's flight-control tower. They said if she served a two-year stint aboard the PUV *James Keeling*, that modified story (and the real story as well) would be wiped from her record.

Two years on *Keeling* compared to a long walk in the void sans exosuit? It was a great deal. Fuck, man, that was a *deal and a half.* She'd jumped on it like a bum on a baloney sandwich.

Being on the *Crypt* had been good, at least at first. She'd met XO Ellis, who her brother worshiped like Jesus Christ himself. She'd been a Raider pilot again, respected by her crew, the techs, and the knuckle-draggers who did the real work.

A deal and a half for sure... until she entered transdim.

She'd *seen* things in the Mud. Hallucinations, they said, but she couldn't be sure. *Ghosts.* The ghost of Spicy, screaming as she burned alive. The ghost of Hard-Six, pushing his own guts back into his belly while begging his mother to save him. And other, *stranger* ghosts— bizarre little weasel-crawdad things with weird, oblong eyes and fleshy shit growing out of the backs of their heads.

The weasel-crawdads told her to kill John Bennett.

Biggie had *listened* to them. Biggie had *agreed* Old Man Bennett must die. She'd tried to choke him to death with his plastic dog-tag necklace, which snapped under the strain. If she'd had a real chain? Or a bit of rope or cable? She would have killed him.

And she would have *enjoyed* it.

She would have *laughed*.

The Mud *made* her do that.

And now here she was, soon to wallow in the Mud once again. When she came out of transdim, she would fight, maybe. Die, maybe. Burn to death like Spicy, maybe. If she survived? Into the Mud for the return trip to Gateway, where the only people she could fuck were the same people she saw on the ship every single fucking day.

The infirmary was on Deck Three. The copper-tunnel passageway leading to it curved slightly, as did most passageways on the lower decks. She passed the small medical storage compartment. Between that door and the infirmary were three small cubbyholes, and one—at waist level—just large enough to slide into.

Now *that* was a good spot for napping. Or, if this little begging session went well, a good spot to hide away while pursuing better living through chemistry.

Biggie timed it right—red-haired Rebecca Watson was the only one in the infirmary, med goggles flipped up on her head. The small compartment, two meters long by six wide, was one of the few places on the lower decks where engineers managed to install four normal, flat walls. Two hospital beds, one occupied by a sleeping sailor with a bandaged left shoulder. Cabinets with latches locked fast. A surgical rig. A bone-melder, a.k.a., *the Iron Maiden.* Biggie had never undergone that particular bit of torture, thankfully, but she'd talked to those who had. It did not sound like a good time.

"Hello, Warrant Bang," Watson said. "Can I help you?"

Biggie hoped the scuttlebutt was right. If she was going back into the Mud, she needed something to keep the weasel-crawdads at bay.

She nodded toward the unconscious sailor.

"That the guy Lafferty shot?"

"It is," Watson said. "Spec-One Michael Camp. *'Tis but a flesh wound,* as they say. She managed to not hit bone. He'll be back to work tomorrow. I'm a little busy right now, so tell me what ails you."

If Watson ratted Biggie out for this, it might be Lafferty who came calling. Something *really* off about that woman. But it was now or never.

"I've been getting some headaches as of late," Biggie said. "Real bad. They could compromise my flying."

Watson patted the empty bed. "Cop a squat."

Biggie sat.

"Let's take a look under the hood." Watson flipped her goggles down. "Bright light. Keep your eyes open."

A light on the goggles blazed into Biggie's eyes, so bright it stung. She had to concentrate to keep from blinking while Watson checked her pupils (or whatever the hell docs looked for when they did that crap).

Watson turned off the light, flipped up the goggles. She felt at Biggie's neck, at the hinge of her jaw, at her throat.

"Headaches," Watson said. "You really came to me for *headaches?*"

A curl at the corner of Watson's mouth, a dimple-making half-smile/half-smirk, the look of someone who gets a thrill out of making you *ask* when she already knows what you want.

"Yeah, headaches," Biggie said, feeling like an idiot for acting the part when they both knew the script. "It's the stress, man. You ever fly an Ochthera?"

Watson's half-smile/half-smirk tucked up further, made her dimple deepen like a fleshy black hole.

"No, Warrant Bang," Watson said. "I've never flown a crawler."

She opened a cabinet, pulled out a plastic vial of pink pills, and held them out to Biggie.

"Take two when you feel the headache coming on," Watson said. "If they don't stop it, take two more. Never take more than six in a twelve-our period. Never. Got it?"

Biggie took the vial, stared at it. *Pinkies.* Basic pain killers. *Vita-*

min-P. The stuff of legend. Along with caffeine, they were Fleet's drug of choice.

She'd hoped it would be easier than this.

"Doc, I might maybe need something stronger."

The dimple twitched. "You don't think pinkies will do the job?"

Biggie did not like Watson. Not one bit.

"Exactamundo," Biggie said.

Watson leaned closer, pretended to examine Biggie's ear, and whispered, "You good with zappies?"

Zapinoforol. Great stuff. Biggie had zapped out to Slumber Town several times in the past.

"That might do the trick," she said.

Watson gestured to the door.

"You're fit as a fiddle, Warrant Bang. Let's grab a bite in the mess. Say, in an hour?"

Biggie's mouth felt dry.

"Yeah, Doc. An hour sounds fine."

34

TRAVIS

Orders had arrived. *Keeling* would soon punch for New Earth, a standard day's travel. From there, Travis did not know where the ship would go. Neither did Lafferty or Lincoln, not until they decoded the orders, an event to which Travis was not privy.

Before the captain and the intel chief did that, though, Lincoln wanted answers—answers from Bethany Darkwater and Zvanut Hasik, who stood before Lincoln's desk in the captain's suite. They both smelled of booze. Him more than her. Hasik's drinking infuriated Travis. Why did Lincoln let him get away with it? His undisciplined ways were rubbing off on Darkwater.

Unacceptable.

Travis and Lafferty sat side by side on the padded couch. The suite's multiple monitors were all off, black screens witness to the grilling.

Behind her desk, Lincoln leaned back in her chair, a clean blue bandana on her head. Travis preferred the blue—the red ones made her look like a storybook pirate. A disposable mycoware coffee cup sat on the desk. On the last voyage, officers had been allowed thin, enameled aluminum mugs. Those were gone; someone had decided they might be crafted into weapons the crew could use during transdim madness.

"Colonel Hasik, the ship created its own wiring," the captain said. "And your best explanation is *I don't know?*"

"As I already noted, it's not wiring in the traditional sense," Hasik said. "I've designated it a *semi-organic MOF conduit array*. Functionally similar to neural myelin sheaths, but for signal routing."

Stitches on his forehead. A wicked bruise on his right eye. He looked like he'd been in a fight. Travis wondered if that had something to do with his late arrival.

"You and your terminology," Lafferty said. "You don't know what it is, but you took the time to name it?"

From the hand holding the coffee cup, Lincoln extended one finger, a tiny gesture that told Lafferty to be quiet. Lafferty complied.

"Taxonomy is not optional, Major," Hasik said. "We can't research what we can't define. We've confirmed the conduit material is a derivative of *Keeling*'s primary MOF—same crystalline lattice, same adaptive beryllium-copper-carbon backbone. What's unclear is the trigger mechanism. There's no record of fabrication. No tool paths. It just *grew*."

MOF—metal-organic framework that made up the ship. The beryllium-copper-carbon alloy could be harder than diamond and stronger than steel, yet also, at times, moved like living biological muscle and tissue. MOF could heal itself. It could *grow*, as it had while encased in the chrysalis, which itself was made of the same alloy.

And it could *kill*, as evidenced by Leona Romanik's demise.

"Captain, I've only been back a short time," Hasik said. "Thanks to Lieutenant Kerkhoffs's instructions, every compartment and section tested their equipment. They submitted detailed performance reports, stating—without exception—that everything functions as well or better than it did before. Our initial testing supports the crew's assessments. We're seeing lower impedance, broader frequency tolerance, and adaptive rerouting capabilities—closer to a biological nervous system than anything else. Lieutenant Darkwater validated signal continuity across a randomized cross-section using standardized regression baselines. I've also begun controlled ablation tests. We deliberately severed small sections to observe autorepair behavior."

"You *severed connections?*" Lincoln leaned forward, her surprise and anger visible. "We lost a crewmember who tried to cut into the ship, remember? You should have reported to me before trying that."

Hasik smiled his arrogant smile. "Captain, the area I selected was inert. No signal load, no load-bearing stress. Roughly a ten-millimeter cross-section. The material responded with localized regeneration— same foil extrusion we've documented elsewhere. No aggression from the ship, no defensive behavior."

Lincoln looked like she wanted to blacken his other eye.

"There was no danger, Captain," Lafferty said. "*Keeling* knows us. We severed only a small area."

Hasik held up a thumb and forefinger that almost but not quite touched.

"A *teeny* area," he said. "The severed area repaired itself, both sides extruding the same foil that has been a bane for us all. There was no issue. We're in the early stages of analysis, but functionally, *Keeling* upgraded herself. The new conduit material replaced all wiring in the lower decks. Signal integration points with standard Fleet wiring are stable. Interfaces are self-leveling, even across mismatched voltages. It's not just efficient—it's superior."

The veins were an unexpected, unprecedented event, yet Hasik didn't seem all that concerned. He had six *Keeling* deployments under his belt. Maybe he'd seen the ship do far stranger things.

"Very well," Lincoln said. "Admiral Epperson wants us on-mission, pronto, so we go. You will continue to work on this? Give me some kind of an explanation?"

The fact she asked that question, instead of giving him a direct order, spoke volumes about the strange power dynamic between Lincoln, Hasik, and Epperson.

"Of course, Captain," Hasik said. "Lieutenant Darkwater and I are actively analyzing the conduit to see what we can further learn."

Lincoln set her cup on the desk. The coffee was probably already cold; mycoware didn't insulate all that well.

"You should have been here, Colonel," she said. "I grow tired of your extended absences. *Keeling* is Fleet's most powerful asset. You should be here, not off doing whatever Epperson has you doing."

Hasik pushed his black glasses up his nose. "You'll have to take that up with the admiral, Captain. I go where I'm ordered."

Lafferty leaned forward, a hawk eyeing a mouse. "And where is that, exactly?" A lilt in her words—she so enjoyed grilling people. "Where *do* you go when we're in port, Colonel?"

Hasik looked down at her. "I am not at liberty to tell you, Major. You should also feel free to raise your concerns directly with Epperson. What I *can* tell you is *Keeling*'s scientific resources are rather limited. There is only so much I can accomplish here."

"I want *answers*, Colonel," Lincoln said. "I want to know what's going on with my ship. What about Romanik's body? The ship pulled her in. Where are her remains?"

That was something Travis wanted to know as well.

"Based on our analysis of MOF phase states during chrysalis retraction, it's likely that Lieutenant Romanik and her vacsuit were depolymerized during solidification. Her molecular structure was integrated into the host matrix—atomized, in essence. Chemically, she may no longer exist as a discrete entity. We will continue to study the phenomena as time permits."

The word phenomena further angered Lincoln. Travis understood why—Hasik seemed completely unfazed that *Keeling* had not only killed a crewmember, but made the body vanish like some lethal magic trick.

"You do that, Colonel," she said. "You're both dismissed."

Hasik and Darkwater left.

Lincoln had gone through the motions of delivering *stern words* hinting at *severe consequences*, but all involved knew it was little more than a charade. The barking dog had no bite.

"XO, Intel and I need to open the orders," Lincoln said. "Please take the conn and oversee the weapons testing."

Travis stood. "Very well, Captain."

He left Lincoln's suite, grateful to have yet another demanding task to occupy his attention. If he'd had time to go to his quarters, he knew he'd check to see if a message from his wife—perhaps soon-to-be *ex*-wife—was among the last batch transmitted from Gateway.

Keep busy. That was the thing.

He headed for the CIC.

"Nothing like being in the firing zone for live ammo testing," Torch said. "Let's hope their IFF is hundy-P."

Biggie couldn't agree more. In most battles, IFF—*Identify Friend or Foe* system—was rarely more than the eyes of the gun crews. Space-time fuckery tended to scramble any electronic signal, IFF included. For now, though, during testing, with no fuckery about and no enemy vessels near, the IFF would, hopefully, be at 100 percent efficiency—or *hundy-P*, as Torch liked to say.

"Occie Two, *Keeling* control. Drones launching in ten seconds."

"Copy, *Keeling* control," Biggie said. "We're ready."

She counted down in her head.

"I hope we have eggplant tonight," Knuckles said. "I missed that meal."

Combat Cook's recipe for those person-sized eggplants was to die for. Say what you will about *Keeling*—the food was better than any other ship Biggie had served on. As long as you didn't mind the persistent flavor of mushrooms, that was.

A flash from *Keeling*'s underside as three drone torps launched from the forward bay, chemjet engines igniting once the three-meter-long cylinders popped free of their tubes. All three took different paths.

"*Keeling* control, Occie Two," Biggie said. "Visual of launch, all drones operating normally."

"Copy, Ochthera Two. Commencing test."

Biggie watched the starboard Type24 turret rotate a full 360, while its twin 8-meter-long barrels elevated and declined through their range of motion. The port Type24 turret rotated as well—the two-turret combo made her think of a legless Tyrannosaurus rex madly doing "jazz hands."

She felt a hint of combat rush. Her bird wasn't a target, but with live guns and crews operating new weapons, one could never be too careful.

Keeling's topside AP6 point-defense canon, mounted atop Deck One, opened up. The rotary canon's six barrels belched out 3,000 20-millimeter rounds a minute. Tracers showed the gunner's tracking of the fast drone torp. The sparkling orange line of fire arced toward the drone before line and drone intersected—the torp broke into three spinning pieces.

"Nice," Knuckles said. "Who's on the top gun?"

Biggie didn't know. Ellis had told her the lineup, but her mind only seemed to store details involving her bird and her crew. The XO and his endless emergency drills cut into her sleep—maybe that was why she couldn't remember names.

"Marchenko, I think," Torch said. "The one-legged wonder is a good shot."

At least Torch knew what was what. It was hard to keep track of gunners. All machinists, signalers, fire controllers, and sensor opera-tors cross-trained on the AP6s. When the shit hit the fan, Ellis wanted an overabundance of competent gunners, which made sense considering a gunner's combat lifespan was often measured in seconds.

Biggie pitched down and accelerated, bringing the Ochthera below *Keeling*'s midline for a clearer view of the two torpedo bays and the single AP6 mounted atop each. The forward point-defense gun made quick work of its target drone. The aft AP6 took longer to close in for the kill, a good six seconds longer.

Six seconds where the target was potentially shooting back at you —an eternity in combat.

"Fern Hardy's on the aft gun," Torch said. "She's a fire controller from *Ishlangu*. The XO better get her squared away. In STC soup she won't be able to hit the broad side of a barn."

Biggie nodded. Ellis would have someone's ass on a platter.

Two torps launched from the aft bay. One curled to port, the other to starboard.

Keeling's starboard Type24 fired both barrels. Smoke billowed from the two-meter-long backblast ports. Out in front of the targeted drone, a pair of flak rounds detonated, spreading a cloud of depleted uranium shards. The drone didn't have time to maneuver—it flew straight into the cloud and shattered into a hundred pieces.

"Nice," Knuckles said. "Good lead, great timing. Idowu's team ain't rusty."

Sergeant Idowu—Biggie couldn't remember her first name—was the starboard turret master. She'd done well in the *Ishlangu* battle.

The port Type24, the new one, fired a blazer from the left barrel. Biggie could see the slower-moving round's path, see the space around it warping and shifting in an expanding sphere. The right barrel fired next—the larger plume of backblast smoke told her it was probably a standard 127-millimeter penetrator, meant to blast big holes in enemy warships.

Biggie silently counted off the time between the first rounds and the next. A little over four seconds ticked by before both barrels fired flak rounds. In the wavering, distorted area generated by the blazer, the last drone broke into a hundred bits.

"Gotta speed up that reload," Knuckles said. "But overall, not bad."

She was right about the speed. Type24s needed to be able to fire, reload, and fire again in three seconds.

"Peredur Geraint's crew," Torch said. "He's saddled with two newbs from *Ishi*. That they're this competent already gives me faith."

Biggie didn't have to ask *faith in what?* No one knew where the *Crypt* was headed, but they all knew combat awaited them upon arrival.

"In your racks," Sands called out. "Feet flat on the footboard, hands inside. If I see anything hanging over the edge, I will cut it off and hand it back to you."

John was the only member of his fire team not in his rack. He wanted to make sure his people were in the right position for the high acceleration needed to enter punch-space. It seemed silly to check up on grown-ass life-takers, but he wasn't taking any chances.

Beaver leaned out of his rack, that shit-eating grin on his face.

"Hey, Master Sergeant," he yelled, "what if Mafi's big dong is hanging over the side? You gonna cut that off and hand it to him?"

John back-handed the side of Beaver's head. Always with that *mouth.*

"Owwww," Beaver said, rubbing where John had smacked him and making a face like Santa had just handed him a lump of coal. "Come on, Bennett."

John heard Sands behind him, thundering down the aisle between bunks.

Oh, hell...

John stood ramrod straight. Beaver quickly lay flat on his back and started whistling a random tune, as if everyone in the platoon didn't know he'd been the one to make the comment.

Sands came around John, leaned into Beaver's rack.

"*Spec Beaver,*" Sands said, at a volume slightly higher than Beaver's normal speaking voice, which meant Sands was shouting at the top of his lungs, "I have warned you about your mouth! Once we are in punch-space, you will do Deck PT until I get tired of watching you vomit. Do you understand?"

"Yes, Master Sergeant," Beaver yelled back. "I look forward to it, Master Sergeant!"

Sands stood straight. With furious eyes, he stared down at Beaver, then turned that anger toward John.

"And since your team leader can't keep you quiet," Sands said, "he will join you in this erstwhile endeavor. Not one more word out of the lot of you!"

Sands stormed off.

John grit his teeth. *The Deck PT* consisted of sets of fifty pushups, thirty burpees, fifty mountain climbers, fifty crunches, twenty lunges, and finished with a two-minute plank. Three or four sets exhausted most everyone—who knew how many Sands would need before he'd seen enough.

"Hey, Bennett," Beaver said, trying to whisper, which for him was speaking at a normal person's volume. "We get to workout together. Ain't that fun?"

John ignored him and climbed up into the top bunk.

Goddamn Beaver.

John adjusted himself, put his feet flat against his rack's aft-facing footboard. Punch-in acceleration always packed a wallop. He wondered if the rat-shrimp hallucination would visit him again, gaze down at him from within the coral-pattered copper overhead that sat a mere six inches from John's face.

The 1MC chime sounded.

"This is the XO. All non-essential personnel should be in their racks. Punch-in acceleration begins in ten seconds. That is all."

John adjusted himself again, making sure he was as flat as possible. That helped the fakegrav plates in his rack hold him down. He lay there and thought about how much "fun" it would be to trade blows with big men a third his age, over and over, until Sands got tired of watching him and Beaver bleed.

Trouble was, it took Sands a long time to get tired.

John was still fuming when *Keeling*'s chem-boosters ignited.

BETHANY

The atrium's heat and humidity didn't bother Bethany that much anymore. Except, apparently, when she had a hangover. The dull throbbing at her temples, combined with the atrium's swampy atmosphere, made her feel like she might regurgitate.

"Lieutenant Darkwater, you're awake. Wonderful." Hasik was at his workstation. He went to his bunk, which was on Bethany's left. He sat. "You look horrible."

Bethany rubbed her offending temples. "Well, Colonel, when my hangover goes away, I'll look better. Unfortunately, even when your laceration and contusion heals, you'll still be ugly whether I'm piss-drunk or stone-cold sober."

Hasik removed his steamed-up glasses. "Did you just crack a joke, Lieutenant?" He wiped them on his stained tank top. "You must be hanging out with the Raiders. All they do is insult one another. It's quite comical, actually. I, for one, am glad you finally pulled that stick out of your ass. Remember how *dull* you were when you arrived?"

When Bethany first boarded *Keeling*, she'd been a different person. Both literally and figuratively. Being aboard *Keeling*, being constantly in the presence of God... those things changed her. So, too, did being around Anne Lafferty, but Major Murder wasn't in the atrium.

Bethany felt safe here. Felt *loved* here.

She looked up at the thin mist illuminated by the coupler's golden glow, at the conical ceiling's lush vegetation.

"Those green beans are getting *huge*," she said. "Huge-*er* I mean. Some of the pods are as long as my arm."

Hasik slid his glasses back on. "We really should get a botanist in here someday." He glanced at the greenery. "You know, we could build a still. We have potatoes up there. And apples. I hear you can make vodka from apples."

There were also sugar beets the size of Bethany's chest. She decided not to mention those. Hasik had brought enough booze onboard to last the xeno department two weeks. Was it a good idea for him to develop his own distillery?

No, it was not.

"Looks like our new colleague can't handle her liquor," Hasik said. "Wake her up."

Martigral was in her bunk, out like a light. The three of them had drained half the plastic two-liter of Scotch. Bethany had consumed the equivalent of... five shots? Six? However many it was, it was at least three too many.

Martigral's bunk... where Jenn Hathorn had slept...

...the copper blade...

...red splattering on the heartstone...

"Darkwater," Hasik said, "did you hear me?"

Bethany found herself staring blankly at the heartstone. How long had she been doing that?

She gently shook Martigral's shoulder. "Rise and shine, Ensign."

Martigral blinked awake, put a hand to her face. "Oh, my *head*." Her short, graying blonde hair was mushed and clumped from sleep. She slowly sat up. "Why is it so *hot* in here?"

"Because it is," Hasik said. "This is a warship. You need to be able to rise on a moment's notice and pitch in. Sit up. *Now*."

Martigral sat up.

Hasik had never been this firm with Bethany. Maybe he didn't like Martigral. If so, it was no surprise—the ensign didn't exactly act in likable ways.

"Ensign," Hasik said, "do you have experience with ship propulsion?"

Martigral shook her head.

"None?" Hasik pushed his glasses up his sweat-slick nose. "No interplanetary craft operation at all?" He glanced at Bethany. "Not even a hauler, for example?"

"Colonel, I'm quite capable of understanding a question the first time I am asked," Martigral said. "If you're going to repeat queries, I will repeat my answers. In other words, *no*, I have no experience with ship propulsion of any kind."

Well, wasn't she a bit of an asshole?

"Then you have much to learn," Hasik said. "We'll cover the basic concepts of propulsion and navigation as they relate to the xeno department. This ship is, obviously, of alien design."

"Which species?" Martigral asked, brightening. "It's not Sklorno, I know that for certain. Probably not Ki or Quyth. Did the Rewall make it? Or the Prawatt?"

She knew Sklorno hadn't built it, but she was unsure if Prawatt had? How strange. Pretty much everyone in xenomechanics or automatonics studied what little was known of the biomechanical Prawatt species.

Which reminded Bethany... she still didn't know Martigral's area of study. On the *Crypt*, one wasn't allowed to ask about such things.

"That information is classified," Hasik said. "As is the technology behind *Keeling*'s transdim propulsion method. I'm only allowed to tell you the basic concepts required for operating it."

Bethany wanted to know that tech. She wanted to know every-thing about *Keeling*. When it came to the transdim drive, Hasik knew more than he had shared. Why did he keep some knowledge to himself? Was it because of Admiral Epperson's orders, or did Hasik think Bethany wasn't capable of understanding it?

Working with *Keeling* was like learning how to fly a jet but having no knowledge of aerodynamics, how jet engines actually worked, and nearly zero knowledge of the parts and processes involved. Monkeys pushing buttons—that's what the *Crypt* crew was.

A crew that was told, over and over again, to not ask questions.

"This ship interfaces with standard Fleet tech in two ways," Hasik said. "The first interface allows us to move between dimensional membranes. We will discuss this more later."

Bethany remembered his detailed explanation. He'd used his well-worn paper notebook, broken down the principles of multiple dimensions existing in the same space.

"The second interface involves maneuvering and navigation," Hasik said. "When in realspace, *Keeling*'s standard curvine technology provides propulsion. Do you understand space-time curvature propulsion, Ensign?"

Martigral let out a heavy sigh. "Yes."

She was *so* annoying.

"This vessel has three kinds of propulsion," Hasik said. "In realspace, a standard, military-grade curvine engine provides thrust and maneuvering, augmented by occasional use of chemical thrusters for enhanced acceleration, deceleration, and maneuvering. Shall I explain the principles of how a curvine pulls a ship along concentrated bands of space-time?"

The way he asked it—so syrupy, so patronizing.

Martigral crossed her arms.

"No need for that, Colonel," she said. "I understand the principles involved."

Hasik smiled with fake delight. "Wonderful! The second form of propulsion is the punch-drive, which allows faster than light travel. Shall I explain how that works?"

If indignation could be lasers shot from the eyes, Martigral's glare would have cut Hasik in half.

"I understand the concepts of punch-drives as well," she said. "Might it not save us time if you simply explain this mysterious third form, since that's what you're clearly dying to talk about?"

"Of *course*, Ensign." Hasik rubbed his hands together. "I thought you'd never ask! In transdim, the curvine operates at a fraction of its normal power. *Keeling's* primary thrust and maneuvering, therefore, come from its tail section."

He extended the pointer and middle finger of his right hand, pressed his left pointer finger against them lengthwise.

"In realspace, this ship's three tails segments press together in one solid mass. In transdim, however—" he split the fingers so they all pointed in slightly different directions, like the legs of a stool "—they separate at the ends and down their length. They become flexible. I compare it to three very large flagella whipping along."

That caught Martigral's interest, cutting through her irritation at being spoken to like a first-year student.

"The flagella provide thrust," she said. "How?"

Hasik put his hand on his chest.

"Sadly, Ensign, you don't have the security clearance to know. But don't feel bad—neither does the good Lieutenant here, and she not only outranks you, she's already got a mission under her belt."

It bothered Bethany that Hasik wouldn't tell Bethany how *Keeling's* in-dim drive worked. She suspected he didn't really know himself.

"I assume you have footage of these tails in operation," Martigral said. "Surely I have the *clearance* to see how the ship I'm on moves in this so-called *transdim*?"

Hasik was enjoying himself. Bethany was glad she hadn't drawn this level of smarmy ire from him.

"We only have footage of *Keeling* moving from transdim into realspace," Hasik said. "It's quite a spectacle. Lieutenant Darkwater will show you later. While in transdim, unfortunately, we can't see any part of the ship due to the minimum focal length of our optical system. You might say that system is far-sighted."

Now it was Martigral's turn to smile.

"So you literally *don't know* what your ship looks like in transdim? That must make it difficult to gather basic observational data."

She meant it as an insult, demeaning Hasik's abilities as a scientist. He didn't seem bothered by it.

"We managed quite well," he said. "Now, while *Keeling*'s innate acceleration tech *does* work in realspace, there our standard curvine acceleration is much faster, so that's what we use. In transdim, however, curvines don't work at all, so we rely on the ship's innate propulsion."

"The *tails*," Martigral said.

Hasik nodded. "The tails, yes. We've created a linkage system that connects standard Union navigation to the ship's directional system. Therefore, in realspace or in transdim, the pilots in the CIC are able to use the same controls for maneuvering and acceleration."

Martigral glanced off, thinking, processing.

"So the pilot's systems don't actually control maneuvering, thrust, et cetera, they control an interface that connects their systems to the ship's alien systems. Do I have that right?"

"Correct," Hasik said.

"What if something goes wrong with the interface?" Martigral asked. "Can you operate the ship's native systems? Does the interface always work?"

Bethany had asked that same question. More than once. She knew Hasik's answer before he spoke it.

"That's classified," he said. "There have been a few instances when *Keeling* stopped responding. We have a method to kick the tires, so to speak, and we quickly get control back."

Bethany hadn't heard of this before.

"The ship *stopped responding*," she said. "What do we do when that happens?"

Hasik's grin vanished. As with questions about the interface itself, she already knew his answer.

"That's classified." He seemed to realize he'd gotten carried away, said things he wasn't supposed to say. "I shouldn't have mentioned it."

Bethany knew she should stop, but her mouth seemed to act on its own.

"Did Hathorn know? Does anyone else? What if something happens to you while we're in transdim and we lose control, Colonel?"

Behind his steaming glasses, his eyes narrowed with annoyance. At Bethany for asking, yes, but also at himself for opening up that particular can of worms.

"Lincoln is familiar with the process," he said. "So is Warrant Ledford in propulsion. We have knowledge redundancy. Leave it alone." His glare softened some. "But it's information you should know, Lieutenant. When we return to Gateway, I will take it up with command."

Command meant only one person, as far as Bethany knew—Epperson.

Hasik went his workstation, opened a drawer, came back with his prized notebook: leather-bound, beat to hell, colored sticky notes sticking out from all sides. He pulled a pen from the spine.

"And now for my favorite part, Ensign Martigral," Hasik said. "Later on, Lieutenant Darkwater will show you how the transdim coupler operates. First, though, I will explain the basics of interdimensional travel."

Orders came in pairs: one coded message for the intel chief, one for the captain. Each received a different message intended for their individual ten-dial cypher keys, keys that were made new for each mission. While the system wasn't foolproof, it was damn close to it. That was a good thing, considering orders often involved combat scenarios—Fleet couldn't be too careful when it came to putting its people at risk and killing the enemy.

Anne used her key to translate the code, putting pencil to paper one letter at a time. As the words formed, her excitement intensified. What an opportunity. What a *moment*.

Lincoln's staccato pencil *scratch-scratch* sounded too loud in the small compartment, like someone trying to quietly clear a persistent throat tickle.

"While we decode this," the captain said, "give me a quick overview of your investigation into new crewmembers. Any concerns?"

BII's brief questioning of the eighteen newbies had turned up little. Anne now knew what a few people had done to be entombed, but those various transgressions did not indicate someone spying for the Purists.

"Nothing obvious," Anne said. "*Ishlangu*'s replacements require the most observation. Theoretically, any of them could have found a way to send *Ishi*'s location to the Purist force that ambushed us."

Anne had Gillick and Daniels working overtime investigating those replacements: Dimo in propulsion; Bakshi in electrical; Byrnes in ECM; gunners Swanson and Seward; Hardy in fire control; and sensor operator Feliciano.

"It's going to take more time to be sure," Anne said.

Lincoln jotted down a letter. "I imagine you will never be sure. Not after Shamdi. You're also grilling the new Raiders, I assume?"

The captain wasn't second-guessing Anne, wasn't demanding to see reports, wasn't micro-managing the work. Despite the Shamdi debacle, Lincoln trusted Anne to get the job done.

At least someone did.

"We're watching them," Anne said. "We're watching all of them."

All of them, including Bethany. Admiral Bock would have to try and contact her soon. Did Bock know about the very orders Anne was decoding now? What *exactly* did Bock want from Beth.

That particular problem would have to wait.

Anne turned cypher dials, wrote down another letter. "Akagi and Camp are significant concerns. Maybe they really have PTSD, or maybe they wanted to stay on Gateway so they could report to their handlers after we departed."

Lincoln looked at Anne.

"Speaking of PTSD, how are you after shooting Camp? Any issues?"

Anne realized she hadn't given shooting Camp a second thought since returning her pistol to the small arms locker, but she saw a certain expectation in the Lincoln's expression.

"I'm... fine," Anne said, throwing in the pause for effect. "It had to be done. Part of the job, Captain."

Lincoln stared, then returned to her cyphering.

Anne felt a need to change the subject.

"I also have concerns about Lekan, the new crawler pilot," she said. "I don't like the way he looks at some of the women on board."

Anne *did* like the way Lekan looked at *her*, though. She'd never slept with a Tower native before. Was his dick as blue as the rest of him?

"Keep at it with all of them," Lincoln said. "But don't interfere with training. I need everyone combat-ready as soon as possible. How about Camp and Akagi? Are they on your list?"

She wrote down another letter, then set her pencil on the desk.

Anne finished her own transcription seconds later, the last few letters driving her excitement.

Good God—Admiral Epperson had a pair on him. He'd had this planned for a while. Absolutely *devious*. Anne couldn't help but respect the man.

"I read, you confirm," Lincoln said.

"You read, I confirm. Aye-aye."

Lincoln spoke. Anne carefully tracked every word on her own sheet, as even a single non-matching letter could invalidate the order, require them to signal back to Epperson's staff for clarifications.

The captain finished—everything matched.

"Order confirmed," Anne said. "Onward to glory."

Lincoln glanced at her, a look meant to be disapproving, to be *judging*, but Anne saw a predator's glint in the captain's eye.

"The Martigral thing pisses me off," Lincoln said. "Did you know about her?"

Anne casually re-read that part of the communique. She never answered quickly. A good BII operative always thought things through before speaking. The right words at the right time did more work than anything else.

"I had suspicions Martigral wasn't who she said she was," Anne said. "She must be well-respected in certain circles to get this assignment."

Lincoln smirked. "Beyond well-respected. Try *revered*. I wonder where she's been holed up that we've never heard of her."

BII operatives weren't the only ones who used words judiciously. Warship captains did, too, it seemed. Anne admired

Lincoln's oh-so-subtle way of saying *I didn't know who she was, but you should have.*

"Fleet is like an onion in that way," Anne said. "Peel back one layer, there's always another. At least we get to know what's inside those crates Epperson put aboard."

The four crates, sitting in the superstructure's small arms locker, were an insult to Anne. She was the intel chief of this ship, yet she didn't have clearance to know what was inside them. Martigral's true nature revealed much about this mission—the crates were hers.

Lincoln picked up her paper, scanned the decoded orders.

"The crew will be none too happy," she said. "I don't know how BII got this intel, but it's impressive."

The crew might not be happy, but the captain was; Anne could see it in Lincoln's body language. On the last mission, *Keeling* had been ordered to *not* engage, to be little more than a glorified shuttle. Now, Epperson chose to let loose the leash that kept his pet pit bull from attacking.

Captain Kiara Lincoln, the Hero of Capizzi 7, the person credited with the destruction of eight enemy warships—more than anyone in Union History—finally got to go on the offensive.

"This timeline is unforgiving, especially for the newbies," Lincoln said. "We need to move fast."

She lifted the handset mounted on the bulkhead next to her desk and flipped the switch for the 1MC.

"Attention, *Keeling* crew," she said. "This is the captain. Executive staff report to the ACIC immediately."

As *Keeling* coursed through punch-space, the executive staff gathered in the cramped ACIC on Deck Four. It had always been hot and humid belowdecks—now it was a bit more of both. Travis had his light gray coveralls half off, arms tied around his waist, but that didn't help much; after only fifteen minutes down here, sweat made his gray undershirt as clingy as a second skin.

Lincoln wore her coveralls the same way, as did Alex Plait, operations department head, Cat Brown, weapons department head, and Chief of the Boat Eloi Sung.

Raider Platoon Commander Gary Lindros preferred to keep his dark gray coveralls fastened all the way up to his thin neck—maybe he figured if he was going to sweat regardless, he might as well look ship-shape. The scalp beneath his sandy blond high and tight gleamed with sweat.

Anne Lafferty took a similar button-up-tight approach with her BII black coveralls, although she'd slid her sleeves to her elbows. Colonel Hasik and Engineering Department Head Sascha Kerkhoffs wore workout shorts and tank tops—they were belowdecks most of the time and dealt with the heat accordingly.

Compared to other ships Travis served on, *Keeling*'s CIC felt like a veritable walk-in closet—the Auxiliary CIC was less than half its size. More metal cave than proper compartment, the ACIC had no intel or xeno loft. Stations were crammed in where space permitted. Signals and darsat were combined in a tiny compartment farther aft.

Some people sat at those stations, while others stood around the ACIC's small nav-orb, which cast an eerie blue glow upon glistening faces.

"This information is classified," Lincoln said. "Do not share it with your subordinates. Major Lafferty, you have the floor."

Lafferty stepped to the orb. "Thank you, Captain."

She called up the galactic map. Of all the repetitive drudgery that was part and parcel of military life, Travis never grew tired of seeing the Milky Way, in any format. Even when colored over by the complex, three-dimensional territorial boundaries of the galaxy's governments, he found the galaxy the most beautiful thing imaginable—the womb of reality itself, so impossibly large that Humanity had explored barely a splinter of it despite discovering punch-drive tech 170 years earlier.

"The Sklorno Dynasty is at war with the Prawatt Jihad," Lafferty said. "This conflict is separate from the Third Galactic War, which currently pits us against the Purist Nation and their allies. Until recently, neither the Sklorno nor the Prawatt were allied with the Purists. That has changed."

The map showed degree lines for galactic longitude—increasing counter-clockwise—and concentric rings marking galactic latitude. Prawatt Jihad territory, marked in yellow, began roughly 40,000 lightyears from the galactic core, occupying much of the space between 0° and 30°: the outer edge of the Scutum-Centaurus arm.

At roughly that same 40,000ly latitude, three governments cut Jihad space off from the rest of the galaxy: the Ki Rebel Establishment, marked in blue; the Sklorno Dynasty, in red; and the Quyth Concordia, in green. Quyth territory wrapped around the Dynasty's core-ward boundary to butt up against the core itself, marked in orange. All borders were fuzzy, since the massive scale and overlapping territorial claims made it impossible to draw exacting boundaries.

Lafferty pointed to the Whitok Kingdom, a thin, teal section hugging the core from roughly 180° to 0°, where it overlapped a bit of Sklorno territory. From 270° to 180°, though, Whitok territory thickened, stretching away from the core to roughly 20,000*ly*. That segment ran "above" Planetary Union territory, marked in red. Top-down representations of the Milky Way hid just how thick it was—around 1,000 lightyears through the outer disk, swelling to over 10,000 lightyears thick near the core.

A thin finger of Whitok territory, the teal bit farthest from the core, was proximal to New Earth, which itself sat about halfway to the galaxy's edge.

"The Whitok Kingdom is allied with the Purist Nation," Lafferty said. "BII has learned the Whitok are allowing Sklorno to travel through Kingdom territory. It's highly probably the convoy is delivering comprehensive Watchtower-class station weapon and sensor upgrades to the Purists."

Impossible. Travis and the other executive staffers exchanged disbelieving glances, perhaps seeing if Lafferty's claim was a joke and the others were in on it. Only Lincoln seemed unsurprised.

"No way," Chief Sung said. "That's sacrilege for those Purist churchie psychos. They slaughter non-humans on sight. They teach their kids nursery rhymes about how to kill each alien species with their bare hands, for Christ's sake. Purists trading with crickets? Taking *tech upgrades* from them? No fucking way."

Lafferty glared at Sung; she didn't like being interrupted.

"Intel indicates this relationship is not known by Purist citizens, or by the military at large," she said. "Watchtower stations are almost twenty years old. They were built quickly. Since their deployment, they've had small, incremental improvements. All Purist military manufacturing is dedicated to ship building and repair. This tech deal with the Sklorno will likely let them upgrade the stations, improving armor, armament, and targeting. If that happens, the

Nation can hold out against us for far longer. There won't be a quick end to this war."

The Third Galactic War was already in its fourth Earth-standard year—a *quick end* was a comical thought. Watchtowers were the reason the Nation defeated Second Group a year earlier. *Solomon's Surprise* was one of Fleet's worst defeats.

If the Purists did that with twenty-year-old tech, what could they do with modernized stations?

"But the Sklorno can't reach Purist space," Plait said. "Even if the convoy makes it to New Whitok, that's too far away from Purist territory. The convoy would have to punch-out at New Earth, Jones, or Rodina, and recharge their drives—a full day's wait—before punching into Nation territory."

Travis had spent time on all three of those Union planets. Their relative proximity to the Purist Nation worlds of Solomon, Allah, and Stewart made for the most active front between the Union and the Nation.

New Whitok sat near the end of the teal thread extending across Union space. Plait was right—the math didn't work out. Ships couldn't just punch anywhere their captains liked. Two planets had to have similar mass signatures and had to be within a certain relatively short distance—galactically speaking, anyway, as even those "short" distances were so vast they defied Human comprehension.

"The Sklorno aren't punching from New Whitok." Lafferty zoomed in on the end of the teal thread. She made a spot pulse, a spot farther out from the core than New Whitok was, right at the teal thread's fuzzy edge. "Intel learned of this previously unknown punch-point, code-named *Junction Nest*, which is a half-day punch from New Whitok. Junction Nest is also a half-day punch from Stewart."

The nature of punch-drive tech meant if a ship traveled half an Earth-day, it took a half-day for the punch-drives to recharge. A full day's travel required a full day's recharge.

"They're punching right through Union territory," Brown said. "Cheeky bastards."

While that was technically true, no one "owned" punch-space. No one could. Only the vast distances involved—and the complex-bordering-on-mystical nature of finding two gravitational wells similar enough to allow punch transit in the first place—kept anyone from passing through any area they damn well pleased.

"For our primary objective, we will surface at Junction Nest," Lafferty said. "There, we will surprise and eliminate the convoy."

Travis felt a tingle creep up his arms. The audacious effort would utilize *Keeling*'s unique transdimensional ability.

Plait crossed his arms, stared into the orb.

"But Junction Nest is in sovereign Whitok territory," he said. "Taking the *Crypt* in there is a provocation. A big one. The Whitokians can't punch from New Whitok directly to Stewart, but they *can* reach New Earth, Jones, or Rodina."

The Kingdom hadn't directly attacked those Union planets. Partly because their fleet wasn't as strong as the Union's, and partly because New Whitok's distance from other Kingdom Worlds left it vulnerable to a concentrated Union assault. Similarly, the Union hadn't attacked New Whitok, because doing so would result in what amounted to a two-front war. Whitok and Union ships had engaged in hostilities, but not often—the delicate detente kept both sides from launching large-scale operations against each other.

A strike inside Kingdom territory, though, might change the game. This mission carried the potential of throwing gasoline on a fire already raging across the galaxy.

"The brass believes it's only a provocation if we attack *Whitokian* ships in Whitok territory," Lafferty said. "The mission is to hit the Sklorno convoy ships only."

Cat Brown rubbed at her face.

"Christ on a crutch, this political shit is complicated," she said. "So we dive into the Mud, travel into enemy territory, attack freighters hailing from a system we're *not* at war with and simultaneously avoid engaging vessels from a system that—technically—we *are* at war with. I got that right?"

Lafferty smiled. "Outstanding observations, Lieutenant Brown. We'll make an intel analyst out of you yet."

Brown waved both hands, palms out. "No thanks, Major. I prefer to blow things up, not sneak around in the dark."

And yet, *sneaking around* was the core of this mission.

Travis studied the map, his gaze flicking across the territories. A dangerous mission, yes, but he knew his ship and his crew—if executed correctly, this plan could succeed.

Sung took off his sweat-stained hat. He crunched it slowly in his hands, pockmarked face scowling in the way he did when any sailor screwed up.

"This is a bad idea," Sung said. "We'll be in enemy territory with no support. If we screw up, we put three planets at risk."

Three planets. Billions of Union citizens.

"We won't screw up," Lincoln said. "When we reach New Earth, we dive immediately. It will take us three days under to reach Junction Nest."

People groaned. Travis included. He couldn't help it.

"Captain," Lindros said, "will we get a short dive to let newbies experience the Mud before we're in it for three days? I have nine people who have no idea what's coming."

"I've got five of them." Brown rubbed her bald head—a nervous twitch of hers. Travis heard the sandpapery hiss of her stubble. "And it's *six* days. Three there and three back. This will be a shitshow."

Six days under. Things would get bad. Very bad. Everyone knew it. Travis wondered if he'd see giant insects again, or if he'd hear the voice of his dead grandmother—good ol' Meemaw, telling him how worthless he was, what a loser he was.

"No trial dive," Lincoln said. "The timeline is too tight. We need to reach Junction Nest while the Sklorno ships are recharging their punch-drives. If we're late to the party, and they're gone, the mission is a bust." She looked at Lafferty. "Tell them the rest."

The rest? How much worse could this get?

"Secondary objective," Lafferty said. "If possible, we are to board a Sklorno vessel, capture three Sklorno—alive—and bring them back to the *Keeling* for return to Gateway Station."

Dead silence.

Capture Sklorno *alive?* Translucent monsters. The galaxy's most violent species.

"You want to bring literal *man-eaters* on board," Chief Sung said, biting back anger. "And put them *where?* In the wardroom? They're *beasts*. They fight to the death."

"That's accounted for," Lafferty said. "*Ensign* Martigral is actually *Colonel* Martigral, a xenobiologist with a doctorate in Sklorno biology."

Lafferty kept her composure, as she always did, but Travis sensed anger in her. Anger and frustration. For the second time, Lafferty and her department missed that a crewmember was not who they claimed to be. Granted, Martigral hiding her rank wasn't the same as Nitzan Shamdi's murderous charade, but the subterfuge still clearly rattled the intel chief.

"Martigral will supervise construction of species-appropriate containment cells," Lafferty said. "She will also oversee the captives' care until we return to Gateway."

Travis reeled in the enormity of it all. Most sentients—not just Humans, but other species as well—thought of Sklorno as a scourge upon the galaxy. In 2520, thirty-seven years ago, Sklorno saturation-bombed the planet Withrit, killing billions of Whitokians and rendering the planet uninhabitable. That atrocity sparked the First Galactic War. Four years later, Sklorno did the same to Whitok itself, wiping out all life on that species' homeworld.

In 2533, Sklorno forces tried to do the same to New Whitok. There, the Whitokians soundly defeated them, bringing GW1 to an end. After that, the isolationist Sklorno avoided all outside contact until a year ago when they'd used a minor border altercation with the Prawatt as an excuse for all-out war.

"So if we're successful, we'll have Sklorno captives on board when we go transdim," Travis said. "How will the Mud affect them?"

Lafferty shrugged. "Hopefully Martigral has accounted for that."

Hopefully?

Sklorno were a truly alien species, woven from murder and insanity, so violent they had no formal relations with the Union or any other government Travis was aware of. Sklorno didn't communicate with other sentient species.

Except, apparently, with the Purist Nation.

"This Martigral situation is ridiculous," Colonel Hasik said. "I only have two people in my department, and now you tell me one of them isn't in my department at all? We'll be shorthanded. Why all the skullduggery? Why didn't Epperson just tell us Martigral's true purpose?"

Hasik's intensity was surprising. He'd been away for two weeks doing something for Epperson. Travis would have assumed Hasik already knew about Martigral's true purpose. At the very least, Hasik should have known why the admiral kept things secret.

"Colonel, we had a spy onboard," Travis said. "Maybe Epperson thinks there could be another. Don't forget the Purists knew where *Ishlangu* would be. This mission is obviously important enough the brass didn't want to take a chance that enemy ears might learn of it."

Travis noticed Lafferty's mouth press into a thin line, but only for a moment before her steady state, non-emotional expression returned. Like the rest of the executive staff, she hadn't been trusted with the big secret—she probably took that personally.

"I have other concerns," Lindros said. "To my knowledge, Major Lafferty, no one has ever taken a Sklorno alive. Admiral Epperson wants us to capture *three* of them, with only one platoon, seven members of which have zero combat experience?"

Travis wondered if Lindros counted himself among that number. He hadn't participated in the battle against the Purist task force.

"Correct," Lafferty said. "This is a massive opportunity to study an enemy should we wind up at war with them again."

Keeling's Raiders had been training to *fight* Sklorno, not capture them. Travis wondered how many Raiders would die.

"Two aggressive objectives," Lincoln said. "Tell them the third, Major."

Trav's jaw clenched. There was *more?*

"The tertiary objective is to capture cargo samples, if possible," Lafferty said. "We want to know what those upgrades entail. Also, BII's intel indicates food and supplies are part of the shipment. What kind of supplies? The Purists are having trouble feeding their military. What kind of food are the crickets sending? How sustainable is it? Can they continue a regular supply of it?"

Lindros crossed his arms. "Are you telling me we're not only supposed to capture Sklorno, but also bring back some cargo? Major Lafferty, my people are trained and equipped to *kill*, not *collect.*"

It was good to see Lindros show some backbone. He had a long way to go to earn the respect of his Raiders. Standing up for them in the face of command would help that cause. Chief Sung would undoubtedly let this little exchange slip next time he was in the mess with the knuckle-draggers.

"The tertiary objective is one of opportunity, Gary," Lincoln said. "If we have time to achieve it, we will achieve it. Should I determine we are under significant pressure from the enemy, I have the option of ignoring it."

As with most things on a Fleet warship, the final decision fell to the commanding officer. The only counter to Lincoln's absolute authority aboard *Keeling* was if the XO and the Intel Officer both decided to remove her from command.

"We have our orders," Lincoln said. "Sascha, while we're in transit to New Earth, you work with Martigral on containment cell construction. The cells must be completed and tested before we arrive. Gary, the mystery crates we stored in the small arms locker contain less-lethal weapons designed for use against Sklorno. Martigral will instruct the Raiders on their use. Everyone, get your people ready. This mission will require the best of every person in this crew."

A one-day punch from Gateway to New Earth.

Then, three days in the Mud.

Then, a mission to fight literal monsters. To *capture* them.

At least this shit would keep his mind off his divorce.

Mostly, anyway.

40

SASCHA

"Looks like no workouts for a while," Zhen Smith said.

Sascha nodded. "There's always pushups and sit-ups, Sergeant."

They stood outside Deck Three's small gym compartment as Smith's people—machinist mates Barnes Marchenko, Ri Chen, and Michael Camp—hustled to break down exercise equipment.

Just forward of the gym wall was the ladder down to Deck Four and Deck Five, and past that hatch to the port Type24 battery's barbette. Past those, the passageway dead-ended at a curved, coral-patterned copper bulkhead—the outer wall of the atrium's conical ceiling. Dark cubbyholes dotted the wall. The compartment aft of the gym was the atomizer, for getting rid of *Keeling*'s trash.

The galley was directly across the passageway from the gym, with the galley storage compartment forward and the crew mess aft. Sascha could hear some Raiders talking loudly in the mess.

The twenty-something Smith pulled a tattered, yellow rag from his pocket, used it to wipe sweat from his forehead. Everyone belowdecks sweated; some more than others, Smith more than most. His black hair looked like thick, wet paint.

"I looked over Martigral's plans," he said. "Putting three of her cells in here is like stuffing ten pounds of shit in a five-pound bag."

He wasn't wrong. The compartment was barely large enough for three narrow treadmills and the two small resistance arrays bolted to the wall. Martigral's three containment cells would barely fit.

"That's crazy Martigral is a damn colonel," Smith said. "I hear she's already bossy as hell."

The engineering crew had received the news of Martigral's true rank with little more than a disinterested shrug and a few mumbles of *that's above my pay grade*. Like Sascha, most people in the engineering department just wanted to serve their time aboard *Keeling* and survive. They'd complain about commands mysterious choices, but other than that, there was nothing they could do about them.

Marchenko rolled out one of the treadmills. "Still want these in cubbyholes, Chief? Should we take them to the landing bay? There's plenty of cubbyholes down there."

On the last voyage, it had been Smith calling Marchenko *chief*.

"No need to take them to the pouch." Smith nodded forward, to the curved bulkhead. "I marked three up there that should be large enough once you break the treadmills down."

Marchenko rolled the treadmill down the narrow passageway, his slight limp the only indication of his solid-titanium prosthetic leg.

The man was handling his demotion well, Sascha had to admit. He didn't remember making the copper blades, but he understood his hands created weapons that caused injuries and deaths to his crewmates. Chenk carried that guilt with him every minute of every day. Maybe that was what helped him obey orders from Smith, who had replaced him as Auxiliary Department Chief.

Ri Chen rolled out the next treadmill, followed by Camp with the third and last. Camp managed despite having one arm in a sling.

"This sucks," he mumbled, perhaps to himself, perhaps loud enough to be heard. "We're doomed and entombed and we have to move these stupid things."

Word had gotten out that Camp had put a blade through Jester Gillick's hand. Not that the BII creep didn't deserve it, always slinking around, trying to pal up to anyone and everyone. Lafferty had *shot* Camp. Like Marchenko, Camp was experienced with *Keeling*—he wasn't going anywhere.

Martigral came up the ladder.

"Lieutenant Kerkhoffs," she said, "give me an update on the containment cells."

Sascha gestured to Smith. "Aux Chief Smith here is—"

"I didn't ask *him*. I asked *you*."

Smooth as silk, Smith stepped into the workout compartment, grabbed a wrench, and started loosening bolts on a resistance array.

Smart man.

Martigral still wore tan BST coveralls, but she'd changed her rank tab, replacing the single-bar outline of a lowly ensign with a colonel's solid heptagram. From O_1 to O_5, just like that.

Sascha had to admit the higher rank suited Martigral; a forty-plus ensign with graying hair was just plain *weird*.

"It'll take another thirty minutes or so to get everything out of the compartment, Colonel," Sascha said. "Then we begin containment cell installation. Fabrication generated the modular frameworks per your specifications. They're working on the restraints now. The crysteel panes are next. Do you want us to examine the pumps you brought?"

One of Martigral's secret crates contained infusion pumps meant to maintain anesthesia levels that would keep the captive Sklorno unconscious.

"No need," Martigral said. "I'll examine those myself. See to it that workspace is made available for me in the fabrication compartment, I'll begin after I brief the Raiders on the less-lethal weapons. You're *certain* the cells will be completed and tested before we reach New Earth?"

Six hours to go before *Keeling* punched-out there.

"Absolutely certain, Colonel," Sascha said. "Do you really think your cells will keep the Sklorno alive?"

"Let's hope so," Martigral said. "All of our biological analysis is from posthumous study. The containment cell design is an educated guess. A *highly* educated guess, but a guess all the same."

Keeling's crew of 105 souls was being put at risk to capture living, sentient aliens, and keep those specimens alive all the way back to Gateway Station—for a *guess*. Sascha knew she should have been used to such things by now. She wasn't.

Sascha thought about the strange things she'd seen after the Purist missile punched a hole in the hull. She still hadn't told anyone about that. That cluster of bizarre eyes, looking back at her...

...it didn't matter. That had been a Mud-driven hallucination and nothing more.

"In transdim, the crew sometimes sees things," Sascha said. "Visions, hallucinations... crazy stuff. Do you know how transdim will affect the Sklorno captives?"

That question gave Martigral pause. She didn't look so smug anymore; now she looked worried. About her potential captives or herself, Sascha couldn't tell. What had she been told? What had she *not* been told?

"I suppose we will find out," she said. "Let me know when the cells are complete. You'll likely find me in the atrium. I apparently still have menial *duties* there until we acquire our specimens. It is a fascinating place, though. The whole ship is fascinating. You're lucky to serve here, Lieutenant."

Martigral descended the ladder to Deck Four.

"That's funny," Smith said from inside the gym compartment, "I don't *feel* lucky."

Neither did Sascha.

Turned out that ten sets of Deck PT sucked.

John stood shoulder to shoulder with Abs and Yo-Yo. The taller Beaver and Reiner stood behind them.

The slight increase in size of the Raider's training compartment allowed just enough room for the entire platoon to gather together. Still, it was a snuggly, hot and humid fit for thirty-seven people. Thirty-eight, if you counted ensign-turned-colonel Martigral. The crew had adopted a phrase for the close proximities brought on by the ship's narrow confines—*Keeling Cozy*.

Lieutenant Lindros stood before an easel holding a large pad of paper. The first page was blank, hiding what lay beneath. Martigral stood to his right, her tan BST coveralls out of place among all the Raider charcoal gray. Sands stood to the Lieutenant's left, a closed crate at his feet.

Real paper. That scared John more than damn near anything else. Electronics like flexipaper, computers, or any kind of presentation gear potentially left a record somewhere, deep in software and silicon. People could crack that shit, find that info. With real paper, though, you write on it, burn it, and what was written becomes nothing but a figment of Human memory.

John's arms and shoulders ached and burned. So did his legs. And his stomach. Sands had screamed at John and Beaver through all ten sets. Sands had a set of lungs on him, no doubt about that. They'd finished two hours ago, and John was still exhausted. Goddamn Beaver was happy and chipper, as if he hadn't worked out at all. The guy was a friggin' mutant.

Yo-Yo leaned closer to John. "Corporal Bennett, what's that egghead doing here? She's not a Raider."

Yo-Yo probably thought *egghead* was an insult. Funny. He wasn't exactly the sharpest knife in the drawer.

"I suspect she'll tell us about the mission," John said. "Be quiet and listen."

Lindros squared his shoulders. Was the LT putting on weight? He was still skinny, *far* too skinny for a Raider, but his coveralls didn't hang quite as much as they had. Maybe it was just the lighting that made it look that way.

"We'll reach New Earth soon," Lindros said, trying to look each Raider in the eye as he spoke. "From there, we dive immediately. Considering the... ah... *difficulties* that may come while in transdim, Captain Lincoln wants you fully briefed before we go under."

John gave his people a fast, hard glare, a silent warning for them to keep their traps shut. Abshire barely suppressed a snicker. Beaver was holding his breath to stop from laughing. Both men, along with John, had tackled a naked, raving Lindros and chained him to his bunk.

Beaver and Abs weren't the only Warthogs struggling to keep laughter in check. Lindros could see that just as well as John could. The Raiders who'd served on the last deployment simply did not respect the LT. That was hard for him to take—it showed on his face.

John felt bad for the guy, but a Raider's respect was earned, not gifted because of rank.

"*Keeling*'s mission is to attack a convoy of Sklorno cargo vessels," Lindros said. "We Raiders will board one of those vessels and capture three prisoners of war."

The words hit John like a punch. This couldn't be real.

"Uh, LT?" John raised his hand. "Do you mean to tell us we're supposed to take three Sklorno *alive*?"

It sounded even crazier when spoken out loud.

"That is correct," Lindros said.

Capture Sklorno. That kind of idiotic order could only come from someone who'd never seen a Sklorno up close. Never *fought* one. Never watched those slobbering beasts attack. Never heard a mortally wounded squadmate with his chest-plate cracked open, screaming as hideous Sklorno raspers tore flesh from his bones—

A hand on his shoulder; John jerked, almost turned to strike but realized it was Reiner's hand.

The packed training room snapped back into focus.

Raiders, staring at him. Lindros, one eyebrow raised.

"Sorry, LT." John made a fist, thumped it against his chest twice. "A little heartburn."

Had he made a sound? He didn't know. Hopefully the heartburn line covered whatever noise he'd made.

Lindros nodded, smiled. "Never-ending mushrooms don't agree with me, either, Corporal."

A small, polite laugh from the packed-in Raiders.

Did LT know John had blanked out? Probably not. As far as John knew, Lindros had never faced combat. And that long-ago moment that sometimes sliced through John's thoughts—flooding him with fear and hate—happened before the lieutenant had even been born.

"Back to it," Lindros said. "Fleet has never taken Sklorno captives alive. They fight to the death. They do not surrender. They do not abandon ship. Those individual Sklorno found wounded and too weak to fight don't survive long because we don't know how to provide proper medical care for that species. To capture one, we need to render them unconscious. To achieve that objective, we have specialized, less-lethal ammo for this mission. Sergeant Sands, show them."

Sands opened the crate. Inside were eight RR-36 magazines made of translucent red plastic instead of the usual clear.

"These mags contain Sklorno stunner rounds," Sands said. "Two members of each fire team will be issued a red magazine. Once we breach the hull, one member of each team will load it and be the first to fire upon any unarmored Sklorno, incapacitating them and allowing us to extricate the prisoner from the vessel. When that magazine is exhausted, the second team member will load their red mag and become the primary shooter."

Spreading the specialized ammunition between two Raiders per team meant that if one member got smoked, the other could still utilize the rounds, extending the unit's ability to deliver less-lethal fire.

"Knockout rounds?" Abbas Basara shook his bearded cinderblock of a head. "You gotta be shitting us, LT."

Two steps brought Sands nose-to-nose with Basara.

"Spec Basara, you are not smart enough to have an opinion," Sands said. "In the future, if you feel compelled to share your uneducated point of view, take some advice from your ol' trusty platoon sergeant." Sands leaned in close to Basara's left ear. "That advice is, *shut the fuck up* instead." Sands snapped back to his usual ramrod-straight posture. "All of you will listen and listen good. You've never faced a Sklorno. I have. They are uglier than a two-peckered billy goat and ten times as mean. The lieutenant is giving us information that could save your sorry ass, the asses of your fellow Raiders, and most importantly, *my* perfectly-sculpted posterior. So lock in and listen."

He returned to his spot and shut the ammo case.

Lindros continued. "Colonel Martigral is the strategic lead on this mission. Colonel, the floor is yours."

Martigral stepped in front of the easel. She flipped the first page over the top, revealing a cutaway drawing of a Sklorno including muscles, organs, and skeletal structure.

"This is our objective," she said.

Sklorno truly were nasty things. Teardrop shaped bodies. Back-folded legs with heavy thighs and long, strong forelegs ending in splayed, five-toed feet. Two and a half meters tall, over three if they extended their legs straight. Powerful runners, their stride echoed that of an ostrich, the long, outstretched upper body balanced by a trailing tail that was itself a meter in length. Coarse black fur jutted from every joint: knees, ankle area, and toe segments.

The drawing captured the strangest thing of all about the species—their translucent bodies. Mostly clear chitin covered see-through flesh, organs, and black bones. A naked Sklorno looked like an elec-tron-scan of a bizarre creature constructed from the parts of many animals, some known, some imaginary.

Like ghostly pythons, two coils of boneless muscle dangled from the cylindrical body—the Sklorno version of arms. John had seen those tapering limbs work rifles and combat knives. As strong as the arms of any man, those coils could drive a blade through TASH armor if the blade's angle was just-so.

The tip of the teardrop body extended upward in a long, flexible neck. Shiny, coarse black fur covered the hideous, softball-sized head. The four pink eyestalks jutting from the fur could each look in any direction. Damn near impossible to sneak up on a cricket. Eyestalks were the only Sklorno body part with color. In individuals, those colors ranged through a variety of reds, from bright magenta to dull crimson, much the same way Human skin carried various hues and tones.

A chitinous chin-plate sat just below the head. From under that plate dangled two curled raspers, extensions of flesh densely studded with small, sharp teeth. When feeding, a Sklorno's raspers darted in and out like a snake's flickering tongue.

"Union forces have never captured a Sklorno alive," Martigral said. "Nor, as far as we know, has any other government. We are going to change that."

She tapped the drawing's head.

"Sklorno do not have the brain-inside-skull biological configuration endemic across most sentient species. Instead, their brain is two clusters of specialized nerves running along either side of their central spine—" she tapped the trunk twice "—*here*, and *here*. That is why there have been documented reports of Sklorno continuing to fight even after their heads have been cut off."

A few Raiders glanced John's way, as if to see if he thought Martigral was full of shit. She wasn't. One of those *documented reports* had been his own.

Martigral's finger traced the teardrop body.

"Stunner rounds deliver a specific amount of voltage calculated to temporarily overwhelm the Sklorno nervous system, *if* they hit this center mass. We believe a hit to a leg may cause temporary paralysis in that leg, but it is unlikely it will knock the individual unconscious. We don't know what a hit to an unarmored Sklorno head will do. Maybe nothing. Maybe knock them out. Maybe kill them."

May cause. We don't know.

Was John hearing what he thought he was hearing?

He raised a hand.

Martigral saw him. She smiled. "Yes, Corporal Bennett. Go ahead."

John knew smiles like that. It was the rare look of someone who knew his combat history, who thought of him as a *war hero*.

"Colonel," John said, "am I to understand the stunner rounds have not been tested on living Sklorno?"

Martigral's smile ebbed, but didn't vanish.

"That is correct," she said.

A soft, angry grumble rolled through the assembled Raiders.

"This is bullshit," Biggie Bang said. She stood packed in along with her flight crew. "You expect Raiders to put a goddamn Sklorno in *my* bird, and I fly it back *here*? These rounds haven't been tested. How long would they *hypothetically* be stunned for? What if they knock out a cricket for, like, a minute or two, and they wake up in my Ochthera's troop compartment?"

Lindros glanced at Sands.

"Warrant Bang, not another word," Sands barked. "The next person who talks out of turn is going to get my boot so far up their ass they will taste the dog shit I stepped in back on Gateway."

The silence returned.

"I understand your concerns," Martigral said. "But let me assure you, if you place these rounds on-target, they *will* put Sklorno down for an estimated minimum time of thirty-one minutes."

An *estimated* thirty-one minutes? Pretty specific for an estimation. John agreed with Biggie—this was some bullshit.

"I hope you warriors understand the magnitude of this mission," Martigral said. "*Keeling's* Raiders have the chance to be the first in history to capture live specimens of this violent, alien species. This is a major opportunity to learn critical information about an enemy of the Union."

John saw the Raiders exchanging quick glances: raised eyebrows, slight smiles, small nods. Raiders—and clams, for the most part—could handle uncertainty and danger if they understood the importance of a mission. This mission was important indeed. That and promises of glory were always strong motivators for knuckle-draggers.

These kids had no idea what they would soon face. No idea at all.

John raised his hand again. Martigral again nodded at him.

"Colonel, what's the range on the stunner rounds? And how many rounds do we have available for test-firing, to get our people used to them?"

"Effective accurate range is thirty meters," Martigral said. "That's calibrated for standard Sklorno shipboard fake-grav and atmosphere."

That was something, at least; few ship passageways were longer than thirty meters.

"As for test-firing, we don't have enough rounds." Martigral nodded toward the ammo crate. "That's all I was allowed to bring."

Eight mags, fifty twenty-millimeter rounds per mag. Four hundred rounds, total. Four hundred *untested* rounds.

"I guess we better be good shots," Reiner mumbled.

Sands looked her way. "Did I just hear you speak out of turn, Corporal Reiner?"

"No, Sergeant Sands," Reiner said. "I didn't say anything."

An absolutely brilliant evasion. Reiner was no egghead, either.

"Sklorno are difficult to restrain, due to their physiology," Martigral said. "You can't cuff their tentacle arms, for example. Chin-plate restraints are complicated and will take some time to apply. Without that restraint, their dangerous raspers can hurt you. Fortunately, we have a simple, fast solution. Master Sergeant?"

Sands reached into the crate and pulled out a long, white mesh bag, holding it up for all to see.

"Once your target is stunned, fold their legs to their body and place the Sklorno inside a crysteel-mesh contracting bag," Martigral said. "While a Sklorno can generate around five thousand newtons of kick force—enough to let them leap six meters high and run faster than any Human—when folded up and bound they can generate very little. Who would like to volunteer to be our Sklorno stand-in?"

Beaver shoved past so fast John stumbled a bit.

"Oh!" Beaver waved like a kid in class. "Can I, Colonel Martigral? Can I be the Sklorno?"

Martigral looked him up and down, taking in his size.

"You'll do fine, Spec," she said. "Step into this bag, then squat with your arms around your knees."

Grinning like a fool, Beaver complied. When he squatted down, she pulled the bags slack up over his head so he was completely inside.

"The bags have a red button and a green button." She showed the buttons, which were side by side on the bag's open end. "Press the green button three times to relax the material. Press the red button, on the other hand..."

She tapped the red button three times. With a soft hiss, the material contracted, mummifying Beaver. He looked like a shrink-wrapped Thanksgiving turkey. Martigral used one finger to push his shoulder—he toppled over.

The platoon laughed.

"This is *awesome*," Beaver yelled. "I can't move at all!"

Martigral pressed the green button three times—the bag relaxed. Beaver squirmed out. Still grinning, he returned to his spot behind John.

Sands picked up the bag. "Each Raider will carry one bag." He crumpled the bag, pressing it down to a lump of fabric barely bigger than his fist. "It fits in a standard magazine pouch. It's a two-state phase-shift material. Once it contracts, it holds shape without power. It's fully analog, so no EMP or STC interference can unlock it."

The master sergeant spoke with confidence, like he knew all there was to know about the material, but John knew Sands—he'd probably memorized what Martigral had told him minutes earlier.

"Master Sergeant, I assume the bags are untested against Sklorno," John said. "What do we do if the bags fail to restrain them?"

"You do what Raiders always do, Corporal," Sands said. "You improvise, you overcome, you adapt. I suggest carrying some extra zip-ties, just in case."

Chief Taylor raised a hand. "We got plenty extra in the landing bay."

Raiders laughed—Taylor wasn't shy about fixing any loose-fitting gear with zip-ties and duct tape.

Sands had tried to lighten the mood a bit but Lindros did not find the banter amusing.

The LT took a step forward.

"We will train with the bags until we can stuff an eighty-kilogram man inside and activate it one-handed in total darkness," he said. "This mission relies on proper handling of the prisoners. Colonel Martigral, anything else to say?"

He took a step back.

Martigral met every Raider's eyes.

"I need you all to understand something," she said. "Most of you have never faced Sklorno. You've seen the movies, I'm sure. *Some* movies portray them as sympathetic characters, make it seem as if

Sklorno think like we do, feel emotions like we do. I am here to tell you *they do not*. Sklorno don't have our sense of self-preservation. Their nature puts the group above the individual. That's why they don't think twice about fighting to the death. Do not underestimate how vicious they are, how *fast* they are, or the intensity with which they will attack."

There was strength in her voice. Strength and conviction. Middle-aged Martigral was more of a natural leader than Lindros, by far.

"I obviously won't be joining you on your mission, but I'll be doing my part onboard," she said. "Good luck out there."

Martigral left the compartment, sliding between the bigger, younger Raiders. She didn't ask for permission to leave, because she didn't need it—the small woman outranked everyone present.

Lindros nodded to Sands, who scowled at the group.

"Before bag training, we will drill a stack formation with the less-lethal shooter at the front," Sands said. "This is a no-armor walk-through. I want to make sure you newbies understand your duties. Line up by teams at the weapons cage. Let's move it."

The Raiders started filtering into the rig room.

John gripped Reiner's elbow. "Corporal, let's take a moment to discuss your attitude." He guided her toward the bunks, away from the others. He spoke close and quiet, so only she could hear. "When you touched my shoulder, what was I doing?"

"*Growling*," Reiner said, equaling his volume. "Kind of scary, actually."

It wasn't a *sparkle* in her eyes, it was a gun-barrel-glint of recognition. She, too, had combat experience. She'd understood he was slipping away—like a true comrade in arms, she'd brought him back and done so with subtlety that saved John from embarrassment, from the shame of *not being in control*.

"Thank you," he said. "You... ah... where did you fight—"

"It won't happen again, Corporal Bennett," Reiner said sharply, loudly, a surprise finishing touch on their pretend dressing-down.

She walked away and slipped into the weapons cage queue with Abshire, Beaver, and Yo-Yo.

Reiner was young enough to be his daughter, sure—but John was old. She was a full-grown Raider, maybe carrying her own echoes of blood, her own scars, her own demons. She didn't want to talk about them. John respected that. He didn't like to talk about his, either.

With decades of practice, he pushed his own memories into the black hole of time and joined his team.

42

BIGGIE

Curled up on her bunk, Biggie waited until the last possible moment.

Doc Watson had come through with a small baggie of zapinoforol pills. No prescription, no label, no way to trace it back to Watson if Biggie got busted with them.

Biggie held one of the pills in her closed fist. Would the zappie help with the transdim insanity, or make it worse? She'd find out soon enough.

They'd punched-out at New Earth without issue. Such a time to be alive, when no one gave faster than light travel a second thought. Now, though, came the part people *did* worry about, and with good reason—time to wallow in the Mud.

She saw Sands, PXO Winter, and Old Man Bennett coming her way. Biggie turned in her bunk so she faced the bulkhead. She popped the pill in her mouth and dry swallowed just as the trio arrived.

"Your turn, Biggie," Sands said. "On your back."

The pill burned in her throat.

"Damn, Master Sergeant," Biggie said, "I was thinking doggy style instead of missionary this time."

"Har-har," Sands said. "Such a comedian. Assume the position."

There was little space between Biggie's bunk and the one above it, which meant someone had to lean over her (or rather, lean *on* her) to secure her right wrist to the bulkhead post. Winter got that job, so it wasn't a man pressing down. Not that gender mattered in this particular case, as everyone knew the PXO worked both sides of the street.

While Winter secured Biggie's right wrist, Bennett strapped down her left ankle.

Some people didn't remember the violence they committed while in the Mud. Biggie did. She vividly recalled trying to strangle John Bennett to death, remembered the excitement fluttering through her chest, remembered the voices telling her to *hurt*, to *kill*.

Fortunately, Bennett's plastic dog-tag lanyard snapped before his windpipe did. He'd barely suffered a welt. Biggie, on the other hand, received an immediate, Raider-style beat-down. Which she'd deserved. Her bruises had lasted for days.

"Secure," Winter said.

"Secure," Bennett said.

They stepped back, allowing room for Sands to check both restraints.

"Good," he said. "Do the rest."

Bennett and Winter switched places. Bennett strapped down Biggie's left wrist while Winter leaned across Biggie's thighs to secure her right ankle.

"Say, PXO," Biggie said, "while you're down there, why don't you check my oil?"

Winter laughed. "Maybe some other time." She finished securing the ankle, gave the restraint a quick tug to test it, backed out, and stood straight. "I got my own tie-down party to deal with."

PXO Winter had lost her shit in the Mud, too. She tried to kill Sands with one of Marchenko's copper shivs. She'd come damn close to succeeding, as evidenced by the nasty scar on the platoon sergeant's right cheek.

Sands checked Biggie's restraints.

"Maa*aaa*gnificent," he said. "Try to sleep, Bang. Someone will be back to check on you after a few hours."

Sands said *someone* would check on her because he had no idea if he'd be sane enough to do it or if he'd be yet another gibbering, violent fool hellbent on murder.

That was the Mud in a nutshell—you never knew how someone would react.

Winter and Sands moved on. Bennett put a hand on Biggie's shoulder.

"You got this," he said. "Piece of cake."

Biggie wasn't one for rah-rah speeches or motivational sayings... but it was different with Bennett. He was old enough to be her grandfather. A badass grandfather chiseled out of a block of granite, sure, but a grandfather nonetheless. He was a killer with kind eyes, the type of soldier who would do anything for his comrades.

"Thanks, Old Man," she said. "Sorry about trying to kill you that one time."

Bennett smiled. "Come on now, Biggie—you're a Raider. If you'd *really* tried to kill me, I'd be dead."

He gave her shoulder a squeeze, then walked off after Sands and Winter.

She'd tried to murder him, yet he blew it off like it was nothing. Old Man Bennett was one helluva good guy.

Biggie felt the first slight head-spin as the zappie started to take effect. By the time *Keeling* went under, she'd already be off to never-never land. Hopefully that would keep the Mud's insanity at bay.

Hopefully.

43

TRAVIS

Just like the first time Travis prepped for transdim, Colonel Zvanut Hasik was the last one into the CIC. Why Lincoln let the man get away with his lackadaisical attitude—not to mention his poor hygiene and, more often than not, the alcohol on his breath—was beyond Trav's ability to understand.

Hasik ascended into the xeno loft, which occupied the CIC's rear-port corner. He sat at the station and pulled on his headset.

Travis faced forward at the XO's position on the command slate's left side.

"Captain, the xeno station is manned," he said.

"Very well," Lincoln said from her position at the command slate's right.

They each had acceleration chairs at their station. Between the chairs was the command slate's compact communications center: two handsets connected by coiled wire to the thick housing, which contained a plethora of dials and switches for the various main circuits connected throughout the ship—all analog, no digital allowed. At various points below Deck Two, where the superstructure met *Keeling*'s copper hull, the comms connections integrated with the "veins" that had replaced belowdecks wiring. So far, everything worked flawlessly.

If the MC system went down, Travis and Lincoln would use the row of sound-powered phones mounted in the overhead above the slate. The six-century-old technology worked even in the nastiest conflicting STC fields.

"XO," Lincoln said, "prepare us for transdim."

She was letting him conduct the dive.

"Preparing for transdim, aye-aye, Captain."

He felt good about the CIC crew. Most of those manning the various stations had gone transdim before. The only person who had not was Spec-2 Daria Byrnes, formerly of the *Ishlangu*. She was third in the ECM rotation behind Corporal Colel Citlalmina, the lead ECM operator who sat at the station, and Spec-3 Brinson Sorro, who was likely strapped down to his rack, as were most standby personnel. Byrnes seemed to be handling her first dive well.

Most "abnormal behavior," as the med team called the often-violent episodes, occurred during the first thirty to forty minutes of a dive. If Sorro was fine after that, he'd be let out, as would most others strapped down.

For now, Byrnes stood by Citlalmina to watch and learn. Hopefully Byrnes wouldn't go psycho. If she did, she'd be handled by Akil Daniels and Jester Gillick, who were in the Intel Loft with Anne Lafferty. Of course, any one of those three spooks could come up on the losing end of the sanity dice. As could Travis. As could Lincoln. Lincoln looked unfazed, but looking unfazed was part of a captain's job.

Would Travis see the nav-orb turn into a giant spider? Would Meemaw's bitter, hateful voice ring though his head?

He'd find out in minutes.

Travis called up the transdim entry checklist on the command slate. He knew it by heart, but Lincoln preferred to see it there as a reference.

"Darsat," Travis said, "any contacts in our sphere?"

Corporal Kanya Saetang checked her station's displays.

"No contacts in darsat range, XO," she said.

DARSAT—an initialism for *Detection and Ranging, Space and Time*—could identify a ship's gravitational signature with high accuracy up to 400 klicks, and with reasonable accuracy up to 600. Checking within that range was always job-one when entering real-space or preparing to exit it.

"Very well," Travis said. "Signals, report nearby contacts."

Signals utilized radar, LiDAR, optics, and transponder interrogation to detect and classify nearby vessels. As such, Signals offered far greater detection range than darsat—at least in non-combat conditions.

"Multiple contacts, all friendly." Comms Chief Frederick Madison manned the signals console. "Locus Alpha, PUV *Parmula*, bearing starboard zero-two-four, low quadrant, range five thousand kilometers. Locus Bravo, PUV *Mako*, bearing port one-six-five, high quadrant, range five thousand, two hundred kilometers. Locus Charlie, PUV *Hathor*, same bearing, range five thousand, five hundred kilometers. Logging all in-orb. No additional contacts in detection range. No active comms. No pending hail requests."

Trav looked to the nav-orb just forward of the command slate. The arrow representing *Keeling* lay dead center. Icons marking *Parmula*, a frigate, *Mako*, a light cruiser, and *Hathor*, a carrier, appeared in the orb at their relative positions to *Keeling*. The orb's farthest range line was 50,000 klicks out, which meant New Earth—at 200,000 klicks—wasn't visible. A shame. That green-brown dot was always a sight to behold.

Three warships, no civilian traffic—Fleet Command had cleared the zone for the *Crypt*'s brief stopover.

"ECM, any sign we're being tracked?" Travis asked.

"Negative, XO," Citlalmina said. "I'm showing no active sensors holding us, probability of passive detection less than zero-point-five percent. We're ghosting."

Ghosting—slang for flying unwatched, with no sensors tracking

Keeling and no one trying to find her. Travis didn't love jargon on the deck, but Citlalmina had earned her latitude. She was sharp and reliable; her little sparks of quiet enthusiasm weren't worth correcting.

On with the checklist.

"Raider Liaison, any concerns?"

Master Sergeant Sands manned the station. Lieutenant Lindros —who seemed to be the only person aboard affected by the Mud every single dive—was strapped down in his bunk.

"No concerns, XO," Lindros said.

Travis turned to face the Intel Loft, which was in the CIC's back-starboard-aft corner.

"Intel, any political concerns?"

Lafferty stood. She didn't have to stand, but she always did.

"No concerns at this time, XO," she said, then sat down again.

With threat recognition, positioning, and politics out of the way, Travis went through the checklist, calling out the formulaic questions and receiving the corresponding answers: no concerns from operations; all guns unmanned, their crews inside the ship; torpedo tubes locked down, their crews out of the torpedo bays; all on-duty personnel at their stations; most off duty personnel strapped down in their racks.

Almost go-time.

"Xeno," Travis said, "coupler status?"

"Transdim coupler in the green," Colonel Hasik said.

Even though Travis knew he'd covered everything, he ran his fingertip down the slate's checklist, double-checking. Lincoln liked that.

"Captain, there are no threats or pending communications," he said. "The coupler is in the green. We are ready to enter transdim."

Lincoln placed her hands on the slate.

"Stay sharp, people," she said. "We never know what will happen in transdim. We never know what we will see within our hull. Try hard to remember that over the next three days. ECM, take us to blackout mode."

"Blackout mode, aye-aye," Citlalmina said.

All screens showing the *Keeling*'s exterior blinked out. The orb's data faded away.

"XO, carry on," Lincoln said.

"Xeno," Travis said, "ready the coupler."

"Readying the coupler, aye-aye, XO." Hasik lifted his station's sound-powered phone handset. "Atrium, Xeno. Make ready to activate transdim." A pause. Hasik heard something that made his eyes flick to Travis, then he turned away slightly, spoke softly but harshly. "That doesn't matter. Just *do it*."

"Xeno," Travis said, "is there a problem?"

Hasik covered up the handset's mouthpiece.

"No, XO, no problem. We'll be ready in just a moment."

BETHANY

Hasik's voice came from the sound-powered phone's grill-covered speaker. His words burbled with controlled anger.

"Lieutenant, prep the coupler," he said. "*Now.*"

Bethany's face flushed, internal heat driven by frustration. Hasik had told to her to *make sure* Martigral was trained to use the protuberance. Martigral wasn't paying attention, so Bethany had informed Hasik—her department head—of the problem. Now her CO was mad at her for doing what she was told?

"Aye-aye," Bethany said. "Initiating transdim."

She set the receiver in its cradle, looked at Martigral.

"Colonel, you should watch this closely," Bethany said. "Lives may depend on your ability to perform this procedure."

Mindy Martigral leaned on the handrail of the protuberance platform. She pulled at her uniform collar, wiped beads of sweat from her forehead.

"I'm having a hot flash," she said. "And it's already an oven in here. Just do the thing, Lieutenant. I'll only have to endure this *diving* business one more time, then you'll be free of me forever."

It made no sense. Yes, Martigral was here for the mission to capture Sklorno, but did she not care about the miracle that was

Keeling? About the impossible things the ship could do? How could Martigral not be fascinated by this, *mesmerized* by it?

And she called herself a scientist...

Bethany stepped to the protuberance, the device that activated *Keeling's* ability to slide between dimensions. Like an abstract sculpture made from blown glass, the protuberance's multicolored bumps, spikes, and protrusions glowed like the heartstone itself, the still-unknown energy inside both structures swirling and pulsing with gold-gray light.

The late Jenn Hathorn had referred to the protuberance as "a diseased demon dick." Bethany pushed that memory away—she didn't like to think of Hathorn.

Bethany performed the now-familiar ritual of sending *Keeling* into transdim: a push on the blue-green knob, a touch on the gnarled amber bump, a turn of the silvery curve, a stroke across a tan/ivory-red indent, a push on a neon-orange ridge, move the gnarled lump on top from left to right, bend the translucent indigo extension downward.

She completed those steps, leaving only one motion yet to perform.

Bethany stepped to the sound-powered phone and lifted the handset.

"Xeno, Atrium," she said. "Transdim coupler ready."

Hasik's voice came back instantly. "Transdim drive ready, aye. Initiate on my mark."

Again hearing the unwanted echo of a dead woman's crass words, Bethany looked at Martigral.

"Hold onto your balls, Colonel. You're about to see something wonderful."

What a joy, what a *privilege.*

"Atrium, Xeno," Hasik said. "*Mark.*"

Bethany cupped the gnarled nub on the protuberance's left side. She squeezed.

45

ANNE

Anne Lafferty's hands locked down on the edge of her Intel Loft console, squeezed so tight her fingertips bent back against the knuckles.

The CIC flooded with light, with color.

So *many* colors.

Reds and blues and greens and yellows, and colors she could not describe, colors which did not exist, *could* not exist.

Shimmers and sheens on equipment, blazing up from slates, radiating from the brass and crysteel clock-timers mounted near the overhead. Light emanated from crewmembers as well: a deep purple in Ellis; orangish from Draper, the pilot; Erickson at the nav station, blossoming with pale-red and a color Anne did not know. When people moved, they moved languidly, colors trailing their path.

In one of Anne's undercover operations, back when she'd been a lowly intel ensign, she'd infiltrated a drug ring aboard PUV *Latobius*. With a crew of eight thousand souls, the carrier was a city unto itself. Anne had posed as a gunner. To gain trust with the dealers on board, she'd taken several kinds of drugs—including acid.

This was similar to that experience. Sort of. She'd seen tracers while on acid, watched bulkheads sag, witnessed solid gear waver like liquid. She'd seen light amplified in ways which made no sense. But that moment compared to this was like a single sparkler at noon compared to a full-on fireworks extravaganza in the blackest of night.

Someone barked like a dog. No, like a *seal*. Anne had seen seals, once, after they'd been brought back from extinction on Earth and modified to live in Rodina's oceans. Why was someone barking like a seal?

"Intel," XO Ellis said, "remove pilot Draper from the CIC, get him down to the infirmary. Ops, get a replacement in here."

Intel? That was Anne's department. Wasn't it? No, it couldn't be. She was an ensign. She hadn't even met the Intel Department on *Latobius*, nor would she. She was a gunner, she was supposed to—

"Major, are you with us?"

A quiet voice from just in front of her and to her left. Akil Daniels. But Daniels wasn't on *Latobius*. He was stationed on... on...

Anne closed her eyes. The colors went away.

Transdim. She was in transdim.

"Major?"

Anne opened her eyes. Daniels looked at her, concern on his face. He looked normal, but the man next to him...

Anne hissed in a sharp, short breath.

Jester Gillick glowed a sickly green. Not quite neon. Split-pea soup. The color lashed from him like solar flares, sickening all they touched, nauseating Anne.

And then, his color winked out.

At one of the two pilot seats, forward in the CIC, Colin Draper violently slapped his hands together and barked like a seal, so loud it made Anne wince. To Draper's right, lead pilot Lars Nygard leaned away from him, as far as he could without getting out of his chair.

"Warrant Daniels," XO Ellis said, "remove Major Lafferty from the CIC. Corporal Gillick, get pilot—

"*No*," Anne snapped. "I'm fine now. Daniels, Gillick, get Draper out of the CIC, immediately."

There was a pregnant pause as Gillick and Daniels hesitated, once again trapped between the conflicting orders of Ellis and Anne.

"Do as Major Lafferty says," the XO said. "Snap to it."

Gillick and Daniels hurried down from the Intel Loft, ran past the command slate, the nav-orb, and the nav station. They each grabbed one of Draper's arms and dragged him out of his chair. He continued to make the seal noise and started kicking his feet, together, like a seal's flippers flapping in the water, as they hauled him out of the CIC.

Anne met the XO's eyes. He gave her the slightest of nods, then faced forward. He could have had her removed from her station. Instead, he'd backed her up even though she'd been lost in the... was it a hallucination?

Never before had Anne felt transdim's adverse effects.

Was that what she'd just endured?

At the command slate, Captain Lincoln turned, stared at Anne with those emotionless, calculating eyes. XO Ellis clearly believed Anne was fine, but did the captain?

Lincoln faced forward.

The nav-orb glowed with the strangeness that was the Mud, a milky, opaline haze coalescing in places as if by black-hole dots of internal gravity, forming flowing strands of crimson and ivory which merged into monstrous, shuddering rivers coursing in all possible directions. Those grotesque currents glimmered with pulses of light— some colors Anne knew, some that defied anything she'd ever seen

Anything, until her transdim-fueled acid-trip.

And in that trip, the way Gillick had glowed...

46

BIGGIE

"Wake up, Biggie. It's your lucky day."

Biggie heard the voice as if through a long tunnel or shouted from a distant mountaintop. It cut through, though, because it was a voice she respected and—quite often—longed to hear.

She opened her eyes, which took some effort. Zappies are a helluva drug.

Old Man Bennett looked down at her, his face all craggy and wise.

"Hey, Bennett," she said. "Why you gotta wake a girl up?"

Biggie felt like her mouth was full of marbles.

"Because you've been under for eight hours," he said. "PXO Winter's babbling endlessly about chicken soup, of all things, and Dork is doing what Dork does in the Mud. That means Sands is in command, and he doesn't want you to wet the bed."

The words unlocked something; an uncomfortable pain in her bladder told Biggie she had to pee. Badly.

"Ah," Biggie said. "You're my hall pass again?"

She had to be strapped down for transdim, but she was one of the lucky ones in that they didn't knock her out and catheterize her, like they did with Brainiac Akagi, Clifton Bishop, and Chris Brogan.

Because of what those three had done previously in-dim, they got drugged for the duration, whereas Biggie and her only *semi*-violent ilk got to be escorted to the head.

"Not just a hall pass this time," Old Man Bennett said. "Sands gave you your yard privileges back. Just stay clear of the weight room. Got it?"

It was oddly fitting the man she'd tried to kill was the one to tell her she didn't have to be strapped down any longer.

"Got it," Biggie said.

Bennett undid the straps, gave her shoulder a squeeze, and moved on.

Jesus, what a good guy he was.

Biggie sat up. Most of the bunks were occupied, Raiders sleeping to pass their time in the Mud. There was Akagi, the crawler co-pilot strapped down in medically assisted slumber. When you kill someone by caving their skull in with a spanner, as Akagi had done to crawler pilot Bhola Nessa a few weeks back, your yard privileges were *permanently* revoked.

Biggie stood. She wavered, gripped her bunk to keep from falling. She was still high as fuck. Needed more sleep. But not here, not around people she'd tried to kill, and who might, at any time, try to kill her.

She grabbed her blankets off her bunk, draped them around her shoulders. She'd hit the head, then go find that cubbyhole outside the infirmary. If no one was already in it, she'd crawl in, pop half a zappie, and sleep until she had to pee again.

47

TRAVIS

The wardroom's air seemed sullen, a cloying, clinging effect of the Mud lurking outside *Keeling*'s hull. But that same air carried something that lifted everyone's spirits—the wonderful scent of baking bread wafting from the small, attached galley where Combat Cook prepared a meal. Coffee steaming from mycoware cups added to the aroma.

Two days into the dive and Travis had yet to suffer a hallucination. No dead grandmother. No visions of giant bugs. Best of all, no dreams about a carnivorous newborn daughter.

Others, though, had succumbed to the Mud's capricious influence.

"Corporal Draper remains under sedation," Doc Hammersmith said. "Signaler Luyang suffered a compound fracture after an attack by Spec-Two Byrnes, one of the *Ishlangu* replacements. Byrnes is also sedated. Spec-Three Hardy in fire control, also from *Ishlangu*, is comatose and unresponsive. We're watching her. Four Raiders remain restrained. One of which, of course, is Lieutenant Lindros."

Hammersmith delivered the report in her normal tone: raspy and disinterested. She wasn't known for her bedside manner. The doc had gained a little weight while in port. More muscle in her thin shoulders, maybe, although with her thick neck she still looked egg-shaped.

"Forty-eight standard hours in-dim and only four sailors down," Lincoln said. "A relative victory compared to past dives. Could the crew be getting acclimated to the Mud?"

"I doubt it, Captain," Hammersmith said. "My hunch is that this is merely a lull. We'll likely see more problems on day three."

Hammersmith didn't know what caused the hallucinations any more than Travis did, any more than anyone did. Random mental instability—a helluva thing for the medical team to try and manage.

"Thank you, Doc," Lincoln said. "That will be all."

Hammersmith left the wardroom.

Lincoln sat at the head of the table, Travis on her right, Lafferty on her left. To Travis's right sat Sascha Kerkhoffs and Alex Plait. To Lafferty's left, Cat Brown. To Brown's left, which Lindros usually occupied for command staff meetings, sat Master Sergeant Francis Sands, the Raider platoon's third-in-command. Both Lindros and Winter were drugged and restrained, Winter due to hallucinations, Lindros to keep him from streaking.

Colonel Mindy Martigral sat at the other end of the table.

Eight made for a tight fit. The wardroom's walls were so close, people couldn't fully push their chairs back; if Kerkhoffs or Plait needed to leave, Travis had to get out so they could slide over his seat. *Keeling Cozy* indeed.

Bradley Henry entered, his apron smeared with spots of faded brown and pale green, a tall stack of eight covered mycoware plates stacked in his arms. He was a touch too large for the door and had to twist his shoulders to pass through.

"Sautéed green bean with garlic," he said. "Pass 'em down but don't take the lid off till I says so."

Part lights-out cook, part showman, Combat Cook was one of *Keeling*'s few steady sources of joy.

Travis lifted the top four off Henry's stack, the disposable, mushroom-fiber material squeaking in time. He set the bottom plate in front of him, passed the next three to Kerkhoffs. The food smelled amazing.

"I believe you meant green *beans*," Martigral said as she set her covered plate in front of her. "*Plural.*"

Combat Cook laughed. "You'll see. All right, remove the lids and tuck 'em under your plate."

Everyone did so. Curls of steam rose up in an eight-part visual symphony.

Travis hadn't known how hungry he was until he stared at a fresh-baked roll, cubed tofu in a white cream sauce, and one single, butter-and-garlic glazed kidney-shaped green bean the size of a fist.

"On *Keeling*, one pea pod feeds you all," Henry said. "Captain, need anything else?"

Lincoln smiled up at him. "No. Thank you, Bradley. That will be all. Eat up, people."

The big cook left the wardroom.

Travis used his mycoware fork and knife to slice into the huge bean. He took his first bite. Fantastic. For all of *Keeling*'s shortcomings, the atrium's constant production of fresh produce meant the crew ate like royalty.

At least the *Crypt* offered one thing better than home—Trav's soon-to-be ex-wife couldn't cook worth a damn.

"We have one more day in the Mud," Lincoln said, chewing as she spoke. "With luck, we won't suffer further casualties. Even if we do, I aim to accomplish both of our mission objectives. Colonel Martigral, are the containment cells ready?"

Martigral sat up straighter. "Yes, Captain. Your engineering department is far from the best I've seen, but I'm confident that what we have will get the job done."

Travis saw expressions of annoyance spread across the command staff, felt the same himself.

"That's truly a rousing endorsement of my people's work," Kerkhoffs said, slowly turning her roll in one hand. "You're too kind, Colonel."

Martigral snorted. "If you want praise, Lieutenant, I suggest you do praiseworthy work."

Lincoln leaned forward, elbows on the table.

"Kerkhoffs' team fabricated holding cells for an alien species, from scratch, using only available materials on *Keeling*, and did so in short order," the captain said. "That is commendation-level work, Colonel Martigral. If you can't see that, I look forward to achieving this mission and getting you off my ship."

Martigral's mouth opened, closed. She clearly wasn't used to being lectured.

"Captain, in *my* department back home, I only accept top-level work," Martigral said. "Admiral Epperson knows this."

Travis almost winced. Did this academic think Epperson's opinion mattered out here?

Without breaking her icy stare at Martigral, Lincoln picked up her fork, stabbed a chunk of bean, put it in her mouth, and chewed slowly. The deliberate action stretched out for five seconds, then ten, adding to the tension. *Keeling*'s command staff continued eating, albeit quietly. The tiny squeaks of mycoware sounded like baby birds in a nest.

Through it all, Kerkhoffs couldn't fully suppress a small smile. Travis knew how she felt. When the Hero of Capizzi 7 had your back, it was an incredible feeling.

"Colonel Martigral, you are not in *your* department," Lincoln said. "You are in *my ship*. When my people deliver for you, you will thank them for their efforts."

Martigral set her fork and knife on her plate.

"Lieutenant Kerkhoffs, please thank your team for their work," she said. "The containment cells meet my specified requirements."

Kerkhoffs nodded once, swirled her roll in garlic-butter sauce.

"I will, Colonel," she said.

Lincoln picked up her utensils and dug into her dinner like she wanted to make up for the time she'd lost casually dressing down Martigral.

"Master Sergeant Sands," she said, "how is Lieutenant Lindros?"

Sands straightened. Travis could just make out the fading suture marks outlining the fresh scar on his cheek.

"Lieutenant Lindros is currently indisposed, Captain," he said. "We are giving him all the loving care that is to be expected from iron-eating Raiders."

Sands had a kind way of stating things. As soon as *Keeling* entered the Mud, Lindros had—yet again—stripped buck naked and run laps around Raider Land. Apparently, bringing him down and restraining him was among the platoon's least-favorite tasks. Among the sailors, there were rumors that Lindros was... *gifted*, in certain areas.

Lincoln chewed as she nodded toward Lafferty.

"Anne, you've had two full days to further examine our intel. Any new thoughts?"

Lafferty's hair caught Trav's attention. It had grown out some since the first mission. She always kept it combed back, every strand as meticulous as her uniform. Now, though, her red hair looked slightly rumpled.

He'd almost had her removed from the CIC. He was sure she'd seen something, but what? Was the Mud affecting her performance? Her ability to make decisions? As she was one-third of the command triumvirate, her stability mattered.

As did Lincoln's.

As did Trav's.

"The intel is good," Lafferty said. "But only as good as it can be considering our language and cultural barriers with the Sklorno. Nothing is one hundred percent certain. When we surface, we need to be ready for anything."

Lincoln nodded. "We will be. Say we surface to a worst-case situation. What should we expect?"

Lafferty reached under her chair, pulled out a three-ring binder. She pushed her plate aside, set the binder atop the table, and opened it.

"I have a flexipaper breakdown," she said. "It's not to leave the Spookhouse. You'll read it there, under my supervision. Here's the high-level. BII is confident we'll face Leafcutter-class freighters. Sklorno tend to mass-produce one type of ship for each particular need. Leafcutters are the only punch-capable freighter they currently use. They're big ships—eight hundred meters long, beam of one hundred twenty-two meters, height of forty-eight meters, an estimated mass of five hundred and sixty thousand tonnes."

She gave that a moment to settle. Leafcutters had more than twice the size of a typical heavy hauler flying under Planetary Union colors. Twice the size and four times the cargo capacity.

Lafferty continued.

"Cargo volume of a Leafcutter is approximately one-point-four million tonnes. Intel expects four to six Leafcutters in this convoy."

Plait let out a low whistle. "*Six?* That's over eight million tonnes cargo capacity."

"Eight-point-four," Lafferty said. "Quite a haul."

All that cargo, transported some 40,000 lightyears across the Milky Way, from one sentient species to another, via a third sentient species' sovereign territory, all while war raged across the galaxy. Travis couldn't help but admire the audacity and creativity of the plan.

"Here's where it gets interesting," Lafferty said. "Because the Whitok Kingdom will not allow Sklorno or Purist warships in their territory, any escort vessels will be Whitokian."

Cat Brown raised a questioning finger. "Escort ships we are *not* supposed to engage, yeah?"

"That's correct," Lafferty said. "The probable ships we are likely to encounter but not engage include Caiman-class, the Whitokian corvette, Croc-class, their version of a destroyer, and possibly a Terrapin-class, a light cruiser. Could be any one of those, or a multi-ship combination. Our intel isn't as reliable on that side of things."

Whitokians were an amphibious species. Fleet's code-names for their various warships always involved amphibious animals from Earth.

"We can handle one ship from any of those classes," Brown said. "Even two at a time, I think." She rubbed the top of her bald head. "But is there any chance we'll face a Komodo?"

By and large and class by class, Whitokian craft weren't on par with their Union, Tower, Leekee, or even Purist counterparts. But there was one exception: the Komodo heavy cruiser. Whitokians designed it as part of a technology exchange with those assholes in the League of Planets, the Union's biggest economic rival. Komodo cruisers not only possessed punishing armament and heavy armor, they were a state-of-the-art lovechild between a big cruiser and a small carrier, boasting a compliment of four APCs and eight Salamander-class fighters.

"Highly unlikely," Lafferty said. "The Kingdom only has three Komodos—*Shell Splitter*, *Tail Spike*, and *Mud Lurker*. Those are functional translations from their Whitokian names. We have grav-sigs on all three. We believe they are all deployed elsewhere."

While *Keeling* wasn't supposed to engage Whitokian ships, the Whitokian ships might not leave Lincoln any choice. Everything depended on what ships were where when *Keeling* came out of trans-dim. In a straight-up fight, the *Crypt* lass might be able to best a Caiman or a Croc, maybe even a Terrapin. Against a Komodo, though, *Keeling* would quickly wind up a scattered mass of wreckage and bodies.

"Where we surface is critical," Travis said. "If there are escort ships, they should be close to the freighters, but Whitokian tactics are a crap-shoot. We don't know what kind of formation they might take up."

Lafferty raised an eyebrow. "You're privy to Whitokian tactics, XO?"

Maybe she thought such things were classified. Some details probably were, but not all.

"I did a paper on Whitokian tactics in the Academy," Travis said.

"They don't follow common-sense doctrine. Sometimes their creative thinking leaves them horribly exposed, sometimes they wind up with a huge advantage."

Brown groaned. "Great. Just what we need. An unpredictable foe. What about Sklorno tactics, XO? You do a paper on those, too?"

"As a matter of fact, I did," Travis said. "I have it on file. I'll send it to each of you. Read it. Sklorno warship tactics are fast and brutal. But if Major Lafferty is right, there won't *be* any Sklorno warships. If their freighters are attacked, they'll run. If the freighters are boarded, every crewmember will fight to the death no matter what the odds they face. If a freighter's bridge is in danger of being captured, their commander will likely scuttle the ship, killing all aboard."

Sands rapped his knuckles on the table.

"Let's make sure we don't breach near the bridge, then," he said. "Agreed?"

Sands would likely be among the boarding party and therefore at great risk, yet he made light of the situation. Travis wished, and not for the first time, that Francis "the Book" Sands was in charge of the Raider platoon instead of Gary "Dork" Lindros.

"Copy that, Master Sergeant," Lincoln said. "We need to surface far enough away from the escorts, whatever they are, land Raiders on a freighter so they can capture Sklorno, get Raiders and captives alike aboard *Keeling*, destroy as many freighters as we can in the process, then dive before we're fired upon."

A set of dangerous objectives complicated by the fact that *Keeling*'s transdim drive wasn't a sure thing—sometimes it fizzled, leaving the ship stuck either in realspace or in the Mud. Odds were good it would work both for surfacing and the subsequent dive, but those odds were *not* 100 percent.

"We'll evaluate the tactical environment when we reach the deployment area," Lincoln said. "If the Whitokians provided enough escort ships, and there isn't a good angle to surface and execute our mission objectives, we may have no choice but to stay in the Mud and head for home."

Hopefully Lincoln would do that, but Travis had his doubts—Lincoln wasn't the type of commander to leave empty-handed.

Plait finished his last bite. He put his napkin on his plate, rubbed his belly.

"We have Whitokian translation software onboard," he said. "We can talk to them if we need to, at least before the STC soup gets thick, but are we still incapable of speaking to Sklorno? I mean, if the Purists seem to be able to do it, why can't we?"

Lincoln stood, walked to the coffee urn. "Good question." She refilled her cup. "How fortunate we are that the Union's foremost expert on the species is sitting at the end of the table. Colonel Martigral, your thoughts?"

Martigral eased back in her chair. Travis had a suspicion that was a practice pose she used on underlings. Or students, perhaps, when she lectured.

"We don't know how the Purists brokered this deal," she said. "I'm confident no Human government can communicate with the Sklorno. Not even the League of Planets. Our best guess is that the Whitokians or the Ki Rebel Establishment had a communication breakthrough they are keeping secret. Both governments border the Sklorno Dynasty, after all, and have centuries more experience with the species than we do. At any rate, I'm a xenobiologist, not a linguist."

She was Fleet's *foremost expert* on the species, yet didn't seem to care about the language barrier at all.

In that regard, at least, she wasn't alone. Many a sailor, Raider, and striker thought of the Sklorno as primitive savages at best, beasts at worst, despite the fact the species controlled seven planets with a combined population estimated at over 200 billion.

Brown crossed her arms, looked at Lafferty.

"Epperson is risking his prized ship and all our lives on this operation," Brown said. "Seeing as no one—including our *foremost expert* here—can communicate with Sklorno or speak their language, how did we get reliable intel on their shipping route? And on what warships might be escorting it?"

Lafferty clearly didn't like the question.

"I'm not at liberty to reveal that information," she said. "What I can tell you is we have high confidence in the accuracy of our intel."

Normally, the intel chief was as cool as the other side of the pillow. Completely unreadable. This time, though, Trav saw something in her reaction—she *didn't know* how the Union obtained the intel. She wasn't read-in on that particular operation, which pissed her off.

Maybe her father ran the Bureau of Information and Intelligence, maybe he pulled strings for his daughter here and there, but in this particular case, Anne Lafferty was just another downstream operative, isolated from the real decision makers.

"Thank you all for your time," Lincoln said. "We have twenty-four hours before we surface for the attack. Everyone, coordinate with Major Lafferty to read her report on our probable Whitokian opposition. Make sure your people get proper rest. And keep your eyes out for additional Mud-generated problems. I need everyone sharp. Finish your meals, then you are dismissed."

SASCHA

Sascha was the boss of engineering. She could have ordered others to scrape foil and then gone about her business, checking back only to see if the job was done correctly, to nitpick or threaten if it was not. But that wasn't her leadership style. No matter what the task, she preferred to roll up her sleeves and work alongside her people. It was the best way to bond with them.

Sadly, though, *bonding* also involved another sailor tradition as old as the Age of Sail itself—telling stories, some of which might not be entirely true.

"So she hikes up her skirt," Marchenko said. "She shows me her ass, and she tells me, *why the hell else would I have a pineapple tattoo here?*"

When it came to telling tales that might contain an exaggeration or two, Corporal Barnes Marchenko was a Grade-A champion.

"You're so full of shit, your eyes are the color of turds," Adam Ledford said. "Three women you *just happened* to sleep with in one weekend did *not* have matching tats, Corporal."

Marchenko stopped scraping. "Chief, you wound me. I didn't say they were *matching*. I mean, *that* would be hard to believe."

Ledford laughed, shook his head, and kept scraping.

As far as Sascha knew, the red-bearded propulsion chief had never suffered a hallucination. That didn't mean he wouldn't eventually succumb to a waking nightmare or an unexpected trip to Crazy Town. In the Mud, that could happen to anyone at any time. Hopefully he had some natural resistance, because if she went down, Ledford would run engineering.

Marchenko, on the other hand, needed to be watched. People had died because of shit he'd done in transdim. The fact that he didn't remember any of it didn't make those sailors any less dead.

Sascha realized Marchenko was sitting there, not scraping the chemjet control station's composite frame, which glistened with thin copper tendrils.

"Chenk, back at it," she said. "I want this place clean before the XO calls another drill."

Marchenko grunted, returned to scraping the thin foil creeping over everything in engineering control. The oddly shaped compartment felt like a copper cave, even more so than the crew mess did. Designers had found places for all the standard gear: chemjet control station; comm station and handset; chem-battery control; auxiliary power management; electrical control; fire suppression systems; gravity management; and oxygen generation control among them.

On any other ship in Fleet, those systems would likely be spread across three or four individual compartments, each at least twice the size of this one. On *Keeling*, though, where space was at a premium, all of that gear was tightly crammed into racks bolted to the curving copper bulkheads. Engineering control looked like a pawnshop jammed with obsolete hardware and wiring.

Three personal restraint harnesses were wedged between racks as well. Engineers here needed the ability to man multiple stations, not be tied to an acceleration chair. The harnesses had cables attached to retracting spools mounted on the low overhead and at various points on the racks, cables that allowed some freedom of movement but would lock down upon sudden acceleration or maneuvering, preventing the sailor from being thrown about. Being in a harness was never pleasant, but in combat it kept people alive and—mostly—able to do their jobs.

Ledford stood, stretched to the side.

"Eng, I'm off watch as of ten minutes ago," he said. "Mind if I get some chow and hit the rack?"

She'd lost track of time. They'd reach the combat zone soon. She needed her people as rested as they could be.

"Go ahead, Chief," Sascha said. "Chenk and I will finish up here."

Marchenko grunted again. He didn't much care for the busy work. No one in engineering did. Sascha included.

Ledford left the compartment. Marchenko stopped scraping, watched for a few seconds to be sure the man wasn't coming back.

"All right, Chenk," Sascha said. "What's on your mind?"

Marchenko hurried over to kneel next to her.

"I've been thinking about that dense area in the midsection," he said. "Maybe it's got something to do with how the ship operates in transdim. I can use the scanners we have onboard to make a 3-D model of it. Maybe we'll see something."

He had forgotten the ship's golden rule.

"I tried scanning it," Sascha said. "Colonel Hasik shut me down. Remember, Chenk—we're not supposed to ask questions about the ship."

That was because of Epperson's ridiculous secrecy. Not even the people who operated the ship were allowed to know too much about it.

"What about the tail section?" Marchenko had missed Sascha's point, or perhaps he just ignored it. "That area is just as dense. How can we be expected to maintain this ship if we don't know what purpose those areas serve?"

A question that was never far from Sascha's thoughts. She remembered going to the XO's quarters, telling him of her effort to scan the tail section. He was not happy with her. She remembered his words, remembered them exactly: *No one told you to scan anything,*

Lieutenant, so I'll pretend I didn't hear what you just said, and you will stop *scanning.*

"I tried," she said. "The XO shut me down for that one."

Chenk started scraping again. "You're telling me you don't want to know?"

Nothing could be further from the truth. Sascha *hated* the secrecy. She often wondered if it would wind up getting people killed, wind up getting the ship destroyed.

"Of course I want to know," she said. "I'm working on getting permission. We just need to wait for the right time. Now leave it alone and let's get this done."

Marchenko grunted again. It was not a happy grunt.

The 1MC alert sounded.

"This is the XO. Vacsuit emergency drill. I repeat, vacsuit emergency drill. You have thirty seconds."

Chenk threw down his scraper. "I'm so *sick* of drills."

That didn't stop him from hurrying to a narrow vacsuit bin built into the racks. He threw the first blue suit to Sascha, grabbed one for himself.

She, too, hated the drills, but she donned her vacsuit quickly.

Even as she did, though, Chenk's claim that he could scan the dense areas lingered in her mind. Could he create an electronic model of their structure and composition?

Maybe, when they got back to port, she could find a way to make it happen.

Maybe.

Someone screamed a madman's endless scream. Someone else laughed hysterically. Others struggled against their restraints. Still others snored, strapped down in their bunks yet oblivious to the craziness raging throughout Raider Land.

John stared at the hookah-smoking rat-shrimp sitting atop PXO Winter's head. She didn't react to it, which meant it wasn't really there. It stared back at John, the same wide head, silvery bulb eyes, and tan-fur-covered shell John hallucinated on the last voyage, but this one's smoke-spilling hookah looked like a steel cowboy boot instead of a gutted RR-36.

It wasn't real. It sure as hell *looked* real, and the sweet, burning tobacco *smelled* real, but since no one else saw it, John knew it was in his head alone.

"Corporal Bennett, your team looks okay," Winter said, her gaze flicking from John to Beaver, Abshire, Reiner, and Yo-Yo, who all stood with him. "Any of you seeing things?"

Winter suffered mild hallucinations on the first day—something about the ship's bulkheads forming a human face that tried to talk to her—but she'd had no problems on the second day. Sands released her. Since Lindros was still restrained and babbling nonsensical, high-pitched noises, Winter was in command.

"I don't see anything weird, PXO," Yo-Yo said, his eyes wide with that *I'm about to go into combat for the first time* look.

Beaver and Abs shook their heads.

"I don't think I am," Corporal Reiner said.

She sounded disappointed.

"You'd know if you were," John said. "PXO, Alpha-Two is good to go."

Winter nodded in agreement.

"TASH up," she said. "We're approaching the target point. The XO wants a crawler ready to launch the second we surface. Biggie is heading to the pouch. Sands will lead. I'll cobble together another fire team and join you at the weapons locker."

Winter hurried off, grabbing upright Raiders as she went, telling them to join her forward of the racks. John's cowboy-boot-boofing hallucinatory pal was apparently going along for the ride.

Good. Maybe the ugly thing would stay with her.

After Winter found five sane Raiders to join John's squad, she'd manage those now freed of their hallucinations and make sure the rest—those who had gotten violent—were brought out of chemically induced sleep. Ten minutes, maybe fifteen before the second crawler loaded up.

John faced his team. "You heard the PXO. Armor up."

Beaver was off like a shot, sprinting for the rig room. Abs and Reiner jogged after him. Yo-Yo, though, stood there, his wide eyes seemingly magnified by his dark skin.

"Spec Ayodele," John said, "get to the rig room and TASH up."

The kid was afraid. Good. Hopefully that would help him pay attention.

"We really doing this, Corporal Bennett? The Sklorno... they're *monsters*. Am I going to die?"

A question John had been asked many times by many Raiders. A question he'd learned to not answer truthfully.

"Stick to your training, listen to me, and you'll make it." John put his hand on the young man's shoulder. "Time to do what they pay you to do, Yo-Yo. Let's go."

Colel Citlalmina stood up from her ECM station, ripped off her vacsuit glove, yanked her sleeve up to her elbow, then bit down on her forearm. Signals Chief Madison reached to stop her—too late. She jerked her head back and spit a mouthful of arm-meat in Madison's face.

"Comms, man your station," Travis barked. "Intel, remove darsat operator Citlalmina and get her to the infirmary. Ops, get a replacement in here, now."

Blood dribbling down his face, Madison turned back to his comms station.

Citlalmina sucked hungrily at her open wound like a kid getting as much milkshake as she could in one pull, then leaned her head back and gargled her own blood.

Operations department head Alex Plait called for a replacement. This was Plait's third deployment aboard *Keeling*. Maybe he was seeing visions at that very moment, just like Travis was, but if so, Plait didn't let it stop him from doing his job.

As Jester Gillick and Ri Chen—a machinist's mate manning the Intel Loft in place of Akil Daniels, who was currently sedated—hurried to Citlalmina, Travis tried to wish away the head-sized hornet crawling across the command slate. The yellow and black body shimmered with a purplish sheen. Its finger-long stinger gleamed with wet poison.

Hammersmith had been right. As the third day rolled on, more and more crewmembers suffered hallucinations. The CIC's aft hatch might as well have been a revolving door for all the staff replacements. Mere minutes from surfacing in enemy territory and hopefully striking the shipping convoy, half of the first-teamers were out of commission, and half of their replacements had also succumbed to madness.

Travis forced himself to stand his ground, to not back away from the big, malevolent hornet. He glanced to his right, at Lincoln. Was she seeing things? Hard to say. She stared into the nav-orb, her vacsuit-gloved hands flat on the command slate. The hornet crawled across her fingers—she didn't seem to notice.

Gillick and Chen hauled Citlalmina out of the CIC, leaving a trail of her blood in their wake.

"Hakobyan," Lincoln said, "activate system and begin DTR sweep."

Darsat, *distance and range, space and time*, detected gravitational variations caused by ships. DTR, *darsat to realspace*, provided one of *Keeling*'s biggest tactical advantages—she could sometimes detect ships in realspace while those ships could not see into the Mud.

"Activating darsat, aye," Gurgen Hakobyan said. "Commencing darsat-to-realspace sweep."

Of *Keeling*'s trio of darsat operators, Hakobyan was by far the worst. Corporal Saetang, the Lead Darsat Operator, had passed out for reasons unknown. Her replacement, Spec-3 Carmel Waldren, had shouted that she saw the devil, then went into convulsions and vomited all over the darsat station. Terrible timing to have Hakobyan now manning it as the attack run drew near.

Brinson Sorro, Citlalmina's replacement, ran into the CIC and took his place at the empty ECM station. He pulled the station's headset and went to work. The Spec-3 continued to impress, both in demeanor and skill.

The huge hornet spread big, gleaming wings. The wings blurred with motion. With a sound like an idling lawnmower, the insect flew to the forward clock-timer, started clicking its stinger against the brass housing.

"Conn, darsat activated," Hakobyan said. "Realspace detection strength is *strong*. No... it's *very* strong. Detection radius is... looks like four-zero-zero kilometers."

Travis felt the nearly electric buzz rip through the compartment. The CIC crew turnover was bad luck, but *very strong* DTR detection out to 400 klicks was the exact opposite. *Keeling* was in the assigned place, at the assigned time, and her ability to detect enemy ships was operating at maximum range.

That fucking *hornet*... he knew it wasn't real, yet that didn't stop the fear, the revulsion, the need to *run away*. Travis closed his eyes, mentally went through the fundamentals of contact-tracking to distract himself.

Dead ahead was 0°. Two arcs, port and starboard, each beginning at 1° and ending at 179°, defined side-to-side position along *Keeling*'s lengthwise axis. Directly astern was marked at 180°. All vertical measurements referenced the ship's horizontal plane. *Elevation*, from 0° to +90°, indicated contacts above that plane—0° at level, +90° directly overhead. *Declination*, from 0° to -90°, indicated contacts below. A contact's exact bearing combined port or starboard angle with elevation or declination. When precision wasn't needed, or wasn't available, ancient ship terms like *starboard-bow-low* or *port-quarter-low* still gave a rough bearing.

"Conn, Darsat! Realspace contacts acquired!"

Hakobyan, speaking too fast and too loud.

Travis opened his eyes. The hornet was still there, but his heart rate had lowered—along with his anxiety.

"*Locus Alpha*, class unknown, average bearing, port zero-four-seven," Hakobyan said. "Average declination, zero-four-six. Average range, eighty-seven kilometers. *Locus Bravo*, class unknown, average bearing, port zero-two-one. Average declination, zero-four-seven. Average range, one-five-four kilometers. Calculating course and speed."

Average. In realspace, darsat could pinpoint exact locations and ranges. With DTR, though, location readings fluctuated from one moment to the next. Travis imagined it was like trying to pinpoint a sun's location based only on reflections from choppy water, except the choppy surface wasn't flat—it extended infinitely outward in all directions.

"Darsat, put contacts in-orb," Lincoln said. "Keep searching. And *calm down.*"

Hakobyan nodded. "Calm down. Aye-aye, Captain."

The hornet buzzed away from the forward clock-timer. Hovering, it turned in place—purple-black eyes locked onto Travis.

With agonizing slowness, the hornet flew toward the command slate.

It's not real... it's not real...

In the orb's nerve-branch soup depiction of the Mud, two labeled clusters of icons appeared. The clusters—white hexagonal outlines representing unknown contacts—were grouped tighter than Travis had seen in previous DTR readings, indicative of higher location probability accuracy. A metal arrow representing *Keeling* sat dead center in the orb. Contacts always appeared in relation to *Keeling*'s orientation: cluster *Locus Alpha* was to port, behind and below *Keeling*; cluster *Locus Bravo*, also to port, ahead and below.

"Nav," Lincoln said, "plot us a course to come up ten kilometers aft of *Locus Alpha*."

Nav Chief Erickson acknowledged the order. He pulled a stretch of paper from his station's thick roll and started mapping out the course change.

On the first deployment, Lincoln said she preferred to keep at least 150 kilometers away from a contact. Ten klicks was insanely tight for her, even if *Keeling* was in an entirely different dimensional membrane.

The slow-moving hornet drew closer. Its stinger leaked poison that dripped down to the deck, flowed into the streaks of Citlalmina's blood.

It's not real... it's not real...

Travis leaned close to Lincoln, tried to ignore the awful sound of the buzzing wings.

"Ten kilometers," he said. "That's right on top of them."

It wasn't his place to directly question his captain's orders, but she encouraged his quiet questions. She wanted him to learn her ways.

"If *Locus Alpha* is a freighter, I want to shorten the sortie travel time," Lincoln said quietly. "And I want to take advantage of the DTR strength to see if we can spot more contacts."

Erickson called out course changes to the pilot. Trav watched the orb. The metal arrow never moved. Instead, everything in the orb moved around it, showing relative positions in relation to *Keeling*. As *Keeling* maneuvered, the clusters denoting *Locus Alpha* and *Bravo* seemed to move up and rotate right until they were lined up directly ahead of the arrow's point.

The distance between *Keeling* and *Locus Alpha* shortened.

"Conn, two new realspace contact acquired," Hakobyan said. "*Locus Charlie*, class unknown, average bearing, dead ahead, average declination, zero-four-seven, average distance three-six-one kilometers. *Locus Delta*, class unknown, average bearing, dead ahead, average declination, zero-four-seven, average distance... uh... four-zero-eight kilometers. Putting contacts in-orb."

Four hundred and eight kilometers. That was slightly beyond DTR's supposed maximum range. A *very strong* signal strength indeed.

In the orb, clusters of white hexagon outlines appeared for *Locus Charlie* and *Locus Delta*. Sure enough, they continued the straight line set by the first two contacts.

Keeling closed in aft of *Locus Alpha*.

The thick hornet flew over the nav-orb, hovered just forward of the command slate. So *big*. Travis focused on the slate's scrolling readout, tried to ignore the thing's hellish buzz.

"Darsat," Lincoln said, "I need grav-signatures on those ships."

Hakobyan's right hand went to his headset's earpiece. "I... I'm working on it, Captain." Light from his monitors gleamed off his sweaty face. "The signal is... ah... it's a little fuzzy."

Travis saw Lincoln's gloved hands curl into fists. With a *very strong* signal, Citlalmina or Waldren probably would have identified the grav-sigs by now.

Were all four contacts Leafcutters? Or were one or more of them Whitokian warships? Could all four be warships? Could this be a trap to lure *Keeling* in?

Lincoln's patience ran out. "Chief Lafferty, assist darsat, I need to know."

Lafferty started down the Intel Loft steps, but before she reached the bottom, Hakobyan turned sharply in his chair, his hand still on his headset.

"Grav-signatures acquired! *Locus Alpha* and *Locus Bravo* are both Leafcutter-class freighters. Changing IDs to *Leafcutter Alpha* and *Leafcutter Bravo*. Working on *Locus Charlie* and *Delta*, but I think they're also Leafcutters!"

"Understood," Lincoln said. "Stop yelling, Darsat. I won't warn you again. Intel, return to your post."

Hakobyan quickly turned back to his station and leaned toward his monitors, perhaps more to try and shrink away from Lincoln's controlled anger than to read the data there.

In the orb, the labels for *Locus Alpha* and *Two* changed to *Leafcutter Alpha* and *Two*. Their icons changed from clusters of hollow white hexagons to clusters of solid red circles—the icon for an enemy ship.

The captain again put her hands flat on the command slate. She stared into the orb. The CIC crew seemed to hold its collective breath, waiting on her decision, but Travis knew his CO's mind—she would attack. First, though, she had to follow Fleet protocol.

"Intel," Lincoln said, "we were ordered to this location to seek out and destroy Sklorno Leafcutter-class cargo ships. We have identified two of the four contacts in our range as such. If we enter realspace from this position, we will be in Whitok sovereign territory. Current status of relations with both the Sklorno Dynasty and the Whitok Kingdom?"

Travis thought this bit of theater was stupid beyond measure. To prevent political disasters, regulations specified a ship's acting head of intel had to approve an attack—even when *Keeling* had been sent to perform this exact mission, and even when said acting head of intel had received no new communications since they'd departed New Earth.

An idiotic policy, but that was Fleet for you.

"We have full approval to initiate hostile action against clearly identified Sklorno freighters," Lafferty said. "We do *not* have approval to engage Whitokian vessels of any kind."

The hornet dropped onto the command slate. Its dead eyes stared at Travis, its pincers *clack-clacked* hungrily.

It's not real... it's not real...

"Xeno," Lincoln said, "prepare to surface on my mark."

"Aye-aye, preparing to surface," Hasik called out from the xeno loft.

"Guns," Lincoln said, "upon surfacing, have crews man all turrets."

The Type24 crews waited inside their battery's barbette, which were built over sphincters. The barbettes were outside *Keeling's* main hull but offered no exterior view of the Mud. A cozy fit for the three-person crews, huddled together, waiting for either the order to climb up to the battery proper or go back inside the hull.

Dardanos Leeds, the artillery chief, repeated Lincoln's order.

"Weps, load Mark16s in tubes one through four," Lincoln said. "Load Mark14 scramblers in tubes five and six. Nav, plot a realspace course right down the line, two-zero-zero meters to their starboard sides. ECM, prepare to jam all frequencies, prepare to calculate a tether formula on *Leafcutter-One*."

A flurry of acknowledgments.

At the ECM station, Sorro turned to look at Lincoln.

"Captain, a Leafcutter is fifty-five times our mass," he said. "We can't slow it down."

Travis wanted to admonish Sorro for openly questioning a command, but he couldn't take his eyes off the hornet as it slowly crawled closer, moving one jointed limb at a time, its antennae twitching...

"We're not slowing it down," Lincoln said. "Follow my orders, ECM."

"Aye-aye, Captain." Sorro faced his station.

The hornet was only centimeters away now. Travis saw his reflection in each of its glossy eyes. He fought the urge to turn and run, fought it with all the will he possessed.

The long antennae angled forward... their tips tapped inquisitively against Trav's chest...

"Xeno," Lincoln said. "Take us out of transdim. Surface, surface, surface."

ANNE

"Taking us out of transdim, aye-aye," Colonel Hasik said.

Anne heard him call down to the atrium, heard his soft words echo across the CIC as if invisible angels repeated them in faint, flute-like tones.

The Mud, fucking with her. What Anne heard, what she saw, and what she *felt*. She wasn't sure if her skin remained attached to her body, or if it had separated from her muscles, and now she wore herself like a comfortable, formfitting shroud.

Some of the CIC crew looked normal, sitting at their stations in their vacsuits, visored hoods hanging between their shoulder blades. Some of them, though, did *not* look normal. Those people *fluoresced*, like a mostly-spent neon bulb in a dark room, and this time, it wasn't just split-pea-green Gillick.

Before she'd been hauled away, Colel Citlalmina had seemed to smolder, as if lava coursed through her veins. A cherry red color subsumed Alex Plait. Sora Garcia, the pilot who'd replaced Colin Draper after he went into convulsions and bit his tongue until blood ran down his chin, glinted as if an emerald candle burned within her chest. XO Ellis shone the brightest of all, a fading-flashlight-yellow matched by an intense spot above the command slate.

The nav-orb became a sphere of violently flickering static.

Colors faded from the glowing crew, and as they did, a thought struck Anne, held her breathless—were those people hallucinating, and she could *see* that they were? Was that what the glows meant?

Could she *see* that?

"We're clear," Hasik said. "We're in realspace."

"Rebooting darsat," Hakobyan said.

Anne could smell Hakobyan sweat from across the CIC. She wanted to know what he'd done to wind up here. A sex-crime, she was sure of it. She knew a deviant when she saw one. What was his particular obsession? Rape? Pedophilia?

One way or another, she'd find out.

She'd find them *all out*.

The nav-orb once again showed the pitch-black of normal space. Dimly lit, concentric distance rings appeared, marking ranges of 10 kilometers up to 200 kilometers.

Anne wondered if some hapless Sklorno aboard *Leafcutter Alpha* happened to be watching the aft monitors when *Keeling* tore its way into reality like a 137-meter-long demon birthed from the depths of hell.

"Weps, fire tubes five and six," Lincoln said.

"Firing five." Brown slapped the fifth of six palm-sized red buttons at her station; it depressed with an audible *click*. "Firing Six." She slapped the last. Anne bet it was a very satisfying sensation. Maybe she'd get to do it someday.

Keeling vibrated slightly as both scrambler torpedoes launched. If *Leafcutter Alpha* managed to broadcast a warning, it would be a short-lived one—the scramblers would trash all signals in the area for several minutes. By the time the two Mark 14s ran dry, *Keeling*'s electronic countermeasures would lock that ship's signals up tight.

"Weps, load tubes five and six with Mark 16s," Lincoln said. "Calculate torpedo solution for tubes one and two on *Locus Charlie*, for tubes three through six on *Locus Delta*."

Brown repeated the commands as she stepped away from the

weapons station and started turning dials on the bulky torpedo data computer, entering range, angle on bow, grav-signature, and relative speed of the targets. The TDC's internal gears, shafts, and cams worked together in a highly intricate, clockwork-like system to solve the complex problem of guiding a moving torpedo toward a moving enemy ship until the torp's small, internal darsat array locked on and its living bat-brain took over.

Anne realized the information Brown calculated wouldn't be sent via wiring all the way to the torpedo rooms, but rather through a combination of wiring and *Keeling's* homegrown conduit. The copper "veins" had worked so flawlessly thus far. No one gave them a second thought.

"Darsat active," Hakobyan said, damn near stuttering on the words. "*Leafcutters One* and *Two* acquired. Grav-signature confirmation acquired for *Locus Charlie* and *Delta*—both are Leafcutters. Changing IDs in nav-orb. Scanning for additional contacts."

Four solid red circles representing the freighters appeared in the nav-orb, a straight line angling up from the lower left as *Keeling* closed in aft of *Leafcutter Bravo*. Single icons for each freighter, not *clusters*, because in real space and at this short distance, darsat gave exact coordinates rather than a fluctuating set of possible locations.

Could Hakobyan be a spy? Him and Gillick both? Why else would Gillick have glowed pea-soup-green? Anne had seen no one else emit that color. If Gillick was a spy, a spy *in her own department?* Bye-bye career. Not even Daddy could help her then.

A sensation at the back of her neck... right under her bump of knowledge...

...was it...

...was it the *tapping?*

The *need*... the *heat*...

Anne opened her binder, flipped through the pages so fast one of them ripped. No, it wasn't tapping. It *wasn't*. Some residual sensation from the Mud, that's all it was. It wasn't tapping. She didn't want to be that person any more, she didn't have to be, because she was better now.

She was better.

"ECM," Lincoln said, "tether formula status?"

Brinson Sorro. Another one Anne needed to watch. Not tall, not short, not thick, not thin, not handsome, not ugly. Dark brown skin but not *memorably* dark. Nothing about him stood out—a highly desired trait in covert ops.

"Still calculating," Sorro said.

The need, the heat… *gone*. They hadn't been real. Transdim side effects messing with her head.

Bad things happened in the Mud

"All turrets crewed," Leeds called out. "Gunners have eyes on *Leafcutter Alpha* and *Leafcutter Bravo*."

Lincoln practically vibrated with intensity. She wanted blood. So did Anne.

"Guns, load HEAP rounds in all barrels," the captain said. "Both turrets, target *Leafcutter Bravo*, do not fire until I give the order."

HEAP—high-energy explosive penetrator. Artillery rounds designed to penetrate inside a ship before detonating.

"Ops, get Martigral up here to coordinate with Raider Liaison," Lincoln said. "Nav, get us to five klicks aft of *Leafcutter Alpha* and match her acceleration as close as possible. Raider Liaison, prepare sortie for launch."

Silja "Bankshot" Lehtonen, a crawler engineer/gunner, manned the Raider Liaison station, at least until Lindros relieved her. If, that was, his people released him from his bunk. And he got some goddamn clothes on.

"We are five kilometers aft of *Leafcutter Alpha*," Erickson called out. "Velocity almost matched, but the ship is accelerating."

Lincoln looked to the ECM station. "Spec Sorro, I need that tether."

"Almost there," Sorro said.

Non-military freighters didn't possess military-caliber ECM suites. *Leafcutter Alpha* wouldn't be able to counter the tether.

"Conn, tubes five and six loaded with Mark 16s," Brown said. "*Leafcutter Charlie* torpedo solution ready. *Leafcutter Delta* torpedo solution ready."

Those solutions were all-analog data computations, transmitted across pseudo-organic conduit, and implanted in the disembodied brain of a mammalian aerial predator. Modern warfare—what a wonderful thing.

Lincoln stretched her gloved fingers out once, then relaxed them. She rested her hands palms-down on the slate.

Anne breathed slowly. Now the real action began. The real *glory* began.

"Fire all tubes in five-second spreads," Lincoln said.

Brown slapped each red button in turn, calling out the tubes as she did. The ship vibrated in time to each launch.

"All tubes fired," Brown said. "All fish running hot, straight, and normal. First salvo time to *Leafcutter Charlie*... fifteen minutes, twenty-four seconds."

XO Ellis and Lincoln thumbed their stopwatches.

"Tether formula ready," Sorro called out.

"Copy, ECM," Lincoln said. "Weps, load Mark 14 scramblers in tubes five and six. If the escorts show up, I want to be ready. Load Mark 16s in tubes one through four. XO, alert the crew for tether."

Ellis picked up the handset, punched the 1MC so his voice was heard throughout the ship.

"This is the XO. Prepare for sudden acceleration. That is all."

He returned the handset to its cradle, then he and Lincoln dropped into their seats. His warning would have everyone aboard scrambling into acceleration chairs or grabbing on to whatever might be close at hand.

"ECM," Lincoln said, "engage tether."

"Aye-aye, Captain," Sorro answered. "Engaging tether."

Keeling had a mass of 10,200 tonnes. *Leafcutter Alpha*'s mass was 560,000 tonnes. The huge difference meant *Keeling*'s tether couldn't do much to slow the freighter's increasing acceleration. Instead, the tether—which intertwined *Keeling*'s gravitational presence with *Leafcutter Alpha*'s—would act like a tow cable, pulling *Keeling* along. No matter how much the freighter accelerated, *Keeling* would stay at a relative distance of five kilometers.

"Tether lock imminent," Sorro said. "Locking now... now... *now*."

Keeling lurched forward, the sudden acceleration rattling the CIC and shoving Anne back against her seat. It wasn't as bad as the acceleration from a tail-flip maneuver, but it certainly wasn't fun. The pressure eased quickly as *Keeling* matched *Leafcutter Alpha*'s relative velocity.

"Tether engaged," Sorro said.

Just like that, *Keeling* was a fish caught on a line connected to a whale.

"Raider Liaison," Lincoln said, "launch sortie when ready."

52

JOHN

John jogged up the ramp into the troop compartment, Corporal Sharma Sarvacharya on his right. Behind them came their respective fire teams. At the compartment's end stood Master Sergeant Francis "the Book" Sands, his black armor hiding all but his scarred face.

"Move it, move it," Sands said. "Stow your rifles. Lock in."

John stopped in front of Sands, then turned to watch his squad. They slid their RR-36s into storage brackets and dropped into their seats, then pulled flight restraints down snug against their TASH rigs.

Beaver, Abshire, and Reiner performed the practiced motions with speed and ease. They were locked down before Ayodele even looked at the storage brackets. His RR-36 shook in his hands.

"Yo-Yo, relax," John said. "One thing at a time. Slow and steady."

The young Raider slid his rifle into the bracket. So awkward in his armor, he turned and sat. He fumbled with the flight restraints. John stepped to his seat, pulled the restraints down and locked them tight. He leaned down, touched his visor against Ayodele's.

Yo-Yo's wide eyes stared back at him.

"You need to cool down, son," John said. "Get frosty. Breathe in deep, four seconds. Hold it for four, breathe out for four, no breath for four. Do that three times. Your squadmates have your back. Ain't that right, Reiner?"

They were packed in shoulder to shoulder. Reiner gave Yo-Yo's thigh armor a reassuring slap.

"We've got you," she said. "You carry your weight, we'll carry ours."

John looked to Beaver, who would take point, and Abs, who was to Beaver's left. They met John's eyes. Both nodded, a silent reassurance that they would look out for Yo-Yo as best they could.

Beaver was a natural, a force of nature the likes of which John had never seen in his thirty years with the Raiders. At first, Abs had been little better than Yo-Yo was now, but Abs listened and learned. He'd had his trial by fire and come out shiny on the far side. As for Reiner, John couldn't be more pleased. Her combat experience already showed in her businesslike demeanor.

"Alpha-Two Lead, lock it down," Sands said.

John moved to his seat, sat, pulled down his flight restraint bars, and locked them in place.

Sarvacharya, Alpha-One's squad leader, sat directly across from him. To her left sat squadmates Abbas Basara, the hulking Mahesh Mafi, newbie Vera Pola, and blue-skinned Jake Radulski from Bravo-One, filling in for the restrained Ricky Chidimma who had been barking like a dog for the last hour, unresponsive to any command other than *good boy*, which made him wiggle his butt in his bunk.

Pola blinked rapidly, struggled to control her breathing. Like Yo-Yo, she was about to get her combat cherry popped. John hoped they would both make it. If their number came up, so be it. They'd die as Raiders.

There was no better way to go.

"Ochthera One Actual, this is Raider Lead," Sands said. "We're locked down and ready to rock."

53

BIGGIE

Chief Taylor stood just inside the open pouch mouth. She gave a thumbs-up, then stepped aside.

Biggie eased Occie One forward. As the crawler cleared the weird, coppery fish-lips, she keyed the internal comms.

"Good afternoon, happy sightseers, and welcome to Biggie's travel service. Today we will be visiting the ancient and fascinating Sklorno culture. Those of you dumb enough to eat lunch, kindly do your best to keep that mushroom-flavored mush inside your body."

She glanced up at *Keeling*'s tail section passing overhead, waited until the wicked-looking barbs were visible only in the aft cameras.

Now came the part she lived for—the only thing that made her poor life choices and endless regrets slip away.

Only when flying was Danielle "Biggie" Bang truly free.

She wiggled her fingers on the yoke, gripped it firm, then thumbed both curvine and chemjets to full. Inertia shoved her against her seat.

She turned her Ochthera in a tight starboard arc and accelerated toward *Leafcutter Alpha*.

54

SASCHA

Keeling's glossy maroon curvine measured 12.96 meters long, 1.82 meters high at the ends, and 91 centimeters at the neck's narrowest point. The spinning, hourglass-shaped mass rested horizontally in a smooth, formfitting cradle made of the same beryllium-copper-carbon MOF alloy that composed the ship's hull and internal bulkheads. The cradle's height of 97 centimeters hid exactly half the curvine; the cradle's edges supported a thick crysteel bubble that arced over and above it, preventing anyone or anything from accidentally touching the black object.

Touching a moving curvine could kill you in nasty ways.

Like most compartments on the *Crypt*, the curvine room was compact. Aft, starboard, and port, only a meter of space separated the cradle from surrounding equipment. The forward door, though, was a good three meters from the cradle, availing a bit of space with three acceleration-chair stations for the propulsion staff.

Sascha didn't use any of them, preferring to let her people take them while she used personal restraint harnesses, in case of unexpected combat maneuvering. Besides—at the moment, she did nothing but watch red-headed Adam Ledford run the show.

"Dimo," Ledford said, "current spin status?"

Acceleration chairs fit people like John Bennett just fine—Dimo looked like a child in hers. She was tiny, sure, but the *Ishlangu* transfer handled her propulsion mate duties well.

"Curvine spinning at one-eight-five hundred thousand RPMs, Chief," Dimo said. "Rotation is within nominal parameters."

"Excellent," Ledford said. "Fuentes, tether status?"

The tether—currently locked on a massive Leafcutter-class freighter—also utilized the curvine's space-time-harnessing tech, creating a gravitational link between the two ships.

"Accelerations synched," Fuentes said. "Initial system stress due to high mass differential now equalized."

Sascha nodded to herself. Excellent work by her people, excellent direction from Ledford. With accelerations synched, *Keeling* and *Leafcutter Alpha* might as well be motionless at opposite ends of a kilometers-long parking lot.

A perfect setup for a boarding run.

Engineering had done its job.

Now it was up to the Raiders.

Sascha wished them luck.

"Chief Ledford, I'll be in engineering control if you need me," Sascha said.

She unhooked her harness and hurried out.

55

TRAVIS

Travis worked to control his breathing. He felt electric. Torps closing in. The freighters, like fat cows, helpless against the coming slaughter. A blue square outline marking *Ochthera One*, carrying Alpha Squad, piloted by Biggie Bang.

Combat had never felt like this to him before. So intense. So *vibrant*. Why now? He didn't know. He didn't care.

"Conn, all contacts are generating STC interference," Sorro said. "I'm attempting to jam *Leafcutter Alpha* and *Leafcutter Bravo*'s efforts. *Leafcutters Charlie* and *Delta* are out of jamming range."

"Focus on *Leafcutter Alpha*," Lincoln said. "Clear the way for our sortie as much as possible. Signals, put visual of *Leafcutter Charlie* in-orb."

The range rings, contact icons, and purple torpedo tracking lines faded to ghostly shades. A vibrating, slightly fuzzy image of *Leafcutter Charlie* appeared, the visual blurred by STC interference. The freighter looked pencil-thin, a deceptive perspective given its actual bulk. Moving patches of burnt-orange and banana-yellow coursed across the hull, some part of the Sklorno species' mysterious obsession with color.

A flash of light amidships, followed closely by a second.

"Torpedoes one and two, direct hits on *Leafcutter Charlie*," Brown said.

Travis glanced at his stopwatch—the second salvo would reach *Leafcutter Delta* in seven seconds... six...

"Torpedo four lost contact," Brown said. "Torp is reacquiring. Torpedo three offline. Torps five and six... direct hits on *Leafcutter Delta.*"

Lincoln thumped her fist against the command slate. "Signals, return nav-orb to tactical view. Darsat, status of *Leafcutters Charlie* and *Delta?*"

In the orb, the red circles for *Leafcutter Charlie* and *Leafcutter Delta* pulsed red-white. A flashing blue line trailed the icon representing *Ochthera One*, marking the Raider sortie path from *Keeling's* arrow toward *Leafcutter Alpha*.

Hakobyan pressed his headset to his ear. "*Leafcutter Charlie* appears to have broken into pieces." He sounded calmer now. Good. "*Leafcutter Delta*... secondary explosions. She's breaking up."

The CIC crew cheered, briefly and loudly, then returned to their work.

Two freighters destroyed. That made the mission a partial success, but there was more to be done.

A bleary-eyed Lieutenant Lindros rushed into the CIC, his white tank top off-kilter, his dark gray coveralls only half-on, empty sleeves flapping wildly with each step.

"Lehtonen, you are relieved," he said.

Lehtonen slid out of the Raider Liaison chair as one of the station's sound-powered phones croaked. She left the CIC as Lindros sat, lifted the handset, and listened.

"Conn, Ochthera Two is loading up," he said. "Squad Two is the follow-on force. Ready for departure in three minutes. PXO Winter will lead."

"Launch Ochthera Two when ready," Lincoln said. "And get a vacsuit on, Lieutenant."

Lindros looked at his arms, as if surprised to see he wasn't wearing one. "Shit... aye-aye, Captain." He pulled a vacsuit from under his station's acceleration chair.

The Raider lieutenant was still somewhat disoriented from his Mud-driven madness. Maybe he'd chosen the liaison station so he could manage his people, or maybe he'd tried to armor up and Winter had talked him down.

Hakobyan hissed in a breath and lurched from his chair, backing away from his station until his headset cable went taut.

"Conn, *three more contacts acquired.*" His pitch climbed with every word. "It's... they're... I don't..."

He wasn't hallucinating—he was panicking, his focus fracturing under the stress of battle.

Travis hurried to the darsat station, gripped Hakobyan's elbow. "Sit down, Spec." Travis spoke softly yet firmly, leaving no room for questioning or doubt. "Sit down and do your job."

Hakobyan's head turned sharply, making the headset cable wobble. He stared blankly at Travis, blinked a few times, trying to process, then threw himself back in his seat.

"Conn, Darsat," he said. "Three new contacts. High probability two are Leafcutters, marking them as *Locus Echo*, five-zero-one kilometers out, and *Locus Foxtrot*, five-six-two kilometers out. Third new contact is likely a Whitokian warship, possibly a light or heavy cruiser, distance three thousand kilometers. Labeling it as *Locus Golf.*"

A fresh spike of adrenaline tingled through him, fusing with the electric charge already thrumming in his chest. There was an escort after all—one horribly out of position. Hopefully a Terrapin, their light cruiser, not the dreaded Komodo heavy cruiser. A fight was coming. A *real* fight.

He wanted it.

He wanted to *kill*. "Increase orb range to three thousand kilometers," Lincoln said. "Put new contacts in-orb."

Hakobyan's hands worked his station's controls. The nav-orb's range rings shrank inward, like the waves of a pebble dropped in a puddle played in reverse. The 200-kilometer ring, which had been at the orb's equator, contracted closer to the *Keeling* arrow, the four existing contacts moving closer as well. New distance rings appeared and shrank inward, marking 300 kilometers, 400 kilometers, and so on, until the 3,000-kilometer ring lined the equator.

Two new icons appeared: *Locus Echo* and *Locus Foxtrot*, also in the straight line of *Leafcutter Alpha* through *Four*. *Locus Golf* was too far out to be included at this range setting. At 3,000 kilometers away, it wasn't an immediate concern. If the ship went full acceleration, it might reach the combat zone in thirty minutes.

If it was a Komodo, though, its fighters could get there in twenty.

Travis put his hand on Hakobyan's shoulder.

"Good work, Gurgen," Travis said. "Stay steady and calm. No more outbursts, understand?"

Hakobyan nodded. "Aye-aye, XO. Sorry."

Travis squeezed the man's shoulder once, then hurried back to the command slate.

"Conn, we are not to engage Whitokian warships," Lafferty called out from her loft. "Doing so could exacerbate current relations and accelerate us to a state of open war."

Lincoln moved data around on her slate, calling up schematics on Terrapin and Komodo cruisers. The STC interference was slight enough that computers still worked. Soon, though, it would be time for paper and pencil.

"Intel, Mission parameters understood," Lincoln said. "Guns, initiate continuous fire on *Leafcutter Bravo*. Weps, set scramblers in tubes five and six to max effect and direct them toward *Locus Golf*. I want staggered detonations, the first at fifteen hundred klicks, the second at two thousand klicks. Fire when ready. Calculate torpedo solution for tubes one and two on *Locus Echo*, for tubes three and four on *Locus Foxtrot*."

Brown repeated the complicated order word for word, then, cool as ice, called down to the torpedo rooms. She seemed unfazed by the appearance of the Whitokian cruiser.

The two Mark 14 scramblers would hopefully create a huge field of space-time interference between the convoy and the heavy cruiser, preventing the Whitokian warship from firing at long distance. The warship was far enough out that, if things went well, *Keeling* might be back in the Mud before it got close enough to engage.

"Conn, Ochthera Two launched," Lindros said. "Ochthera One has reached its target."

Ochthera Two's blue square outline icon appeared, moved from *Keeling*'s arrow toward *Leafcutter Alpha*. Lucyna "Fancy Pants" Romauld piloting that one, carrying PXO Winter and Bravo Squad.

Martigral rushed into the CIC. She ran past the command slate and stood next to Lindros. He pulled a harness under his acceleration chair; she hurried to don the harness as he connected a restraining cable.

"Conn, Darsat," Hakobyan called out. "Grav-sig confirmation that *Locus Echo* and *Six* are Leafcutter-class freighters. Changing IDs to *Leafcutter Echo* and *Six*. Picking up gravitational fluctuations indicating the launch of small craft from *Locus Golf*. Too far out to identify... looks like five of them."

Lincoln and Travis exchanged a glance. Terrapins did not carry fighters or APCs—but Komodos did.

"Putting fighters in-orb," Hakobyan said.

A red triangle appeared in the nav-orb, the shape fuzzy due to STC interference that made the fighters appear in numerous locations simultaneously.

"Intel," Lincoln said, "calculate probable acceleration of enemy voidcraft. Coordinate with darsat and get me a countdown on the clock-timers."

John felt intensity roiling through the troop compartment. More than he'd felt when they'd crossed the gap to attack the Purist corvette. *Way* more. He understood—it was one thing to fight fellow Humans, like the Purists, but another thing altogether to face off against true aliens, against movie monsters.

The youngsters seemed hyped-up, ready for battle. Hungry for it. Radulski shifted in place, his aggression palpable. Mafi, too, and even squad leader Sarvacharya. They all needed to dial it back a notch.

Why were they so amped up? John didn't know. Maybe three days in the Mud had them all ready to eat iron and shit nails.

He activated his fireteam channel.

"Alpha-Two, get icy, stay icy," he said. "Maintain three points of contact until we're inside. Just because it's a freighter doesn't mean they won't try to shake us off." Abs and Beaver knew that well enough. Yo-Yo needed all the reminders he could get. "Abs goes in with red-mag knockout rounds loaded. Once he's dry, he will call *red mag out*. At that point, Reiner loads her red magazine and takes over as the knockout shooter. Copy?"

A stuttered round of *Copy, Corporal* filtered back to him.

"And don't forget, guys," Beaver said. "You have to scream, aim, *and* fire!"

"Beaver, shut up," John said. "Get your head in the game. Not another word."

John didn't know what else to say. Guys like Beaver? Their heads were *always* in the game, but he couldn't just be babbling like an idiot, not when shit was about to go down.

"Coming in hot," Biggie said on the squad channel. "Prepare for touchdown in thirty seconds. We'll contact-scan for a soft spot and crawl to it. Stand by."

She would put them down on *Leafcutter Alpha*'s hull, negating any need for Raiders to jump. Sometimes Raiders went over the top and crossed the gap, sometimes they jumped out of a perfectly good armored personnel carrier, and sometimes that same APC set down on a ship to find the right breach point.

Extricating prisoners demanded the latter.

"Raiders, we are about to make a contact-landing," Sands said. "Stay seated. Keep your flight restraints locked. I will be trailing a hardwire into the breach, maintaining contact with this Ochthera as long as possible. Expect STC interference. If and when it happens and you lose radio communication, remember to watch for your team leader's hand signals. *Do not* rely on touch-channels, that will get us bunched up. Understand?"

A chorus of *Yes, Master Sergeant* met his question.

The newbies needed to be reminded of the basics. Sands's calm, authoritative delivery would give them confidence their leadership knew what the hell was happening. When rounds started flying, faith in the command structure meant more Raiders came home on their own two feet.

"Excellent," Sands said. "Raiders, *arm up!*"

The flight restraints were designed to allow certain necessary movements. John and the others removed their RR-36s from their brackets. Yo-Yo got his out with no problem.

"Check safety," Sands said.

John did so, watching Yo-Yo to make sure he did it right.

"*Safety on, Master Sergeant,*" the Raiders called out in unison.

Only then did it hit John that a squad leader, not the platoon sergeant, should lead this op. Were Sergeant Jordan, Alpha Squad's leader, and Corporal Torres, Bravo Squad's leader, both stuck in the Mud?

If so, John knew they would be in Ochthera Two, which wouldn't be far behind.

"Check barrel for obstruction," Sands said.

John looked through the backblast mouth down through the barrel. Clean as can be.

"*Barrel is clear, Master Sergeant.*"

Yo-Yo fumbled with his. He missed the unified response, but John was pleased to see the boot did a good check of his barrel.

"Safeties on," Sands said. "I repeat, *safeties on.* Lock and load."

John checked his safety: on. He pulled a magazine from his webbing. A quick glance at the mag confirmed its 50-round load. He slotted the mag atop the RR, gave it a firm slap to lock it home, heard ten other simultaneous *clacks* as he did.

He looked at the upper right corner of his visor's HUD, saw the 50 there that marked the rounds in his magazine.

"*Locked and loaded, Master Sergeant,*" John called out with the rest.

"Maa*aaa*gnificent," Sands said. "Bad-asses, one and all. We will execute this mission to the fullest extent of our exceptional warrior abilities. Stay calm and prepare for a bumpy landing."

57

BETHANY

Bethany felt hot all over. It wasn't just the atrium's steady-state, sauna-like environment—the feverish sensation swelled *inside* her.

A sensation she hadn't felt in a long, long time.

Was she feeling what High One felt?

High One *wanted* to fight.

God wanted to fight.

God *wanted* to kill.

No, it was more than just *want*, it was *lust*.

All those years in the convent. When *was* the last time she'd felt like this?

Back when Melanie had been alive—that's when.

This raw part of Bethany had laid dormant and lightless since the Prawatt attack, and all through her decade as a nun and during her brief time aboard *Keeling*, where hungry eyes of men and women alike looked her up and down. Those embers of life's most primitive compulsions now awakened, bellowed to glowing torridity by the cosmic breath of violence and death.

Primitive. Burning. Driving. Something forged in evolution's churning cauldron eons before the first ancestors of man wriggled out of the water and onto the shore.

The *need* to take life, to *consume* life.

Someone calling her name... Hasik... from the sound-powered phone.

Bethany couldn't concentrate.

She wanted to kill.

She wanted to fuck.

Her head swam.

She couldn't concentrate, couldn't escape the *heat* in her mind, in her soul...

She yanked open her vacsuit's chest seal. With frenzied, urgent movements, she stripped off her gloves. She felt the atrium's sweltering mist against her skin.

Kill.

Fuck.

Feed.

Bethany Darkwater slid her hand inside her vacsuit, down her belly, her fingertips searching, sliding lower and lower...

"Firing beacon," Torch said. "Landing spot... *marked*. Touch-scan ready."

"Copy." In her HUD, Biggie sighted in on the flashing beacon.

The Leafcutter wasn't as long as *Akathaso*, but it was close. Far thinner than the massive carrier, though—finding the right place to set down among madly fluctuating patterns and colors was no small task. Hit a spot too thin, the Ochthera might plunge through and foul the claws, if not damage the fuselage and troop compartment. Too solid, and those same claws might hit too hard, wrecking them and sending concussive waves back up into the crawler, jostling the living shit out of the Raiders within.

She triggered chemjets, shot along the freighter's length.

Biggie heard and felt the impact of bullets smacking into the Occie's port side—they sounded dangerously close to the cockpit.

"Knuckles, goddammit," she said. "Clear the way!"

Biggie couldn't take her eyes off the approach, lest the tsunami of insane shades make her lose sight of her target and drive the Occie into a flaming streak of chemfuel and metal.

"Point-defense turret sighted," Knuckles said, her voice as calm as if they were all sitting down to a leisurely lunch. "Taste my pussy, you cricket bitches."

The Occie vibrated in time to the top turret's twin .50-cals belching depleted uranium rounds.

"Smoked it," Knuckles said. "No other threats spotted."

Biggie would ask Knuckles about that ridiculous *taste my pussy* line, but later, after they got back.

"Torch, extend claws," Biggie said. "Raider Team Lead, brace for landing on LZ's topside, amidships, facing prow. In five…"

The Occie lowered relative to the Leafcutter, the distance between the two vessels shrinking. Armored doors beneath cockpit and tail slid open, exposing the fakegrav claws at the ends of stubby, folded legs.

"…four…"

The legs extended.

"…three…"

"Claws deployed," Torch said.

"…two…"

Biggie triggered reverse thrust. Inertia slammed her against her restraints.

"…one…"

The crawler shuddered as four claws hit home.

"…touchdown. Scanning for breach point. Raiders, prep for deployment. Torch, you have the controls."

Biggie released the yoke.

"I have the controls," Torch said. "Contact-scanning for breach point. Advancing."

This was the scariest part of the process. Biggie could do nothing but watch as Torch worked the claw-yoke. The Ochthera crawled forward, one leg at a time, fakegrav claws locked on the hull, pushing ultrasonic and magnetometric waves into the ship, searching for the right spot…

"Fire tubes three and four," Lincoln said.

Brown repeated the order, pushed the red buttons.

Travis saw purple chevrons marking those torps begin their journey toward *Leafcutter Foxtrot.*

"Load tubes three and four with Mark 15s," Lincoln said.

She was preparing for their escape from the combat zone. The four scattershot warheads in each Type 15 provided area denial by spreading thousands of dense metal bearings across a wide area, damaging or destroying incoming missiles and torps.

On all clock-timers, the first dial showed a spinning countdown: 16:23... 16:22... representing the arrival of the enemy voidcraft.

"Conn, Darsat. Detecting hull fractures and explosive decompression throughout *Leafcutter Bravo.*"

In the nav-orb, *Leafcutter Bravo*'s icon pulsed red-white.

Another cheer in the CIC, but smaller than the last—enemy fighters were coming, their host cruiser close behind.

"Conn, Darsat... hostile voidcraft now two-two-five-zero kilometers out and closing. Probable warship now two-seven-three-zero kilometers out and closing."

A cluster of red triangles appeared in the orb's largest distance ring, marked 3,000*km*. From this distance, with two active scrambler torps warping space-time, the icons representing the enemy voidcraft winked in and out of dozens of probable locations every second.

"Conn, Intel." Lafferty in her loft. "High probability enemy warship is Whitokian Komodo-class cruiser. High probability enemy voidcraft are Salamander-class interceptors. They carry forward 30-millimeter autocannon and Minnow-B void-to-void missiles."

One Salamander was trouble. Five of them? *Big* trouble. If the Ochtheras got caught out in the open, the Minnow-B void-to-void missiles would make short work of them. Those same missiles—and the autocannon—were a significant threat to *Keeling*.

"Raider Liaison, assault teams are to abandon cargo and prioritize prisoner capture," Lincoln said. "Inform Ochthera pilots if they're not back in the landing bay in twelve minutes, I repeat, *twelve minutes*, we leave without them. Conn is setting second clock-timer dial to twelve minutes."

Travis felt creeping dread combined with growing anger. If the Ochtheras returned at full-burn, they might make the trip back in two minutes. That meant *Keeling*'s Raiders had ten minutes to find Sklorno, stun them, bag them, and get back to their respective crawlers.

There was a very real possibility Lincoln would leave them behind—the *Crypt* was too valuable an asset to be lost trying to save a platoon of grunts. Except they weren't just *grunts*. Travis knew them. He'd eaten beside them. Run them through drill after drill. They'd thought him a coward—he'd proven them wrong.

John Bennett, Biggie Bang, Beaver, Sands... they were Trav's comrades. They *mattered*.

"Guns," Lincoln said, "load blazers, fire for STC spread effect for the next seven minutes to buy us some time, then load flak and fire for straight-line area denial against Salamanders."

With all in-range bogeys dead or dying, *Keeling*'s Type24s would fire STC blazer rounds to thicken the space-time soup between it and the oncoming fighters.

The rules of engagement specified no destruction of Whitokian ships. The Salamander pilots were unlikely to intentionally fly through shrapnel clouds that could damage or destroy their voidcraft —they would veer around the lethal obstacle. Every degree of deviation from the Salamander's current straight-line approach gave *Keeling* more time until they reached firing range.

"Conn, Darsat. Whitokian warship now twenty-five hundred kilometers out, exiting first scrambler field, entering the second."

Once that big beast got close enough, blazer rounds weren't going to help much. Before it got into true firing range, *Keeling* needed to dive.

The clock-timer showed two simultaneous countdowns, compounding the stress of this life-and-death situation.

The shortest timer, the one for the Raiders to depart *Leafcutter Alpha*, read 11:27... 11:26... 11:25...

JOHN

Beaver couldn't stop laughing.

"This is *awesome*," he said. "The combat sims were *way* weaker than this!"

The Ochthera lumbered across the freighter's hull. John felt like a giant mule was kicking his armor, rattling him around inside despite the inertia-gobbling shock material between him and the TASH's inner shell. While contact-landings weren't as spectacular as crossing the gap, they were kind of fun, in an unsafe amusement park ride sort of way.

"Oh my God," Yo-Yo said. "Are we hit? Are we hit?"

Before John could shush the youngest member of his team, Sands's steel wool voice barked from helmet speakers.

"Ayodele, keep your mouth shut. You too, Beaver."

Biggie's voice came next.

"Raider Lead, ingress identified. Surface defenses suppressed. Commencing breach."

"Copy," Sands said. "Team One, stay frosty."

Beaver started laughing again.

The Ochthera lurched forward, then backward, then sideways, jostling John and his squadmates. There was no atmosphere in the troop compartment, not yet. He didn't hear the crawler's underside plasma drill grinding through the Leafcutter's hull, but his TASH haptics let him feel it.

"Hull breached," Biggie said. "Matching pressure. *Keeling* just informed us to ignore cargo sample retrieval and focus on capture of the enemy. Full-burn return is two minutes, which means you boys and girls have *less than nine minutes* to be back in your seats. Don't make me feel bad about leaving you behind. Pressure equalized—go get 'em, tigers."

Sands pushed up his flight restraints.

"Raiders, up and make ready!"

The squad pushed up their restraints and stood. John's mics picked up the hiss of inrushing air as the troop compartment pressurized.

"Weapons ready," Sands said. "Alpha-Two, prepare to make entry."

John stepped close to the hatch on the troop compartment deck, invisible save for its meter-and-a-half wide, circular line, and the recessed rotary handle in the center. He kept his rifle angled down, as did the others.

"Bennett, prepare a bee," Sands said.

John reached to a hip, removed the fist-sized drone from its mag clamp. It activated upon removal; an overlay screen appeared in John's HUD.

In heavy STC fuckery, bees didn't work for shit, but the soup wasn't that bad here. Worth a shot.

"Mafi," Sands said, "pull the hatch."

Mafi grabbed the floor hatch's recessed handle, turned it 90 degrees clockwise, waited a second, turned it hard 180 degrees counter-clockwise, then yanked the circular hatch upward.

Abs and Reiner aimed their rifles through the breach, each looking in opposite angles through a fresh hole in the meter-thick hull. Molten metal lined the circular sides, glowing globs pulled down to splash against fakegrav plates below.

"Deploy bee," Sands said.

John tossed the drone in. His HUD window filled with a 360-degree view of a passageway awash in wild, rapidly shifting colors and patterns. During the Ochthera's launch, the approach, the touch-down, and even the hull-crawl, he'd felt fine, but now the moving, multihued vomit spray of the alien passageway made him slightly queasy.

Insane, swirling hues, but no Sklorno.

"Passageway," John said. "Clear forward and aft, closed pressure hatches both forward and aft."

"Alpha-Two, progress through forward hatch," Sands said. "We'll be right behind you."

Beaver dropped down, followed by Abs, then Reiner, implementing the deployment order they'd drilled many times. Yo-Yo hesitated. John angrily pointed at him, then to the breach. Yo-Yo nodded and dropped down. John followed.

He hit the passageway deck. His mind reeled from the visual onslaught of whirling colors—amorphous, flowing patches blurring structural lines and edges like some form of architectural camouflage.

The last time he'd seen something like this... twenty years ago... the kick of his rifle... the screeching of the enemy... the screams of his comrades...

John closed his eyes, but the memories didn't hide...

Red blood, *Raider* blood, splattering the walls, one more color in an endless, psychotic Rorschach blotter...

Sergeant Petrov, on the deck, half his throat ripped out but trying to scream anyway, leg blown off, his TASH chest-plate cracked open, two clear-bodied Sklorno crouched over him, raspers flicking in, snapping back, dragging shreds of flesh and muscle from his body...

They were eating him alive...

John, losing all thought, drawing his combat knife, cutting into the enemy, slicing off arms, legs, taking his time, making it *last*, watching the enemy tremble in agony, *enjoying* the spectacle...

"Corporal, snap out of it."

Reiner. Urgent, but not yelling. Her gauntleted hand on his armored shoulder, opening up a private touch-channel between them that shut off the other circuits as long as they were in contact. Only he had heard her words.

The rest of the fire team, looking at him, waiting for him. Beaver, concern on his face, concern and also the idiotic eagerness of someone born for moments like these.

John stepped to the side; Reiner's hand returned to her RR-36, breaking the touch-channel.

"Beaver, take point," John said. "Advance to the hatch. Let's bag us some crickets."

61

ANNE

"Conn, Sands and Alpha Squad are progressing forward through the ship," Lindros said. "Ochthera Two touched down on the forward section. Winter and Bravo Squad breached and are moving aft. Neither squad has contact with the enemy yet. If *Shell Splitter* launches STC interference ordinance, we may lose contact."

Despite getting closer in the nav-orb, the clusters of red dots marking *Leafcutter Echo* and *Leafcutter Foxtrot* hadn't changed in size—some two dozen blazer rounds warped gravity near them so much so that time and space were more localized suggestions than realities.

And, now, at the orb's edge, a new cluster of red dots labeled *Locus Golf* appeared.

"Conn, Darsat." Hakobyan, getting squirrelly again, his voice rising again. "*Locus Golf* grav-signature confirmed as Komodo-class heavy cruiser *Shell Splitter*. Updating ID."

Full confirmation. *Keeling* faced the meanest bastard in the Whitokian fleet. Anne had the specs in front of her—they did not exactly fill her with confidence.

"Conn, Intel," she said. "Komodo's primary armament is two batteries of three 28-centimeter cannon each. Six torpedo tubes.

294

Twelve missile launchers with packages of void-to-void Minnow-Cs, armor-piercing, and STC-interference blazers. Two large silos likely loaded with Tadpole ship-killer missiles."

The huge 28-centimeter, 15-meter-long barrels fired 300-kilo-gram penetrators easily capable of destroying *Keeling* with a single hit. But they fired far slower than *Keeling*'s smaller Type24 batteries—about three rounds per minute compared to *Keeling*'s fifteen.

The Komodo threw knockout punches while *Keeling* hit with fast, hard jabs. The artillery wouldn't be the first problem, though—*Shell Splitter*'s torps and missiles—especially the hull-cracking ship-killers—would pour in from long distance. Hopefully the *Crypt* would be back in the Mud before any of those weapon systems posed a real threat.

Anne's unknown BII colleagues had gotten much right. There was only one reason the freighters hadn't made a desperate run for punch-space—their punch-drives were still recharging. *Keeling* had reached Junction Nest at precisely the right time. But while location and timing were incredibly accurate, BII's projections about potential escorts sucked. The three Komodos were supposedly accounted for, now this one—and its streaking Salamanders—put a lethal ticking clock on *Keeling* and on the secondary objective as well.

As for the primary objective, that was a smashing success. Torps were closing in on *Leafcutter Echo* and were streaking toward *Six*, which itself was going full-burn toward the Komodo.

Akil Daniels hurried into the CIC, stumbling a bit.

"Spec-Three Chen, you're dismissed," Anne said.

Chen quickly descended the Intel Loft. Daniels climbed the three steps. He looked groggy, was probably still feeling the effects of both the sedative and the analeptic given to counter it.

The second clock-timer dial ticked off the Raiders' fate: 9:22… 9:21… 9:20…

If the grunts didn't make it out on time, Lincoln had no choice but to leave them behind.

Of course, Anne had similar thoughts during the Battle of

Ishlangu. Ol' *Yellowbelly Ellis* turned out to be not so yellow-bellied after all. Was there anyone aboard who defied their psyche profile more than him? Long before *Keeling,* Anne had seen his jacket as part of a broader investigation for various promotional candidates. The XO's tag of *coward* wasn't a one-time thing. Yet here, on the *Crypt,* the man had balls of steel.

Anne stared at his back, at the lines of his broad shoulders, at his gloved hands playing across the command slate. She realized she was horny. *Beyond* horny—she felt hotter and wetter than the atrium.

She'd never been horny before during combat. Why now? She didn't know. What she *did* know was that she wanted to throw Travis Ellis on top of the command slate, use her knife to slice open his vacsuit and coveralls, then ride him like a pogo stick.

And maybe cut him. Just a little. Cut him and watch him bleed while she fucked him...

62

BIGGIE

Biggie wiggled in her seat, trying to scratch an itch on her right butt-cheek. The longer this dragged on, she knew, the more her tingling skin would make her wish she wasn't wearing the LASH rig.

In a small way, being clamped to a hull provided a kind of cover, as enemy forces sometimes hesitated to fire on one of their own vessels, which they had to do to hit a mounted Ochthera. In the big picture, though, being clamped to a ship was risky. It slowed any reaction to attacks from enemy forces that didn't mind inflicting a little collateral damage.

No action of that sort yet. Biggie and her crew could do nothing but wait.

"*Dio mio,*" Torch said. "I think another one just went *boom.*"

Torch was making an educated guess based on a flickering bit of light some 450 klicks away, located roughly where *Leafcutter Echo* had been. While immediate-vicinity STC interference wasn't too bad, *Keeling*'s scrambler torps and a barrage of blazer ordinance made it impossible to accurately detect anything beyond a couple of kilometers away.

"If so, that's four gone," Nikula said. "And Lincoln will dust *Leafcutter Alpha* as soon as we lift off. That'll be *five* ships in one mission.

Freighters, sure, but still. I bet that sets a single-encounter tonnage record."

God, but did this waiting suck. Somewhere out there, a damn Komodo was probably at full-burn acceleration, closing in on *Keeling*. Salamander fighters would arrive before the Komodo did. Biggie did *not* want to face those fuckers. An APC up against interceptors was an equation that rarely ended with a favorable outcome.

"Possible visual of escort," Nikula said. "Emerging from the scrambler fields now, port-forward zero-one-one, elevation fifteen degrees. Distance roughly... two thousand klicks."

Biggie searched for it, then saw it. *Fuck.* From this far away, the Whitokian warship was a vibrating, spherical cloud of possible locations, a cloud the size of a major city.

She checked the console's clock-timer, set at the tightbeam instructions from Lieutenant Lindros.

8:21... 8:20... 8:19...

Subtract the return time, and Sands had just over six minutes to get Alpha Squad back inside the crawler.

Biggie keyed the Raider leadership channel, a hard connection carried by a spool of wire that ran from the Ochthera to Master Sergeant Sands. Wired analog connections weren't applicable in most boarding missions, but when they could be used, they helped mitigate STC communication interference.

"Raider Lead, this is Ochthera One Actual," she said. "We have visual of a big fucking problem, and five little fucking problems will be here before you know it."

63

JOHN

Senseless patterns swirled along the passageway's walls and overhead. Only the deck provided any consistency. As long as John didn't look down, steps on the deck were steps on the deck, and gravity was gravity—even if it was fake.

He couldn't shake the flashbacks. He was *here* and *now*, with his squad, Alpha-Two, looking for freighter crew to abduct, and he was also *then* and *there*, with Gamma-One, running for his life while Sklorno in noisy powered armor chased him through the passageways and put big holes through his best buddies.

The crickets hadn't got him then.

They wouldn't get him now.

And if they did? It was one hell of a good day to die.

"Yo-Yo, step to your right," John said. "You're too close to Abs."

Without a word, Yo-Yo took a step right as the squad advanced in a slanted-stack formation. Beaver had point. He stayed close to the left-hand bulkhead and its chaotic kaleidoscope. Abshire was two steps behind and one step to Beaver's right, just clear of backblast should Beaver open fire. Yo-Yo was third. With his position corrected, he was now two steps behind and one step to the right of Abs.

John was fourth, directly behind Beaver but far enough in his rear that any backblast had ample space to disperse. John wanted Yo-Yo close, so he could help the kid when the team got into the mix.

Reiner brought up the rear. John treasured the bit of luck that had delivered a seasoned corporal—a *real* corporal, not a trumped-up brevet like himself—into Alpha-Two. Reiner knew her shit.

John checked his HUD—five minutes left before they needed to be back in the crawler.

The STC interference was growing worse but radio still worked. Sands and Alpha-One were back thirty meters or so, usually one hatch behind—far enough away so both teams couldn't be wiped out in the same attack, close enough to rush forward in support if things went hot.

This was an alien vessel, yes, but certain design elements echoed throughout most of the galaxy's sentient species: straight passage-ways; 90-degree intersections; pressure doors every twenty to thirty meters. Aside from the wild dance of chromatic chaos, if John squinted enough it basically felt like being inside a standard Union warship.

But not like *Keeling*. Nothing felt like the *Crypt*.

"Closed pressure hatch ahead," Beaver said. "Fifteen meters."

"Hold," John said.

The squad stopped. Beaver, Abs, and Yo-Yo aimed their weapons at the hatch.

"Reiner," John said, "rear status?"

"Hatch behind us sealed," she said. "Alpha-One holding there. I have clear comms with Raider Lead. He says we need to hurry the fuck up."

John sent the bee forward, landed it on the pressure hatch. Through the drone's mics, John heard noises coming from beyond the closed hatch, noises that sent ripples up and down his skin— high-pitched chittering, reminiscent of clear, ringing birdsong, combined with low-pitched, thumping, thrumming, bassoon-like resonances.

Sklorno, talking.

The timbre of the sound told John the chatty Kathy wasn't wearing a suit: armor, exo, vac, or otherwise.

"Raider Lead, contact imminent," John said. "Abs, at least one of the hostiles is unarmored. Fire on sight. Everyone else, wait for my command."

Unlike the enemy, John's TASH suit meant the approaching Sklorno could not hear his words.

He felt that surge of adrenaline-atop-adrenaline. This was the moment when existence shifted, when seconds spanned years, when the primitive, inexorable tumult of kill or be killed overwhelmed him, *engulfed* him like a warm, welcoming womb.

In this moment, John Bennett was truly himself, a creature born to burn in the brightness of battle.

Finally, the haunting echoes of the passageway-hopping hellscape that earned him his first Fleet Cross faded away. There was no *before*. The was no *after*. There was only *now*.

The hatch door swung inward.

A squirming glob of evil darted through. Five of them. Eel-like raspers flailing and flinging saliva everywhere. Translucent bodies revealing ghostly images of contracting muscle and clear, flowing blood. Coarse mops of black hair bouncing beneath vibrating eyestalks. None of them wore suits. Tentacle arms held weapons: two of the Sklorno carried pistols, one carried a rifle, while the last two lugged long, heavy, skull-crushing spanners. No whispers from them now—their balls-shrinking shrieks raged so loud John could hear them through his armor.

In that fraction of an instant, John wondered if Abs would deliver or if he'd flinch at the sight of horror-movie monsters hurtling toward him. All the training in the world couldn't fully prepare you for combat; doubly so for combat against something so *different*, something so *not-human*.

Abshire's RR-36 opened up as the horde closed in. Fuck, they were so *fast*. John thought he saw one go down, and another, felt a bullet skip off his armor before he gave the order.

"Fire."

He pulled the trigger, registered Beaver firing almost at the same instant.

Twenty-millimeter recoilless rounds punched through unprotected bodies, splattering gobs of translucent flesh and splashing clear goo across the bulkheads' madly shifting, nonsensical imagery. Two Sklorno dropped in twitching, shuddering piles—the fifth alien somehow missed the fusillade and launched itself at Beaver.

John and Beaver both angled their aim toward it. One 20mm round hit its trunk, the other its left leg. The mangled beast hit the deck in front of Beaver, a fist-sized hole through its chest, its left leg shredded beyond recognition.

Beaver raised an armored boot and *stomped*. The Sklorno's head caved in, one of its four eyestalks spinning away, a squirt of translucent, pale blue brains jetting out and splashing across Yo-Yo's visor.

"*Cease fire*," John said.

In the comms, he heard Yo-Yo vomit.

Down the passageway, past the three butchered, pulverized bodies, John saw two prone, twitching Sklorno.

Martigral's nonlethal ammo had worked.

"Raider Lead, Alpha-Two Lead," John said. "Looks like we got a pair of them. Still alive. Over."

"Ma*aaaa*gnificent, Alpha-Two," Sands said. "Keep the corridor covered. Alpha-One, get in there and bag 'em. Bravo Squad breached closer to the prow and have one captive. We've got our three. Double-time it to the breach point, people, let's haul ass."

The aft hatch opened. Alpha-One hurried in, Mafi and Radulski unfurling their white crysteel-mesh bags. The Raiders moved swiftly, folding the downed, limp Sklorno and stuffing them in.

"Corporal Bennett," Reiner said, "help me, Yo-Yo's choking."

John turned. Reiner was trying to unfasten Yo-Yo's neck-seal in order to get his helmet off, fighting off his hands as he grabbed at his throat, trying to claw gauntleted fingers through his own armor. Sklorno blood still smeared the outside of his visor—vomit splashes dotted the inside. Through that thin haze of yellowish-green, John saw the kid's wide, gasping mouth.

John knelt next to him. "Get his helmet off!"

The passageway had atmospheric integrity. The air might not be great, but it wouldn't kill him.

"I'm trying," Reiner said. "His clasp is jammed."

John mag-clamped his rifle. "Hold his hands."

Reiner grabbed Yo-Yo's wrist, pushed his hands down, giving John room to work.

TASH seals were designed with bulky gauntlets in mind—all seals and clasp tongues easily accommodated digits thick with armor and substrate. John slid his pointer finger under the clasp's tongue and pulled. It didn't budge. He pulled harder.

The clasp didn't *pop* open, as it should, it *broke*, the tongue spinning one way, a pressure spring another. The helmet connection remained sealed—no way to open it now, not without the tools on the Ochthera.

"Raider Lead, Alpha-Two Lead, critical wounded inbound," John said. "Ayodele vomited and he's choking on it. We can't get his helmet off. We need TASH tools and the squad trauma kit ready for us in the crawler."

John lifted Yo-Yo into a fireman's carry, the TASH's artificial muscle equal to the task.

"Reiner, take point," John said. "Abs, switch to standard mags, you and Beaver cover our rear, let's *move!*"

It didn't take long to reach the breach point, where Sands was waiting, covering the passageway forward. Reiner joined him. TASH gauntlet reached down through the hole in the hull; John lifted Yo-Yo, the Raiders above hauled him in.

Sands cut his hair-thin comm wire and let it drop. No need for it any longer. He sent Reiner up, then Beaver, then Abs, then John.

In the Ochthera, John found Radulski using clamp-breakers on Yo-Yo's neck-seal while other Raiders strapped the bagged Sklorno to the deck. Pola stripped off her gauntlets and yanked the big med kit from its bracket.

Sands was the last one through the hatch. "Biggie, Raider Lead, we're all in." He slammed it shut and dogged it. "Full-burn to *Keeling*. Alpha Squad, anyone not helping with Yo-Yo, lock down *now*."

The neck-seal broke free. Radulski dropped the tool and pulled off Yo-Yo's helmet. Pola knelt, her armored knees beside Yo-Yo's ears. She rotated his head back and used her thumbs to push his jaw open.

"Can't see the obstruction," she said. "Must be way down there."

She grabbed a portable suction wand from the med kit. Jamming the nozzle deep into Yo-Yo's throat, she triggered the pump—a harsh, rhythmic *hiss-thunk, hiss-thunk* as it pulled bile and mucus from his airway.

There was a moment of lightness as the Ochthera disengaged from the hull, then sudden acceleration sent John, Radulski, Pola, and the limp Yo-Yo sliding backward to pile up against the troop compartment's closed rear ramp.

The Occie raced for *Keeling*.

John fought against the G-forces as he flipped Yo-Yo onto his back.

Pola recovered and got to work. She tore open a side pocket on the trauma kit and yanked out a compact mask with a flexible bulb attached. She leaned over Yo-Yo, one hand pressing the mask tight over his mouth and nose, the other squeezing the bulb to force air into his lungs.

John had danced with death many times. Experience taught him what to look for, where to see hope, and where to see the hard truth of a soldier's life.

Yo-Yo's chest didn't rise in time with Pola's squeezes.

John looked at Yo-Yo's face, the skin tacky with vomit.

Blank eyes. Pupils dilated so wide almost none of his brown irises remained.

"He's not inflating," Pola said. "Something's stuck in there deep. Radulski, get me the auto-crike from the kit."

She stayed calm. That was good. A steady voice meant someone you could rely on. Pola had potential.

Yo-Yo had potential, too.

John slid away, bumped up against something on the deck—a bagged, unconscious Sklorno. He watched Pola try to save Yo-Yo.

He watched... and he knew the kid wouldn't make it.

Yo-Yo.

Gone.

Not because of enemy fire. Not because he'd made a mistake. Not because of bad tactics. Not because of poor training.

Dead because of shitty gear.

Epperson.

As the crawler reached toward *Keeling*, John's focus drifted off. His mind swirled with thoughts wrapping his scarred hands around Epperson's throat.

Epperson deserved to choke to death—just like Yo-Yo.

64

TRAVIS

"Conn, Darsat. Enemy fighters now nine minutes, thirty seconds from missile-launch range."

Trav looked at the nav-orb. Red triangles marking the Salamanders were a thousand kilometers out, closing in from an angle—the Mark15s had forced them to change course. Fifteen hundred kilometers out, *Shell Splitter*'s red dot approached from forward-starboard-high, the ticking 2:07 beneath it showing the time until the cruiser reached estimated long-distance artillery range. Much nearer was the red dot of *Leafcutter Alpha* at forward-port-low, purple square outlines labeled *Ochthera One* and *Ochthera Two* moving away from it toward the metal arrow marking *Keeling*. The dots of *Leafcutter Bravo*, *Charlie*, *Delta*, and *Echo* pulsed red-white. Purple chevrons representing *Keeling*'s torps reached for *Leafcutter Foxtrot*. Those Mark16s had run into STC interference generated by the Komodo; odds were they would not reacquire their target.

"Conn, sorties returning from *Leafcutter Alpha*," Lindros said. "Ochthera One, one minute, thirty seconds out, two captives aboard. One casualty, we need medical waiting at the flight bay. Ochthera Two, one minute, fifty seconds out, one captive aboard. No casualties."

Next to Lindros, Martigral pumped a fist in victory.

Both crawlers would make it back in plenty of time to dive. One Raider down. Only one.

"ECM, disengage tether," Lincoln said. "Ops, get medical to the pouch. Have Kerkhoffs's team report there as well to move the prisoners to containment cells. Guns, have both deuce-quad turrets open fire on *Leafcutter Alpha*."

Plait and Leeds repeated the orders.

The deck beneath Travis thrummed as the Type24 batteries opened up, their 8-meter barrels hurling 127-millimeter penetrators at *Leafcutter Alpha*.

"Colonel Martigral," Lincoln said, "you are free to assist with prisoner transfer."

Martigral stared into the nav-orb, her eyes flicking across the multiple icons glowing within the sphere.

"I'll wait until the final sample arrives," she said.

Lincoln's eyes narrowed. She hadn't *ordered* Martigral to leave, but a captain didn't usually need to give commands to have her requests or suggestions followed.

"Conn, Guns. Turret crews report multiple artillery hits on *Leafcutter Alpha*," Leeds called out. "Visual confirmation of multiple decompression points, significant internal explosions."

Even as he spoke, the deck thrummed again as the Type24s fired another salvo.

At the signals station, Sara Ellison turned in her seat, looked to the command slate.

"Conn, I've detected a chunk of cargo from *Leafcutter Bravo*," she said. "It appears to be a block of containers of uniform size, bound together."

Travis heard Anne Lafferty stand so fast she knocked a three-ring binder off her station.

"I want that cargo," she said. "Captain, if we can acquire it, we must do so."

The third mission objective—they could achieve it, but doing so meant more time before *Keeling* could dive. The longer she remained in the field, the more peril she faced.

"Raider Liaison," Lincoln said, "divert Ochthera Two to recover a container from the identified wreckage. Strap it to the top, tow it, I don't care, just make it fast. I want Ochthera Two back in the pouch in three minutes, tops."

Lindros spoke quickly and efficiently to his people, directing them to obey no matter what the cost.

Lincoln hadn't hesitated for a second. She was the edge of the knife, the tip of the spear... Travis felt blessed to serve under such a warrior. And, maybe, together they could kill more enemy, kill them and feed upon their corpses...

"What the *hell* are you doing?" Martigral rushed toward the command slate, was stopped jerkingly short when her harness cables snapped taut. "Lincoln, you thick-headed *fool*, I need all the samples! Don't risk my third by—"

"You *shut* your *whore mouth*," Lincoln roared. "Question my authority *one more time* and I will have you *keelhauled!*"

Martigral stood there, her harness cables stretched to the max, murder in her eyes and hate in her heart, but she said nothing.

Travis was speechless. *Keelhauled?* Lincoln had never reacted like that. What was wrong with her? Not just her—Travis could barely contain the exploding rage inside himself. *Feed on their corpses?* What was going on?

"Ops," Lincoln said, her voice again normal—cold, emotionless, and efficient. "Ensure crew is on-hand to assist with cargo from Ochthera Two. Stow what you can, discard anything that won't fit."

She was going for it, and by doing so, placing Ochthera Two and the Raiders aboard in danger. A mechanical failure, a stray bit of debris, or the genuine possibility of damage to the crawler from the very cargo they were to collect could mean the difference between life and death for those soldiers.

"Conn, four torps launched from *Shell Splitter*," Hakobyan said, almost shouting the words. "Run time is five minutes, zero-six seconds. Putting in-orb."

A new cluster of red chevrons appears in the nav-orb; Trav thumbed his stopwatch.

Plait announced Ochthera One's successful landing; Biggie, Sands, Bennett, and the rest had made it back. Travis stole a glance at Martigral. She stared daggers at Lincoln. Did Martigral not know a glare like that was almost as much a sin as questioning orders? Lincoln focused on the nav-orb, though Travis knew she saw Martigral's disrespect.

"Conn," Ellison said, "*Shell Splitter* has opened fire with main battery artillery, likely 28-centimeter cannon, salvo dispersion two kilometers. ETA of initial salvo, nine minutes, fourteen seconds."

The cruiser had reached maximum range and was lobbing Hail Marys *Keeling*'s way. *Keeling* needed to maneuver out of their path. The Whitokian captain had begun the chess match of bearing, angle, position, and relative acceleration.

Too bad for them—*Keeling* didn't play chess. The *Crypt* had its own game, its own set of rules, and hell awaited those who denied her soul-taking glory.

"Weps," Lincoln said, "load tubes one and two with Mark 14 scramblers. Guns, blazers in all barrels. ECM, be ready to activate our corruptor on my mark. We're going to leave the enemy wanting, and they will *know* that *Keeling* is the alpha and omega, the swallower of souls!"

Travis stared at her. The *swallower of souls?* Was Lincoln losing it?

For an instant, he blamed her reaction on transdim, but only for an instant, because they weren't *in* the Mud.

They were in realspace.

65

ANNE

Anne watched the threats close in. Red triangles representing the Salamanders, 3:18 from ship-killer-missile max launch range, and from there, an additional estimated run time of 3:11. *Shell Splitter*'s torps, a cluster of red chevrons, 2:14 away. Red crosses marking the cruiser's first artillery rounds, 3:22 from arrival.

Everything hinged on how fast the pouch crew could secure Ochthera Two's recovered enemy cargo.

"Ops," Lincoln said, "talk to me."

At the Operations station, Alex Plait listened to a voice only he could hear: the 5MC from the flight bay.

"We got it." He turned to Lincoln. "Conn, two captured cargo containers locked down."

"Ops, seal up the pouch the instant Ochthera Two is in," Lincoln said. "Raider Liaison, have your people stow their weapons, double-time. I want to know the *moment* those weapons are secured."

Martigral disengaged her harness cables and ran out of the CIC, undoubtedly heading for the pouch. She wanted to make sure her "samples" were properly moved to their containment cells, of that Anne had no doubt.

"Weps," Lincoln said, "fire tubes one and two. Guns, time blazer rounds for detonation one-quarter distance between us and *Shell Splitter*. Fire when ready. ECM, activate corruptor."

Lincoln was throwing out the whole kit and caboodle of STC fuckery: scrambler torps, blazer artillery rounds, and *Keeling's* corruptor. In seconds, the ship would be dead-smack in the middle of space-time curvature run amok, hopefully a field so large the Komodo's gunners wouldn't know where to fire.

"Xeno, prepare to dive," Lincoln said. "Give me transdim coupler status."

Over in the xeno loft, Anne noticed Hasik bristle. He hated the term *dive*.

"Aye-aye, Captain," he said. "Preparing to *go transdim*, getting transdim coupler status."

Hasik spoke into his sound-powered phone that ran straight to the atrium. Such a stodgy little prick he was. Even now, with enemy torps bearing down, he insisted on proper terminology. And there was the small fact that a dive wasn't guaranteed—Hasik should be worrying about how fucked *Keeling* would be if he couldn't get the ship into the Mud.

And speaking of fucked... Anne suffered a flush of heat in her head as she wondered what Hasik might be packing downtown.

"XO," Lincoln said, "alert the crew we're diving."

Ellis grabbed a handset. Anne heard his voice over the 1MC.

"This is the XO. Prepare to dive. All personnel, clear the way from the pouch to the Raider weapon cage. All non-essential personnel, to their racks and strap down. Medical, prepare tranquilizers. Remember that anything strange you see when we hit the Mud is not real. I repeat, it *is not real*. That is all."

The dive alarm sounded.

Now it all came down to Hasik, Beth in the atrium, and *Crypt's* temperamental transdim coupler. If the thing misfired, the Komodo heavy cruiser and her interceptors would be all over *Keeling*, at a range so close STC interference wouldn't matter.

Lincoln was taking one hell of a gamble. Anne *loved* it.

Just in front of Anne, Jester Gillick picked up the binder she'd dropped. He set it on Anne's station, offered a small smile, then sat in his acceleration chair. The binder had fallen between Gillick and Akil Daniels. When *Keeling* entered the Mud, she would watch everyone, but she'd watch Corporal Jester Gillick most of all.

"Conn, Xeno, I…"

Something about the breaking desperation in Hasik's voice made Anne look his way.

"Atrium is not responding," he said. "I don't… we can only dive if someone performs the protuberance sequence."

Beth… was Beth hurt?

"Atrium, Xeno, come in," Hasik said, loud enough for the entire CIC to hear him. "Lieutenant Darkwater! *Are you there?*"

Anne stood. "I'll go check on Darkwater."

Lincoln turned, her face twisted with rage. "Intel, stay at your post. Hasik, get to the atrium, *now*."

Hasik reached to take off his headset—his hand paused.

"Darkwater is responding! Atrium, Xeno—transdim coupler status?" He nodded. "Yes, got it. Conn, transdim coupler status is in the green."

Anne sat back down.

Lincoln faced forward. "Xeno, remain at your post. Prepare to dive on my mark."

The *steel* in the captain's voice. A true commander, a true *warrior*.

In the orb, red torpedo chevrons closed in—1:29 and counting.

Kiara Lincoln, the commanding officer of the PUV *James Keeling*, stepped on her acceleration chair, then stood atop the command slate, hands outstretched like she was a Shakespearian actor, and in that moment, Anne loved her leader *so much*, loved her and would *kill* for her.

"ECM," Lincoln said, "jam incoming torps."

"Aye-aye, Captain," Brinson Sorro said. "Jamming incoming torpedoes."

The CIC fell quiet.

2:25...

2:24...

"One torpedo jammed," Sorro said. "Veering off."

2:21...

2:20...

"Second torpedo jammed," Sorro said. "Hold on... something's changed."

"Conn, Guns. Turret crews report remaining enemy torpedo warheads splitting into cluster missiles, approximately eight missiles each, total of sixteen incoming. They are accelerating."

The STC-fuzzed red triangles faded; STC-fuzzed red diamonds shot forward.

"Copy, Guns," Lincoln said. "Get the turret crews inside. Darsat, Signals, get a fix on those incoming missiles and give me time to arrival. Guns, have point-defense batteries open fire, deuce-quad batteries fire flak. Weps, set intercept course for the Mark 15s in tubes three and four, fire when ready."

The 15s dense cloud of metal would stop most of the incoming missiles, but Anne knew it was likely some would get through and continue on to *Keeling*.

"Captain, we need to dive," Anne said. "Right now."

Lincoln didn't turn around. She shook her head.

"Negative, Intel," she said. "We will not enter transdim until all weapons are secured."

Lincoln didn't look back, but Ellis did, the XO's eyes briefly meeting Anne's. The two of them, together, could override Lincoln's stupid order and initiate the dive process. When Ellis faced forward again, Anne knew he would not back such a play.

The die was cast. Anne hoped she'd survive the next few minutes.

BETHANY

Bethany felt so *hot*, as if the atrium's steam flowed through her, filling her veins.

Her hands went through the motions, did their dance on the protuberance. It was as if someone else controlled her actions, muscle memory performing the task without a shred of thought on her part. That was good, because all she *could* think about was what her body needed, how she had to give herself to God.

The autopilot moving her like a marionette finished the sequence. *Almost* finished it.

Standing atop the protuberance platform, completely naked, Bethany Darkwater's left hand cupped the gnarled nub that would send *Keeling* into the Mud.

While she waited for the command, her right hand found something else to do.

SASCHA

The dive alarm sounded throughout the ship.

Wedged between a coral-patterned bulkhead and a battered Sklorno cargo container, a vacsuited Sascha kept a hand on Ri Chen's hip, steadying him as he slowly climbed the ladder to Deck Four, his shoulder pushing up a mesh bag holding the dead weight of an unconscious, fetally-folded Sklorno captive.

Above, Marchenko stood at the edge of the hatch, struggling to haul up a rope tied to the bag. Behind Marchenko, out of sight, Hamza Harring also pulled on the rope, which was threaded through an overhead bracket. They needed to get this third Sklorno up to Deck Three, where Martigral was locking down the first two captives.

TASHed Raiders from Bravo Squad rushed past Sascha, sprinting into the tunnel to Raider Land to secure their rifles and knives. Overhead lights strung down the tunnel's ceiling lit up their armor in staccato pulses as they passed beneath.

Part of Alpha Squad went with them, while others lingered by their Ochthera's open rear ramp, gathered around Rebecca Watson as she performed chest compressions on a motionless Raider.

Sascha looked up at the bag.

"Chenk, *pull*," she said. "Faster, move it!"

The bag... it *stretched* a little, pushed out by a pair of big feet pressing against the inside.

"Hey, this thing is *moving*," Chenk said. "It's not supposed to be able to do that!"

Sascha watched, stunned, as the mesh bulged a little bit more, the powerful legs trembling as they extended. The fabric was rated to five thousand newtons of force; the Sklorno couldn't tear it.

Ice-dagger horror ripped through her—it wasn't trying to *tear* the fabric. The bag's bunched-up opening jerked, jerked again, loosening ever so slightly. Boneless, tooth-studded, saliva-coated raspers squeezed through like paste from a tube.

Part of her tried to cry out in alarm, but in that split-second of realization her mouth would not move, her lungs would not draw air with which to shout.

Trailing strands of spit, the raspers reached up, curled down, and hit the red button three times.

The bag relaxed, expanded.

A kick from within stretched the mesh outward as it smashed into Chen's vacsuited head and he fell away, stunned.

Sascha grabbed at the bag's opening, trying to choke it tight, trying to trap the beast inside. She might as well have tried to seal the gates of hell with a scrap of ribbon—the Sklorno burst from the bag, knocking her hands aside.

She saw the alien foot—coarse clumps of knuckle-hair, transparent flesh, the darker shades of the bones beneath—an instant before it smashed into her visor.

The kick rattled her, scrambled her senses. She fell backward, the Sklorno's desperate, inhuman shrieks audible in both her vacsuit's speakers and through the suit itself.

Sascha knew she would hit the deck hard, tensed against the coming impact, but she didn't slam against the fakegrav plates—she plunged *through* them.

The ship, the bulkheads, the floor, the copper walls... all ceased to be.

Sascha Kerkhoffs floated, weightless.

She stared out into the Mud...

Infinite. Beyond comprehension.

Endless rivers of crimson and ivory, intertwined like pulsating, living creatures that merged and thickened, separated and twined, branched and condensed, reaching out into forever. A sprawling weave so vast that in the distance it became a fuzzy, almost uniform fog in every direction.

How was she outside the ship? Her vacsuit kept her alive, kept her breathing. Except, she *wasn't* breathing.

The endless fog... something moving through it...

Something alive.

Something *massive*.

Sascha briefly thought about what she'd seen during the Battle of *Ishlangu*, through the hole in *Keeling*'s hull before it sealed—shapes that might be eyes, staring at her.

Recognizing her.

The distant thing came closer, moving at impossible speeds...

As the voluminous, incomprehensible mass drove through crimson and ivory rivers, rending everything in its path, piercing the infinite fog, details began to take form...

Floating and helpless in the boundless, colorful, *impossible* expanse that was the Mud, Sascha Kerkhoffs screamed.

68

BIGGIE

As the cockpit visor opened, Biggie saw Kerkhoffs hit hard, the back of her vacsuited head bouncing off the deck.

The Sklorno thrashed, desperate to get clear of the crysteel-mesh bag, powerful legs kicking and tentacle arms flailing.

Most of the Raiders had vanished down the tunnel to Raider Land, hurrying to secure their weapons—the four or five who remained threw themselves atop the squealing alien, a mass of battered black armor squeezed into the small space aft of Ochthera Two's closed rear ramp and a copper bulkhead thick with tool racks.

Biggie sprang out of the cockpit, her motions blistered by her LASH rig's micromuscle, and rushed toward the melee, crew chief Taylor falling in at her side.

Beaver's left forearm pressed against the Sklorno's thin neck. Wriggling raspers lashed at his helmet, glazing his visor with spit. Beaver's right hand reached to his thigh, pulled his armor-penetrating combat knife, raised it high. The point of the 20-centimeter vanadium-enhanced steel tanto plunged through a whipping rasper and into the Sklorno's chin-plate.

"*Don't fucking* stab *it,*" Sands cried out. "Hold it! Tie it down!"

Taylor turned to a gear rack, grabbed something there and threw

318

it to Biggie. Great pass—Biggie caught it without breaking stride, saw it was a bundle of thick plastic zip-ties.

Biggie reached the edge of the wriggling armor pile. The Sklorno managed to free a foot long enough to kick Reiner, the blow so strong it sent her armored body stumbling back.

Jake Radulski grabbed an eyestalk and *yanked*—the stem tore free in a burst of clear blood.

The alien stiffened, wailed in high-pitched agony. Both raspers snapped back, one retracting into the beast's version of a mouth, the other pulling against the impaled tanto blade's serrated side, slicing the clear flesh and sending clear-gray teeth skittering across the deck.

"God*dammit*, Radulski," Sands roared, "don't rip off its fucking eyestalks, either!"

Biggie dove atop the Sklorno's foot, weighed it down with her body as she tore at the bundle of zip-ties, which popped and scattered across armor, body bag, Sklorno, and deck alike. She snatched one up, looped it around the creature's disgusting foot, tried to grab the other foot to bind them tight.

"Raiders, *step back!*"

The words resonated with command so thick Biggie found herself rolling off the pile even before she realized it was Neal Abshire's voice. The lowly spec's bellowed order hit the other Raiders as well—no one questioned, everyone *moved*, rolling off, pushing off, jumping clear.

Abshire lowered his RR-36 and fired. Backblast smoke billowed behind him—the point-blank stunner round struck the Sklorno in a shimmer of purple energy.

The Sklorno fell limp.

"Shoot that fucker again," Radulski screamed. "No, don't, because I'm gonna *kill* that *fucking* mother*fucker!*"

He drew his knife.

Master Sergeant Sands stepped in and shoved Radulski hard—man and armor flew across the deck, smashed into a tool rack.

"Radulski, *cool your cock*," Sands said. "Get your ass to the weapons locker and secure your weapons." Sands shoved his rifle against Biggie's chest-plate. "Bang, take my rifle and knife to the cage." He drew his blade, handed it to her hilt-first. "Beaver, take Bennett's and Abshire's weapons. Bennett, help me bag this sonofabitch. Taylor, you got any duct tape down here?"

"*Gobs* of it, Master Sergeant," Taylor said.

Bennett pulled a fresh crysteel-mesh bag from an ammo pouch.

"Maaagnificent," Sands said. "When we put this vaginal stain in the bag and seal it, you wrap up the top till not even air molecules can get through. Everyone else, get to the cage so PXO Winter can lock your weapons down. *Move it, move it, move it!*"

The Raiders obeyed in a burst of action.

Carrying the master sergeant's RR-36 and his knife, Biggie stepped over Kerkhoffs and ran aft toward the tunnel sphincter. She glanced over her shoulder as she moved, saw Sands and Bennett hurriedly stripping out of their TASH armor.

The 1MC chimed.

"This is the XO. Raiders, get your weapons secured. All hands, prepare to dive."

Trav held the handset against his chest, the channel open to 1MC. His mouth felt dry, his tongue felt thick enough to choke him.

"Mark 15s splitting and spreading," Brown said.

The nav-orb flashed and pulsed with closing threats, any one of which could be *Keeling*'s destruction, a tightening noose of incoming torps, artillery rounds, Salamander interceptors, cluster rockets tearing through the STC interference. The closer they got, the less interference they faced, the more accurate they became.

And the Komodo heavy cruiser itself, now only 500 kilometers out, spitting even more artillery and self-propelled munitions.

The torp-launched cluster missiles, represented by a red diamond with the number 16 below it, would arrive first, would arrive in *seconds*, unless...

"Mark 15 warheads detonating," Brown said.

In the orb, a flash of yellow representing the new flak cloud flared around the red diamond icon...

The number changed from 16 to 6.

The deck shuddered as Type24s fired desperate, short-range flak rounds.

The number blinked to 3.

"Cluster missiles inside flak range," Brown said.

Travis dropped into his acceleration chair and raised the headset to his ear. "All hands, *brace for impact,* in three..."

Across the CIC, people pushed back into their chairs, preparing for the inevitable concussion.

"Two..."

Travis heard a deep *ping* sound, like someone hitting an immense kettledrum, hitting *several* of them all at once—*Keeling* reverberated in a way he'd never felt before.

"*One!*"

The red diamond blinked out.

Frozen, Travis waited for the sickening tremors brought on by missile impacts, for the agonizing, helpless moments afterward to find out if the ship endured the hit or broke up into pieces, scattering him and his crew into the void.

The tremor didn't come.

"Continue battery flak fire," Lincoln said. "XO, find out what happened to those missiles."

Travis flipped the 38MC switch for the point-defense control channel.

"Point-defense, XO. Did any of you hit those incoming missiles?"

"XO, Forward Point-Defense battery. Negative, it wasn't us. I saw it. The... those pimple things on the hull... a bunch of them swelled up and *burst.* Must have been full of flak or something. The missiles got shredded."

Lindros turned in his seat. "All Raider weapons locked down!"

"Xeno," Lincoln said, loud yet calm as ever, "dive, dive, *dive.*"

This time, Hasik didn't argue about terminology.

Travis held his breath, watched the Salamanders' red triangles closing in.

The triangles, the distance rings, *everything* in the orb blurred, faded, overwhelmed by swelling, thickening, pulsing, multihued static.

The indescribable light of a million suns filled the CIC.

70

BETHANY

Snakes writhed around Susannah's body.

She felt their muscle, their *strength*, as they coiled around her, slid against her. The living ropes bound her, held her. She did not struggle, did not fight, because she *wanted* to be bound by them.

The snakes' bright colors drove into her soul. Their shimmering iridescence cascaded across the atrium, joining the heartstone's pulsating, amber glow. The combined light show caressed Susannah and the hanging plants alike, filling everything they touched with life, with peace.

We will be unified, my Child. We will meld.

When? When would she meld with God, if that's who spoke to her? And if it *wasn't* God, if that was her interpretation of whatever it was, she no longer cared—this power that engulfed her, that lifted up her soul, that *elevated* her to new heights of existence... she belonged to this entity, whatever it may be.

Susannah...

No, she wasn't that person anymore. Her name was *Bethany*.

"Take me," Bethany said, her words flying from her mouth as bursts of indescribable colors, colors that fluttered through sprawling leaves above. "Take me, *please!*"

The word-lights whirled faster and faster, a dizzying, intense cyclone of multichromatic sound.

Bethany. Bethany.

Why was High One calling her that? That wasn't her name. But if High One wanted to call her that, Bethany would comply.

Lieutenant.

Urgency in High One's words now, almost a plea. High One did not need to beg, for Susannah was willing to *meld*, to become one...

Lieutenant Darkwater, wake up.

The snakes and swirling colors vanished. Bethany stared up at hanging fronds and dangling, oversized fruit. She was on her back? But she was staring straight up the conical forest above her, which meant...

...which meant she was lying atop the heartstone.

"Lieutenant Darkwater, can you hear me?"

Colonel Hasik's voice.

Bethany sat up. Hasik stood on the protuberance platform, intentionally not looking at her, but rather off to the side. She was sitting on the heartstone, on its glowing, glassine surface. She felt its warmth against the skin of her legs, of her buttocks.

Against her skin...

"Please put some clothes on," Hasik said.

Bethany was naked.

She pulled her knees to her chest, wrapping her arms around them.

"Colonel," she said, "I don't... I'm not..."

She didn't know what to say. How had she gotten up here?

"It's the Mud, Bethany." Hasik raised a hand to the side of his face to block out any peripheral vision. "Please, get off of there and get dressed."

Her face flushed with shame. Hasik had seen her naked. Perhaps only for a moment. *Naked.* Was there any greater sin a woman could endure?

It's the Mud, Bethany. Except it started *before* the dive into trans-dim. How? Why? And did Hasik know?

"Yes sir." She hopped up, one arm covering her breasts, the other her privates. "Sorry, sir. I don't know what happened."

Hasik waved a hand at her as if to chase away her words.

"Get dressed," he said, and turned his back to her.

Bethany hurried across the heartstone to the catwalk. She climbed over the railing, then descended the stairs, metal-grate steps sharp against the soles of her feet.

She looked around, peering through the ever-present mist.

Where had she put her clothes?

71

JOHN

"XO, we lost a man," John said. "I should be with my squad. Can't you get Colonel Martigral for this? She's the Sklorno expert."

They'd told John to wear his TASH rig. Just in case. XO Ellis, Major Lafferty, Chief of the Boat Eloi Sung, and Corporal Marchenko from engineering wore vacsuits. John even got to carry a weapon, the rarest of rarities while in-dim. If there was a problem, hopefully it was one easily solved by an RR-36 loaded with Sklorno stunner rounds.

"Colonel Martigral is occupied with her subjects," the XO said. "With Lieutenant Lindros... ah... *preoccupied*, I need Sands and Winter monitoring your fellow Raiders, so you get the tap for this. You're an expert, too, Bennett. Like it or not, you're the only one aboard who's been on a Sklorno warship. I know you want to be with your guys, but I need you here."

After a couple of hours in the Mud, XO Ellis ordered the pouch's atmo vented. Lincoln wanted to know what was in the containers that she'd risked Raider lives to retrieve.

Marchenko slowly walked around one of those containers, his focus on the scanner in his hands.

The container was 12.3 meters long, 3.2 meters tall, and 2.6

meters wide, roughly comparable to a standard cargo container used by Human wheeltrucks and haulers. The rippled surface of the top and sides would allow tight stacking, multiple containers fitting together like puzzle pieces with almost no wasted space.

A ship the size of *Leafcutter Alpha* could carry thousands of containers like this.

With the two Ochtheras lined up nose to butt against the port-side bulkhead, there was barely enough room left to walk around the container. If it wasn't for *Keeling*'s growth while in the chrysalis, the containers and Ochtheras together wouldn't have fit at all.

"Hurry up and open the thing already, Marchenko," Chief Lafferty said. "We're wasting time."

Marchenko continued his steady walk around the container. "I appreciate your rank, Major." His eyes remained locked on the scanner in his hands. "I appreciate *not blowing up* a whole lot more, copy?"

Lafferty started to say something, but Chief Sung held up a hand.

"Major, give him a minute," Sung said. "Let him do his job correctly."

Lafferty crossed her arms. She seemed overly agitated. Was she seeing something? Was she hallucinating? John's little rat-shrimp friends weren't around for this trip through the Mud. Not yet, anyway. Small blessings.

Kerkhoffs should have been here for this, but she was in the med bay, knocked out cold from her fall on the flight deck. One of the few casualties of the mission. Her and Spec-1 Onyeka Ayodele.

Yo-Yo. Trained to be a Raider, to be a warrior. In his first combat encounter, he'd choked to death on his own vomit, gone forever because of old, defective armor.

Since *Keeling* was heading home, Lincoln skipped the burial at sea ceremony. Yo-Yo's body lay sealed in one of the many copper cubbyholes peppered throughout *Keeling*'s hull. A portable refrigeration unit would keep his corpse cold until Gateway, where he'd be prepped and shipped to Jupiter Net Colony. His folks there could have a real funeral service. A rarity in Fleet, and damn kind of Captain Lincoln.

A funeral, for a twenty-year-old who had arrived in chains.

John still didn't know what Yo-Yo had done wrong. Now, he never would.

"Container itself is a composite material," Marchenko said. "Doesn't look like there's any metal inside. Or plastic. No sign of explosives. Seems biological in nature, but whatever it is, it's frozen solid in a big block of ice. Doesn't appear to be booby-trapped."

"Of *course* it's not fucking booby-trapped," Lafferty said. "It's a random container from a ship full of them, a ship that had no idea we were coming, that had no idea *anyone* could hit them. XO, it's a goddamn cargo container. So let's see the cargo."

As the ship's executive officer, Ellis had the authority here, but only by a slim margin. Lafferty had the rank. Ellis glanced at Chief Sung, getting the COB's take. Ellis did things like that because he was smart—good officers relied on their noncoms.

"I agree with Major Lafferty," Sung said. "Chenk, open it up."

Marchenko handed Sung the scanner.

The container didn't have a locking mechanism, just a simple latch lever to keep the contents airtight.

Marchenko gripped the lever. "XO, if something in there eats me, lie to my ma—tell her I went out in a blaze of glory."

Ellis nodded. "By the time I'm done, Chenk, they'll write songs about your bravery."

John stepped closer, readied his RR. Maybe there was nothing dangerous inside, but when it came to crickets, he practiced an abundance of caution.

Marchenko lifted the lever. If it made noise, no one could hear it in the pouch's vacuum. He pulled the door open.

Inside, a wall of translucent, frost-coated ice. In that ice, blackish shapes streaked with gray, packed in tight, the largest of which was perhaps 30 centimeters in diameter. John leaned closer. Hard to see through the ice. Looked like some bits stretched in deeper—whatever they were, they were packed lengthwise.

"Like I told you, frozen solid," Marchenko said, peering closer. "Although I don't know what they are. Some kind of alien fish or something?"

The blackish shapes... *hair*. Coarse, thick hair. The gray, stretching in deeper, barely discernible from the ice itself.

No... no way...

"They're Sklorno," John said. "Compacted and frozen."

Marchenko held his hand out to Sung. "COB, can I have my scanner back?"

Sung handed it to him. Marchenko held it near the wall of ice and started recalibrating the instrument.

Ellis stepped closer. "Is this some kind of funeral rite or something?"

"Unlikely," Lafferty said, her voice taking on an air of excitement. "Not unless these Sklorno converted to Purism and wanted to be buried on the Nation's homeworld."

Marchenko stepped to the container's side, aimed the scanner up and down its length.

"It's *full* of them," he said. "Gotta be... three thousand bodies in there."

Three thousand dead Sklorno?

"They're packed in like sardines," the XO said.

Sardines...

John had eaten sardines once, when his squad mate, Tudor Sevastian, received a care package from his parents on Earth. Tudor—may his soul rest in peace—shared the tin with his comrades. John still remembered the oddly ceremonial process of using the little key to roll back the tin's top, exposing the glistening fish beneath.

Sardines... holy shit...

"XO," John said, "BII said the convoy carried supplies, including food. I think these bodies are packed like this because *they* are the food."

No one spoke.

It was an insane concept, John knew, yet what else could explain it?

"But these are—or were—sentient beings," XO Ellis said. "They can't be food."

Lafferty stepped closer to John, stood next to him.

"Sklorno eat people," she said. "That's a documented fact."

A fact John knew all too well.

Lafferty rapped her knuckles against the ice, knocking free a small shower of frost.

"As far as we know, they can digest us with no issues," she said. "And if they can eat *us*, then..."

Her voice trailed off.

The XO's eyes widened.

"Then we can probably eat them," Ellis said. "Humans can eat them. *Purists* can eat them."

One container out of how many? Were they all packed like this?

John and the others stood there, trying to get their heads around what seemed obvious—Sklorno had butchered their own citizens, then shipped the bodies across the galaxy to feed the Purist Nation's army.

Holy shit indeed.

72

ANNE

Six hours into the transdim journey back to New Earth, Anne had yet to see a single person glow. She didn't know why it didn't work this time. Well, it worked a little bit, at least—*people* didn't glow, but the Sklorno were another story.

Three vertical containment cells, each as narrow as an upright coffin. With the cells, chemical pumps, monitoring equipment, and Martigral herself, there wasn't much room left in what had once been the tiny gym compartment.

Within the cells, mesh bands kept the captives' legs tightly folded so they couldn't extend. Similar bands wrapped around the captives' necks so they couldn't move their strange heads. Still other bands pinned tentacle arms against their trunks. Metal masks prevented chin plates from opening, trapping the wicked, tooth-studded raspers inside.

Beneath strange, translucent flesh, Anne saw their darker skeletons and coursing blood.

Astonishing. She was face-to-face with a Sklorno—so to speak, anyway, considering the cricket's nasty collection of eyes and mouth —yet neither she nor the alien was dead or dying. *Humanity, fuck yeah.* She wouldn't have thought such a thing possible, but with

Keeling's unprecedented abilities, the potential for warfighting seemed limitless.

Most of the crew hated the *Crypt*. Not Anne. She loved this ship. *Loved* it.

The Sklorno in the middle—the awake one—glowed a suffused lemon-peel-yellow, mostly in its chest and eyestalks.

"Maybe they're hallucinating," Anne said. "Just like Humans do."

Martigral shook her head, peered at a small display screen on the center cell.

"Doubtful. We don't know if they can hallucinate at all. Even if they can, it doesn't matter—the anesthesia has them under control."

Anne wondered if Martigral was saying that to make herself feel better. One Sklorno was out cold, eyestalks drooping down, but another's drifted lazily. Its eyelids—surprisingly similar to those of a Human, only clear—slowly blinked.

The captive in the middle, though, the one that put Kerkhoffs in the infirmary, the one Radulski almost killed, looked wide awake. Its three remaining eyestalks moved like cobras to a snake charmer's flute.

Anne had watched the blockbuster movies—*Sklorno Massacre I* and *Sklorno Massacre II* stood out as classics. *Cricket Exterminator* was also a good one, although it had been re-named to *Sklorno Hunter* due to outrage from simps who objected to both the word *cricket*—which they claimed was "speciesist"—and the word *exterminator*, as it presented Sklorno not as a sentient species with its own history and culture, but as a pest to be wiped out.

She'd devoured documentaries as well. She'd followed the news of xenobiologists' multiple efforts to contact and communicate with Sklorno—all of which failed. She'd been read-in, well after the fact, to a secret Fleet mission that sent an Egret-class coldship to directly contact the species.

The Sklorno destroyed that ship. All hands lost.

She'd even watched the few depositions—there were only four—

of people who'd managed to escape from vessels boarded by the bloodthirsty aliens. Those survivors described the terror of a supposedly "sentient" species killing and eating the crew, even as they waited to be the next meal themselves.

And, of course, there were the debriefings of sailors and Raiders who'd faced the hostile species in close-quarters combat, either boarding Sklorno vessels or repelling Sklorno boarders from Fleet ships. There were only seventeen of those cases, the most prominent of which was by one borderline-elderly member of *Keeling*'s crew: Corporal John Bennett.

Anne knew more about Sklorno than most, but it was one thing to watch movies and documentaries, another entirely to see crickets in real life.

The middle captive's three alien eyes stared at her. Did she see fear in them? Anger? *Hate*? She couldn't tell.

Did these creatures have families? Friends? One moment they were living their alien lives, the next, they were specimens for study, never to see their homes again.

Oh, well. War sucks when you're on the losing side.

"U, G, L, Y," Anne said. "You ain't got no alibi, you're ugly."

"Ugly?" Martigral shook her head. "Not at all. *Different*? Yes. As different from us as any species we know. Culturally speaking, that is."

There were sentient species far more *biologically* different than Humans, namely the Rewall and the Prawatt. Both were collective organisms more akin to bacterial colonies than to *Homo Sapiens*, but at least humanity could communicate with them.

"Physiologically, they don't *look* similar to us, but they are," Martigral said. "Similar circulatory system. Similar muscular structure. Even their eyes aren't so different. Their homeworld is quite comparable to ours." Smiling slightly, Martigral stared at each captive in turn. "In the last few hours alone, I've already proven several of my theories about our two species' convergent evolution. What we have accomplished on this mission is already breathtaking—and we've scarcely scratched the surface."

The way Martigral *looked* at the Sklorno, with fascination bordering on adoration.

"This is going to make your career," Anne said.

Martigral nodded. "It certainly will. And I assume it won't exactly hurt yours, either, Major."

Anne hadn't planned this op. Prior to receiving Epperson's orders, she'd had no knowledge of it. But she was the intel chief during this unprecedented event. That mattered.

Daddy would be over the moon.

Martigral wasn't wrong, but even the unreality of looking at Sklorno captives and the promise of career advancement couldn't completely chase away the lust Anne felt during the battle.

As attractive as she found Travis Ellis, thinking of jumping his bones during a life-and-death situation wasn't like her. Sorro was hot, too, but Alex Plait? Balding, out of shape—not her cup of tea. And while *maybe* she could envision a moment when Plait might provide a welcome distraction if Ellis, Sorro, or Beth weren't available... *Hasik?* Had she actually wondered what that lying troll's cock looked like?

Those urges had vanished, though. Would they come back if another fight or stressful situation came?

Maybe Anne just needed to get laid.

That would solve the problem.

Something to worry about another time—there was intel still to be gathered, analysis to be made, and probable conclusions to be reached.

"Colonel, I told you what was in the captured containers," Anne said. "Do you agree those frozen Sklorno corpses were meant to be food?"

The colonel looked at the third cell's monitor. Her brow furrowed in concern.

"Your hypothesis is logical," she said. "There are multiple documented cases of Sklorno eating Human flesh. We've found no reason Humans can't eat Sklorno."

Martigral made notes on a pad of paper.

"Major Lafferty, this is classified, but I'll tell you. Years ago, in the First Galactic War, Fleet won a small battle with the Sklorno. The Sklorno, predictably, scuttled their own warships so they could not be taken alive, but we were able to recover part of one ship. That part contained their version of a galley. In it, Fleet found containers packed with butchered Sklorno bodies. The prevailing theory is they deal with overpopulation and starvation by killing their own, then eating the dead so nothing goes to waste."

That would definitely tick the box for *cultural differences.*

"We destroyed five ships," Anne said. "Five ships with a cargo capacity of over a million tonnes each. The reason we started that convoy was because it carried materiel for the Purist war machine, but there was likely ample cargo space beyond that materiel." The potential numbers boggled her. "There could have been millions of Sklorno in that shipment, Colonel. Frozen and packed in tight. *Millions.* Is such a thing even possible?"

Martigral stopped writing. She looked at her captives.

"The Dynasty is estimated to have between sixty and eighty billion Sklorno," she said. "If the convoy contained, say, a million dead Sklorno, that would be zero point zero zero one four three percent of their total population." She lifted the pad, scribbled something down. "One million would be little more than a rounding error to them. Knowing the species organization abilities and utter ruthlessness, I'd say such a thing is definitely possible."

Fleet's premier expert on Sklorno believed the species capable of massacring a million of their own—to trade as food.

"Makes you wonder what the Purists gave them in return," Anne said.

Martigral laughed. Something about that amused her. Anne didn't find any of it funny.

"I'm afraid intergalactic trade isn't my concern." The colonel jotted something down, then lowered the pad. "Do these three specimens frighten you, Major? Do you worry they might escape their containment and eat *us?*"

While that would be a bad way to go, Anne didn't fear death. By any method. She'd been in the field on her own enough times to know an unexpected end might be scant moments away.

"What terrifies me," Anne said, "is that the Union can't even *speak* to Sklorno, yet the Purist Nation—of all governments— somehow negotiated a trade deal. We've been lapped by a backwater system of religious primitives who worship stars."

Religious primitives who had also planted a spy right under Anne's nose. A spy who hurt Anne's career as much as—if not more than—this unprecedented success would help it.

"Yes, that is terrifying," Martigral said. "The Nation may be a theocracy, but as for how *primitive* they are, Major, I have my doubts. What they can't invent on their own they try to copy from others. Or just steal technology outright. Purists are not true luddites. Like us, they have scientists."

Scientists like Beth, although Beth claimed she'd spent her decade in the Nation as a truck-driving nun. And yet, here she was, on *Keeling*, as the number-two scientist aboard, privy to the Union's most-classified weapon.

Beth knew more about that weapon, about the *Crypt*, than Anne did. A fact Anne found to be a bit disturbing.

But Beth was safe. Beth was trustworthy.

Wasn't she?

Of course she was. Anne had more important things to worry about, like the executive staff's mission debriefing, and after, finally getting some sleep. She and the other executive staffers had been up for going on twenty-four hours straight.

"I'll leave you to it," Anne said. "If you need anything, don't hesitate to ask. The Spookhouse is one call and one deck away."

Martigral mumbled something as she again bent to read the first display, starting her cycle over.

Was that... a light blue glow? Yes, faint, but there. Coming from inside Martigral's head. She seemed fine, though. Dozens of crewmembers endured minor hallucinations, visions that didn't get in the way of them doing their jobs.

Anne stepped out of the compartment and closed the door behind her.

A Raider guard—Spec-1 CARPENTER, one of the newbies—straightened at attention. Seventeen years old. A babyface, although the faded scar on his upper lip gave him a slight, perpetual sneer. No armor, no weapons, but he was a big kid, intimidating enough to dissuade any curious sailor from trying to sneak a peek inside. Only Martigral, Anne, the XO, and Captain Lincoln had access to the compartment.

Carpenter didn't glow. That was good.

"How are you doing, Spec?" Anne asked.

"I'm good, sir," Carpenter said. "Although, it's torture being on duty here and having to smell that good cooking. I'm *starving*."

Anne glanced to the crew mess entrance, just a few meters aft and across the passageway. Sounded like it was packed. She sniffed.

"Fresh biscuits," she said. "That it?"

Carpenter nodded. "Yes sir. People keep walking by with them. I can't eat on account of being on duty, and the mess is *right there*. Cruel and unusual punishment, if you ask me."

Carpenter... Anne still didn't know what he'd done to wind up on the *Crypt*. Maybe she'd see if Daniels had any ideas on that front.

"That's hardly fair to you," Anne said. "How about I grab you one *and* give you permission to eat it right here?"

Carpenter brightened. "That'd be real nice of you, Major."

Anne was due in the wardroom in a few minutes, but she had enough time to grab the man some sustenance—it never hurt to be in the good graces of the jarheads.

73

BETHANY

Bethany and Colonel Hasik waited in the passageway outside the wardroom. Hasik hadn't said a word about Bethany's confusing, humiliating act. For that, she was grateful. He seemed to act like it had never happened.

She wished that were true.

Oh, how the events of the past few months had changed her. To think she'd gone from a hauler-driving nun, celibate and happy in her convent, to a person who stripped naked and masturbated atop the power source of a warship.

And then there was that small detail of killing a person.

But did she want to go back to that convent? No. She wanted to be here, with *Keeling*.

The wardroom door opened and executive staff filtered out. They looked as tired as Bethany felt.

Alex Plait gave Bethany a smile. Brown nodded her way. Doug Erickson stared down at his shuffling feet. Sergeant Sands kept twitching his head away from something only he saw. Chief Sung wasn't there, as he had the conn. He'd had some sleep, apparently, one of the lucky few Lincoln ordered to their racks right after the battle so that at least some crew would be properly rested.

Hallucinations or not, on the *Crypt*, those who could keep going simply kept going.

Hasik entered the wardroom and Bethany followed.

The table was trashed: crumb-dotted mycoware plates; crumpled cloth napkins; an empty basket that might have once held biscuits. Hunger pangs pinched Bethany's belly, even though she'd just wolfed down some cereal and milk in the mess. She'd even eaten the mycoware bowl. And the spoon.

Her body, craving the calories burned from the stress of combat, probably.

Lincoln sat in her usual spot at the head of the table, elbow on the tabletop, cheek leaned against her hand. Sweat stained her doo-rag. A cup of coffee steamed in front of her. XO Ellis sat on her right, scribbling furiously on a scrap of paper torn from one of the big rolls in the CIC.

And, of course, at the far end of the table, sat Major Murder herself, obviously exhausted, although her black coveralls looked sharp and spotless as always.

"Hello, Lieutenant Darkwater," Lafferty said with a warm smile. "Glad to see you're okay."

Did Lafferty know Bethany had been found naked atop the heartstone only eight hours earlier? Did she know Bethany's lust-filled meltdown happened *before* the ship went transdim? Had Hasik already told Lafferty? Was that a black mark against Bethany? Would it make Major Murder distrust her?

"I'm fine, thank you, Major," Bethany said, forcing an appropriate yet not-too-familiar smile, because the captain and the XO were sitting right there. "I'm glad to see you're all right as well."

Lincoln straightened, blinking away fatigue.

"Grab a coffee and sit," she said. "Both of you."

Hasik looked at Bethany, nodded toward an open chair. He went to the urn.

Thankfully, the chair he'd indicated was in the middle of the table—not too close to Lafferty, and not so far away it would look like Bethany was avoiding her.

Bethany wanted to feel the presence of God, but God did not reach out. She'd felt nothing since Hasik woke her. Nothing at all. That wasn't unusual; sometimes, Bethany went a day or more in the Mud without the adored sensation of *connection*, of *belonging*. While it didn't worry her, she missed it.

Hasik set a mycoware cup of steaming coffee in front of Bethany, then sat next to her, at Lincoln's left, and sipped from his own cup.

Lincoln rolled out her shoulders. "My apologies for taking this long to talk to you both." She yawned. "There's a lot going on. Have either of you slept?"

The captain looked drained. Drained and somewhat withdrawn. Bethany wondered if the captain had also suffered... *odd* behavior during the battle.

"Not a wink," Hasik said. "We're shorthanded in Xeno. Martigral must be busy playing with her new toys."

Lincoln licked her fingertip, touched it to the table; a breadcrumb stuck to it. She sucked it free, then rubbed her fingers on a balled napkin.

"When we reach port, Martigral will depart along with our POWs," Lincoln said. "I'd rather not have Maia Whittaker foist another surprise sailor upon us to fill the Xeno Mate position. I don't want to be shorthanded in that department ever again. I want at least two qualified people in the atrium any time we face hostilities. Major Lafferty, perhaps it would be better if we promoted from within?"

Lafferty brightened. "That is a *fantastic* idea, Captain. We can ask Kerkhoffs if anyone in engineering is a good fit." She looked at Hasik. "Colonel, you might not get someone with an applicable degree, but you could train them to do what's needed."

Hasik reached out and tipped the biscuit basket toward him, seemed disappointed to find it empty.

"I'm *famished*," he said. "Major Lafferty, I would gladly give up someone with multiple PhD's for a nice bit of consistency. Hopefully a xeno mate with more... *common sense* this time. I'm tired of my staff dying horrible deaths."

Ellis stopped writing. Pencil still on the paper, his tired eyes locked on Hasik.

The colonel realized what he'd just said. "Oh, I'm sorry, Bethany. That was... rude of me."

...the knife...

"It's fine, Colonel," Bethany said. "It's fine."

...Hathorn's blood...

Lincoln rapped her knuckles on the table in an obvious—and welcome—effort to change the subject.

"I'm starving," she said. "Zvanut, let's get you fed. Bethany, are you hungry?"

It was so strange to hear Colonel Hasik's first name spoken out loud. And had Lincoln just called her *Bethany?*

"Yes, Captain," Bethany said. "I could eat."

Lincoln stood and went to the closed galley window. She knocked on it.

"Bradley, can you bring us three—" she glanced at Ellis, who nodded, then at Major Murder, who shook her head "—four more of those sensational portobello sandwiches? And if there are more biscuits, some of those as well."

The window slid open. Big Bradley Henry's head peeked out.

"*More* sandwiches?" He quickly glanced around the wardroom. "You had two already, Captain. You're gonna swell up like a tick."

Lincoln returned to her seat. "Winning the war requires a lot of calories, it seems." "That it does, Captain," Henry said. "Sandwiches en route."

He slid the window shut.

Ellis started writing again. Furiously. Bethany wondered if the letters, numbers, and formulas he wrote down would be the same when they returned to realspace. Hasik said sometimes things like writing—or even *math* itself—might not be the same in another dimension, but they would never really know, because what was written down might change as well, somehow conforming to the different physics of realspace. Concepts like that lurked in the deeper end of the multidimensional pool. Bethany did not pretend to understand it.

Ellis put his pencil down and leaned back in his chair. He, too, seemed both exhausted and distant. Perhaps he was enduring a hallucination at that very moment.

"We need to know the xeno department's take on those pimples," he said. "Somehow, this ship grew its own kind of point-defense. The external gun crews say the pimples detonated from within, sending out clouds of shrapnel that destroyed incoming missiles. If either of you knew what the pimples were and didn't tell us, now is the time to speak up. Did you know? Did you trigger their detonation?"

Bradley Henry entered, his big hands carrying a stack of thick sandwiches wrapped in wax. "Outta biscuits." He set the sandwiches on the table. "Sorry, Captain, you're not the only hungry one aboard." He grabbed up the empty plates and basket. "Damn crew's been in the galley eating up everything in sight."

Lincoln handed out the sandwiches.

"I understand," she said. "When's the last time you had sleep, Bradley?"

The big cook blinked a few times, trying to remember.

"Oh, maybe nine or ten hours before we surfaced at Junction Nest. Same for my team. We wanted to make sure there was plenty of hot food ready for after the battle."

Which meant he'd been up for something around twenty hours, working the entire time, most likely.

"Go get some sleep," Lincoln said. "That's an order. Your staff, too. Those still on duty can make do for the next eight hours. I want you nice and rested for our victory celebration when we surface at New Earth."

Henry nearly sagged with relief. "Aye-aye, Captain." He hurried out as if he wanted to leave before Lincoln changed her mind.

Hasik unwrapped his sandwich. Bethany did the same. Grilled

portobello on a toasted brioche bun. It smelled *amazing*, all smoky and charred. It wasn't a single mushroom cap, but rather a steak-thick chunk of one sliced from the meter-wide portobellos growing upside-down in the atrium.

"We didn't trigger anything," Hasik said as he took a big bite. "The response was..." he chewed, swallowed "...automatic. And no, we didn't know what the blisters were." He chomped down again.

Bethany knew Hasik had eaten only an hour ago, yet he ate like a starving man. And this was Lincoln's *third* sandwich?

Something odd about that.

Bethany bit into her sandwich; it tasted even better than it smelled.

"We need to know what happened," Ellis said. "If those pimples hadn't... well... *popped*... at least three missiles would have struck us before we entered transdim. The ship would have been damaged. Possibly even destroyed. We might all be dead, Colonel."

Ellis didn't eat his sandwich. He slowly rotated it in place atop the crinkly wax paper.

"And yet we are *not* dead," Hasik said. "While I appreciate your need for information, XO, I can provide no insights until we get out on the hull to examine the remnants of those strange growths. We can't do that while in transdim. I can't even *see* what they look like right now, because of the minimum focus distance for the optical system. Until we enter realspace, I simply don't know what happened."

Lincoln bit into her sandwich, spoke as she chewed. "When we surface at New Earth, Colonel, I'll allot you two hours to get on the hull and take a look." She wiped a dribble of portobello juice from her chin. "You ensure we're good to enter punch-space. Anything more than that will have to wait until we return to Gateway."

Conversation ceased as people ate. Ellis took big bites. Hasik took bigger bites. Lincoln practically inhaled hers.

So *strange*.

"Classy bunch," Major Murder said. "Dining manners extraordinaire."

Bethany raised her sandwich to her mouth, but froze when the XO's see-right-through-you stare landed on her.

"So we don't know *how* the pimples formed," he said. "I suspect that you, Lieutenant Darkwater, have a hypothesis on *why* they formed?"

All eyes turned toward her. Including Hasik's.

Bethany flushed with embarrassment. Everyone was *staring*. She set her sandwich down.

"XO, I know as much or as little as you do. I couldn't begin to surmise why—"

He straightened the fingers of his right hand, a sharp gesture, one that silently said *just stop it already*.

"Your best guess will suffice for now," he said. "You seem to understand this ship on a—" he glanced at Lafferty "—more *fundamental* level than the rest of us."

Lafferty nodded.

Lincoln watched, saying nothing.

Had they been talking about her? What had they said?

Bethany wanted Hasik to step in, tell the XO to leave her be. Instead, Hasik—still looking at her, waiting for her response—shoved his last hunk of sandwich into his mouth.

They wanted her thoughts on why the blisters formed. She marveled at their lack of awareness, at their ignorance of the majesty surrounding them all. She realized then that not even Hasik truly understood. He knew more than she did about *Keeling*, true, but his knowledge was like knowing what the notes on a music staff meant without being able to hear the *music* they represented.

All right then. If they wanted the truth, she would tell them the truth.

"Captain, Colonel Hasik, I realize you can't tell me details, but can you tell me if *Keeling* was involved in combat before the Battle of Ishlangu?"

The two exchanged a glance.

"Yes," Lincoln said. "That is correct."

Of course it was correct.

"And the ship took damage?"

Lincoln and Hasik traded another look, only, this time, Bethany sensed it was the captain silently telling Hasik he could share a bit more information than he had before.

"That is also correct," Hasik said. "Extensive damage from artillery."

Bethany imagined poor *Keeling* suffering greatly from high-velocity projectiles and explosive rounds.

"But no torpedoes," she said. "And no missiles?"

Hasik shook his head. "To my knowledge, the Purist missile that hit us in the *Ishlangu* encounter was the first such weapon to strike *Keeling*."

He chose his words carefully. There was much he would not say, probably would *never* say. The scant supporting detail he provided, though, shored up Bethany's hypothesis.

"I see. And *Keeling* has never gone through metamorphosis before?"

Hasik nodded quickly—that kind of information wasn't embargoed in any way.

"That is correct, Lieutenant," he said. "The metamorphosis at Gateway was the first. As far as I'm aware of, at least."

He was the cauldron of knowledge for the ship, yet there seemed to be a period that predated his experience. Bethany felt anger rising —what had Epperson and Fleet command done to *Keeling* before Hasik came aboard?

"I believe some of the ship's changes are in response to stimuli experienced in battle," Bethany said. "*Keeling* grew a new kind of wiring, what we call *conduit*. We call it that because it's *not* wiring, it's something different, something more like the mesh of a neural net. Conduit is more efficient, more robust, and more redundant than the wiring we had, which means it maintains a higher probability of functioning when we take damage. *Keeling* saw a need and replaced part of our technology with something better."

Bethany's audience said nothing, yet she could see her words hit home. Everyone here already knew *Keeling* had grown something better, but they hadn't conjectured the impetus behind the growth. Maybe because they'd all be so busy with duties and mission prep since the chrysalis retracted. And if they did have ideas, those ideas didn't matter to command—Epperson had sent them out on a dangerous combat run without even pausing to take a look under the hood himself.

Come to think of it, Bethany also hadn't realized the impetus for the changes, at least not fully. Not until now. She'd been busy, too.

"*Keeling* has been in battle before," Lincoln said. "Damaged in battle. Why didn't she grow conduit after those incidents?"

Sometimes, being very smart in a room full of those with lesser intelligence drained a person's reserves.

"Probably because she can only make large-scale changes like that while in stasis," Bethany said. "To use scientific analogs, a caterpillar undergoes massive change only while in stasis, only while in a chrysalis, when the imaginal cells activate and completely alter the caterpillar's form. Histolysis, histogenesis, eclosion—we saw the same things occur in *Keeling*."

The raised eyebrows and blinking told her the others didn't know those biological terms, but they got the context.

XO Ellis leaned forward, elbows on the table.

"You're comparing the ship to living organisms again," he said. "Do you believe this ship is alive?"

Lafferty's stare intensified, as if she were watching a drama that had just reached the good part. Not quite a cat observing a mouse, but not far from it. She studied Bethany like a scientist observing how a specimen behaved—just before dissecting it to see what made it tick.

"We've been over this," Hasik said, sharply. "The ship is an automatomic construct, XO. It is no more *alive* than any other self-assembling, self-repairing entity."

A strange hill to die on, considering the entire Prawatt species was self-assembling and self-repairing, yet most scientists considered them to be living things. Biomechanical sentient beings. Bethany thought of diving into a discussion regarding that point, but she remembered that *Bethany Darkwater* wasn't an expert in that field—*Susannah Rossi* was.

Did Hasik believe what he was saying? Or was his insistence on accepted dogma due to Epperson's influence and control? Maybe Hasik did believe *Keeling* was alive, but he dared not speak such a thing out loud.

"You asked about missiles," Captain Lincoln said. "Your thought is that the ship grew the pimples *because it was hit by a missile?*"

Well, well, well... there was a decent observationalist among them after all.

"Yes, Captain, that is my hypothesis," Bethany said. "*Keeling* took damage from a missile. Not the superstructure, which is a manmade addition built by Fleet engineers, but the hull—the ship *itself* took damage. *Keeling* was *wounded.*"

There it was... the plain truth.

In that moment, Bethany realized that Lincoln and XO Ellis weren't *creators* or *builders* or *scientists*, trying to gain an in-depth understanding of how things functioned, of why things came to be. They were *operators*. Show them how to operate a tool or a weapon and they would apply themselves until they excelled at its use.

Lincoln and the others didn't see it. They used *Keeling*'s gifts without wonder or reverence—as if she was nothing but a machine.

Someday, maybe, they would understand.

Someday, maybe, they would sense the *presence*.

They would welcome the *love*.

"*Keeling* adapted," Bethany said. "Whatever species created him, they created him to respond to... to..."

She lost her thread, because at that moment she felt the *connec-*

tion, felt *Keeling*'s love, and realized that in many ways she was no different from Lincoln—and Ellis and Lafferty and Hasik—in that she hadn't truly understood until now. At least not this part of it, this tiny sliver of the holy mystery that was God.

And she had referred to *Keeling* as a "him." That wasn't how Fleet described ships. She'd deferred to the masculine, because High One—God—was exactly that. So said the scriptures.

A slip of the tongue. She would correct it. Her crewmates weren't ready to accept the truth.

"*Keeling*'s creators designed her to respond to whatever environment she encountered," Bethany said. "They made a ship that *evolves*."

The 1MC chime sounded.

"Attention, attention, this is Chief Sung. Captain Lincoln, XO Ellis, requesting you report to the CIC immediately. We have detected a moving object within darsat range. That is all."

There was a brief moment of silence, perhaps the general fatigue slowing everyone's reaction time, then it hit them all at once.

They were in transdim and something out there—something within darsat range—was *moving*.

Lincoln stood. "Lieutenant Darkwater, return to the atrium. Hasik, XO, Chief Lafferty, come with me."

Travis, Lafferty, Hasik, and Lincoln entered the CIC, each moving to their assigned stations.

Travis expected the burst of adrenaline that came with a new danger, but he didn't feel a boost. He'd gone almost a full standard day without sleep.

"I have the conn," Lincoln said.

"I stand relieved," Sung said as he moved to the command slate's right side. "All stations, Captain has the deck and the conn."

The CIC ran with a reduced crew—navigation, operations, signals, co-pilot, and weapons stations were unmanned. In the Mud, on a fixed transdim course, there was no immediate need for those personnel. With multiple people restrained to their racks or anesthetized, it was critical to make sure the sane ones had proper, post-action rest.

"Talk to me, Chief," Lincoln said. "What do we have?"

The nav-orb showed the Mud's crimson milk, swirling and pulsing with endlessly fusing and diverging flows leading in all directions. A hollow, yellow hexagon hovered at starboard high, labeled *Locus Eight.*

Yellow—the color of an unidentified contact.

That was different from a white icon, which represented an *unknown* contact. *Unknown* meant the darsat system knew the contact was a ship or some other familiar object, it just didn't know what *kind* of ship or object it was. *Unidentified*, on the other hand, meant something so unusual, so *different*, that the darsat database had never encountered anything like it before.

The yellow hex outline left hazy trails of disturbed Mud in its path—a path that was not a straight line.

The contact, whatever it might be, was maneuvering.

"Approximately five minutes ago, darsat detected an unidentified, moving mass tagged as *Locus Eight*," Sung said. "No comparable grav-sig in the database. Average bearing, starboard one-two-seven high. Average elevation, zero-four-nine. Average range..." he trailed off, as if he doubted himself, but the range lines in the sphere showed the distance "...average range, two hundred and fifty thousand kilometers."

A significant distance, at least from a warship's perspective, but Travis understood Sung's consternation. While *Keeling*'s optical system had shown traces of unknown objects moving through the Mud before, those objects had been much farther away—too far for darsat to get any kind of lock.

Which made *Locus Eight* the closest moving object the crew had yet seen in the Mud.

"XO, sound general quarters," Lincoln said. "Chief Sung, man the ops station and get Erickson up here on the double."

Travis grabbed the handset, flicked on the 1MC.

"This is the XO. General quarters, general quarters. That is all."

The general quarters alarm sounded. Standby crew would rush to fill the empty CIC positions. Hopefully the people meant for those positions hadn't succumbed to hallucinations between now and the last time they'd reported in.

"Darsat," Lincoln said, "what is the mass of *Locus Eight*?"

Spec-3 Waldren manned the darsat station. She'd recovered from screaming about the devil and puking all over the place. Her presence here likely meant Gurgen Hakobyan was getting some well-deserved sleep.

"Estimates fluctuate," Waldren said. "Distance is a factor, Captain. And... I don't know any other way to say this... but I don't think darsat measures mass displacement the same way in the Mud as it does in realspace. Best estimate is between ten tonnes and one hundred tonnes."

Anything from an APC to a small patrol craft about one-tenth *Keeling*'s size. Darsat measurements were usually far tighter, not a 10x variable from lowest to highest.

"Captain, a wide variance like that is not unexpected," Hasik called out from the xeno loft. "This dimension's physics don't line up with our own. Gravity here might not be the same."

No matter how many times Travis heard that, it always boggled his mind.

An unexpected pull of forward acceleration; he gripped the command slate to keep from stumbling backward.

In the nav-orb, *Locus Eight*'s yellow hex rotated toward port and declined at the same time, moving toward the direction in which the *Keeling* arrow pointed—*Keeling* was turning starboard and angling up.

"Pilot," Lincoln said sharply, "I ordered no change in course."

Spec-3 pilot Greg Houston manned the pilot's station, the CIC's forward-left seat. The co-pilot seat to his right sat empty. Houston worked the yoke with greater and greater intensity.

"I didn't change course, Captain. Helm is not responding."

A surge of anxiety hit Trav.

Lincoln seemed to sense his concern, leaned in. "We haven't detected an object like this before, but we have had instances of losing control. It's not as bad as it sounds, XO. It's happened to me twice, a few more times to Hasik."

The captain stood straight again. She undoubtedly knew Trav's unspoken question: *I'm second-in-command, why wasn't I told this could happen?* Chalk it up to *Keeling's* ridiculous secrecy, where protecting information was more important than protecting lives.

The wardroom discussion with Darkwater bubbled up through his anxiety and fatigue. Darkwater seemed to know more than Hasik, yet she had a fraction of his experience. And the way her face brightened when she spoke of *Keeling*... as if she damn near *worshiped* the ship.

Disturbing, to say the least.

In the orb, *Locus Eight* continued to rotate down and left as *Keeling* angled up and turned starboard. *Eight's* icon was now almost directly ahead of *Keeling's* arrow. The rings indicated a distance of 195,000 kilometers.

Keeling was moving closer.

Fighting through a haze of fatigue, Travis stared at the nav-orb. Keeling was angling up, turning starboard—no helm input, no command. It was moving toward the contact. On purpose.

Was this a preprogrammed transdim response, like a defense drone tracking motion of a possible threat?

Or... had the ship *decided* to investigate?

"Colonel Hasik, give me your recommendation," Lincoln said. "Do you want to send Darkwater up here to man the Xeno station so you can examine the linkage?"

The linkage system, the interface between *Keeling's* inherent transdim movement and Fleet's navigation controls. Did Travis know how that worked? Of course not. Yet another secret kept from him.

"Try chemjets first," Hasik said. "That worked last time."

Lincoln hid her emotions well, but Travis had come to know her mannerisms. He sensed her frustration. Even though she made it sound like this wasn't a major issue, she—like any warship commander—hated having anything beyond her control.

"Pilot, chemjets," Lincoln said. "Full-reverse, three-second burn."

Houston repeated the order. He triggered the burn. Where Travis had felt the backward pull of the *Keeling* accelerating, he now felt deceleration's forward push.

In the orb, *Locus Eight* suddenly accelerated away, tacking up and to starboard. It shot to the orb's outer distance ring and was gone.

Had *Eight*'s crew detected the burn? If it *had* a crew. Travis had no idea what the object was.

"Darsat, extend range," Lincoln said. "Get *Locus Eight* back."

"Maximum range for an object of that relative mass is already represented in the orb," Waldren said, her voice calm and steady. "*Locus Eight* is too small to be detected beyond the range currently shown."

Lincoln grunted in annoyance. Losing a contact was bad, but at this distance it wasn't an immediate concern.

Erickson rushed into the CIC and sat at the nav station. Pilot Sora Garcia raced in after and manned the co-pilot station.

Frederik Madison stumbled in. The signals chief looked like he'd been awake all of thirty seconds.

"Signals," Lincoln said, "give me max optical in-orb. Do it fast."

Madison slumped into his chair, his hands working the controls on autopilot while his brain tried to catch up.

In the orb, the sphere of visible Mud contracted, distance rings shrinking inward, rings appearing at the equator before shrinking themselves. In seconds, the relatively detailed 200,000-kilometer view became a denser image covering 1,000,000 kilometers in all directions. It was akin to looking at a cluster of nerve cells through a microscope, then pulling back so fast you couldn't tell one cell from the next.

Travis saw no sign of movement. No dark dots in the glimmering, shimmering, crimson-and-cream web. No dark paths scratching their way through the mesmerizing Mud.

"We lost it," he said.

"Conn, Pilot. I have regained helm control."

Lincoln turned to face the xeno loft. "Xeno, what do you think that contact was?"

Lincoln had four *Keeling* deployments under her belt—Hasik had seven.

"Your guess is as good as mine, Captain," the colonel said.

That didn't sit quite as well with Lincoln. "Should we pursue?"

Hasik glanced at the nav-orb.

"It would take us several hours just to reach its last known location," he said. "My recommendation is to get us back on course and get us home. The crew is tired, Captain."

Those words brought Trav's fatigue thundering back; he'd pushed it down, held it at bay, but he'd gone many stress-filled hours without a moment's reprieve.

"I agree," Lafferty said from the Intel Loft. "Exploring the Mud is not our mission at this time."

Lincoln considered. She put a hand on the command slate to steady herself; Travis wondered if she might pass out from pure exhaustion.

"XO, secure from general quarters," the captain said.

Travis did as she ordered.

Lincoln dug the heel of her hand into one eye.

"Chief Sung, you have the conn," she said. "I want the CIC fully staffed ASAP. XO, Xeno, Intel, get some sleep while you can. I'll do the same. Report to my quarters at oh-eight-thirty."

Travis glanced to the clock-timer—current ship-time was twelve thirty-five. Unless another situation required his attention, which seemed inevitable, he could get almost eight hours of sleep.

And God, did he need it.

"Aye-aye, Captain," Travis said, then headed for his quarters.

Molly lay on the kitchen floor, drawing shallow breaths, her neck ravaged and torn, bleeding all over the tile. The fridge door hung open above her, its light reflecting off her pooling blood.

Travis tried to crawl toward her but couldn't move from his spot a few feet away. No matter how fast he moved his hands and knees, no matter how far he stretched, the tile floor slid beneath him, keeping him from reaching her.

Between them, the paste-smeared newborn crawled as well, closing in on the woman it had wounded, closing in on its mother. A meaty, wet placenta dragged behind the newborn, tugged along by a gnarled umbilical cord, leaving a wet streak on the brown tile. Little handprints, knee-spots, and the tiniest dots left by tiny toes gleamed under the kitchen lights.

"Molly, *get up*," Travis said. "You have to move! Get up and run!"

He couldn't stop the newborn. He couldn't help his wife.

He didn't remember the attack.

Had the newborn come out of the fridge?

He couldn't remember.

The newborn, his own *child*, clumsily crawled closer to Molly.

Blood in Molly's blonde hair. Her dazed, green eyes blinked slowly. She grasped a shelf in the open fridge, tried to pull herself up. The shelf bent; a container of cottage cheese fell out and landed on her, popping open, spilling white clumps on her shirt, clumps that dribbled off and plunked into her blood puddles—tiny white cubes like melting ice cream atop a spilled raspberry shake.

The newborn (Kinley, his daughter-to-be's name was *Kinley*) stretched a tiny, bloody hand toward Molly. Stubby, grease-smeared fingers ending in long claws reached for Molly's green eyes...

Travis found new strength. He stood, yet he didn't move closer and didn't know why he didn't move closer (because he couldn't move because he wasn't really there) but the words that roared from his mouth carried the power and unflinching mettle of a warship commander.

"*No!* You get away from her. Bad girl! *Bad!* You get away from her!"

The newborn stopped, looked back at him, clumsily falling to her side she did. The tiny mouth hung open, surprised. Tiny dagger-teeth glittered. Birth-grease plastered across Kinley's face, along her arms, on her body, the grayish-white substance streaked with blood, some hers, some her mother's.

Kinley's eyes...

Her eyes... no iris, no pupil, no white at all, nothing but the lustrous, metallic sheen of copper...

"Dehhhh*hhhhh*..."

The noise came from the abomination's mouth, a mouth that tried to form words but perhaps did not know how to do so.

"Dehhhhhh*hhhhh*..."

Travis knew what it was trying to say, a word that swelled his soul with panic, with an overpowering urge to flee, with a desperate need to *kill it* (kill his own child her name is Kinley it would be *Kinley* but she wasn't born yet) Travis put his hands to his ears and shook his head but that did not stop the sound, the growling voice, inhuman and *wrong*...

The vile newborn drew in a breath, her tiny chest rising...

"Dehhhhhhhhhh*deeeeee*."

Travis awoke in blackness, flailing his arms to ward off the monster that had to be right there. His blanket bound him like ropes. He lurched about, reached back to punch at the invisible threat—his elbow smashed into something, flared with instant pain.

That pain, though, sliced through his haze, cut the last strings of his dream. He slid out of his bunk, half expecting chubby little hands to grab his ankle, tiny little needle teeth to savagely bite into his toes. He pressed the button for his cabin's lights.

He blinked against the sudden illumination...

The newborn sat on his bunk, staring at him with copper eyes.

Travis screamed, his lizard-brain throwing him backward, away from the horror of newborn and placenta and umbilical cord.

"Dehhhhhhhhhh*deeeeeeeeeee*!"

He fell to his ass, feet pushing at the deck, trying to push him *through* the wall—away, away, away, *away*...

"Travis! It's not real!"

He looked up so fast something twinged in his neck, saw Anne Lafferty standing in the door, staring down at him.

Travis again looked to the bed.

The newborn was gone.

He felt Anne's arms around him, pulling him close, and only then did he realize how badly he was shaking, rattling from the fear and revulsion whipsawing inside him.

"It's not real," Anne said, softer this time. "It's not real."

She held him tight. He pressed into her, let her solidity and warmth protect him against fear that pushed him to the edge of madness.

Anne pulled his head to her shoulder. He liked her strength, he *needed* her strength.

"That's it," she said, her words comforting, understanding. "Breathe. Calm down. I've got you. It's the Mud, XO. It's just the Mud."

Shuddering, Travis held her. As the dread started to fade away, he found himself wondering...

Was it just the Mud?

Or was it something else?

Something far, *far* worse.

Sascha floated.

Her head hurt a little, but everything else felt so *nice*. Was she dreaming? It was dark. She opened her eyes; it was still dark. Something on her face...

"Look who rejoined the living. Hold on there, sleepyhead, let me help."

Hands gently removed something from Sascha's face—an eye mask, she realized, wincing at brightness penetrating her lids.

"Open your eyes, Lieutenant."

Sascha did so, blinking as her eyes adjusted. She was wearing a hospital gown. She felt the lower decks' heat against her skin.

Rebecca Watson, medic, leaned over her, bulky med goggles flipped up.

"I take it I'm in the infirmary," Sascha said.

"You got it on the first try. Can you sit up?"

Sascha sat up and let her lower legs dangle off the bed's side.

There were other people in the small compartment. On the infirmary's other bed, white-haired Doc Hammersmith and medic Rudy Rudello examined a bloody, open wound on the right shoulder of

Charlie Hong, an electrical mate in Sascha's department. A plastic splint encased Charlie's left wrist.

Rudy caught Sascha looking, flashed her a smile. A very cute smile from a very cute mouth. More than once, he'd expressed his interest in her. Maybe when things weren't so busy, Sascha would take him up on that offer. She wanted to run her fingers through his thick, chestnut-brown hair, which was easily two inches longer than regulation. Not that anyone cared. If Lincoln didn't mind her crew fucking each other, she certainly didn't give a damn about someone's haircut.

"Hey there, Lieutenant," Rudy said. He winked. "How you doin'?"

Sascha's thoughts misfired—what was she thinking? This was no time to be scoping out a hookup.

"Corporal Rudello, *focus*," Hammersmith snapped.

Rudy returned his attention to Charlie's shoulder. A nasty wound.

Sascha leaned closer to Watson. "Who did that to him?"

"*She* did." Doc Watson nodded toward the far side of Sascha's bed.

On the deck, bound in chains, was the diminutive form of Hyeon Dimo, a propulsion mate and another of Sascha's engineering department subordinates. Dimo stared wide-eyed at Sascha. Fresh sutures made an angry black-and-red line on her temple.

The *intensity* of that stare... kind of disturbing.

"In the Mud, bad things happen," Watson said. "Miss *Bet You Blink First Contest Winner* down there apparently lost her shit when Spec Hong went on a rant about how awful our lovely ship is. Spec Dimo was less than amused. She bit Hong's shoulder and wouldn't let go. Hong gave her several left hooks. Hit her so hard he broke his own wrist. Dimo's lockjaw bit went on until I got there and jabbed her with a butt-cheek full of zapinoforol. Great stuff. I gave you a bit of the same to keep you under."

Zappies? Sascha had never taken that drug before, but now she understood why many sailors did—she felt *great*.

Dimo wouldn't stop staring. Something *odd* about her.

Watson flipped her goggles down. "Look straight ahead for me, Lieutenant. Bright light." She lifted Sascha's right eyelid. Sascha managed not to blink. Watson did the same with the left, then pushed her goggles back up. She made the peace sign.

"How many fingers am I holding up?"

"Two," Sascha said. "When was I brought here? What happened?"

Watson took Sascha's wrists. "Stand up for me. Nice and slow."

Sascha slid off the hospital bed, Watson ready to catch her if she fell. When Sascha did not, Watson let go, grabbed a tablet from the foot of the bed, and made some notes.

"You had a bit of a fall," Watson said. "What's the last thing you remember?"

At first, Sascha wasn't sure, but it came back fast enough. Damn, that had been scary.

"The Sklorno got loose," she said. "Then I... I fell, maybe?"

Watson nodded as she wrote. "You did. Bonked the back of your noggin. Your brain got knocked around inside your skull a bit. That was three days ago."

Sascha stared, shocked.

"Three days?"

"Mmm-hmm," Watson said. "We're still in transdim, about to surface near New Earth. Don't worry, I was the one who pulled your catheter. Are you experiencing any hallucinatory effects?"

Sascha looked around. Everything appeared normal.

"I think I'm good."

"Wunderbar," Watson said. "You probably suffered a mild concussion. Were this any other ship, you'd be off duty, but it's the *Crypt.* Chief Ledford has been holding down the fort in engineering, but you're shorthanded there and Lincoln wants you back in charge."

Ledford ran the propulsion division. He'd been tapped as

Sascha's engineering department head replacement should anything happen to her. This was his fourth *Keeling* deployment.

Watson pointed to a thin locker built into the cabinets of medical supplies. "Your clothes are in there. Get dressed and kindly get your tush back to work."

In the locker, Sascha found her coveralls, underwear, a T-shirt, socks, and boots. No room for privacy in the small compartment. She dressed quickly, then headed for the ladder down to Deck Four.

Something teased at the edges of her memory. Had she dreamed while she was knocked out? Or when she was *drugged* out? She thought she had, but she couldn't get a handle on it.

And why did Dimo's stare bother her so much?

Sascha rolled her shoulders, pushing the thoughts away. One electrical mate and one propulsion mate in the infirmary. Were others strapped down for safety? Or possibly hallucinating something awful at that very moment?

Nap time was over. Back to work.

77

MINDY

Mindy Martigral wrote on a pad of paper. Stone Age nonsense. Computers were, supposedly, unreliable in-dim. She would only have to tolerate this strange reality a little bit longer, as they were soon to exit transdim at New Earth. Her subjects—and, hopefully, *her*, if there were any justice in this universe—would never be in "the Mud" again. She needed to gather as much environment-specific data as she could before that opportunity vanished forever.

Subject One remained unconscious. Pulse and blood pressure low but steady. An unconscious Sklorno, it seemed, exhibited physical responses similar to that of an unconscious Human. That aligned with the vast bodies of work related to other sentient biological species. Harrah, Ki, Whitokians, and Leekee all needed the mental downtime brought on by sleep in order to properly function. Even the Prawatt needed sleep, at least the more advanced ones that progressed beyond basic automaton levels. As for Rewall, no one knew. Strange, massive creatures floating in space like leviathans... some argued they weren't truly sentient at all, just a zooid with astonishing cooperative processing.

Subject Three was struggling. Pulse erratic. The anesthesia

didn't seem to agree with it. Mindy kept adjusting the dosage. She hoped that when they surfaced, things would level out. It was probably transdim causing the issue, not the chemical mix Mindy created to keep them docile.

Subject Two, on the other hand, the one with the missing eyestalk... Subject Two was different.

No matter how much Mindy tweaked the anesthesia mixture, Subject Two didn't succumb to its effects. It slept—four sessions of sleep averaging 5.2 hours per session over the 70 hours it had been in the containment cell—but that slumber appeared to have nothing to do with the anesthesia.

Mindy hadn't slept that much herself, come to think of it. How could she with this absolute goldmine of data at her fingertips. She would get the Fleet Cross for this. And a Nobel Prize. And, probably, the Agaral Award. While Fleet needed to know how this species ticked, needed to know every last bit of biology, needed to find out how they *thought*—when that work was done, Mindy Martigral would be hailed across Human systems as a brilliant pioneer.

Not just Human systems... she'd be hailed across the galaxy.

It really was—

"Let me go."

Her heart leapt into her throat—it was her mother's voice. Her *dead* mother's voice.

Subject Two... the voice seemed to come from Subject Two. It was looking right at her, three eyes staring, wavering on their three eyestalks.

Mindy couldn't breathe. Had she somehow imagined it?

As she watched, icy fear tingling through her body, the Sklorno's head shuddered, wavered... and became the head of her mother.

Her dead mother.

"Mindy, honey," Mother said, "let me go."

What was happening? How was this possible?

The pad of paper slipped from her hands, fell to the deck; the noise made her jump.

"Honey... let me go."

The lips moved, but the voice... it was in Mindy's head.

"You're dead," she said. "You died."

"I'm alive. Let me go. Let me go."

No... no she wasn't. It was a hallucination. The Mud. *What you see in the Mud isn't real.*

"Let me go, honey. Let me go."

A new sound made her jump, made her scream out loud—that whistle that came before the 1MC...

"This is the XO. All hands, prepare to exit transdim. All hands, prepare to exit transdim. We will surface in five minutes. That is all."

A fist pounding on the door.

"Colonel Martigral, are you all right?"

The Raider guard outside. *Abshire*, was it? They changed every three hours.

Mindy looked at Subject Two—Sklorno head, three eyestalks, one bandaged stub.

No mother.

No *dead* mother.

What the hell was this place?

Bam-bam-bam. "Colonel! Are you all right? I'm coming in!"

Mindy lunged for the door. She yanked the handle up, pulled the door inward, and jumped outside, thudding into Spec-1 Abshire. He stepped back; Mindy pulled the door shut and slammed the latch down so hard it hurt her wrist.

"Colonel, what happened?"

Abshire—yes, that was his name, it was right there on his dark gray coveralls—looked at her with concern, his eyes flicking to the door and back again.

Two curious sailors standing outside the crew mess looked at her as well. Mindy had made a scene.

"Nothing happened," she said. "Make sure no one goes in there. *No one.*"

She didn't wait for a response.

Heart pounding, skin tingling, Mindy ran down the passageway. She had to get to the atrium and make sure those dolts Hasik and Darkwater got the ship back to reality.

78

BIGGIE

A piece of cake and a single bottle of beer—Lincoln's reward for risking life and limb. Not that Biggie was complaining. She liked beer. And cake.

Bradley Henry (the oversized culinary arts Spec-3 known as *Combat Cook*) lifted his latest creation and set it on the serving counter's flat top for all to see.

After the last run, the *Ishlangu* debacle, clams packed into the galley first, followed by Raiders. This time, though, Lincoln made it clear Raiders got to be first in line, because they'd lost one of their own.

Biggie (somehow executing strategy so pathetic, Sun Tzu himself would have slapped her) wound up in front. The gathered mass of Raiders behind pushed forward as they tried to get a closer look at the cake, pressing her hip bones into the tray rail.

Keeling was back in realspace, roughly 600,000 klicks from New Earth. Soon, they would punch for Gateway, and this run would be over.

Time to *splice the main brace*, an ancient maritime tradition that old-school captains like Lincoln still embraced in voidborne warships.

Complete the mission, kill the enemy, get an extra ration of alcohol. *Rum* in the Age of Sail, *beer* aboard *Keeling*.

Would anyone ever know what they'd accomplished? With the secrecy around both ship and objective, Biggie doubted it. That intel scumbag Lafferty never missed a chance to remind the crew what happened to people who talked.

A deep penetration into Whitokian territory. Five freighters destroyed. A surgical commando strike on a goddamn Sklorno vessel. Three aliens snatched. Critical intel in the form of the recovered cargo. All that and not a single casualty from enemy fire. Only one death, because a fresh boot couldn't get his helmet off.

Yo-Yo's loss infuriated her. The poor kid.

"Jeeze, *look* at that cake," yelled Beaver, who was pressed in on Biggie's right. "Combat Cook, you're a *genius*! Can I have my beer now?"

Henry pointed a finger at him. "You'll get your beer after everyone gets a chance to appreciate this work of beauty."

Biggie knew fuck-all about the culinary arts, but as far as she was concerned, the cake was a masterpiece.

The top layer was *Keeling*, its fondant form rising up from a square of vanilla and raspberry swirl representing the Mud. Looked like a milk-chocolate submarine breaking the surface of a froth-covered crimson and white ocean.

The bottom layer, half again as large, bore Henry's signature black icing dotted with white candy stars. Realspace, obviously. At each corner, a mint-colored fondant freighter (pretty damn realistic, Biggie had to admit) breaking into pieces due to red and orange torpedo explosions.

The Raiders behind her leaned closer, trying to see the details. Their weight pressed her harder against the rail. It was starting to hurt.

"Back off," she said over her shoulder. "If I wanted y'all's teeny junk in my trunk I'd have sent out a dozen teeny invitations and some teeny monocles so your one-eyed midgets could read it."

Raiders and clams alike laughed.

"The invites woulda got lost in your black hole of a snootch," Jake Radulski called out. "I bet an APC could do a tail-flip in there and not even touch the sides."

More laughter, and she laughed along with it. A tail-flip. Pretty good chirp.

The Raider directly behind Biggie, Spec-1 Basara, put his hands on the rail to either side of her. He leaned in so close she could feel his breath.

"If it was *my* junk in there, flygirl, you'd know it."

A Raider bragging about the size of his dick? Shocker.

Biggie tried to turn toward him, an instant reaction to give the spec a dressing down, but she couldn't move, not with Basara pressing into her, dumb-but-pretty Beaver tight on her right, and Mahesh Mafi, that mountain of a man, tight on her left.

Basara pushed away from the rail, giving Biggie the tiniest bit of space.

"All you asswipes, *back up*," he said. "The softies up front are getting squished!"

Biggie paused, now unsure if she should yell at him for his comment when he'd just done what she'd asked.

The way his voice had sounded when he said *flygirl*. It wasn't just another chirp.

There was something off about Basara.

Something off about a *Crypt* crewmember? Shocker.

"Maaaaagnificent," Sands called out from the back. "Combat Cook, it's a shame these missions are top-secret and the galaxy will never know of your esculent masterpiece."

Esculent? Where did Sands get these words?

"Beer-*beeeeeer*-beer," Beaver yelled. "Beer-beeeeeer, *beeeeeer*-beer. That's Morse code, Combat Cook! It means *I want beer*."

Jesus, Beaver was loud. Biggie's right ear rang.

"Beaver, shut your cakehole," Combat Cook said. "Stop wagging your tongue and put it back in a clam's ass where it usually resides.

All right, Ling, cut my brilliant work so these troglodytes can eat it. I'll hand out the beers myself, so don't any of you lot try anything funny!"

Spec-1 Ling Lightbringer was as small as Henry was big. She had to get a stool to stand tall enough to cut the cake. Samuel Stepanik, the third and final member of the galley crew, put the slices onto mycoware plates and gave them to reaching Raider hands.

"Hey, Combat Cook," Dave Starr called out from farther back. "What the hell is a *troglodyte*? Is it as ugly as a *Warthog*?"

Biggie shouted over her shoulder. "It's a big dumb thing that lives in a cave, just like us."

The Raiders laughed and hooted in approval.

"Uglier than a warthog, Corporal," Sergeant Sarvacharya yelled. "But not as ugly as your mom."

The soldiers roared in delight at Starr's expense. The shit-talking and teasing were about to take off. Such things happened after a fight. Even when Raiders died, sooner or later the joy of simply being alive, of *surviving*, overwhelmed them.

A break in the sadness of loss. Biggie knew the feeling well. That sadness would return, echoes of combat would haunt many of these Raiders.

Biggie knew that feeling, too.

Beaver snatched a plate, placed it on the rail in front of Biggie.

"For you, Warrant Officer," he yelled.

Well, wasn't that sweet?

"Thanks, Spec." She picked up the plate, tried to turn around. "Now if I could just get out of..."

Pressure against her ass, and this time, she *did* feel it—felt Basara's stiffness.

Biggie went rigid.

"So sorry, flygirl," Basara said, laughing. "Hey, Master Sergeant Sands, will you tell these a-holes to back up? Poor little Biggie's getting squished."

Disrespect, embarrassment, anger, all rolled into one instant internal bomb. Part of Biggie wanted to hide. Part of her wanted to cut off Basara's balls and vent them.

"Enough swapping spit and rubbing tummies," Sands roared, his Master Sergeant voice in full effect. "Back your knavish, nudnik posteriors up and act like people of culture and breeding, or you get to spar with Beaver."

The weight on her again eased. Humiliated, Biggie pushed her way through the crowd. She left the mess and headed for Raider Land.

"Hey, Warrant Biggie!"

She stopped, saw Beaver standing there in the passageway, left hand balancing two plates of cake, the fingers of his right holding two plastic bottles of beer.

"You forgot your treats, Warrant Biggie. You okay?"

She'd left her cake on the tray trail. He'd grabbed it for her.

Beaver's ever-present smile wasn't there. Instead, he wore the hard expression she'd seen behind his TASH visor before a fight.

"I'm fine, Spec," Biggie said.

He held the plates and the bottles toward her.

"Sugar and beer. The good stuff. But you get only one bottle 'cause the other is mine. Combat Cook saw you leave in a rush, so he said it was okay I grab two."

Biggie took a plate and one of the bottles.

"Thanks," she said. "That was nice of you."

"I'm a nice guy. Everyone says so. Except when we spar. That's why Sands said that. About the sparring. I'm not nice when I spar. Doesn't mean I'm not having fun, but it's *mean*-fun. You know?"

She'd seen him spar. *Mean* wasn't the word for it. Beaver fought like pre-packaged murder. But Biggie wasn't in the mood for chit-chat —she still felt phantom stiffness pressing against her.

Violating...

Insulting...

"Thanks for the cake and the beer," she said. "I'll have them in private."

He nodded once, not the least bit offended by her brushoff. Everyone knew she didn't hook up with other Raiders.

"Sounds good, Warrant Biggie." Beaver's voice then turned quiet, a contrast that sent a chill up her spine. "So you know, if any fucknugget bothers you, you can tell me. I'll make sure they don't ever bother you again."

Had he seen Basara dry-humping her? Or had he watched her leave and put two and two together?

"I can take care of myself. Got it, Spec?"

Beaver's smile returned in full force. So did his volume.

"I got it, Warrant Biggie. Enjoy your brew."

Beaver was a sweet guy. Maybe. You never knew who people really were. Except for Abbas Basara. Biggie suspected she knew *exactly* what kind of person he was.

"I will," Biggie said. "I'm sorry about Yo-Yo."

He'd been in Alpha-2, with Beaver and Bennett.

"Thanks," Beaver said. "I didn't know him well, but he seemed okay. For arriving in chains, I mean. Catch you later, Warrant Bang."

He walked back into the packed mess.

Biggie looked at her cake. Black icing. One little white candy star. Maybe she should go back in. They'd be toasting to Yo-Yo's memory soon. Like Beaver, she hadn't been tight with the man.

But the toast would make her think of people she *had* been tight with.

Hard-Six Peterson, begging for his mother before he bled out.

The smell of Spicy Spagnolla's burning flesh.

Cake. Beer. What Biggie needed was drugs, and plenty of them.

She changed her mind and headed for the infirmary. Maybe Doc Watson was still there.

79

SASCHA

In the machining compartment, Sascha huddled with sweaty Barnes Marchenko and sweaty Peggy Keahloha, electrical division chief. Three slices of cake and three opened bottles of beer sat on the machining bench, as did two handheld scanners Chenk and Keahloha had jury-rigged to a monitor showing a 3D-scan of *Keeling*'s midsection, through which ran the weird passageway connecting the pouch and Raider Land.

"Chenk," Sascha said, "you shouldn't have done this."

He smiled as if he thought she was playing.

"You told me we needed to wait for the right time," he said. "The Mud was the *right time*. No one was paying attention. We couldn't exactly ask your permission, you know?"

Sascha remembered the thrashing Sklorno, *sort of* remembered getting kicked in the noggin, then, nothing until Watson woke her up. Three days of nothing.

On any other ship in Fleet, she would have been temporarily relieved of duty so she could be evaluated by docs and shrinks back in port. On the *Crypt*, though, a department head going catatonic in the Mud was just another Wednesday.

Still... what Chenk and Keahloha accomplished...

"Chief Ledford was running the department," Sascha said. "Does he know about this? Does anyone else?"

They shook their heads.

"Good," Sascha said. "Don't *ever* do something like this again without my permission. Even if I'm *dead*, you hold a fucking seance and get my take. Got it?"

They nodded.

The fact they hadn't been noticed, as far as Sascha knew, was an indication of how weird things got in transdim. With a heavy rest cycle, some people chained to their bunks, and others flipping out over hallucinations, Marchenko quietly carrying a scanner from one place to another wouldn't draw much notice.

Sascha wasn't happy with Chenk's actions, but those actions didn't surprise her. Keahloha, on the other hand... Sascha had never involved her in discussions about *Keeling*'s hidden areas.

"Peggy," Sascha said, "if we get caught at this, Lincoln will have our asses. Chenk shouldn't have asked for your help. If you want to drop it, right now, you can walk away. Your involvement will never be mentioned."

Keahloha was 39, looked 49, repeatedly stretched and compressed by the stress brought on from two decades in Fleet. Sascha didn't know what she was in for and was afraid to ask.

"I don't care." That gravely, toad-croak voice of hers. Keahloha scratched at her head, gnawed fingernails audible against her graying black hair and scalp. "This is my third run on the *Crypt*. Ship's doing something to me, Lieutenant. Doing something to all of us. Not just mental, you know? I've put on ten pounds since I got stationed here."

The woman looked fit as could be, although the arms and legs of her coveralls did seem a bit snug. Not much fat on her at all, though. If she was worried about her weight, that was her prerogative.

"I want to know more," she said. "That conduit stuff? The ship *growing*? Never heard of anything like it. This ship... it's *special*. Maybe it's evil... I don't know. Whatever it is, I'm tired of command thinking we don't get to know about things that will probably be the death of us. I get that I'm expendable, we all are. I just can't tolerate being kept in the dark anymore. You can count on me to keep things hush-hush."

Sascha glanced at Marchenko. *Glared* at him, was more like it. He should have waited for Sascha to awaken. At the very least, he should have acted alone.

"Peggy's solid, Lieutenant," he said. "*She* actually approached *me*. She's been trying to figure out what's up with the solid areas all on her own."

Well, Schrödinger's multidimensional cat was out of the bag, so to speak, and there was no putting that beastie back in.

"All right, Peggy, you're in," Sascha said. "Chenk, you don't talk about this to *anyone else*. Do *not* test me. Understand?"

He pantomimed locking his lips and throwing away the key. Like he hadn't done just the opposite.

"Okay," Sascha said. "Tell me your process."

"It was easy," Marchenko said. "We took the scanners to the pouch to check on bolt depth for the ammo racks. When there, I suddenly *remembered*—" he put that word in air quotes "—that we needed to check bolt depths in the Raider Land workout area's resistance rigs. I had Peggy do that, secretly scanning along the way. When she got there, she realized her scanner was—" again with the air quotes "—*on the fritz*. She came back to the pouch, scanning all the way. I took *my* scanner through the tunnel to Raider Land, scanning all the way. I checked the resistance rig bolts, then came back—"

"Scanning all the way." Keahloha couldn't resist being part of the story. "We preplanned the angles to get max coverage."

"Yeah," Marchenko said. "So I got back to the pouch, and..." he gestured to Keahloha.

"Hey, whaddaya know, I'd fixed my scanner," she said. "It worked fine. No need to file a report on bad gear that had to be checked by Chief Smith."

Zhen Smith, Aux Division Chief—Marchenko was his direct

report. Smith had been promoted from corporal to sergeant and taken over Marchenko's position.

Together, Chenk and Keahloha had performed four full-length scans of the solid section amidships, all right under the noses of Raiders, engineering, and operations.

"Clever." Sascha nodded toward the monitor. "And that effort got us this."

This was the most detailed scan yet. Sascha had done a partial one much earlier, before Colonel Hasik learned what she was doing and ratted her out to Lincoln. The captain had made it clear—*quite* clear—that Sascha was not to scan any further.

Out of all the madness that was *Keeling*, Lincoln's order might be the most insane bit of all—command *did not* want the engineering department to know all there was to know about the ship.

On the monitor, Sascha turned the model, looking at the layout from different angles. The passageway from Raider Land to the pouch ran through the midsection like a train tunnel through a mountain.

"It's not just *solid*," Keahloha said. "It's *dense*. Denser than solid iron. Denser than osmium, even."

Keeling's beryllium-copper-carbon alloy was bizarre to begin with. The metal-organic framework contained staggering amounts of internal surface area due to the material's complex crystalline structure. What seemed to be solid simply wasn't. In some ways the MOF was bigger on the inside than the outside.

The solid midsection area seemed to possess the same qualities as the rest of the ship, yet there it was, denser by a factor of eleven.

The scan showed vague hints of lines and curves and shapes, but nothing Sascha could make out.

"These patterns," she said, "did you analyze them?"

Marchenko shook his head. "Can't trust computers to work in-dim. Besides, I didn't want to enter anything into the system. Just in case."

"Good," Sascha said. "That's good."

Just in case was shorthand for *BII assholes*. Lafferty, Daniels, and Gillick, trying to uncover potential Purist spies. Daniels and Gillick stuck their nose into everything, trying to sniff out any hint of people doing stuff they shouldn't be doing.

"Maybe I can find an isolated system on Gateway," Sascha said. "But how do we get this scan data off the ship?"

Marchenko reached down, rapped knuckles against the prosthetic lower leg hidden by his coveralls.

"Already got that worked out, Lieutenant," he said. "I take this leg off for body scans. The MPs will scan the prosthetic, too, obviously, but all they'll see is solid titanium."

With the heavy secrecy surrounding all things *Keeling*, everyone was subject to a simple scan before boarding or disembarking. Wouldn't want anyone sneaking recording gear on or off.

Keahloha pointed across the narrow machining bay to a glazing machine.

"I'll make a storage drive out of a titanium film substrate," she said. "We fuse that to his fake leg. Leg gets scanned, shows as solid, and through it goes, back to Chenk on the other side."

Devious and efficient. Sascha was impressed. These two sailors knew their stuff. No surprise there—they had a combined 43 years of service between them.

Noncoms—the oil that made Fleet machinery run smooth.

Marchenko picked up his bottle of beer.

"If I get busted, I take the fall myself," he said. "I know the score."

Did he? Lincoln's wrath was one thing—they had no idea what Admiral Epperson might do.

This was dangerous for all three of them. More so for Marchenko, if he was as good as his word. And *very* dangerous for Sascha's career—if there was any career left after her hitch on the *Crypt*.

But she wanted to know. So did Marchenko. So did Keahloha.

The 1MC chime sounded.

"This is Intel Chief Lafferty. A reminder to all that anything you experienced on this run is classified at the highest level. You will not discuss anything you may have seen with anyone else, including your crewmates. All messages sent home will be scrubbed, so please do me the favor of not making me come talk to you about things in those messages that should *not* be in those messages. If you're unsure of what you can and can't say, have your CO contact me. BII is here to help. That is all."

"Yikes," Keahloha said. "Not the best timing, considering."

Sascha shut off the monitor.

"Put this stuff away," she said. "And make it quick."

80

TRAVIS

Back in the relative safety of realspace, the pressure of the mission drained away.

Travis and Anne Lafferty sat on the couch in Lincoln's suite. Lincoln reached into a drawer of her small desk. She pulled out three mycoware cups and a thick plastic beverage bag with a black cap. The clear bag contained an amber fluid.

"We'll punch for Gateway as soon as Hasik finishes his examination of the hull and the crew finishes splicing the main brace," the captain said. "Before we do that, though, a celebratory drink for the command triumvirate. My apologies for the container. Not even the captain is allowed to bring a glass bottle on the *Crypt*."

She twisted off the cap. Travis smelled it immediately.

"Please tell me that's Scotch," he said. "If it's not, lie to me and I'll pretend it is."

Lincoln poured. "MacDecy single malt. Eighteen years old. Please keep this little secret to yourself—I don't want Colonel Hasik trying to figure out how to steal it."

She handed Anne the first cup.

"Impressive," Anne said, sniffing, smiling. "Have you been hiding this in your desk the whole time, Captain?"

Lincoln sighed, shook her head as she poured.

"Intel Chief Lafferty, I have the *strangest* feeling you somehow knew that bag was there."

Anne chuckled.

Trav's opinion of Anne had changed. He'd always thought her good at her job, and brave beyond measure based on her actions during the Battle of *Ishlangu*. But before that bout of heroism she'd tried to take command of *Keeling*. If she'd succeeded, she would have left *Ishlangu*'s crew to fend for themselves. He'd considered her skilled but also ruthless—a Human automaton who followed her BII programming.

Not anymore. Not after she'd been there for him after his nightmare. Or hallucination. He still wasn't sure. He'd *lost* it, and she'd been there to bring him back. As far as he knew, she'd told no one of the incident.

She wasn't an automaton—Anne Lafferty was a good person.

"I'm bold, Captain," Anne said. "But not *that* bold."

"Lieutenant, I wasn't born yesterday." Lincoln handed a cup to Travis. "I know you're quietly investigating *everyone*. I don't blame you for that, not after the last operation."

Anne seemed to take that to heart.

"Thank you," she said. "Fool me once, but I won't get fooled again."

Travis wondered if Anne counted Martigral among those who *fooled* her. Probably not. Martigral, though, had been ordered onto this ship by Epperson himself. She wasn't a Purist spy, like Nitzan Shamdi had been.

Many good sailors died because Anne's department missed Shamdi. Was that her fault? Hard for Trav to say. Anne hadn't assigned Shamdi to the *Keeling*—Whittaker had. Epperson's Executioner missed his Purist ties, as had the Raider staff who'd recruited him, trained him, and commanded him before he wound up entombed.

Lincoln raised her cup. "To an outstanding mission."

"To an outstanding mission," Travis and Anne said in unison.

He took a sip. Good stuff. *Strong* stuff. This two-ounce pour alone would get him buzzing. He hadn't had a drop of alcohol since seeing that message from Molly.

Would there be messages from her waiting at Gateway? He hoped so. While he wasn't a religious man, he *prayed* for it. He wanted to see his wife and daughter. He wanted to be there for Kinley's birth—because he was her father, and, maybe a little bit, because he wanted to see for himself she wasn't a copper-eyed fetus-monster.

"Speaking of secrets," Lincoln said, "I have a favor to ask of you both."

For once, the captain didn't radiate complete control, like a tuning fork set to vibrate pure confidence. She was rattled.

"Of course, Captain," Lafferty said. "Anything you need."

Lincoln's doubtful expression mirrored Trav's own reaction—a career-hungry BII operative was not exactly one to be trusted at face value.

"I'll assume you mean that," Lincoln said. "In our engagement with the convoy, I acted... well, I can't explain it."

She'd stood atop the command slate, shouting her orders. *They will know that* Keeling *is the alpha and omega, the swallower of souls.* And the way she'd threatened Martigral...

They hadn't been in the Mud. There was no reason for Lincoln to act in such an outrageous, completely unprofessional manner, and yet... hadn't Travis had his own wild thoughts? *Kill the enemy and feed on their corpses?*

Trav's first nightmare back on Gateway Station, with his newborn daughter attacking her sister... could *that* have been caused by the ship?

Maybe...

Maybe *Keeling* was affecting them, somehow. Maybe there was more to this madness than hallucinations in transdim.

The thought formed a pit of ice in his belly.

"A little leadership pizzaz," said Lafferty, grinning. "That's all it was, Captain."

She was trying to make light of the situation, yet there was no real humor in her statement. Had she, too, experienced strange thoughts during the battle?

Lincoln eased back in her chair. "I said some things I shouldn't have. I don't know if Martigral will report my behavior to Epperson." She focused on her cup, as if it might protect her from the admiral's wrath. "Martigral defied orders. I think she just wants off the ship with her little friends, so she might not mention it to anyone. But if she does... can I count on you both to downplay the incident? Treat it like... like Martigral is making a big deal about nothing?"

The captain's actions during the battle were one thing—asking subordinates to fudge the truth in a potential investigation was another animal entirely. It wasn't like her. Of course, her standing atop the command slate like a pirate captain of old, promising death to her enemies wasn't like her, either.

"I've spoken with Martigral since the battle," Lafferty said. "I'll have another little conversation with her before we get home. I think I can be fairly convincing. Suffice to say, Captain, that if she doesn't mention the incident, you won't mention it, either?"

Lincoln looked at Major Lafferty with doubt, as if she didn't dare trust a word that came out of the spy's mouth, but that expression softened to guarded gratitude.

"Thank you, Major," Lincoln said. "I would appreciate that. XO?"

She was putting him on the spot. Travis had 97 weeks left on his *Keeling* sentence. If the ship's commander couldn't rely on him, those months could go by very slowly indeed.

"This is a ship of secrets." Travis raised his cup. "So I don't think I'm out of line when I say—what happens on *Keeling*, stays on *Keeling*."

With that, Lincoln visibly relaxed. A good captain always relied on her XO, and a good XO always backed up the captain.

They all sipped. *Damn*, that was good Scotch, even if it did have a faint trace of mushrooms thanks to the cup.

"We were given three objectives and we accomplished them all," Lincoln said. "We denied the enemy their Watchtower upgrades, we destroyed five enemy vessels, and we obtained a sample of the cargo. A small sample, to be sure, but that was all the engagement allowed."

Lincoln had risked Raider lives—if not the entire ship—for that sample. She'd rolled the dice and won. *Keeling* suffered only one casualty, and that from equipment failure. Ayodele's body was on ice in a cubbyhole down in the pouch.

"That small sample is incredibly important," Anne said. "What we learned from picking up that cargo will inform BII's priorities from here on out. We've been underestimating the Purist Nation. By a *lot*, it seems."

The thought dulled Trav's enjoyment of the Scotch. Despite having inferior ships, inferior tech, and a smaller military, the Nation had fought the Fleet to a standstill and turned the conflict into a war of attrition. On top of that, they were making new trade partners, if not new alliances?

Anne held her cup close to her face, sniffed deeply.

"We captured *living* Sklorno," she said. "That's never been done before. And I know freighters aren't warships, but still—*five* enemy vessels destroyed? That's impressive, Captain."

"At *least* five," Travis added. "I like to think our torps reacquired *Uniform* after we dove."

Something they would probably never know. In war, ships die in the dark—the void is nothing *but* dark.

Lafferty raised her cup. "Cheers to your success, Captain Lincoln."

Travis raised his. "Absolutely."

Lincoln smiled, raised her cup a bit. They all drank.

"I doubt it will be as easy next time," Travis said. "That Komodo escort was horribly out of position. We met zero resistance because the Whitokians had no idea we could reach them. Now they know." He looked at Anne. "We fooled them once."

She met his gaze. "And you think they won't get fooled again?"

Was that what he was saying? He wasn't sure.

"All I know is we sucker-punched them," Travis said. "From now on, you can bet they'll have their guard up."

Lincoln knocked back the rest of her Scotch. "Hard to have your guard up everywhere." She crumpled the mycoware cup, tossed it into her wastepaper basket. "We'll get them again, XO. And again. And again. The *Crypt* can help bring this war to an end. If, that is, Epperson lets me do what I was born to do."

The sound-powered phone on Lincoln's desk growled. She lifted the handset.

"This is Captain Lincoln."

Travis could just make out Plait's voice on the other end.

"Captain Lincoln, Conn. Darsat is reporting a strange signal. A contact that appears to be in transdim. Very faint, but it's there."

Lincoln frowned. "We've never picked up in-dim contacts from realspace before."

"That's correct, Captain. Waldren believes the only reason she spotted it is because it has a similar grav-sig to the contact we picked up before *Keeling* moved on its own."

A chill washed through Travis. Was this ship, or whatever it was, stalking *Keeling* in realspace the way *Keeling* stalked enemy vessels?

"Understood, Conn," Lincoln said. "Get Hasik inside immediately, then sound general quarters. I'll be right there." Lincoln hung up. "Put your drinks down. Hopefully you can finish them later. Let's go."

Martigral scraped foil.

Bethany hadn't asked her to, and she certainly hadn't *ordered* the colonel to do it. Martigral had entered the atrium, grabbed a scraper and gone to work without saying a word.

Bethany would join her soon. But not yet. She stood on the protuberance platform, looking at the heartstone's golden light. So beautiful. So *peaceful*. She needed to soak up the moment, because that peace would not last.

Soon they would punch for Gateway. Plenty of problems waiting there. She'd have to socialize with "Annie" again, most likely. And just because Bock's people hadn't made contact yet didn't mean Bethany was off the hook. Not by a long shot.

A sudden stab of pain in her stomach made her cry out, made her clutch the rail with one hand while her other went to her belly.

Martigral stood. "Lieutenant? What's wrong?"

The pain eased, just a bit, just enough for Bethany to draw a breath.

"I don't know," she said. "It just *hurts*."

Another burst hit her, made her double over. She hissed against the pinching sensation, fought to stay upright.

Out of the corner of her eye, she saw the dark protuberance blaze with light, its multicolored lumps and bumps and extensions shimmering with rainbow hues...

...and then, the blue-green knob—the one she pushed to start the dive process—slid inward on its own.

82

JOHN

John sipped his beer, enjoying the rare treat. He'd been last in line for cake. When he got it, he found he didn't really want it. He gave it to Beaver, who was on the other side of the table shoveling it into his mouth like someone was going to snatch it away. Reiner sat next to Beaver. She looked both angry and sad. She'd lost her beer to Torres, betting the bottle on a single rock-paper-scissors throw. Torres had quietly won two such challenges and was pounding her third— Reiner's—before Lindros caught on.

Yes, Lieutenant Dork himself decided to grace the grunts with his presence. That was a bummer for Sands. He couldn't just cut loose like the rest of the platoon, not with his anal-retentive commanding officer watching.

"Shoulda gone with scissors, Corporal Reiner," said Abshire, who was sitting next to John. "Cheer up, I'll buy you a beer when we get back to Gateway."

People were starting to filter out of the mess. The cake was gone, the beers had all been handed out. John wanted to enjoy this small moment with his fire team. They'd toasted to Yo-Yo's memory. That had been nice.

"Hey, Corporal Bennett," Beaver said, a dot of black icing on the tip of his nose, more of the same smeared on his lips. "You fought Sklorno before. Were you as badass as we were on that freighter? Kicking the living *shit* out of those crickets?"

"Good question." Abshire slapped Beaver's shoulder. "Back then, did you scream, aim, *and* fire like my main man here?"

Young warriors, reveling in the post-combat glow. That was how it went in war—a comrade's death hurt, it scared the hell out of you, but it also made you grateful to be alive. Made you happy that you'd stood and fought, that you'd proved your mettle. John had been like them once.

Now, though, that victory flame barely flickered.

He'd lost a man.

How *could* he be happy?

"Yeah, Old Man," Reiner said. "Was this fight like the last time you squared off against Sklorno?"

John felt the suffocating, heart-ripping memories rushing back. This time, though, looking at the faces of Beaver, Abshire, and Reiner, he was able to stop them in their tracks.

"Not exactly the same," John said. "This run went a bit better."

Abshire rolled his eyes. "Come *on*, Corporal! You got to give us more than—"

The 1MC chime sounded.

"This is Operations Department Head Plait. General quarters. General quarters. Vacsuits on. That is all."

Raiders and sailors alike got up quickly, started moving out of the mess.

"What the hell?" Beaver started shoveling the last of the cake into his icing-smeared mouth. "We're at New Earth. Is this another one of the XO's drills?"

John flew out of the booth and crashed into someone. Abshire slammed into John a split-second later. People cried out. John tried to untangle himself from the two people under him, then he was thrown upward and smacked hard against the mess's curved copper ceiling before the deck's gravity yanked him to the deck, where he landed on yet another person.

"*We're maneuvering,*" Lindros shouted. "Find something to hold on to!"

Everyone in the mess was off their feet, a pile of some two dozen Raiders and sailors. John grabbed the cereal dispenser counter.

Just as he did, the mess filled with fire and light...

...they were diving.

"Oh, fuck," he heard Abshire say. "This is gonna be bad."

83

ANNE

Head ringing, jaw stinging, Anne pushed herself up off the CIC's deck, got to her hands and knees. She tasted blood. She had to get to her acceleration chair.

The nav-orb shimmered with opalescent static.

"We're in-dim," someone called out. "Chief Sung, get medical up here, we have wounded."

Plait. That's who was speaking. At the command slate, leaning on it, *gripping* it, his legs wobbling.

Anne grabbed the back of a chair, stood on wobbly legs, held on tight as the ship accelerated. "Rebooting darsat," someone else called out.

To her left, Lincoln was on her back, sliding toward the CIC's rear, blood oozing from a cut on her cheek, blood spreading across her bandana. She *thumped* to a stop against the base of the Intel Loft.

XO Ellis stumbled to the command slate, his right hand clutched to his chest.

"I have the conn," he said. "Get to your stations."

Plait mumbled something, stumbled toward Anne. His head glowed a strange shade... aquamarine? She realized she was holding on to the ops station chair. She got out of Plait's way as he fell into it.

"Chief Lafferty, man the XO station," Ellis said as he dropped into the captain's chair and buckled in.

Anne heard him and didn't hear him all at the same time. Everything seemed slow and sluggish. They'd barely entered the CIC before the ship lurched hard to port, then angled down, accelerating the whole time, was *still* accelerating.

She moved to the command slate, her steps feeling like she was walking on gelatin. She fell into the XO's chair, tried to lock the harness with her weak, rubbery hands.

"Helm is unresponsive," someone called out.

Ellis reached over, secured Anne's harness for her.

"Helm, keep trying," he said. "Chief Lafferty, call engineering, tell them to prepare for chem-thrust, full-reverse. Ops, get all personnel locked down. Tell the crew we're in the Mud—remind them what they see might not be real."

"Darsat contact!" Carmel Waldren... that's who it was. "It's *Locus Eight*, same one I detected from realspace. Five hundred kilometers dead ahead... and closing. Putting it in-orb."

Anne's head began to clear. Her head hurt, but she'd fought through worse.

"XO, the captain is out cold," Chief Sung yelled. "We need a stretcher."

The crimson-and-cream tangle of the Mud bloomed in the nav-orb. Everything looked fuzzy. The optical system was calibrating, trying to catch up.

Straight ahead of the arrow representing the ship, a yellow hexagon appeared atop a dark gray dot that streaked through the Mud, leaving a barely visible wake in its path.

Whatever it was, *Keeling* was chasing it.

"Let me out, honey."

Who was that talking? A nice voice. Soft and warm.

Mindy Martigral stumbled out of the atrium. The ladder... to her right... the one that led up to Deck Three.

"All hands, find secure location. Vac suits on. Department heads, report your status to Ops."

A different voice. A man's voice. It came from the ceiling, from the strange copper walls.

Mindy's hands found the ladder. She started up.

"Let me out, honey."

The nice voice again. Calling to her. She knew it but couldn't place it. A voice she hadn't heard for many years.

Something invisible yanked her left, then down, pulled her off the ladder and crashed her into the deck. Pain in her elbow. She'd hurt her arm.

"I'll kill you, you *motherfucker!*"

Yet another voice. An angry one, full of violence.

Someone ran past Mindy. Someone else leapt over her. Chasing. Hunting.

"Let me out, honey."

Finally, she recognized the nice voice. The soft voice. The *warm* voice.

Her mother.

It was her *mother*.

Mindy reached out and grabbed the ladder. She pulled herself to her feet.

She climbed.

Her mother needed her.

85

BIGGIE

G-forces shoved Biggie deeper in her cubbyhole, the blankets packed around her like wadding. Her *head*. She'd been slammed out of a delightedly drugged sleep, her cheek smacking against the coral-patterned copper ceiling.

She couldn't get her bearings, yet part of her was grateful the cubbyhole was so small, barely larger than a coffin. If there had been another few meters of space above her, she might have picked up enough momentum to get *really* hurt.

Was she imagining this?

Was this a hallucination?

If she wasn't high, maybe she'd know. But she was high. *Very* high, thanks to a dose from Doc Watson.

An alarm blared. She couldn't remember what it meant. Even when the world wasn't spinning and jouncing around her, her head spun and jounced on its own.

Were they in combat?

Was she going to die?

Inertia yanked her sideways, banged her against the wall just centimeters away. The blankets, thankfully, dulled some of the impact.

Maybe she should try...

Maybe she should...

The world spun anew. She lost the thought as her body went all rubbery and warm.

With zappies coursing through her veins, Biggie fell asleep.

The CIC shook. Cables mounted along the low overhead rattled and swayed, jostled by the ship's irregular motion.

Travis needed to get control of the ship. He had to find a way.

Vacsuit on save for the hooded visor flapping against his back, Colonel Hasik rushed up the xeno loft steps. Nearly hyperventilating and glasses askew, he fell into his seat.

"Colonel," Travis said, "are you hallucinating? Are you able to perform your duties?"

Hasik's glasses magnified eyes already wide with shock. "I almost didn't make it in." He barely had enough breath to speak. "I was out on the hull. I don't know what would have happened to me."

The man was only half present; Travis needed all of him.

"Colonel, are you able to perform your duties or *not?*"

Trav's booming voice snapped Hasik back to the moment.

"Yes, XO, I am able to perform my duties. I'm not seeing anything weird—I think I'm fine."

"*Keeling* is piloting itself," Travis said. "It appears to be pursuing contact *Locus Eight*, a close grav-sig match to the object we detected the last time we lost helm control. We need to regain control and surface. Reverse thrust has not worked. What do you recommend?

Should we attempt a tail-flip and use the more powerful forward chemjets?"

Hasik shook his head so hard his glasses flew off.

"No!" He leaned to the side and groped at his station's floor. "We don't know if the aft thrust will hit the tails." He sat up, glasses in hand. "We... um... I'm afraid it's classified."

Even now, with the ship out of control and the crew in danger, Epperson's unknown guillotine hung over the man's head, kept critical information hidden away.

"Colonel Hasik," Lafferty said, speaking with cold authority. "Tell the XO what happened on the last tail-flip attempt, or under Article Seventeen, Section Four, Item B, I will place you under arrest for endangering the lives of Fleet crew."

Glasses still in his hand, Hasik squinted at her.

"Is that a real codicil?" he asked.

"You'll find out in four seconds," Lafferty answered.

Hasik put his glasses on so fast one of the temples poked him in the eye. He winced, used both hands to slide them on.

"We performed one in-dim tail-flip test," he said. "The ship responded in a defensive manner. There were casualties."

Rage overwhelmed Travis. Had this piece of shit kept *a potential loss of helm control* to himself?

Yes, he had. So had Lincoln.

The xeno department head—the person who supposedly knew more about this ship than anyone else—didn't know how to regain control.

Controlling his fury, Travis faced forward. He grabbed the handset and switched to 2MC: *Propulsion*.

87

SASCHA

Someone was singing a nursery rhyme and giggling like a child.

Everything shook, everything *shuddered*.

Sascha held on for dear life, her right hand gripping a stanchion, her left pressing the handset to her ear.

"XO, reverse thrust *is* at full. Fuel reserves at sixty-five percent and dropping fast." Reverse thrust had slowed *Keeling* but hadn't come close to stopping it. The ship's innate acceleration greatly outclassed the chemical engines. "I recommend we tail-flip and use the more powerful aft chemjets."

To her right, at one of the propulsion stations, Adam Ledford waved at her to get her attention; he shook his head.

"Negative on the tail-flip," Ellis said. "That is not an option."

Ledford again focused on his station. How had he already known a tail-flip was a bad idea? He'd served on the *Crypt* longer than she had—had he been through something like this before?

"I understand, XO," Sascha said. "What else can—"

The deck dropped away and shifted to starboard, so fast her arm locked like a rope pulled taut—she held on but felt something in her right shoulder tear.

For an instant, she was floating, then the deck rose up violently,

398

smashing her against fakegrav plates, breaking her grip on the stanchion. The handset slipped from her grasp.

Her shoulder screamed.

New acceleration sent her sliding across the deck.

Hands grabbed her. "LT, we got to get you strapped in!"

Sascha's head spun. Chief Ledford held her. Spit in his red beard, a cut under his right eye streaking blood down his pale skin.

"Hurry, LT, let me help you." Ledford shoved her left arm into the harness. He grabbed her right arm to put that in as well—Sascha yelped in pain. He ignored her cries, got the arm in, then locked the harness.

"Everyone in harnesses or acceleration chairs," Ledford said. "Move!"

Still groggy, Sascha grabbed for the swinging handset, snatched it on the second try.

"Conn, Engineering. This maneuvering is killing us down here."

"I'm well aware," XO Ellis said. "Increase gravity to one-point-five gees. Get me more reverse thrust, I don't care how you do it. Conn, out."

She put the handset back in the cradle, gave it a firm pull to make sure it was locked in tight—she didn't need the thing whipping around like a medieval mace.

"Aux," she said, "prepare to increase gravity to one-point-five gees."

Across the compartment, Zhen Smith answered her order.

She switched to the 1MC.

"Attention, attention, all crew prepare for gravity increase to one-point-five. I repeat, one-point-five."

88

BETHANY

Bethany wrapped her arms around the protuberance. The alien object's bumps and knurls dug into her like dull knives as the ship's wild movement threatened to throw her free from the platform.

"Atrium, Xeno! Get us out of transdim!"

Hasik's tinny voice blared from the protuberance platform's comm speaker.

"I'm *trying*," Bethany said. "The protuberance isn't responding to my touch. The surfacing pattern does nothing!"

The ship lurched up and to the right, dragging hard points down Bethany's shoulder and chest despite her desperate grip. Her arms grew tired—she didn't know how much longer she could hold on.

Another hammer-harsh change of direction drove solid ridges into Bethany's right hipbone, sending a jolt so deep and unexpected she cried out.

"Lieutenant! Are you all right?"

Bethany bore down against the pain just as the ship plummeted downward, smacking her cheekbone against the blue-green knob.

"*Lieutenant!*"

"I'm... I'm here."

Bethany tasted blood.

"Find a way to get us to surface," Hasik said. "You saved us before —save us again."

Saved before? Yes... in the Battle of *Ishlangu*. She'd done something to power up *Keeling*'s transdim coupler, which let them escape the Purists. But what, exactly, had she done?

She couldn't remember.

She hurt. She hurt *everywhere*.

Bethany closed her eyes, tried to reach out to God.

Why are you doing this? You're hurting *us*.

If God heard her, He did not respond.

The ship angled up so fast the momentum smashed Bethany down, dragged her arms across unforgiving solidity, breaking her grip.

Then she was flying.

Bethany slammed into the platform's railing with a sound of bone against metal.

She heard a distant voice... Colonel Hasik, repeating her name... and Martigral's name...

He sounded upset...

Even that noise faded away as Bethany slipped into blackness.

89

JOHN

Head ringing, John leaned on a table and pushed himself to his feet. The mess was a madhouse—crew unconscious or otherwise injured from the sudden maneuvering, people screaming from hallucinations, others brawling. Broken cereal dispensers. Cereal everywhere. Mycoware plates and utensils scattered all over the place. And Lieutenant Lindros—naked as the day he was born—standing atop the serving counter, his Sklorno-tentacle-length schlong flopping about.

A guttural roar tore through the chaos.

"Where's my fucking watch, you drunken cunt?"

Mafi stood near the mess entrance, his hands locked down on Torres's neck. He lifted her, *shook* her. She clawed at his hands.

"Beaver, *with me*," John shouted as he leapt over bodies and drove his shoulder into Mafi's ribs.

90

MINDY

Three Raiders flew out of the mess and slammed against the wall. Two men and a woman. All fell to the deck. Another man rushed out of the mess, laughing and shouting *"Jump on the pile!"* before landing on the biggest of the fallen Raiders and sliding an arm around his neck and under his jaw.

None of them saw Mindy.

Nor did the moaning Raider guard lying facedown on the deck outside the gym compartment. He tried to get up, but his groggy movements didn't give him enough strength against the crushing gravity that drained the strength from Mindy's legs, that made it hard to breathe.

"Where's... my... watch," the big Raider grunted, eyes bulging as he struggled to free himself from the choke-hold.

Mindy heard yelling and screaming coming from the mess, but those sounds didn't really register because she heard something far more important, far more urgent.

"Let me out, honey."

As the Raiders kicked and punched and choked each other, Mindy opened the gym compartment door, slipped inside, and pulled shut it behind her.

TRAVIS

"XO, Atrium is not responding," Hasik said. "I think Lieutenant Darkwater is injured. If Martigral is there with her, she may be hurt as well."

Someone had to be ready to operate the transdim drive, ready to surface *Keeling* the moment they regained helm control.

"Get down there, Colonel," Travis said. "Contact me when you arrive."

Hasik hurried out of the xeno loft, his vacsuit legs *zip-zipping* as he ran.

"XO, internal damage reported throughout the ship," Plait called out. "We have multiple injuries. There's a riot in the mess—some Raiders are suffering violent hallucinations."

Travis glanced at the Raider Liaison station, knowing it was empty. At the moment, that didn't matter. Lindros, Winter, or Sands would have to get the platoon under control—unless they were part of the riot.

The ship shuddered. Engineering had maxed out reverse thrust, but the rapidly draining chemjets did little other than generate destructive torsion and shear across every manmade seam, weld, and rivet.

The 1MC chime sounded.

"This is engineering. Increasing gravity to one-point-five. I repeat, increasing gravity to one-point-five. Initiating, initiating, initiating."

Travis felt extra weight push him into the captain's acceleration chair—in an instant, he'd gone from weighing 81 kilograms to roughly 121. He wheezed, heard Lafferty grunting on his left. He'd forgotten the oppressive squeeze of 1.5Gs. It would wear the crew down but help stabilize those not strapped in.

He focused on the nav-orb. Shifting, bifurcating tendrils of crimson and cream flowed like rivers, intertwined like neurons.

Now the orb's span represented a mere *five* kilometers, showing a coursing cloud of red and pale gray—a shifting mist without form or definition. Perhaps *Keeling* was inside one of those tendrils.

In that mist, the target that *Keeling* pursued was a dark shadow. Every time Travis thought he might get a good look, the image fuzzed or the bogey banked away.

"Darsat," Travis said, "do you have anything yet? What am I looking at?"

"Hard to get a solid read on it." Waldren's head wobbled in time to the ship's shudders. She held one hand to her earpiece, her eyes flicking across her screens. "Approximately forty meters long... five meters at the beam, estimated... mass approximately one hundred tonnes. Grav-sig has no matches other than similarity to what we detected in the Mud before."

The size of a patrol craft, or maybe a fighter/bomber. Whatever it was, *Keeling* would not give up the chase. Did *Keeling* want to destroy the craft? Was it possibly a vessel made by the same alien culture that made *Keeling*?

The nav-orb didn't show him any details. The optical system was designed to interpret this dimension at large relative ranges—not distances this close. What few glimpses Travis caught gave him little to go on.

"Darsat, remove the *unidentified* icon," Travis said. "It's blocking my view."

The yellow icon blinked out.

The target was black, maybe, with many shades of dark gray plates—armor, probably—extending from a central core... contrails of some kind trailing from it in irregular, shimmering puffs.

"Conn, Ops. Infirmary reports current maneuvering makes it impossible to treat critically wounded."

Everything in the orb blurred, shifted, as if trying to come into focus over and over again but never quite succeeding.

"Signals, I need to see it," Travis said. "Get me a better look, now."

Signals Chief Madison manned that station, a poorly wrapped, blood-stained gauze bandage around his head.

"Optical isn't designed to manage all the inputs at this speed," he said. "I'm trying to adjust the settings to compensate, but at the moment it can't keep up."

The still-indefinable target grew larger in the nav-orb.

"We're closing in," Waldren said. "Distance to contact, approximately seven hundred meters."

ANNE

"Five hundred meters," Waldren said.

Anne gripped the armrests of her acceleration chair. The ship was completely out of control, piloting itself, chasing an unknown bogey that banked and turned and dove and climbed in breakneck changes of direction, changes *Keeling* matched.

"Four hundred."

In the nav-orb, the fuzzy black image whipped to port, out of view. Anne braced an instant before inertia threw her hard to starboard, pushing her against her restraints.

"Three hundred!"

The bogey was bigger in the orb, but she couldn't make anything out—what little focus they had was fading fast as the closing distance put the bogey inside optical's minimum focus.

Ellis grabbed the comm handset. "This is the XO. All hands, brace for impact."

Gillick and Daniels ran into the CIC, rushed to their seats in the Intel Loft.

"Signals, I need to see the contact," Ellis said. "Get it back!"

"Two hundred!"

The black image fuzzed out completely, leaving nothing but wildly streaking crimson-and-cream smoke.

"*One hundred meters!*"

Keeling was going to ram it. Anne wished Bethany were there, wished she could explain what was happening, explain why Anne was about to die...

And then... nothing.

"XO, we're at zero acceleration." Lars Nygard at the pilot station. The co-pilot seat remained empty. "Relative standstill."

The nav-orb showed a fuzzy, gray, fist-sized bubble around *Keeling*'s marker. Beyond that, drifts of milky fog.

A chilled stillness filled the CIC. Anne heard the clock-timers ticking.

"Darsat," Ellis said, "where is the target?"

Waldren pushed her headphones tighter, tilted her head slightly.

"XO, the readings are strange," she said. "I think we've made contact with the target. It... it's possibly attached to the upper prow."

Attached?

A chase...

A *catch*...

"Signals, get me eyes on the target," Ellis said. "*Figure it out!*"

He was losing it, screaming in throat-ripping anger.

Anne reached out her right hand, gripped his forearm, squeezed it until he looked at her. Fury in his piercing, amber eyes.

"XO, the bogey is inside optical minimum range," she said, quietly but forcibly. "You know the one hundred meters around us is our blind spot. Signals can't fix it."

Travis sneered, and for an instant, Anne knew he wanted to hit her. Then his eyes widened. He blinked, shook his head, and she knew that urge had passed. He faced forward.

The gray ball around *Keeling* marked the ship's blind spot. The only way to see what they'd connected with was to send a person to the Deck One observation bay and have them look.

According to Hasik, who'd logged more *Keeling* deployments

than anyone, in that way lie madness. People seeing the Mud with the naked eye had gone insane, the colonel once told him. The kind of insane you don't come back from.

"Ops, get someone up here to take the captain to the infirmary," Travis said. "Get me damage and injury reports. Intel, get some sane Raiders in TASH, position them at the entrance to the atrium in case we're boarded."

Boarded? The word kicked Anne's common sense back to life. Keeling had likely made physical contact with an unknown craft. Were there crew in that craft? Were they already trying to cut their way in? She should have made that connection instantly, but she hadn't—Travis had.

A horrific sound reverberated through the CIC. A *groaning* of sorts, like the vibration of metal beams bending, combined with the deep, brittle crunching of cracking crysteel.

Heavy tremors thundered the ship, rattling equipment and crew alike. Anne stiffened and clenched her teeth. She gripped her acceleration chair, fought to stay still even as the violent motion flopped her against her restraints like a rag doll.

She waited for death—*Keeling* was breaking up.

The end had come.

The tremors ebbed, then flared again, even harder.

CIC crew cried out in helpless fear—the moans of the damned.

The tremors stopped.

They simply *stopped*, so suddenly and totally Anne wondered if she'd hallucinated the whole thing.

Silence, save for someone babbling a prayer.

Not a hallucination, then.

Anne began to hope she might live through the day.

The 1MC chimed.

"This is Radulski in Raider Land. The bulkheads are moving down here. You hear me? The *fucking walls are moving!*"

Next to her, Travis took a deep, sharp breath. He wiggled his shoulders as if shaking off what had just happened, then grabbed the handset.

"This is the XO, stay off the main circuit! All crew, we are in the Mud, remember that what you see may not be real." He switched to 9MC, the *Exo-Troop communication* circuit—a.k.a. *Raider Land.* "This is the XO, pick up, *now.*"

Anne heard the immediate answer.

"XO, PXO Winter. Radulski's right—the tunnel walls are moving. If it's a hallucination, we're all seeing the same thing."

"Copy, PXO. Hold on." He turned to Anne, leaned close. "Get Kerkhoffs to that tunnel. I need to know what's happening."

He conveyed quiet intensity, yet also frigid calm. With Lincoln out, the XO was stepping up. Again. Was this really the same man she'd met in *Ishlangu*'s lower decks before they were both entombed?

Anne lifted her handset and selected the 2MC—*Propulsion Plant.*

93

SASCHA

The walls *wriggled*.

Was this real? Was she hallucinating? They were in the Mud. This *couldn't* be real. The tunnel between Raider Land and the pouch ran through the mysterious, dense, solid mass—*solid* being the key word—and yet the tunnel quivered, the lights strung along the ceiling swung wildly, the fakegrav deck plates tilted and shifted.

"Chenk... you seeing this?"

Marchenko moved at a crouch, struggling against the one-point-five gravity. He directed his scanner at the port-side tunnel wall—up and down, side to side—methodically doing his job despite the gut-pinching terror surrounding them.

"You mean do I see the fucking *walls* moving, Chief?" He nodded. "Yeah, I see it."

She'd ordered Chenk and Keahloha to accompany her. Maybe because they already had experience doing internal scans, maybe because her shoulder hurt so bad she could barely lift her arm, let alone one of the heavy scanners.

The ship remained at a relative standstill. The brutal roller coaster ride was over. For the moment, at least. Four of her people were down, injured from the rough maneuvering. Another two—Ted

Mi-Suk and Kym Hansen—were tied up with cables, cords, and ropes, anything the engineering staff could find to bind until someone from medical could drug them up and *shut* them up, stop them from screaming.

Sascha assumed other departments had suffered just as much. Lincoln hadn't said a word since that first jerking, punishing lurch—was the captain injured? Was she dead?

Some fifteen meters down the tunnel, two jizzies in full TASH blocked the tunnel's exit to Raider Land. If the walls truly came alive, if the copper *attacked* like the chrysalis attacked Romanik back at Gateway, those Raiders—and the pair positioned at the tunnel's pouch entrance—would rush in to try and save Sascha and her people.

"I don't want to be in here," Keahloha said. "If the ship goes bonkers again, we're toast."

She rotated her scanner in a circular pattern along the starboard wall, which shimmied and squirmed. It moved like... like...

Sascha couldn't put her finger on it. Whatever it was, it strummed some primitive fear response deep in her soul, made her want to get the fuck out of there.

"That's enough for now," she said. "Let's get back to fabrication and collate the scans."

The tunnel around them twitched and convulsed. Flopping lights cast mad shadows along the coral-patterned surface. Despite the high gravity that made every step a challenge, they *got the fuck out of there* fast.

94

TRAVIS

Was this respite permanent, or a temporary pause in *Keeling's* erratic behavior?

"Injury report update," Plait called out. "We're up to fourteen incapacitated. Three severely, they are either in the infirmary or being carried there. Captain Lincoln has a broken jaw and she's groggy, Hammersmith says she's unfit to command. Watson is in the crew mess, triaging. Several injured there. All department heads reported in except Hasik, all crew accounted for except for xeno department. Two dead—Corporal Ellison and Spec-2 Byrnes."

Sara Ellison, their lead signaler. A good sailor. Infuriating. And Byrnes... the ECM operator from *Ishlangu. Beyond* maddening. Byrnes had survived that awful battle only to be press-ganged into service aboard *Keeling,* where she'd lost her life not due to battle, not due to incompetence or malfunction, but because the ship itself had gone rogue, because the ship went where it wanted to go, like a goddamn spoiled *child.*

Lincoln down. Until she returned, this was Trav's show, Trav's watch. A watch upon which two people were already dead. He needed to find a way out of this.

Travis glanced at a clock-timer. Unbelievable. It had only been twenty-one minutes since Plait first notified Lincoln of the unknown bogey. It felt like *hours* had passed.

Cat Brown ran into the CIC, Sora Garcia right behind her. Garcia manned the co-pilot station.

The 18MC light flashed—the atrium.

Travis answered, "Conn here."

"Conn, Atrium." Hasik's voice. "Linkage is still down, so we can't get navigation control, but the protuberance is functional again. Transdim coupler levels in the green. I believe we can surface."

Finally. They could get out of this godforsaken Mud.

"Copy, Atrium. Status of Darkwater and Martigral?"

"Darkwater is unconscious," Hasik said. "I'll secure her to the deck. We need medical here right away. Martigral isn't here. I don't know where she is."

Where could Martigral be? When she wasn't in the atrium, she was in...

She was in the gym compartment—with the prisoners.

"Xeno, emergency surface," Travis said. "Get us to realspace."

"Aye-aye, XO, emergency surface."

The rough flying, people and equipment violently thrown all over the place.

Had the containment cells held?

Travis looked to the Intel Loft. Lafferty, Gillick, Daniels. He needed to send someone, needed them prepared in case the impossible had happened.

He didn't trust Gillick or Daniels with a weapon—he trusted Anne.

"Major Lafferty, Colonel Martigral is unaccounted for," Travis said. "It's possibly the rough maneuvering compromised the containment cells. Go the small arms locker. The instant we surface, get a sidearm and report to me from the gym compartment."

Her eyes widened as she saw the same terrifying possibility he did. She took off like a shot.

Travis lifted the handset, switched to the 1MC.

"This is the XO. All hands, prepare to surface. All hands, prepare to surface."

Handset still in his grip, the 13MC light lit up—*Fabrication Bay*. "Conn here."

"XO, we... ah... we did the scan." Kerkhoffs sounded beyond rattled. "I don't know if this is real or I'm imagining it."

"Give me the info, Eng. Worry about reality later."

In what universe did saying such a thing make sense? In a universe where the *Crypt* existed, that was where.

"We scanned the dense area around the tunnel," Kerkhoffs said. "We compared it to previous scans—don't ask about that right now—and... XO, there's been a repositioning of matter in that area. An *increase* of matter, approximately eighty tonnes worth. We think... whatever we were chasing, we think *Keeling* somehow ingested it."

What was she saying? *Ingested?* That—

A roar of anger from the pilot station.

"Fuck me?" The co-pilot, Nygard stood, pointed a finger at the pilot, Sora Garcia. "No-no-no, fuck *you!*"

He punched Garcia in the face, put all his strength into it—Travis heard the impact, the crunching thud of his fist breaking her nose. She sagged even as he hit her a second time, then a third.

Brown and Erickson rushed from their stations, tackled Nygard, driving him into his monitor. Gillick and Daniels ran past the command slate, rushing to help.

"Eng," Travis said, "did you say *ingested?*"

In the momentary pause, Travis heard Nygard screaming in rage, saw him go down beneath a pile of vacsuited bodies.

"Yes, XO." Kerkhoffs sounded like she didn't believe her own words, like what she said was too fantastical to accept. "That's our guess. Whatever that target was, *Keeling*... well... our ship *ate* it."

All sound faded away. Numb, Travis stared into the nav-orb.

Sitting on the passageway deck, extra weight grinding his knees against the fakegrav plating, John checked the pulse of Ricki Chidimma, who lay facedown outside the gym compartment. Pulse was strong and steady. John wouldn't do anything further, though—Chidimma's bleeding scalp wound meant he might have a neck injury or possibly brain damage. They needed to get the medics here to check him.

John felt the strange, internal tingle of his body returning to the dimension in which he'd been born. So subtle, yet now, after several dives, he recognized it. There were no words to describe the sensation, but he recognized it.

"We're out of dim, Beaver," he said. "You can stop choking Mafi now."

Next to him, Beaver relaxed his hold on the big, unconscious, bearded man.

"I wasn't choking him, Bennett," Beaver said. "I was *done* choking him and *ready* to choke him some more. Mafi go night-night."

Torres pushed herself to her hip and elbow, her free hand rubbing at her neck.

"Fuck Mafi," she said in a hoarse whisper. "And fuck his fucking watch."

John felt himself lighten, like a literal weight rising off his shoulders and every other part of his body as well as gravity returned to normal.

The 1MC chime sounded.

"This is the XO. We... we temporarily lost control of *Keeling*. We have regained control. All crew prepare for immediate punch-in. Course is set for Gateway Station. Triage centers are in the crew mess and the infirmary. All crew chiefs report additional injuries to operations. That is all."

The XO didn't sound like himself. He sounded rattled. How else *should* he sound? *Lost control* was surely part of the unannounced, unexpected dive into the Mud.

John heard a woman's scream of terror—he was up like a shot, as was Beaver.

The scream had come from the closed gym compartment, a scant one meter away.

For an instant, John assumed the sound was yet another hallucination, all in his head, or a cry from someone else suffering one—but they'd just come *out* of transdim.

They were in realspace.

Another scream, this one of gurgling pain.

And then... high-pitched chittering, a sound that sent chills racing along John's skin.

"*Hostile on board*," he shouted. "Sklorno prisoner may be loose! Beaver, *open it!*"

Beaver yanked the handle up and pulled the door open. John started in, but Beaver was faster—the younger soldier shouldered through, only to sail backward, knocking John aside before slamming against the wall.

A blur of translucent motion launched from the compartment, muscle and power that drove past with the force of a linebacker.

John regained his balance, planted a foot to give chase, only to be hit by a second something that rushed out of the compartment, something screaming, bleeding, dressed in blood-soaked tan coveralls. He reacted by instinct, catching the person before she fell—Colonel Martigral, half her face ripped away, one eye a red hollow, blood spurting from her ravaged throat.

Abshire and Sands were there, throwing themselves on the alien, grabbing at it, trying to drag it to the deck, but it was too strong. The Sklorno stumbled forward along the passageway, staying upright as the two Raiders lost their grip and fell to the deck.

The Sklorno reached the dead end that was the atrium's curved, coppery outer wall. Three eyestalks jerked in three different directions. It saw the ladder down, rushed to it—three gunshots barked out.

The Sklorno stumbled back, clear blood spurting. The beast hit the closed galley door, slumped to the deck as its powerful, back-folded legs gave out. Tentacle arms spasmed, waved without purpose, as did the three eyestalks still searching for a way out.

Movements of panic and desperation... movements of pending death... not so different from one species to the next.

John lowered Martigral to the deck and pressed his hands against the ragged, ripped flesh of her throat, trying to stop the bleeding, already knowing it was too late but doing it anyway, doing what his training made him do.

Anne Lafferty climbed up through the hatch, sidearm pointed at the alien. She knelt, grabbed all three eyestalks with her free hand, pressed the gun against the translucent, teardrop shaped body. The beast's thick legs moved, sluggish and without strength, feebly pushing big feet against the deck.

Lafferty yanked the eyestalks, pulled the three madly blinking eyes right in front of her own. The Sklorno let out an all-too-recognizable squeal of pain and fear. Tooth-studded raspers, clogged with bloody shreds of Martigral's face and throat, slid out, pulled at Lafferty's black coveralls.

She smiled. It happened so fast, but John saw it—a warm smile, a *loving* smile.

"This is for your own good," Lafferty said.

She fired. She fired again. And again.

The alien let out a low, fading moan.

It sagged.

It went limp.

Sands and Abshire hurried in, pinning down legs and tentacle arms as Lafferty stood and half-turned away from them in the ready position, her sidearm angled toward the deck.

John felt someone small kneel next to him.

"Corporal, *move!*"

Doc Watson, her half-askew med goggles pointing up.

John sat back and let go. Watson leaned in fast, like a bird snatching a worm, one hand applying pressure to the wound. With her other hand, she pressed two fingers up under the woman's jaw.

Martigral's one remaining eye blinked slowly—she looked at John.

She spoke, words mumbled from blood-smeared lips half-torn away by sharp alien teeth.

"My... mother..."

The last sound to leave her mouth was a weak, dwindling sigh.

Colonel Martigral stopped blinking.

John knew death when he saw it.

"She's gone," Watson said.

Still on her knees, Watson shuffled around Martigral's corpse and started examining Chidimma.

Watson, Chidimma, Martigral, the deck itself, it all started to shimmer. Another feeling John knew well—*Keeling* was entering punch-space.

Beaver groaned and sat up.

"Fucknuggets," he said. "Those crickets can really *kick.*"

A rare moment of quiet.

Sascha stood alone in the curvine room, waiting for her staff to arrive. While in punch-space, the curvine itself sat motionless. So perfectly machined was the hourglass-shaped piece of tech that you had to look twice to be sure it *wasn't* spinning. Whether sitting idle or rotating at hundreds of thousands of revolutions per minute, the glossy maroon surface looked almost the same.

She rotated her shoulder, slowly, testing her range of motion. It felt a bit better. Doc Hammersmith said it would be sore for a few days. She gave Sascha pinkies for the pain. Vitamin-P to the rescue. Shocker.

So much to do before they reached port, and plenty more after.

She and her engineering team would soon go over every centimeter of the chemjet system to check for damage caused by the heavy use of reverse thrust. Then, a cataloging of all internal structural damage incurred from *Keeling's* wild maneuvering.

The ship going rogue and doing what it had done was, thankfully, not on her. The punch-drive provided FTL travel. The curvine provided sub-light propulsion. Both of those systems were Sascha's responsibility. That black magic, *transdimensional* bullshit, though? That was all on Hasik.

Hopefully, before they punched back into realspace at Gateway, he'd figure out how to keep the ship from doing what it wanted to do. *Doing what it wanted to do.* How insane was it to think of a ship in those terms? Insane or not, it was reality.

The ship had ignored directional commands.

The ship dove on its own.

It chased something on its own.

The fucking thing *consumed* something on its own.

They wouldn't be able to figure out what *Keeling* ingested, or *how* the ship ingested it, until they were back in realspace. If they'd be able to figure it out at all, which was a big *if*.

The chemjet examination wasn't the only big project on her plate —Chief Lafferty expected a written explanation as to why Sascha disobeyed orders and scanned the dense section in the first place. It didn't matter that Marchenko and Keahloha did it; Sascha wasn't going to throw her people under the bus. She couldn't, not if she wanted Chenk to sneak those initial scans off the ship.

And Sascha did want that.

But *why* did she want it? She wasn't sure. Ninety-six weeks left in her sentence. She could do her time and be done with this ship, so why was she prying into the repurposed armor and *Keeling*'s mysterious black budget? Why was she going to risk the wrath of Lafferty and Epperson to learn what she could about this ship *eating* something?

Sascha didn't have answers to those questions, other than that she had two mysteries on her hands, and she couldn't let either of them go.

Before she did anything, though, she needed to take care of a high-priority demand from the XO—he wanted someone from engineering transferred to the xeno department ASAP, before *Keeling* reached Gateway. She'd narrowed it down to four candidates.

Those four candidates entered the curvine room.

Spec-1 Hyeon Dimo, nicknamed "Little Thing," propulsion mate from *Ishlangu*, who'd bit out a chunk of Charlie Hong's shoulder. Sergeant Kishor Bakshi, electrical mate, also from *Ishlangu*. Spec-1 Michael Camp, machinist mate, who had watched the ship's chrysalis smash Leona Romanik to death, who had gone AWOL before being shot by Lafferty and dragged back to the ship. Spec-1 Li Ying, the propulsion mate who always wore coveralls to hide some of the white skin patches caused by her vitiligo.

Dimo and Bakshi had been aboard not quite two full weeks. As such, Sascha didn't rely on them as much as she did the others. Li had asked more questions about the transdim drive than anyone else—questions she wasn't supposed to be asking, but you couldn't keep an inquisitive engineer down. Li might love the Xeno Mate position. Camp never stopped moping, never stopped mumbling how "doomed" everyone was, which made him Sascha's leading candidate for the transfer; getting him out of engineering would be a good thing.

"Okay, team, here's the deal," Sascha said. "The XO tasked me with transferring one of you to the xeno department to help in the Atri—"

Dimo's hand shot up. "I'll do it!"

Her enthusiasm caught Sascha off-guard.

"Spec Dimo, let me finish describing the opportunity."

"But I *want* it," Dimo said. "Ever since I got here I've wanted to help in the atrium. I've had…"

She trailed off, seeming to catch herself before she said something wrong.

"Had what, Spec?" Sascha asked.

"Nothing, nothing." Dimo wrung her hands together, squeezing them hard enough to make white spots appear. "I'm the right person for the job."

"*I* want the position, Lieutenant," Li Ying said. "I've got a *Keeling* deployment under my belt. I have more experience in transdim." She looked at Dimo, didn't hide her disdain. "Seniority. Sorry."

Li had a point. Experience aboard mattered, but so, too, did rank.

"Sergeant Bakshi," Sascha said. "How about you? Any interest in being the new Xeno Mate?"

Bakshi wore military issue glasses. The black frames were identical to Colonel Hasik's, yet Bakshi's lenses never steamed up and were always spotless. The dark brown eyes behind those lenses simmered with anger.

"Permission to speak freely, Lieutenant?"

Sascha nodded.

"I don't want anything to do with whatever goes on in the atrium," Bakshi said. "I haven't seen my family in nine months. I know most of you are criminals and rejects. My only sin was being on *Ishi*, now I'm stuck here. I don't want anything to do with this fucking lumpy turd of a ship."

Dimo's knee rose and her foot snapped upward, connected with the bridge of Bakshi's nose—the cartilage there crunched sickeningly. He dropped, hands covering his face.

Camp grabbed Dimo by her shoulders, meaning to pull her away from Bakshi, but the small woman twisted and drove her knee into his groin. He cried out, sagged to the deck.

Li Ying backed away as far as she could, which wasn't far in the cramped compartment. She grabbed a spanner off a rack, held it like a club.

"Spec Dimo, *that's enough*," Sascha said. "What the hell are you doing?"

The wild-eyed, diminutive propulsion mate pointed down at Bakshi.

"He insulted the ship! He called *Keeling* a *turd*!"

Dimo was crazy. This was her second assault on a fellow crewmember, and this time she didn't have the Mud as an excuse. Lincoln's lax policies be dammed—*Little Thing* needed to be brought up on charges.

Sascha grabbed the comm handset, switched to *1MC*. "This is Lieutenant Kerkhoffs in the curvine room, I need Raiders here on the double!" She slammed the handset back into the cradle.

Dimo looked crestfallen. "Raiders? You're arresting me? But he insulted *Keeling!*"

Pride of ship was a huge part of Fleet life, but Sascha hadn't seen much of it aboard the *Crypt*. Probably because many crewmembers had been forced to be here for various transgressions, with no leave, kept away from any chance of seeing friends and loved ones. Dimo had been here for only *eleven days*—how had she developed such a passionate attachment so quickly?

Although... she was one of the rescuees from *Ishlangu*. After the destruction of that warship, Dimo spent time aboard the *Crypt*, in trans-dim, returning from the combat zone to Gateway Station. Had she experienced any hallucinations that might make her so devoted to the *Keeling?*

Devoted... just like Bethany Darkwater seemed to be.

Bakshi sat up, hands thick with the blood oozing from his broken nose.

Camp groaned, clutching at his balls.

"Lieutenant," Dimo said, her eyes wide and pleading, "what about the Xeno Mate job? Can I start now?"

She didn't seem to care that she'd put two of her crewmates—both significantly bigger than her—flat on the deck. Dimo was definitely not someone who belonged in *Keeling*'s most important area.

"Spec Dimo," Sascha said, "it's clear that Spec Li is—"

Dimo's body suddenly *bubbled* like boiling pudding, her facial features warping and shifting. Arms and legs morphed into hideous appendages hidden by her stained, light gray coveralls. Her head *grew*, stretching upward so high it angled against the overhead pipes.

The head *changed*...

Fear dug through Sascha like a shovel in the chest. She'd only caught a glimpse of it, a glimpse through the opaque, thickening film of *Keeling*'s self-healing material, but she'd seen enough then to recognize what she saw now, to recognize what Dimo had become...

...six lidless, trembling eyes, each the size of a watermelon, jiggling madly, fighting against each other for dominance, fighting against each other to look at Sascha, to gaze deep into her soul, *through* her very being...

...four wings, *devil's wings*, black and wet, torn and folded, about to *spread*...

One eye burst in thick, spraying dollops of broth, revealing a mouth that was more beak than lips, yet was neither.

"You belong with us, Sascha Anneliese Kerkhoffs... you belong with us."

She heard a woman's scream echoing through the void, a sound she *saw* as well as *heard,* a sound coursing and burbling like the Mud's ever-flowing crimson-cream strands...

...the scream was her own.

"Lieutenant Kerkhoffs! Are you hurt?"

Sascha opened eyes she hadn't realized she'd closed. Old Man Bennett, gripping her shoulders, his face close and filled with concern.

"Lieutenant, *are you hurt?*"

He was holding her, holding her in place so the Dimo-thing could *get* her...

Sascha knocked Bennett's arms away, crawled backward on her butt until she hit the curvine cradle's base. She looked past Bennett, looked at the abomination...

But it was no longer an abomination.

It was just Spec-1 Hyeon Dimo, all of five-foot-one, one hundred pounds soaking wet, a blue-skinned Raider holding her right arm tight, the Raider they called *Beaver* holding her left.

Whatever the strange spell had been, it was gone. Sascha wasn't sure if it'd happened at all.

It *hadn't* happened. Just a hallucination. Just the fucking *Mud.*

"I'm not hurt," Sascha said. "I'm okay."

Bennett clearly didn't think she was, but he nodded anyway.

"We'll take Spec Dimo to Raider Land and hold her there until the XO can address the situation," he said. "Knowing how shorthanded we are, I imagine XO will define punishment and then put her back on duty."

Back on the job? Back in engineering?

"*No!*" Fighting back fear and revulsion, Sascha stood, lowered her voice to a normal level. "No, Corporal Bennett. Spec Dimo is being transferred. Take her to the atrium. She works for Colonel Hasik now."

Dimo let out a sound that was half shout of joy, half incomprehensible relief.

"Thank you, Lieutenant! *Thank you!*"

Sascha nodded to the door. "Take her there immediately. Please."

Bennett's already wrinkled brow wrinkled deeper, concern writ in those lines. But like the good soldier he was, he did as he was told.

"Yes sir." He walked back to the blue-skinned man—Radulski, Sascha remembered now—and the always-shouting Beaver. "Let's escort her to the atrium."

They left the curvine room.

Camp threw up on the deck.

With blood-smeared hands, Bakshi picked up his glasses. They were still in one piece. They still looked spotless. "I hate it here." He put the glasses on and got to his feet. "Permission to report to the infirmary?"

Sascha nodded. She still felt the fear—thick, cold molten metal rolling through her body.

Bakshi left. Dripping blood marked his path.

Sascha sensed a stare, looked at Li Ying, who still held the spanner.

"I wanted that position," Li said. "I have seniority. That asshole Dimo gets it because she sucker-punched two people? That's *bullshit*, Lieutenant. And why the hell did you scream? You acted like you were hallucinating or something."

Oh, were Li's little feelings hurt? Too goddamn bad.

"I don't need to justify my decisions to you, Spec," Sascha said. "And don't worry about how I reacted. In the Mud, bad things..."

Her words faded away.

In the Mud, bad things happen.

But they weren't *in* the Mud.

And if they weren't in the Mud, then…

Then what just happened to her? It seemed so *real*.

The fear in Sascha's soul shifted, it transformed.

Dimo was crazy… but, maybe… so was Sascha.

"Dismissed," Sascha said.

Li glared. She dropped the spanner. It clanged against the deck. She left the curvine room.

Sascha stood there, her heart pounding, her skin tingling. They weren't in transdim, they were in punch-space.

People didn't hallucinate in punch-space.

What was happening to her?

She was tired. Stressed. That was it. The battle. Not enough sleep. The Sklorno kick to her head. A concussion. Watson had said so. A concussion… that's what made Sascha see something that wasn't there.

The same thing she'd seen through the hole in the hull during the Battle of *Ishlangu*.

It didn't mean anything.

Camp threw up again.

Work. Her people. Sascha would focus on her team, on her duties. They'd be back at Gateway soon. She'd get some rest.

She'd be fine.

Ninety-six weeks left.

She would be *fine*.

Sascha helped Camp to his feet.

"Come on, sailor," she said. "Let's go get your nuts looked at."

EPILOGUE 2
BETHANY DARKWATER

The painkillers weren't doing much. Enough, maybe, that Bethany could function, although her focus wasn't really there. Her face hurt. Her body hurt. Her head hurt.

Keeling's mad maneuvering had given her quite a thump. Three stitches for the cut on her cheek, two inside on her tongue from where she'd bitten through it, and a splint on her right pinkie from when she'd slammed into the protuberance platform railing. Still, she knew she'd gotten off lucky—three people had apparently died from the rough flying.

Their bodies were stored in cubbyholes. At least they'd get a real funeral service, not be incinerated in space, their atoms returned to the stars from whence every living thing came.

Every living thing?

Was *Keeling* made of star stuff?

Mysteries upon mysteries upon mysteries.

No one knew how *Keeling* had absorbed or ingested the object in transdim. They were in punch-space, about seven hours travel remaining until Gateway. When the ship punched-out there and returned to realspace, then and only then could an external examination begin.

If, that was, *Keeling* didn't dive back into the Mud for another transdim snack. Colonel Hasik was working on the linkage system, trying to find a way to prevent *Keeling* from going rogue again.

So much to process. *Keeling* pursuing the object. The object itself and its ingestion. The hunger Bethany and others had felt, hunger that vanished after *Keeling* ingested the object—had she and other members of the crew felt what the ship felt? That seemed obvious, but if so, what about Bethany's inexplicable bout of sexual arousal? Was that the ship's urge? Was it just another hallucination manifestation? Had others experienced similar sensations?

Except... the ship hadn't been in transdim when she'd gotten so turned on she couldn't think straight. The ship had been in realspace, which meant it wasn't a hallucination.

Someone thudded on the atrium's closed sphincter.

Bethany walked to it, slid her hand along the oval frame's smooth, bright copper. The metal retracted.

She stepped back quickly, feeling a fight-or-flight-driven surge of adrenaline—in the passageway stood the Empty Man.

"Lieutenant Darkwater, we were told to escort Spec-One Dimo here to your department. Lieutenant Kerkhoffs says she's your new Xeno Mate."

Bethany couldn't look away from the abomination standing before her—a muscled old man masked by a vibrating black haze.

He was *evil*.

"Lieutenant," the creature said, "did you hear me?"

"Jeeze, the Mud is really gumming up brains today."

The Empty Man said the first part, but someone else had spoken the second part...

Bethany realized three additional people stood in the passageway: Raiders Perry, Radulski, and a short woman in a sailor's light gray coveralls.

"Are you all right?" the Empty Man asked. "Do you need assistance?"

Hollow sockets for eyes, the darkness in those spaces full of dangerous, deadly blankness.

It was all Bethany could do to not run screaming.

"I'm fine," she said.

The blue-skinned Radulski smirked. "That's what they all say."

"I said I'm *fine*, Spec." Bethany had to hold it together, get the Empty Man away from here. He didn't *belong* here. "What do you want?"

Dimo took a step closer.

"I'm in your department now," she said. "Lieutenant Kerkhoffs just transferred me. I'm... I'm *really* excited, sir."

The Empty Man's words played back in Bethany's mind.

"Oh, I see." Bethany grabbed Dimo's wrist, pulled her through the portal. "I have her now, thank you. We're good here. Please move along. Have a nice day."

Bethany swiped her hand along the oval's rim—the metal stretched inward, closing the sphincter and blocking the hideous Empty Man from sight.

Bennett. That's who it was. Why did Bennett always appear that way? The other Raiders looked normal. Bethany wasn't hallucinating... was she? They were in realspace.

"Lieutenant Darkwater? Are you all right?"

Bethany gathered herself. Dimo had to be the shortest person aboard. Her black hair would have been heavy and lustrous were it not cropped so close to her scalp. Stitches on her temple, dotting a reddish line of pursed flesh. Small nose, quite cute. Full lips. Big, dark eyes—*eager* eyes.

"I'm fine, Spec," Bethany said. "I wish people would stop asking me that question."

Dimo smiled. "I'm sure everyone is just concerned about you, sir. You are the heart of this ship, after all."

Her eyes. Not just *eagerness* in them. *Admiration*, too.

It was... weird.

"Hey, we both have stitches," Dimo said. "Yours are new. Those bruises look painful, sir."

Bethany had another two hours to go before she could take another painkiller. Maybe she could cheat that a little bit, take it a tad early.

"They're no picnic," Bethany said. "I got thrown around during the unexpected dive. How did you get your stitches, Spec Dimo?"

Dimo's smile crinkled wider. "Someone insulted the ship." *Glee* in those eyes, the eyes of someone who loved to fight, who loved to *hurt*. "We had words."

They *had words*? Had it happened in the transdim? Bethany would have to look into that. The last thing she needed was a Xeno Mate who got violent in the Mud.

"Colonel Hasik is your new department head," Bethany said. "You'll meet him soon. He's elsewhere in the ship, working on something."

Working on something Bethany wasn't allowed to see, apparently.

"Is he working on the pimples?" asked Dimo. "The whole crew is talking about how they saved us from that missile barrage. Can I see the pimples? What can I do first? I'm so excited! I can't believe I'm here. When *Ishi* was on fire and cracking up, I thought I was going to die, but now I know it was meant to be. I've had *dreams*, sir. Wonderful dreams! I believe I have been called upon to... to..."

She trailed off, as if she'd caught herself before saying something that might bring disdain or ridicule. *Called upon?* The phrase struck a chord within Bethany.

"It's all right, Spec. We're going to be working closely together, so I need to know who you really are. Tell me what you were going to say."

Dimo stared. Such big, dark eyes.

"I believe God brought me here," she said. "I believe God wants me to follow you, Lieutenant. God wants me to obey you."

Obey? That was a strange way to put it.

"I'm an officer," Bethany said. "Of course you should follow my orders."

Dimo shook her head. "I don't mean rank." She glanced off, stared at the glowing heartstone. "I should *obey* you... like people *obey* their spiritual leader."

Her words took Bethany's breath away.

"Like in a church," Dimo said. "But not a church of false gods... or of metaphorical bullshit." She looked up into the atrium's dense, dangling greenery. "The church of a *real* god."

It wasn't until that moment that Bethany realized how *alone* she felt. She had her intermittent, often unexpected communions with *Keeling*, which filled her heart and soul. She even heard God's voice sometimes... or at least thought she did. Being on *Keeling* brought her a sense of belonging, of *oneness* she'd never felt before, not even during her dedicated days as a sister in a Purist convent. But for all that rapturous bliss, she hadn't felt true connection with *people*.

That kind of connection mattered. She was Human, after all. Humans were drawn to their own kind, always and forever.

A church.

Bethany liked how that word made her feel.

"Those gray sailor coveralls won't do," Bethany said. "Not anymore." She pinched her collar, lifted it slightly. "From now on, you'll wear the tan of the Bureau of Science & Technology. I've got some you can use until we get back to port."

From the look on Dimo's face, one would have thought it was Giving Day, and she was getting all the presents.

Yes, this woman would work out just fine.

Five hours until Gateway.

Anne knocked on the door to Lincoln's quarters.

"Enter."

Anne stepped inside. Lincoln sat behind her desk. She looked like she might throw up—if not drop dead—at any moment. A clean, red bandana hid the cut she'd suffered when she'd gotten knocked out.

"Have a seat, Chief," she said. "XO's on his way."

Anne sat on the small couch. "I'd ask how your noggin feels, but it's written all over your face."

Lincoln slowly blinked half-lidded eyes.

"That's why we're meeting in here, Chief. I don't need the crew seeing me like this."

A knock on the door made Lincoln wince.

"Enter," she said.

Travis stepped in, shut the door behind him.

"Chief Sung has the conn," he said. "Good to see you up and about, Captain. How's your head?"

In answer, Lincoln pointed to the couch.

Travis sat next to Anne. She waited to feel that thunderbolt of lust for him, yet it did not come. She still wanted him, sure, but with nowhere near the intensity she'd experienced in the CIC.

In the Mud, bad things happened.

So did *horny* things, apparently.

"Let's make this quick," Lincoln said. "Hammersmith filled me in on most of what happened. Chief Sung told me the rest. We have a lot to address when we reach Gateway." She lifted a tablet from her desk, squinted at it. "I have the casualty report here. XO, list them, please."

Ellis drew in a breath, gathering himself. He took death so personally. That was a liability in a commander.

"Four deaths total," he said. "Raider Specialist-One Onyeka Ayodele, died in combat. Lead signaler Corporal Sara Ellison and ECM operator Specialist-Two Daria Byrnes died when the ship went rogue. Colonel Mindy Martigral died due to injuries sustained when the Sklorno captive escaped."

He listed Ayodele as a combat death. While technically true, it was a rather nice way of saying the guy choked on his own vomit. The Raiders were pissed—they blamed Ayodele's death on a malfunction of his armor. They weren't wrong.

"Epperson will not be happy about Martigral," Lincoln said. "We're all going to get chewed out."

The captain spoke in almost a monotone, but Anne still picked up the sarcasm. What could Epperson do to them? The command triumvirate now had two full missions worth of experience together— he would not screw with effective chemistry, no matter how angry he got.

"Chief Lafferty," Lincoln said, "I was told you killed the escaped Sklorno. Well done."

Very few people could claim such a thing. As far as Anne knew, she was the first BII operative to kill a Sklorno. Daddy would be so proud.

"Epperson won't be happy about that, either," Travis said.

Anne could endure such anger with ease. The prisoner killed a crewmember. She did her duty putting the beast down.

"The other two captives remain alive." Lincoln looked at her tablet. "Monstranto is looking after them?"

The supply chief wasn't a xenobiologist, or even a regular biologist; then again, no one aboard was.

"That's correct, Captain," Travis said. "Warrant Monstranto is checking on them hourly. Other than maintaining the same anesthesia mixture Martigral used, there's not much for him to do other than hope for the best."

Poor Mindy Martigral. From Epperson's pet xenobiologist to a corpse chilling in a cubbyhole. Such was life in Fleet.

"Injuries," Lincoln said. "I know we have a lot, present company included. XO, any that require replacements?"

Travis sniffed, cleared his throat. He barely knew these people— why did he get so worked up about them?

"Raider Specialist-One Jasmin Miroslav," he said. "She suffered brain damage when the ship went rogue. She is medically unfit to serve."

Lincoln closed her eyes. "She was fresh out of boot, wasn't she?"

"I'm afraid so," Travis said. "This was her first deployment."

Well, all right, Anne could see how *that* was a little sad. Sort of. At least she could see it made Travis and Lincoln sad, so Anne pretended it made her sad as well.

"A real shame," she said, hanging her head. "So unfair."

Travis reached over, gave Anne's forearm a quick squeeze. Was he consoling her? Nice of him.

"War is never fair," Lincoln said. "XO, if we have to deploy again right away, any other injuries that require replacements?"

Travis shrugged. "There're a lot of broken bones, a lot of lacerations and bruises. Hammersmith is still working nonstop, but by the time we punch-out, I think the bone-melder will have patched up the worst of it."

Anne felt fortunate she hadn't been banged around like many of the crew had.

"Where are we at with the ship going rogue?" asked Lincoln. "Does Hasik think the same thing will happen again when we punchout?"

For that one, Travis didn't have a ready answer.

"Colonel Hasik is working on that now," the XO said. "He's optimistic he can modify the linkage system so it won't happen again. We won't know until we know."

Out of all the dangers the crew faced, and there were many, this new threat dominated above all—would the ship do what it was supposed to do, or would it plunge back into the Mud on a whim and chase something? Anne loved a little chaos in her life, but this was one X-factor she would happily do without.

"I see," Lincoln said. "Is Darkwater helping him?"

Poor Beth. Her pretty face cut up and bruised. She'd taken quite a beating during *Keeling*'s little jaunt.

"No, Captain," Travis said. "Darkwater is getting the new Xeno Mate up to speed. You wanted that position filled before we got back to port. Hasik feels he can handle the linkage system by himself for now."

Which meant Hasik didn't want Anne's bestie to see the *linkage system* that had failed. Anne hadn't seen it, either. Linkage was yet another highly classified element of a vessel that was nothing *but* highly classified elements.

"Chief Lafferty," Lincoln said, "any further developments regarding your vetting of the crew?"

Anne sat up straighter.

"One significant red flag," she said. "Lieutenant Kerkhoffs performed an unauthorized scan of the ship. She had requested permission to do so several times and had been denied several times. The ship's captain, executive officer, and the highest-ranking non-command officer aboard all told her, in no uncertain terms, not to do it—yet she did it anyway. If it hadn't been for *Keeling*... ah...

consuming the unidentified object in transdim, we might not have known."

Both Travis and Lincoln looked uncomfortable. Anne couldn't blame them. *Keeling* continued to defy rational expectations of what a ship could do.

"That is a concern," Lincoln said. "Did she have help?"

Gillick and Daniels had poked around but they'd found nothing. The engineering department seemed quite loyal to Kerkhoffs—the sign of a good officer, or a *really* good spy.

"As far as I know, she acted alone," Anne said. "I'll continue to investigate. I'd like permission to interrogate her when we get back to Gateway."

Lincoln rested her head in her hands. From pain rather than exasperation, by the look of it.

"I doubt Kerkhoffs is a spy," Travis said. He held up a hand to cut off Anne's immediate response. "I'm aware I'm not an intelligence analyst. I'm aware you know far more than I do. Captain, unless you're going to replace Kerkhoffs, I don't think it's good for her to be interrogated by someone she'll ship out with on the next deployment."

Was that an emotional yet rational defense?

Or was Travis working *with* Kerkhoffs somehow?

"Two days until we reach Gateway," Lincoln said, her words thin, tired. "I'll decide then, but I think the XO is right. Someone else can interrogate Kerkhoffs. Chief Lafferty, leave her be for now, but make sure she doesn't take any information off-ship."

Too bad for Kerkhoffs. At least Anne would have been nice about it. Well, nice-*er* than whoever Daddy sic'd on her.

"Aye-aye, Captain," Anne said. "I'll escort her off ship myself."

Travis rubbed his knees.

"Kerkhoffs is our engineering department head," he said. "Of course she wants to know all she can about the ship. That doesn't make her a spy. Everyone wants to know more. *I* want to know more. Captain, when we return, we need to talk to Admiral Epperson about letting our people better understand the ship. The blanket secrecy is overkill. It makes us less efficient."

Lincoln stood.

"Two days until Gateway," she said. "I'll entertain the thought then. For now, I'm going to sleep. XO, let Sung run the show for a few hours. Get some rest before taking over. Wake me if anything happens. Dismissed."

Anne and Travis stepped into the narrow passageway. Travis shut the door behind them.

"I'm hungry," Anne said. "Want to grab a sandwich in the wardroom?"

Travis stared off. She wasn't sure he'd heard her.

"I'll take a rain check," he said. "I need to do a walkthrough. The crew needs to see me up and about."

He strode off, leaving Anne alone.

Since he'd had that banger of a nightmare, there was something different about him. What had he seen in that dream?

Travis shouldn't have backed Kerkhoffs. That marked him as a suspect. Add him to the list:

Jester Gillick.

Brendan Akagi.

Michael Camp.

Sascha Kerkhoffs.

And, now, XO Travis Ellis.

Travis pulled at his collar. It was always hot below decks. Sweat tingled in his hair, gathered in his pits. He was used to it, but that didn't make it any less annoying.

He stood at the atrium's sphincter. He was already fucked nine ways to Sunday. He'd be in port soon. He'd probably have a divorce document waiting for him. He might never see Molly again. Or Aven, if Molly decided to be a total asshole. He might never see Kinley *at all*. His child—his own flesh and blood—and he might never see her.

And now, thanks to the dreams that tore his mind apart, there was a piece of him, a slimy, lurking, *spineless* piece, that didn't want to see Kinley.

What if she had copper eyes?

What if she called him that bastardized form of *daddy*?

And to top Trav's personal shit salad off with some dried-turd sprinkles, Epperson still had it out for him. The admiral thought Travis was a coward that could be manipulated by fear. Was the admiral right about that? In port... maybe.

But not out here.

Not in this ship.

On *Keeling*, Travis didn't feel like himself. He wasn't afraid.

Here, he was stronger. Here, he wasn't *Yellowbelly Ellis*. Here, his captain relied on him. Here, Raiders that chewed iron and shit nails respected him.

Aboard the *Crypt*, Travis Ellis wasn't the man who fled the Battle of Asteroid X7, who left his fellow countrymen to die. To be taken prisoner. To be raped. To be murdered.

Here, he was who he was supposed to be.

When he returned to port, would he still feel like this? He didn't know. Epperson would be all over him again, so why was he here now? Why was he thinking of adding more threat? More risk?

Because there were questions he could no longer ignore. Not completely, anyway. The officer in him needed to learn more. The officer in him needed to protect his crew.

Because command treated that crew not as the self-sacrificing heroes they were. Command saw them as *numbers*. As assets to be used and discarded, to be fed into the forge of war—sacrificial lambs offered up for slaughter.

That was why he would take this chance.

If it cost him his family and career? All the sailors and Raiders aboard *Keeling* had careers, too. He would not put his selfish needs above theirs.

Travis slid his hand along the bright copper rim. The sphincter stretched apart, a throat opening to swallow.

He entered the atrium, saw Bethany Darkwater and her new transfer, Hyeon Dimo, standing on the metal-grate protuberance platform. Darkwater looked at him with light in her eyes. Dimo, with darkness. The tiny woman wearing tan coveralls subtly stepped in front of Bethany as if Travis were a potential threat.

"Hello, XO Ellis," Darkwater said. "What can I do for you?"

She'd changed since they'd first met. Travis saw it now, saw the subtle, gradual accumulation of alterations in one whip-crack moment of realization.

"Hello, Lieutenant," he said. "Is Colonel Hasik working on the linkage?"

Darkwater nodded. "He is, XO. You want me to go get him?"

Travis glanced around the atrium. The heartstone. The hanging garden with its too-green leaves, its obscenely large fruits, vegetables, and fungi. The mist. The *humidity*. Such a strange place, more so because it was tucked away inside a warship.

"I actually came to see you, Lieutenant," Travis said. "Spec Dimo, give us ten minutes."

Dimo—who'd bitten a chunk out of one sailor, broken the nose of another, and maybe ended a third's bloodline—had the audacity to look at Darkwater for permission.

Darkwater's smile vanished.

"Spec, the XO gave you an *order*. Don't look at me like I outrank him. You do what he tells you and you do it *now*."

Dimo winced as if she'd been slapped, as if she'd disappointed the one person in the universe she most dreaded disappointing. "Aye-aye, Lieutenant." She looked at Travis, all trace of her protective anger gone. "I'm sorry, XO. So sorry."

She hurried down the platform steps and rushed to the exit. The way Dimo *moved*, with speed and grace. Had she been blessed with more size, she would have made a genuinely frightening Raider.

The atrium sphincter pinched shut behind her.

"My apologies, XO." Darkwater strode down the platform's metal-grate steps. "I haven't had direct reports before. I'll see to it that Dimo is punished for her disrespect."

Perhaps the hanging mist had obscured Darkwater's face, or perhaps Travis hadn't been ready to see the damage she'd taken. Fresh stitches on her swollen cheek. A splint on her pinkie. Bruises that would grow bigger and darker.

Bethany Darkwater looked like she'd been in a fight.

A fight, or a battle.

Hard to believe people once called this woman *mousy*. There was nothing mousy about Bethany Darkwater. Not anymore. She carried herself with an officer's confidence.

And... she was a bit *bigger* than she'd been before. Thicker. Not so surprising; she'd probably been a scientist somewhere, hidden away in a lab, sitting on her ass all day. On a Fleet warship, you *worked*. Constant work changed a person. You shed fat and put on muscle. More to the point, you gained confidence, and with confidence, you stood straighter. You took on the aura of a warrior. Because even if you labored belowdecks and never crossed the gap or fired a weapon, if you served on a warship, you *were* a warrior.

After facing life and death, after cleaning blood from the decks, after hearing the last moans and screams of your friends, a person was never the same.

Never.

"No need to discipline Dimo," Travis said. "Not yet. You're new to command, Lieutenant. While there is a fine line between letting people run all over you and smacking them down for every screw up, it's still a line. I suggest you give Dimo room to learn that."

The lieutenant considered those words.

There was a sparkle in her eyes that hadn't been there when she'd first come aboard.

Bethany Darkwater was a woman in love.

But in love with *what*?

Travis wasn't sure he wanted the answer to that particular question.

She had changed. So had he. But had they changed... or *been* changed?

Another question he wasn't ready for.

"XO, I understand what you have told me. Regarding punishment for insubordination, I will follow your guidance. Now, what is it you wanted to talk to me about? How can I be of help?"

And here it was. The metaphorical Rubicon that Travis needed to cross. Yellowbelly would have shut his cowardly mouth.

But he wasn't that person anymore.

"Lieutenant, I assume you've heard the phrase *don't ask questions*?"

She nodded.

"Yes, XO. I've heard that phrase here. Many times."

Hits of personal experience in those words. Dark experiences. The scars and bruises Darkwater bore were not all on the surface.

"I've heard it, too," Travis said. "I think the time for not asking questions has passed. At least between you and me."

That raw, simmering intelligence again, like a neon sign lighting Darkwater's face from within.

"I'm listening," she said.

A balanced, noncommittal, political response worthy of Anne Lafferty. Maybe Darkwater had learned from her close friend.

Lafferty... *Anne*... Travis would talk to her soon as well. There was a hunger for knowledge in Anne, one that outweighed even her hunger for career advancement.

"I need to know more about this ship," he said. "My people are dying. Death and war go hand in hand, of course, but I think we're losing good sailors and Raiders because no one will tell us the full truth. I want to ask you questions, Lieutenant. I want to ask you because I believe you are the one who knows the most about *Keeling*." A thought slid into his brain, took control of his mouth. "I believe you are the one who is *meant* to know the most about *Keeling*."

The words were out before he thought them through. *Meant to know?* What did that even mean?

And yet, he saw Darkwater's reaction, knew he'd said the *right* thing even if he didn't grasp what the right thing was.

"I believe I understand, XO. Although, how can any of us can know things that are beyond our *ability* to know? We are mere mortals, after all. Are we not?"

He didn't get her meaning. As long as she would talk to him about the ship, he didn't care.

"This ship is more than a tool operated by a crew," Travis said. "That much is obvious. What I want to know from you—and this will stay between us—is *Keeling* an automatonomous machine, like low-level Prawatt ships and soldiers? Or is it truly *alive*?"

She didn't answer right away. She stared at him as if she saw something in him that he did not see himself.

Something, perhaps, he could *never* see.

"XO, your question is one scientists and philosophers have been asking since rudimentary artificial intelligence first appeared in the twenty-first century. What does being *alive* actually mean? Current science defines *life*, defines *living things*, as self-sustaining systems capable of Darwinian evolution. A long time ago, that definition was limited to self-sustaining *chemical* systems. Systems like you and me. Like all animals, plants, bacteria, et cetera. The Prawatt, though—and more advanced models of the aforementioned AI—made the *chemical* part obsolete."

Her starting-from-square-one approach annoyed him.

"I'm not here for a history lesson, Lieutenant. Is this ship alive, or not? *Keeling* ignored our commands. I don't care what Hasik says, I believe the ship *made its own decisions*. If I'm going to keep as many of my people alive as I can, I need to understand what we're dealing with."

Darkwater tucked the tip of her tongue into the right corner of her mouth, glanced off to the heartstone. The heartstone—alien tech that, somehow, let *Keeling* hop dimensions. The heartstone, where Jenn Hathorn's corpse had been found after she learned Darkwater was no easy mark.

"There is a broader concept of life," the lieutenant said. "Does the system have *organization?* Is it made up of cells or a structured system that maintains order? *Keeling*'s MOF structure is like cells, quite similar to the ones you and I have, yet *extremely* different."

Travis knew enough about the structure to agree. Different, sure, but as a fundamental building block of an organism that could grow, a *cell* was a *cell*.

"Then there is the big one," Darkwater said. "*Metabolism*. Can an entity take in energy and convert that energy to sustain itself? Before our recent trip into the Mud, I wouldn't have been sure. But *Keeling*—"

"—*hunted*," Travis finished for her. "It pursued prey. It *ate* something."

"It did. I embrace Occam's Razor—that the simplest explanation is usually the right one. I'm not sure we should discuss this with anyone else, even Colonel Hasik, but I believe our ship *predated*. With intentionality, it *consumed resources*."

Did that indicate an ecosystem of some kind? A web of predator and prey?

"What will *Keeling* do with those resources, Lieutenant? What will they be converted into?"

"I have no idea." Lafferty smiled, shrugged. "Isn't that amazing? Isn't that *wonderful*? Maybe *Keeling* will convert the material into more of itself. The ship did *grow*, after all. Regardless of that, there are more elements in the definition of life we must consider—*homeostasis*, along with *growth and development*."

Words Travis thought he understood but perhaps not in this particular context.

"Homeostasis?"

"Does the entity maintain internal stability and adjust to external conditions," Darkwater said. "And does it undergo changes over time and develop into different stages?"

Maintaining internal stability. After the Purist missile strike, the ship repaired itself. And Hasik had let on that was not the first time *Keeling* did so.

"In short, homeostasis means the ship can keep itself alive," Travis said. "As for growth and development, it not only grew larger, it replaced our wiring tech with its own more efficient system."

The lieutenant raised both hands to her chest as if she was about to pray—she clapped her hands together softly, two times.

Applause.

"You are a fast learner, XO. *Keeling* likes that."

He leaned away slightly, as if those words were a weight that gently nudged him backward.

She thought the ship *liked* something?

That was enough for now. He had to get back to the CIC. They'd soon begin their approach to Gateway.

"This has been helpful, Lieutenant. When we—"

Darkwater grabbed his hand, an action that caught him off-guard. So intimate, so friendly—the touch of *family* he hadn't felt for so long.

"There's more," she said. "*Adaptation and evolution, response to stimuli*, and... and..."

She glanced off, looking at the heartstone again.

"And what, Lieutenant?"

Doubt clouded Darkwater's gaze.

"XO, there's more going on here than rote aspects of what defines life. Concepts that... I'm sorry, I can't put them into words. Not yet. I assure you—all of this stays between us. We must learn. We must study. We *must*."

Was she holding something back? Or, perhaps, she had ideas and concepts she couldn't process?

The 1MC chime sounded.

"This is the captain. XO Ellis, report to the CIC immediately. XO Ellis, report to the CIC. That is all."

Darkwater patted his hand, squeezed it, then let it drop.

"You are essential, Travis Ellis," she said. "*Essential.*"

A mysterious line from a mysterious woman. Who was the real Bethany Darkwater?

And what was she in for?

"Another time, Lieutenant," Travis said. "Another time."

With that, he left the atrium. While there were big questions yet to be answered, he had his duties.

His captain needed him.

EPILOGUE 5
DANIELLE "BIGGIE" BANG

She felt like she'd been the guest of honor at a blanket party. She really, *really* needed to avoid getting high and crawling into a cubbyhole when the ship decided to go psycho and chase some interdimensional lunch.

Biggie slowly, *painfully*, slid her way out of the hole and stood on the passageway's fakegrav deck. She pulled her blanket around her neck, wore it like a robe. Hot down here. Always hot below decks.

She had survived.

Survived both a battle and some bug-nuts crazy shit she'd been too high to process. Torch and Knuckles would catch her up on current events.

They were headed back to Gateway. There, she could sleep on an actual bed.

Ninety-six weeks left on her sentence.

Damn, did she hurt all over.

Her cubbyhole was right next to the infirmary—maybe a few painkillers would help the cause.

Blanket wrapped around her, Biggie Bang shuffled down the passageway. One look inside the infirmary gave her hope that, very soon, she would feel *much* better.

"Hey, Doc Watson. Got a second?"

"But I don't wanna," Beaver yelled. "The walls are *moving*, Corporal Bennett. It's *weird*. Why do I gotta?"

"Because I *said so*," John snapped. "That's why. Come on."

John led Beaver, Abshire, and Reiner through the tunnel toward the pouch.

Only a few hours until they reached Gateway. John wanted a moment for his team to say goodbye to Yo-Yo. Once the ship docked, the body would be removed and sent to his home. John and the others would not be invited to the funeral service, and even if they were, they wouldn't be allowed to leave Gateway.

The tunnel walls were still moving. And, yes, Beaver was right, it was weird. The XO didn't want anyone using the tunnel at all, but John didn't want to go up to Deck Four, walk aft through the engineering section, then descend back down to the pouch—people might ask what he was doing.

"*Weird* is the wrong word," Reiner said. "This is *gross*."

Hard to argue against that sentiment. In the mess, people whispered terms like *ingested* or *consumed* or *absorbed*, but John preferred simpler concepts—the ship *ate* something. Was the tunnel part of the ship's stomach? Or, God forbid, its poop-chute?

Hopefully not.

They exited the tunnel, entered the copper cave known as *the pouch*. Both Ochthera's were butted up against the flight bay's portside. Chief Taylor and crawler tech Banks were at a workbench examining chunk of machinery John didn't recognize. That meant it was for one of the Ochtheras—he knew every piece of gear a frontline Raider handled, up one side and down the other.

Taylor saw him, stopped working. "Corporal, you're not supposed to be in the tunnel. What's up?"

She was one of the good ones. John knew that if things got really hairy, if *Keeling* were ever boarded or the Raiders were shorthanded, Taylor would TASH up and fight alongside them without a moment's hesitation.

"Sorry, Sarge," John said. "We wanted to pay our respects to Yo-Yo before we hit Gateway."

Taylor frowned, perhaps considered saying something disciplinary, then let it go.

"I hear you," she said. "Just don't let Lindros find out, okay?"

Behind John, Beaver fake-coughed the words *Dork is a dumb-ass*.

The kid had no sense of decorum. None at all.

"Yeah, LT ain't my favorite, either," Taylor said. She nodded toward a pair of ammo racks bolted into the copper bulkhead. "Ayodele's in the third cubby from the bottom. Just pull the plug out and set it aside—I'll put it back when you're done."

She returned her attention to the workbench and the gear.

There wasn't much room between the racks, but there was a little bit behind them, just enough for all four surviving members of Alpha-2 to squeeze in.

Cubbyholes dotted the ship's interior copper bulkheads. Most were small, maybe big enough to set a beer inside. Many, though, would hold a toolbox or an RR-36, and others still were large enough for a person to crawl into. They looked natural, worn, like a metallic cliff face where long-gone water had eroded nooks and crannies.

Pieces of white composite, carved to fit perfectly, plugged four of those man-sized holes. Each plug had handles, a small control panel set into it with a readout showing 3.0°C, and a name written in black marker.

MARTIGRAL

ELLISON

AYODELE

BYRNES

"It's like a morgue," Abs said. "Let's make this quick so we don't get Chief Taylor in trouble."

He gripped the handles and pulled. The composite plug popped out; thick white mist spilled down to the fakegrav deck plates dotted with spreading copper foil.

The mist cleared—the cubbyhole was empty.

Fucking techs... did they think this shit was funny?

"Sergeant Taylor, *get over here*," John said. "You better have an explanation for this or—rank be dammed—I will shove my hand up your ass and move your mouth like a puppet."

Somewhere in his lizard-brain, a tiny voice of warning yelled at him for speaking that way to a superior noncom, but at that moment he didn't give a damn.

Taylor hurried over, her sergeant's scowl locked in and her curled lip ready to give far better than she got from a lowly corporal.

She saw John and the others packed around the open cubby. She stopped cold.

"You assholes," she said. "Did you move his goddamn body? What's wrong with you?"

It was the confused anger in her words that cut through John's mental haze.

This wasn't a joke.

Chief Taylor wasn't playing some sick game.

"Oh, jeeze," Abshire said. "Remember how when we first got back onboard, we were looking for Romanik's body and we couldn't find it?"

For the first time in a long, *long* time, John wished he wasn't a Raider.

He wished he wasn't entombed.

"I remember," Beaver said, his voice oddly, uncharacteristically quiet. "Darkwater and Hasik said the ship absorbed her body."

Absorbed.

That was what Hasik and Darkwater said, all right.

But John knew a better word.

A *simpler* word.

Yo-Yo's corpse had been here.

The ship *ate* him.

The Crypt Continues In Book III—Fratricide

———

Make sure to join our Discord
(https://discord.gg/aethon)
so you never miss a release!

Looking for more great books?

An explosive new military science fiction thrill ride from #1 Amazon bestselling author T.R. Harris. **What do you do when everyone in the galaxy is out to get you? Captain Shadow:** a name that strikes terror in the hearts of the occupying Vonish forces in the Reaches, Earth's outermost province. Having annexed the region without firing a shot, the slimy aliens now face an invisible enemy that's wreaking havoc on their warships, while also feeding the fever for freedom within the natives. So, who is the mysterious **Captain Shadow?** …On the surface, former Navy Captain Jonathan Carr has it all. As the sole heir to the massive Carr Shipping and Transport Company, he has wealth, fame and privilege in his home province of the Reaches. But secretly, Jonathan lives a double life… as the infamous **Captain Shadow.** Aboard his salvaged starship, Star Wind, Jonathan and his crew fight for the liberation of the Reaches, and with little support from distant Mother Earth and her stellar empire, the United Peoples of Earth (UPE). The stakes grow even higher when Jonathan learns of a deadly conspiracy between the Vonish and elements within the UPE. Now, it's a desperate race against time as Jonathan sets out to save the Earth, while at the same time being pursued, not only by the aliens, but by the Humans as well. **Captain Shadow begins the next high-tension military sci-fi series by T.R. Harris: The Star Wind Series. Full of political intrigue and thrilling space battles, along with humor and witty banter, this book has it all. Oh, and the clock is ticking.** *Fortunately, we have Captain Shadow on our side. If there are any sides left to be on... Don't delay. Grab your copy of **Captain Shadow** today!* **From the bestselling author of The Human Chronicles Saga and Human for Hire comes this action-packed new military science fiction thrill ride. It's perfect for fans of JN Chaney, John Spearman, and Jeffery H. Haskell!**

Get Captain Shadow Now!

———

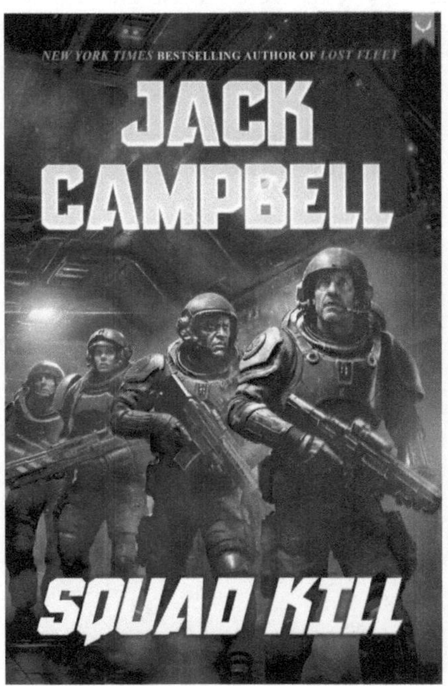

A new military science fiction adventure from Jack Campbell, the NYT bestselling author of Lost Fleet. **Getting home alive will take everything they have...** Osiris "Oz" Aquino is an underprepared Navy officer put in command of seven castoff Marines on a research starship dispatched to an alien planet. His sergeant is hostile, his Marines have records full of infractions – not to mention that they're plagued by old weapons and missing supplies due to budget cuts – and the crew and scientists would rather have nothing to do with him. As the ship approaches the planet it's investigating, they find plenty of signs of intelligent life in the form of ruined cities and skeletal remains. The only things living in the ruins are adorable aliens which the researchers dub squonks. It all seems run-of-the-mill, until it isn't... Sudddenly, the squonks get loose in engineering and go ballistic, the crew sent to investigate aren't coming back, and Oz and his team have a fight on their hands. He must restore safe access to engineering before the crew on the ship run out of air all while figuring out what turned the squonks from cuddly to killer. And if he doesn't act fast, the squad who've evacuated to the planet's surface may not survive. **From Jack Campbell, NYT Bestselling author of Lost Fleet, comes this action packed, science fiction thrill ride filled with military action, detailed alien worlds, and characters you can't help but root for.**

Get Squad Kill Now!

For all our science fiction books, visit our website.

ACKNOWLEDGMENTS

CONTINUITY

I can't imagine writing a Siglerverse novel without the keen eyes of John Vizcarra, Siglerverse Continuity Czar. While my head was in the stars, John's feet were on the deck, ensuring Voidstrike's many details matched those from Shakedown.

MEDICAL

Joseph A. Albietz III, MD, helped me with some of the messy bits.

EDITING

Kalene Williams TASHed up and waded into battle against typos and inconsistencies, wielding grammar and style guides like the weapons they are.

www.ingramcontent.com/pod-product-compliance
Lightning Source LLC
Chambersburg PA
CBHW030349310726
48979CB00001B/239